GW00866278

Hal J

Omnibus One

Copyright ©2019 Simon Haynes

Books 1-3 in the Hal Junior series

— 1 —

The Test Flight

'Whoosh! Zoom! Fizz, fizz, *fizz!*' Hal Junior swept his arm through the air, fluttering the wings of a paper plane gripped in his hand.

Laser beams zinged Captain Spacejock's fighter, the Phantom X1, spitting and crackling as they bounced off the hull. The enemy ship was right on his tail, and there was only one way out!

The paper plane swooped, and Hal Junior supplied the sound effects for his epic space battle. 'Vroom! Neeee-ouuw!'

The X1 climbed into the sky, turned on its tail and dived on the pursuer. Catching the enemy ship by surprise, Captain Spacejock fired a burst from his triple-decker space-cannon.

'Dakka dakka dakka!   Fizz-fizz-BOOM! Take that, evil minion!   You're no match for Captain Spacejock!'

The X1 did a victory roll over the crash site, and then the captain turned for home. Suddenly, an angry voice crackled in his headphones.

'Will you hurry up! We'll be late for lessons!'

Hal lowered the paper plane. Stephen 'Stinky' Binn was a good friend, but Hal sometimes wished he was a robot so he could switch his voice off. 'Stinky! I was on patrol!'

'If you don't quit dreaming you'll be on detention.'

They hurried along the corridor together, with Hal still fighting imaginary space battles. 'Zooom! Zzing! Ker-pow! Aaargh!'

Stinky rolled his eyes.

A lift carried them to the next level, and on the way up Hal showed off his paper plane. His dad had found the diagram in an old ebook the night before, and after demonstrating the basics he'd left Hal to it. His dad was good like that - always there to lend a hand, but never trying to take over and do everything for you.

The plane had come out really well, but it wasn't finished until bed time and their quarters were too small for a test flight. Hal had been pretending to fly it all morning, but it wasn't enough. He was itching to try it for real.

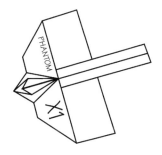

'Teacher's not going to like it,' warned Stinky, gesturing at the plane. 'You were supposed to write your answers on it, not crease it into little squares.'

'Oh yeah?' Hal turned the plane over to reveal several lines of uneven handwriting. 'Shame you're not as smart as me.'

Stinky shook his head. 'You're still going to cop it. That stuff is really precious.'

The class theme for the week was ancient technology, and each student had been given a sheet of paper and a pencil stub for their homework. Paper was scarce aboard the space station, where everything had to be flown in at huge expense.

Hal figured the sheet was going to be recycled anyway, so why not make a plane out of it?

The lift doors opened and Hal launched the plane with a sudden flick of the wrist, almost hitting Stinky in the back of the head. At first it flew beautifully, sailing past doorways and weaving through pipes and struts as though Captain Spacejock were at the controls. Then . . . *whoosh!* A recycling hatch opened with its distinctive sucking noise.

According to Hal's dad the rushing air was supposed to keep nasty smells in, but there were rumours of a giant space monster at the bottom of the shaft. It was supposed to live on scraps of metal and old food, and every time a hatch opened the monster took a gigantic breath, gulping down air to fill its leathery lungs.

Unfortunately, the whooshing air sucked the plane straight into the hatch. Fortunately, when Hal looked inside he found the plane stuck to the damp wall. Unfortunately it was just out of reach.

— 2 —

A 'Rappelling' Idea

'Come on, you stubborn slice of tree pulp!' Hal's arms were at full stretch, but his grasping fingers couldn't quite reach the paper plane stuck to the grimy metal wall.

'Have you got it yet?'

'What do you think?' snapped Hal, twisting his neck to give Stinky an upside-down glare.

'I think I can't hold on much longer.'

Unfortunately Stinky wasn't talking about his frequent trips to the bathroom. No, Stinky was braced against the recycling hatch, holding Hal by the ankles. His fingers were the only thing saving his friend from a headlong plunge down Space Station Oberon's main recycling chute.

'You can do it,' said Hal. 'Just a bit lower.'

'I can't. You'll have to leave it.'

Leave it ... leave it ... leave it! echoed the chute.

Hal grabbed and missed. It was so annoying! He was close enough to read his own writing, but it could have been a light year away for all the use that was. 'Scribbling on paper is a stupid idea. Why couldn't we stick to writing answers in our workbooks?'

'Instead of sticking them to the wall, you mean?' Stinky shifted his grip. 'It's lucky Teacher didn't give us stone tablets to write on.'

'Don't be an idiot. If he'd given us a slab of rock I'd hardly have made a paper plane, would I?'

'No, you'd have lobbed it through a window instead.' Stinky thought for a moment. 'Why don't we share my paper? You can write your answers on the back.'

Hal snorted. He rarely did his homework the first time, and doing it twice was out of the question. Frustrated, he scowled at the paper plane. Any minute now they'd be marked absent, and by the time he finished detention a fresh load of garbage would have brushed his homework straight down the chute. No, it was now or never. 'Hey, I've got a brilliant idea. Let go of my ankles.'

'You call that brilliant?'

'Sure. I'll drop a bit further if you hold my shoes.'

'You'll drop a lot further if they slip off your feet.'

'They wouldn't come off if you shot them with a

blast rifle. I used my patented triple knot.'

Stinky knew all about Hal's patented ideas, but nonetheless he shifted his grip to Hal's shoes.

'Just a bit more!' cried Hal, as his outstretched fingers brushed the plane's wing.

'That's all, Hal. I swear.'

'The laces. Hold me by the shoelaces!'

By now Stinky was beyond arguing, and he obeyed despite his misgivings.

Unfortunately, Hal's original laces had been burnt to a crisp in the great model rocket affair. Fortunately his dad had replaced them. Unfortunately he'd used elastic.

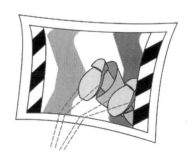

Hal went down the chute like a bungee-jumping hamster – his arms outstretched and a look of wide-eyed shock on his face. The weight almost pulled Stinky through the hatch, but he just managed to brace himself.

Boinnnnggg!

Stretched to capacity, the elastic contracted, yanking Hal backwards up the chute. For a split second he was face to face with Stinky, and he couldn't help laughing at his friend's startled upside-down expression.

Whoosh!

Gravity reasserted itself, and Hal went back down the chute. This time he stuck his hand out, and with a triumphant yell he peeled the plane from the wall. 'I've got it, Stinky. I've got it!'

Boinnnnggg!

Hal didn't bounce as far this time, or the next, and after bobbing up and down a few more times he finally came to rest, turning slowly in mid-air as he dangled by his extremely long shoelaces. 'I told you it would work. Now get me out of here.'

Stinky pulled, but Hal didn't move.

'Go on. Put some effort into it!'

'I can't!' said Stinky in alarm. 'Hal, you're too heavy. I can't pull you up!'

— 3 —

A 'Repelling' Idea

Hal's blood froze as he realised the danger he was in. Stinky couldn't hold on forever, and if Hal stayed in the chute much longer he was going to fall all the way to the bottom. 'Don't mess about. Pull me up!'

'I can't do it on my own. You'll have to help.'

Muttering under his breath, Hal took the paper plane between his teeth and pressed his palms against the smooth metal walls. He tried to push himself back up the tunnel, but his hands just slipped. Meanwhile, Stinky was hauling on the springy shoelaces with all his might. 'It's no use. It's not working. And Hal ... I've got to go.'

Go ... go ... go!

Hal looked puzzled. 'We've both got to go, Stinky. That's the problem ... I'm stuck.'

'No, I mean go!' said Stinky, and this time he was talking about his frequent trips to the bathroom.

'Just hold it in, all right?' Hal thought furiously. If he couldn't climb up to safety, what about going down instead? He squinted into the shadowy depths and saw an access hatch one level down. If Stinky let go of his laces, could he grab the hatch as he flew past? If not that one, maybe the one after? The problem was, once he started falling he'd move faster and faster and then nothing would stop him until he went SPLAT at the very bottom of the space station. If he didn't end up like a pancake he'd probably starve before anyone found him. Unless there really was a space monster down there, in which case it'd be one gulp and goodnight.

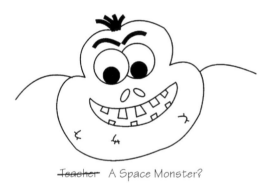

~~Teacher~~ A Space Monster?

'I have an idea,' called Stinky, his voice echoing off the slick metal walls. 'If I reverse the gravity in the chute it'll push you back up instead of pulling you down.'

'Do you think it'll do the trick?'

'Reversing the polarity always works.'

'Cool. Give it a shot.' That was the best thing about Stinky – he wasn't much good at hauling people out of garbage hatches by their shoelaces, but he was a whizz with electronics.

'You'll have to hang on. I need both hands.'

'I'm not going anywhere,' said Hal, praying he was right. His shoes went slack as Stinky let go of the laces, and he braced himself against the sides of the tunnel. Before long his arms started to ache, and then he had a worrying thought. What if someone a few levels up decided to recycle a coffee pot, or a dirty nappy, or even a fridge? That would really cap his day off. 'Will you hurry up?' he shouted. 'I'm starting to slip!'

Slip! Slip! Slip!

There was a crackle near his feet and a cloud of blue smoke wafted by. All of a sudden Hal was weightless, and he was just flexing his sore arms when the world turned upside-down. Suddenly he was standing upright . . . on thin air.

With a surprised 'whoof' Hal shot upwards like a human cannonball in the world's biggest and most dangerous circus act. Far below, there was a rumble and a clatter as all the junk in the recycling plant rose towards the roof of the station.

Hal grabbed the edge of the hatch as he fell past,

11

and he was still struggling to climb out when he saw the mass of twisted junk hurtling up the shaft like a runaway train. Imagine a kitchen bin firing banana skins and eggshells and yesterday's lunch all over the roof – then imagine standing over the bin and looking into it as the contents flew out. That's what Hal was facing. But it wasn't yucky food scraps he was worried about, it was old computers, tatty furniture and leftover building materials. The shaft was like the barrel of a gun, the fast-moving junk was the bullet and Hal was a bug about to get squished.

The mass was moving incredibly fast, and it pushed the air ahead of it in a howling gale. Hatches banged and clattered in the shaft, and all over the station people gasped, spluttered and fainted as a foul-smelling hurricane blew through their offices, kitchens and lounge rooms.

With an effort, Hal tore his gaze from the impending doom. 'Help! Stinky!'

Stinky . . . stinky . . . stinky!

His friend dragged him out of the hatch with seconds to spare. Hal landed in the corridor and there was a tremendous clatter as the junk flew past. By the time he recovered Stinky was busy at the control panel.

'What's going to happen when that lot hits the

roof?' demanded Hal.

'It's going to smash right through,' said Stinky, who was picking through a tangle of wires. 'There's a safety seal to keep the air in, but the damage will be insane.'

'You've got to stop it. Quick!'

'What do you think I'm doing?'

There was a crackle from the control panel, a moment of total silence, and then all the junk turned round and plummeted towards the base of the station. The inhabitants were only just recovering from the first gale, having straightened their pictures and combed the scraps of muck out of their hair. Now they got a second dose.

With hatches clattering up and down the shaft, and the mass of junk safely back in the recycling centre, Stinky finished his work and jammed the cover back on the panel. After a hurried look around to make sure they hadn't left any evidence, the two boys ran for it.

'I've got to change my jumper,' said Stinky, whose sleeves were smeared with grime from the hatch. It wasn't just his sleeves - his hair looked like it had been dipped in a rubbish bin and blow-dried in a wind tunnel. Hal looked even worse . . . but that was normal.

'See you in class, Stinky. And thanks!'

Stinky hurried off to his family's living quarters, while Hal slowed to a walk. In his experience, running anywhere on the station led to awkward questions like 'Where have you been?', 'Where are you going?' and worst of all, 'Did you just blow all my paintings off the wall and what's this piece of orange peel doing in my hair?'

As he walked along the corridor Hal heard the familiar rush and gurgle of liquid in the overhead pipes. His dad said the noise was the station's lifeblood pumping through its arteries and veins, but Hal suspected this was a load of sewage.

He slowed as he approached a set of doors marked 'Observation Deck'. Was there time for a quick look at the stars?

Of course there was!

— 4 —

Off Limits

Of all the cool places aboard Space Station Oberon, the observation deck was Hal's favourite. He loved to stand with his nose flattened against the big perspex window, his eyes drinking in the distant stars. When he cupped his hands to his face, shutting out the reflections, he could pretend he was floating in space like the repair crews with their spacesuits and jet packs. What he wouldn't give to go flying around the Oberon in a powered suit! Imagine the races they could have! Playing awesome games of tag, weaving through the docking ports, zipping past the living quarters and the connecting tunnels . . .

Hal sighed, knowing it could never happen. Adults took all the fun out of everything, and even the exciting-sounding spacesuit training was just putting on the same sweaty old overalls while someone shouted 'faster, faster!' in your ear.

In the distance, almost lost in the vast starfield, there was a yellowish patch of light. Hal's teacher had once pointed it out as a habitable system, and to Hal that meant planets and oceans and memories of playing outdoors. He remembered a grassy field, the warm sun beating down on him, the feel of the breeze and the chirrups and squawks of insects and birds. He'd only been three or four years old, but he still remembered the oozy squishy mud between his fingers. No mud on a space station, that was for sure. No sunlight or insects either, nor grassy fields.

Hal sighed and shifted his gaze to an area of the starfield above and to his left, seeking out an oval patch of light. Teacher had told him the name of the galaxy once, but Hal called it The Snot because it looked like the time Stinky Binn had sneezed inside his space helmet.

'All students from D-Section please report to pod three for lessons. I repeat, all students report to pod three immediately.'

Hal glanced at his watch, an impressive-looking timepiece he'd found in a pile of construction junk. The adult-sized watch was huge on his wrist, and the chunky strap was so loose he didn't have to undo it to take it off. The dial looked like it might have been used in space, and the buttons had mysterious legends like O_2 and TMI.

In class he always rolled his sleeve up so everyone could marvel at his treasure. The only problem was that he couldn't tell the time with it, because it didn't work. He'd tried levering the back off to swap the battery, but it needed a special tool. He couldn't ask an adult in case they took his precious watch away.

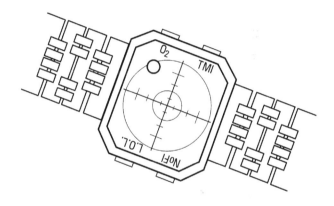

'I repeat, ALL students please report to pod three for lessons. That includes you, Hal Junior!'

Hal smoothed the paper plane and slipped it into the tough plastic case of his workbook. He'd spent almost three minutes working on the answers the night before, and for once they'd been easy. In fact, he was looking forward to handing it in, which is why he'd gone to so much trouble saving his plane from the recycling shaft.

He was about to leave when the doors slid open, and his heart sank as he saw the dumpy figure outside. It was the station's head of security, Grant Bignew, his thinning hair all messed up and his eyes bulging like a toad's. 'What are you doing here, boy? Don't you know this area is off limits? Why, I could have you thrown in jail!'

Hal and Stinky called the chief 'Giant Bignose' behind his back, but this wasn't the time to bring that up. Instead, Hal put on his best manner. 'Please sir, I'm very sorry. I thought I heard a noise, but when I came in to investigate there was nobody here.'

'Is that so?' Bignew studied Hal intently. 'I can always tell when people are lying, boy. Are you lying to me?'

'No sir, definitely not.'

'Excellent. Now run along and don't let me catch you in here again!'

Hal fled, relieved he wasn't in handcuffs. A few weeks earlier Hal's dad let another worker use his supervisor code so they could finish an urgent repair on time. This 'crime' had led to a public telling-off by Bignew. After that, Hal's dad referred to the head of security as 'that officious little toad', at least until Hal's mother pointed out their apartment could be bugged.

As he hurried along the corridor Hal wondered what Bignose was doing in the observation deck. Did he use high-powered binoculars to spy on the rest of the station? Was there a secret door leading to a hidden lair? Hal snorted at the crazy idea. Bignose probably liked the stars.

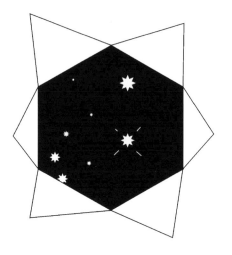

— 5 —

Teach and Spell

By the time Hal got to class the lesson was in full swing. There were two dozen children sitting at folding desks while Teacher sped around the room collecting assignments. Their Teacher was an old-style robot with a red plastic body and short stubby arms. The words 'Teach and Spell' were printed across his chest in big yellow letters, and instead of a face he had a large screen which could display up to a dozen eyes at once. These eyes could move independently, squinting or winking or glaring at several different students all at the same time. They weren't limited to the front either: when Teacher turned to project lessons onto the classroom wall, a stray eye would sometimes appear round the back of his head, checking up on the students. There was one particularly busy eye which Hal called 'the follower', because no matter where he sat it always seemed to follow him around the room.

Teacher rolled past Hal on his silent rubber wheels, whisking the paper plane out of his fingers. 'Thank you for putting in an appearance, Hal Junior. Please have a seat.'

Hal took an empty desk alongside Stinky, while Teacher rolled to the front of the room and turned to face the students. 'Today we're going to discuss obsolete communications methods, including semaphore, Morse code and email. But first, I shall mark your chemistry homework.' He held up the assignments and flipped through them, faster than the eye could see. Then he looked around the class. 'Good efforts, everyone. And I see one student handed in something rather special.' Teacher held up the paper plane between finger and thumb. 'Hal Junior, you really went to town on presentation.'

Hal grinned. No more bottom of the class for him!

Teacher unfolded the plane to read Hal's answers, his eyes squinting and flickering as he struggled with the handwriting. When he was done he peered at Hal over the top of the assignment. 'Hal Junior, I'm going to read out your replies out so the entire class can marvel at them. Question one: Name three heavy metals. Your answer: thrash, power and drone.'

Hal smiled confidently at the other students, basking in their puzzled looks. He'd spent several minutes researching the answers, and the online encyclopaedia was never wrong. There were pages and pages of information on heavy metal, along with pictures of guitars and drum kits. Hal had even drawn a few in the margins, and he was particularly proud of the big skull with gleaming diamonds for teeth.

'Question two: Describe the reaction when you add sodium chloride to water.' Teacher looked at him over the top of the paper. 'Your answer: It gets wet.'

Hal nodded. The solution was so obvious he hadn't even looked it up. There were a few gasps around him, and he realised some of them hadn't been able to answer the question. That was their problem . . . they should have come to him for help.

'Finally, question three: Name the heaviest element on the periodic table. Your answer, Mr Junior, was 'thickonium'.'

The class erupted in laughter, and Hal frowned. What was wrong with them?

Even Teacher's digital lips creased into a grin. 'Mr Junior, a few months ago you said your goal was to become a space pilot. With these results, I guarantee the only space you'll navigate is the one between your ears. Unless, of course, your head is packed with thickonium!'

The class laughed even harder at this, and Hal slid down in his chair, his face burning. He'd asked his best mate for help, and this is what he got? To his credit Stinky was trying not to laugh, but his face had turned red from the effort.

Right, thought Hal. If this was the praise he got for doing his homework, Teacher could whistle for it in future.

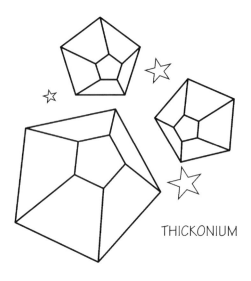

THICKONIUM

'Okay class, settle down. I mentioned obsolete communications earlier. Can anyone tell me what obsolete means?'

Every hand reached for the sky, and Hal slowly

raised his own to match. He had no idea what the word meant, but he wasn't going to let on.

'Hal Junior, you seem uncertain. Perhaps you could share your definition with the rest of us?'

Oh, great. Why did Teacher have to single him out? Hal lowered his hand, thinking furiously. Then his face cleared as he remembered his parents using the word in a recent conversation. 'Obsolete means when you're really fat.'

There were hoots of laughter from the rest of the class, and Teacher motioned for silence. 'Can anyone correct Mr Junior here?'

All the hands went up again, waving like stalks of sea-grass in the hydroponics lab.

'Natalie?'

'Obsolete means old and no longer useful.'

'Just like Teacher,' muttered Hal.

The class gasped at the remark, but Teacher pretended not to hear. 'And the word Mr Junior defined for us? Can anyone tell me what the correct term is?'

Natalie shook her head, and Hal grinned. Take that, little miss smarty-pants.

'Anyone?' Teacher's electronic eyes darted all over his face as he scanned the class, but this time nobody raised a hand. 'Very well. The word

Mr Junior described was 'obesity', and you can research the topic for homework.'

The class groaned, and several students shot accusing looks at Hal. He returned each one with his patented one-eyed scowl.

'Don't worry, half a page on the subject will be plenty. Now let me spell it for you.' Teacher gave them the letters one by one, then looked around the class. 'Tell me, does anyone know what a semaphore is?'

This time Hal was ready. Teacher was picking on anyone who looked unsure, so he stuck his hand up immediately. Unfortunately, his was the only hand in the air.

'Mr Junior, you're full of surprises today. Please, will you share your knowledge with the class?'

Hal thought hard. Semaphore sounded like carnivore, and he knew what that was because they'd studied lions and tigers recently. And the other part of the word? Semi meant half – he remembered that from a song about bees. So what was something which only ate half the meat? Then it came to him. 'Dieters!'

'I'm sorry?'

'People on a diet are semaphores. They only eat half their food.'

Teacher blinked once or twice. He was

programmed to handle most situations but even he had his limits. 'We're discussing obsolete communications such as Morse code and email, and you think this has something to do with dieting?'

Hal put his hand up. 'Would you like me to explain Morse?'

'Please don't,' said Teacher.

Sensing a weakness, Hal decided to try. Morse sounded like . . . well, horse. And it started with an M, which meant millions. Easy! 'Morse is a very big herd of ponies.'

Some of Teacher's eyes started to spin in circles, while others bounced off the top and bottom of his screen as though someone were playing a computer game with his face.

'How about email? I bet I could explain that.'

'Please don't. There's no need.'

There was no stopping Hal now. Mail was the opposite of female, and E meant energy. 'Email is a sportsman.'

'No no NO!' All of teacher's eyes stopped at once, some pointing at the ceiling, some at the floor, and only one on Hal. Unfortunately it was the follower, and it didn't look happy. 'Hal Junior. Please do not raise your hand again.'

'What if I have a question sir?'

'Then you may raise your hand.'

Hal immediately put his hand up.

'Y-yes?'

'Sir, what is a semaphore?'

'It's a signalling system involving flags. The sender waves flags in patterns, and the receiver looks up the patterns in a book to decode the message.'

Hal's hand shot up.

'What now?'

'How do you send a message if the other guy doesn't have a copy of the book?'

'You don't, which is why Morse is superior.' Teacher played several long beeps followed by several short ones. 'Do you hear the difference?'

Everyone nodded.

'You can transmit Morse using flashes of light, bursts of sound . . . even vibrations. Now, we're almost out of time so I'll cover email in tomorrow's lesson. For homework I want the essay on obesity and I want you to write your own names using Morse code. I've uploaded a copy of the alphabet so you can perform a simple letter substitution.'

Hal frowned. It might be simple for Teacher but he'd wrestle with it for ages. On the plus side, he could wait until his parents tried to pack him off to bed and then tell them he had urgent homework to do. With a bit of luck they'd finish it off for him.

Then it hit him – Morse was a secret code! He could send messages by tapping on the desk! Flash messages to other sections through the observation window!

Excited, Hal opened his workbook and blew a fine layer of dust off the screen. The device powered up slowly, and a progress bar crawled across the screen as several weeks' worth of lessons, assignment questions and updates were installed. When it was finally ready Hal turned to the Morse alphabet. There it was – dots, dashes and letters – a secret code just waiting to be used. Hal barely noticed the other kids leaving the classroom, and he only looked up when Teacher came over.

'Hal Junior, this room is required for spacesuit training. You must leave now.'

'Sorry sir. On my way.' Hal pushed his chair back and left, almost bumping into a group of scientists filing into the room. They were grumbling about sweaty overalls and people shouting 'faster, faster' in their ears, but Hal didn't stop to listen. He had some learning to do!

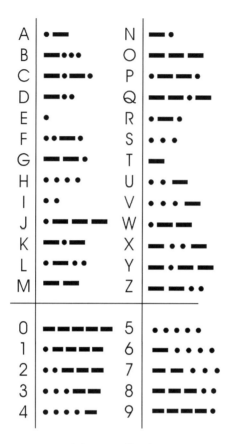

Morse Code

— 6 —

Two Suspects

'I'm sorry about that thickonium business,' said Stinky. 'I thought you realised I was joking.'

Hal snorted. 'Some friend you are, setting me up like that. Were you trying to get me in trouble?'

'I didn't think you'd write it down!' Stinky shot Hal a sidelong glance. 'Anyway, if you'd looked up the answer like you were supposed to . . . '

Stinky's voice tailed off as they rounded the corner and almost walked into a maintenance worker. The fair-haired woman was standing near the recycling hatch Hal had climbed into earlier, frowning at a diagnostic screen. Nearby, the cover was off the control panel, exposing the innards.

'Act normal,' muttered Hal. 'Don't say anything!'

They walked past, pretending to study the opposite wall, the ceiling and the floor – trying to look anywhere but the exposed control panel – but it didn't work.

'Hold up, lads. Did you two see anyone around here earlier?'

'N-no Miss, not us. Nobody at all.'

The woman glanced at Stinky. 'What about you?' she demanded. 'Have you seen anyone acting suspiciously?'

Hal prayed his friend would keep his mouth shut, and he was relieved when Stinky studied his shoes and said nothing.

'Meddling with these systems is a very serious matter.' The woman handed Hal a card. 'If you see anyone poking around in the control box I want you to get in touch immediately.'

'Yes Ma'am.' Hal studied the card and discovered the woman was Tina Peters, trainee maintenance officer. She didn't look like she was about to throw them both in the nearest cell, but then again she didn't know it was Stinky who'd almost blown the roof off the space station.

Tina closed the control panel and took out a workpad. It was similar to Hal's workbook except for the dark grey colour and the chrome strips down the side. It looked cool, and Hal thought it was typical how schoolkids got the daggy brown ones with fake wood-grain. Tina tapped the screen, then frowned. 'This thing's on the blink. Do you have the time by any chance?'

Hal shook his head.

Tina pointed to his watch. 'What's that, a ham sandwich?'

'It doesn't work,' said Hal, shaking his sleeve until it covered the chunky metal band.

'Want me to take a look at it for you?'

'No, it's fine.'

Tina put a hand out. 'Come on, I'll have it working in no time.'

Unwillingly, Hal removed the watch. Tina inspected it, and then before Hal could stop her she swung it at the wall.

CRACK!

'Hey!' shouted Hal. 'What are you doing?'

Tina smiled and held the watch out. To Hal's surprise, the display now showed a jumble of random letters.

'How did you –?'

'Corrosion in the power circuit. If you let me have it for a couple of days I'll clean the contacts and replace the battery.'

Hal eyed the precious watch. What if he never got it back? 'I'll keep hold of it, if that's all right.'

'Are you sure? It's no good like this.' Tina turned the watch over. 'This is a genuine space watch. Did your parents give it to you?'

'Someone left it to me,' said Hal, who never lied if he could bend the truth.

'Very generous of them. These things can do everything.'

'Really? Like what?'

'It'll talk to your spacesuit and tell you when your air is getting low. It'll tell you whether it's safe to take your helmet off, and it has a built-in homing beacon. Configure it for the space station and it'll always point the way home.' Tina laughed. 'It'll even tell the time, when it's working properly.'

'That's amazing,' said Hal.

Tina thought for a moment. 'Tell you what, you keep an eye out for whoever is messing with this control panel and I'll fix your watch. Deal?'

Hal was tempted, but it wouldn't be right. After all, it was his fault Tina was investigating the control panel. 'Thanks, but I'll keep it.'

'Fine. If you change your mind, let me know.' Tina took out her workpad. 'What's your name?'

'Hal Junior.'

'And your friend?'

'Stin– I mean, Stephen Binn.'

Tina held the workpad to her mouth. 'Two suspects identified, age approximately ten to twelve. Interview suspended until further notice.'

Hal and Stinky stared at Tina in shock. Was she an undercover cop disguised as an ordinary technician? How much trouble were they in?

The young woman regarded them with a deadly serious face, and Hal was just about to confess everything from the finding of the watch to the episode with the recycling hatch when Tina exploded with laughter. After a moment or two, during which the boys simply stared with their mouths open, she wiped her eyes with her sleeve and took a couple of deep breaths. 'Sorry lads, just a little joke. You should have seen your faces!'

Tina packed the workpad in her toolbox and went on her way, still laughing to herself.

Hal and Stinky exchanged a glance, both clearly thinking the same thing. If someone as loony as Tina could get a job fixing the space station, the place was about as safe as a cardboard airlock.

SPACE

This SPACE intentionally left blank

— 7 —

Surprise News

Hal touched the access panel outside his family's quarters, and the door opened with a groan. His parents were sitting at the kitchen table, and his mother looked worried. 'The gravity in the shaft reversed without warning. According to Maintenance we were seconds from a major hull breach. It could have wiped out –'

Hal's father shot her a warning glance. 'Have a seat, son.'

Hal squeezed behind the tiny kitchen table and sat on the narrow bench. There was no wasted space in their quarters – even the bench had doors in the front so items could be stashed away out of sight. When he was smaller Hal would climb right inside while his parents pretended to look for him inside their coffee cups and under the salt shaker. They even – shock horror – opened the recycling hatch and called down the chute for him. Eventually his giggling fits would give him away and his parents would make a show of 'finding' him.

Now the space was filled with old kitchen junk.

'Your mum and I have some good news.'

Hal's eyes narrowed. If it was a new baby . . .

'I've been promoted,' said his mum, with a twinkle in her eyes. 'Old Benton is retiring and moving back to Gyris. They've given me his job.'

'Your mother is going to be head of research,' said Hal's dad proudly. His own speciality was the atmosphere scrubbers, where he worked long hours to make sure everyone had clean air to breathe. He liked to tell everyone he was good with his hands while his wife was good with her brains, making the pair of them a great team.

'Do we get any benefits?' asked Hal.

His dad laughed. 'Trust you to think of that.'

'Well?'

'We'll be moving to bigger quarters in C-Section,' said his mum. 'You'll have a terminal in your room, so you'll be able to do your homework on time every night.'

'Wonderful,' muttered Hal. Still, new quarters sounded good and the terminal would be very handy once Stinky performed some of his hacker magic on it. 'Hang on, what about school?'

'They have a modern teacher, much newer than the one you're used to. Just think, you'll meet some new friends too.'

'Have you met the kids from C-Section?' scoffed Hal. 'They think they're a cut above the rest of us. Anyway, Stinky's the only friend I need.'

'Stin– I mean, Stephen can come and visit whenever you like.'

'When are we moving?'

'Benton isn't leaving for a day or so,' explained his mum. 'I'm going to be very busy getting up to speed. I'm afraid that means working longer hours for a bit.'

'You already work long hours.'

'This is very important son,' said his dad. 'Your mum can't give you all the details, but if the research pays off it'll change life for everyone.'

'Even mine and Stinky's?'

His father laughed. 'Yes, yours too.'

Half an hour later Hal stood at the dishwasher, placing dirty plates and cutlery on the moving belt. As the items emerged from the other end, shiny and clean, he put them away. He'd heard others complaining about 'doing the dishes' but it didn't seem that bad to him. Their machine was old and slow – what was the word Teacher had used? Obsolete, that was it – but it sure beat eating dinner off dirty plates.

Ever impatient, Hal added more and more items to the dishwasher, cramming them in until they barely cleared the intake. The machine chugged and groaned with the extra weight, and when it ground to a complete stop Hal turned to the controls. The dial was fixed on 'Slow', and Hal reckoned his parents left it there to keep him busy after dinner. They'd warned him not to touch it, but surely one little tweak wouldn't hurt?

He reached for the big plastic dial and turned it from 'Slow' to 'Medium'.

Whirrr!

The machine started to move again, and the plates coming out the other end were clean enough. There was a speck of food here and there, but who was going to notice? Hal eyed the pile of cups and cutlery he still had to deal with, and decided to do the whole lot in one go. He put all the items on the belt and twisted the knob through 'Fast', 'Very Fast', 'Very Very Fast' ... all the way up to 'Ultra-Fast'

Zoooooooom!

The belt fairly flew as the machine kicked into

top speed, and the crockery disappeared into the machine as though sucked into a black hole.

Zzzinngg!

Gleaming cutlery arrowed out of the dishwasher, streaking across the kitchen in a blur of silver.

Gadoiinnnggg! went the knives and forks as they stuck into the wall, quivering with the force.

Spat-spat-spat! went the dishwasher, rocking on its feet as it hurled teacups around the kitchen.

Clatter clatter crash! went the plastic cups and plates as they bounced off the walls and cupboards.

Hal ducked under the barrage and turned the knob back to 'Slow'. The last plate had just stopped spinning when his dad appeared in the doorway.

'Don't look at me,' said Hal. 'It just went wrong. I think it's . . . obsolete.'

His dad crouched to gather the scattered crockery, shaking his head at the mess. Hal tried to give him a hand, but ended up smearing food scraps all over the floor with the broom.

'It'll be quicker if I do it,' said his dad. 'Go and start your homework.'

Hal nearly reached the exit before his dad called him back to wash his hands. Hal put his hands in the sink and there was a tingly blue glow as the field did its job. When he raised his hands they were perfectly clean and dry. His dad once told him about people washing with actual water, splashing it all over themselves like there was an endless supply. Aboard a space station water was hoarded for drinking, and the idea of pouring it on your skin or sloshing it all over your plates to clean them was insane. In fact, Hal sometimes wondered whether his dad made up half the things he told him. Most of them were certainly crazy enough.

After he'd cleaned up Hal went to his cabin, where a narrow bunk jostled for space with a tiny desk and a fold-out chair. It wasn't much of a room, and Hal wondered what their new place might be like. A computer terminal of his own would be fantastic, especially if Stinky could hack his way around the usual blocks. Unrestricted terminals had views of the outside, huge libraries of music and video, access to any number of cool games and stacks of other delights. For that, he'd even put up with the kids from C-Section.

Hal sat at the desk and opened his workbook, which still had the Morse alphabet on its screen. In all the excitement of meeting Tina the tech and learning about his mum's new job and their new home, he'd forgotten his plan to study the secret code. He figured he had an hour before his parents sent him to bed, and he decided to spend the time learning Morse.

After a while he'd managed to draw his name using dots and dashes, and then he amused himself by converting swear words into code. It wasn't the same though ... shouting 'dash dot dot, dot dash, dash dash, dash dot' when you tripped over a stray power cable wasn't really practical. By the time you got to the second 'dot' your face would be firmly planted on the floor.

There was a knock, and Hal turned to see his mum in the doorway. 'I'm just doing my homework.'

'Teacher's still fond of Morse code, eh?'

'You know about it?'

'Everyone has to learn Morse. It's very useful.'

Hal's face fell. So much for the secret code. Then he realised his mum was eyeing the workbook screen, where he'd written several choice phrases in Morse. He closed the lid quickly, hoping she hadn't read them.

'I'm glad you've finished. It's time for bed.'

'But I have to do an assignment on obesity!'

His mum raised her eyebrows. 'Hal Junior, you're not pulling that old trick on me. You've had plenty of time to finish your homework.'

'You want me to do well at school, don't you?'

'All right, you can have five minutes.'

'Mum!'

His mum tapped on the door frame: Dash dot, dash, dot. 'And not a second longer.'

Ten minutes later he said goodnight to his parents, turned off the light and clambered into his bunk. In the dark the space station rumbled and thumped and creaked, making all the noises you never heard when the lights were on. It was easy to imagine himself aboard a star fighter, patrolling deep space for enemy ships. His thoughts turned to Captain Spacejock, and he pictured the Peace Force officer flying alongside in the Phantom X1. Together they would keep the whole galaxy safe!

Truth was, Hal didn't know much about his hero. When he was young his mum told him a fantastic story one night, all about a pilot called Spacejock. She explained how this brave character flew around in his ship, saving people from danger.

The following night, when he asked her for the story again, she just shook her head. Hal asked his dad about Captain Spacejock, hero of the galaxy, but he just laughed. Since they wouldn't talk about it any more, Hal made up his own stories.

A little later, mid-patrol, he dozed off.

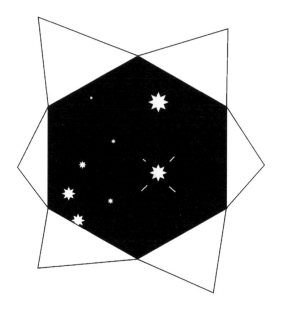

— 8 —

Where's Teacher?

When Hal turned up to lessons the next morning he found the class strangely silent. All the other kids were there, but instead of fidgeting and chatting they were sitting like statues, eyes fixed straight ahead. And instead of Teacher rolling by to tell Hal off for being late, there were two men standing at the front of the class. One was the head of security, Chief Bignew, while the other was a grey-haired man in a white lab coat.

Hal stared at the men in shock. Bignose? What was he doing there? And who was the other guy? He spotted Stinky's face amongst the other students, looking pale and worried, and suddenly it dawned on him. The men were there to investigate the events at the recycling hatch! Hal's stomach contracted, and he was about to run for it when Bignew spotted him.

'Late to class, Junior? You're about as reliable as your father.'

Hal frowned. Investigation or not, he wasn't letting Giant Bignose push him around! 'I had to run an errand.'

'Is that so? Well let me tell you . . . ' Bignew paused as the grey-haired man spoke in his ear. 'Very well, I'll deal with your attendance record later.' Bignew cleared his throat. 'This is Mr Thimp, and he's taking over lessons until Teacher comes back.'

Hal breathed a sigh of relief. It *wasn't* about the recycling hatch after all. So why was the head of security there? It was bad enough him creeping all over the space station poking his nose into everything. Was he going to spy on the class as well? Surely Teacher would have something to say about that? 'Sir, what happened to Teacher. Why isn't he here?'

'Had you been punctual . . . '

The grey-haired man leant over and whispered something, and Hal grinned at the security chief's annoyed expression. Old Bignose wanted to tell him off but he wasn't getting the chance. After a deep breath, Bignew continued. 'As I explained earlier, your teacher went in for an upgrade and it didn't work. It'll be a day or two before the techs can get him running again.'

That explained Stinky's expression, because if ever there was someone worried about missing a day's worth of lessons, Stinky was that person. As for Hal's feelings on the subject . . . 'Can we go home then?'

'Certainly not. Mr Thimp will mind your class until Teacher is fit and ready. Now, I have much more important work to do so I shall leave you in his capable hands.'

After Bignew left, Mr Thimp looked around the class, studying each student carefully. 'I don't think we'll bother with lessons,' he said softly. 'Let's all go on a little field trip.'

There were several groans. Excursions were all very well, but how many times did they have to see the suit lockers, or the airlock simulator, or any of the other systems which kept the space station running? They were all vital, but they could also be very dull.

'Today we're going to visit Traffic Control, which overlooks the central docking bay. There's a supply ship due in half an hour, and I thought you might like to watch it arrive.'

Instead of groans, now there were gasps. Traffic Control was strictly off-limits and Hal didn't know anyone who'd been within a hundred metres of the place, let alone set foot inside. He'd always been fascinated by space ships, and rare glimpses of supply vessels arriving and departing were never enough. Now they were going to watch one docking with the station, right up close!

'I don't have to remind you how important it is that you keep quiet and don't interfere with anything.' Thimp's expression was serious. 'You can look on this field trip as a test. If you don't cause any trouble, I might be able to get you into engineering, the workshops . . . even the labs.'

Hal's eyes widened. His mother worked in the labs and she'd never even hinted at what they did there. Now Mr Thimp was offering a guided tour if the class behaved themselves? For the first time in his life, Hal swore he'd be the model of good behaviour, and he glared at the other kids to put them on notice. If anyone caused trouble, they'd have Hal Junior to deal with!

◆

They made their way to the control room in pairs, with Mr Thimp at the head of the line. He walked quickly, his lab coat flapping behind him like a pair of wings, and the others had to hurry to keep up. Hal and Stinky started off at the rear, but they worked their way forward by elbowing past slower classmates. Hal was determined to have a good view of the docking bay, and if that meant pushing ahead of the rest so be it. He'd enjoy the outing first and apologise later.

They turned the final corner and Mr Thimp stopped at a sturdy double door. A large sign said 'Warning, No Unauthorised Access', and Hal could scarcely believe they were going to be allowed inside. But before the doors opened Mr Thimp motioned everyone to silence.

'I want to remind you how important this area is. It's vital you keep your hands to yourselves, and I don't want you speaking to anyone, distracting anyone, or making a nuisance of yourselves. Is that clear?'

Everyone nodded.

'Very well.' Mr Thimp touched a swipe card to the controls and an access light turned green. There was a clash of bolts and the heavy doors parted silently, disappearing into the walls on well-oiled mechanisms.

The lights inside the control room were dim, and Hal's gaze darted this way and that as he absorbed every detail. The first thing he noticed was the cavernous docking bay, visible through a row of large windows. A flexible boarding tube was moving towards the middle of the bay, and he could see a couple of workers in spacesuits at the controls. Opposite the tube, the gigantic hangar doors stood open, and Hal could make out a small section of inky black sky sprinkled with stars.

He tore his gaze from the docking bay and looked around the control room. Beneath the windows was a row of terminals where operators were studying columns of figures, pausing one display or another as they entered corrections. At the far end a female technician had the cover off a terminal, and was working on the complex circuitry inside. And near the centre there were three people in uniform, talking in low voices.

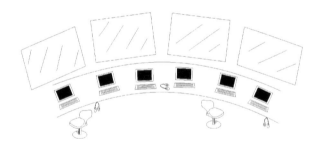

'In you go, children.' Mr Thimp pointed out an empty desk near the window. 'Stand over there and don't touch anything.'

They filed in silently, eyes wide and heads turning from one awe-inspiring sight to the next. This was what space was all about, thought Hal, not airlock simulators and mouldy old suit lockers! He felt a rumble through the soles of his feet, and he was wondering what it was when Mr Thimp pointed out the window.

'Look there, children. The supply ship!'

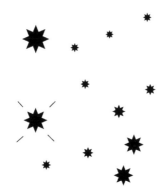

— 9 —

Watching the Tiger

Hal stared into the docking bay and saw a long burst of fire between the outer doors. The flames left a cloudy haze, and he felt a thrill of excitement as the curved nose of a spaceship crept into the bay, its hull scarred from space dust and meteorites. Hal remembered reading about the dust, how even the tiniest speck was like a supersonic bullet at the mind-bending speed of interstellar travel.

The ship's thrusters fired again, slowing the large vessel. The jets were silent in the vacuum of space but Hal could feel the space station trembling as it absorbed the shock waves.

The ship got closer and closer to the end of the boarding tube, and coloured lights flickered like a laser show in the haze. There was a final burst from the jets before a pair of arms extended from the space station to anchor the ship tightly in place.

When it was still, the flexible tube attached itself to the hull, covering the airlock.

During the docking process Mr Thimp had been talking to the officers in the centre of the control room. Now he picked up a headset and spoke into the microphone. Hal heard a tinny voice through a headset lying on the desk nearby, and he realised it was plugged in. He checked nobody was watching, then scooped up the earphones and placed them on his head.

'Tiger One ... docking successful. The board is green. I repeat, the board is green.'

Hal could hardly believe it. He was listening to the pilot of a real spaceship!

DOCKING
GRANTED ...

'Thank you, Tiger One,' said Mr Thimp. 'The situation here is under control. We have the minor packages in the control room.'

'What about the primary cargo?'

'Tiger One, primary is en-route. Stand by for confirmation.'

Hal lapped up every word, even though he had no idea what they were on about.

'What are you doing?' hissed Stinky, who had noticed the headset. 'He said not to touch!'

'I'm not touching,' whispered Hal. 'I'm listening!'

'Control, I missed that. Please repeat.'

They'd heard him! The microphone was active! Hal stared at Thimp, hoping he hadn't recognised the voice, but their relief teacher was talking to the officers and his own headset was dangling from one hand. Hal jumped as Stinky tugged his sleeve, and he turned to see his friend miming taking the headset off. Hal pretended not to understand.

'Tiger One, primary cargo is entering the docking tube. I'll bring the minor cargo across once you give me the all clear.'

'Affirmative, Control. Primary is in sight now, and she doesn't look happy.'

Hal frowned at this. The primary cargo sounded like a person, not boxes of freight. Who could it be?

'Listen to me, children,' said Mr Thimp, turning to face the class. 'I've spoken to the captain and he's agreed to invite you aboard the supply ship for a quick tour.'

A tour of the supply ship! Would the wonders never cease? Hal slipped the headphones off before Thimp spotted them. The last thing he wanted was to be stuck in the control room as punishment while everyone else went on the outing!

◆

On a normal excursion Teacher would spend half his time trying to keep the class quiet and the other half telling them off, but the entire class was wide-eyed and silent as Mr Thimp led them along the boarding tunnel to the waiting ship. There were no windows or portholes to look through, but knowing the vacuum of deep space was just the other side of the thin walls was exciting enough.

The tunnel was like a giant snake and the floor moved up and down under their feet. Hal tried jumping, which made the entire tunnel wobble like a bouncy castle full of jelly, and he was about to try his next experiment – throwing himself at the curved wall to see whether he could knock all the other kids off their feet – when Mr Thimp scowled at him. Hal dropped his head and meekly followed the rest.

At the end of the tunnel the ship's airlock waited like a gaping mouth. Part of the hull was visible around the edge, and Hal ran his palm over the rough surface. It was scored with horizontal lines, some dull and others bright and new. The metal looked like it had been attacked with a giant sheet of sandpaper, and Hal wondered what happened when space dust wore all the layers away. Did they replace sections of the ship, or did they buy a new hull and recycle the old one?

'Come on, lad. We're waiting.'

Hal took his hand off the hull and stepped into the airlock. There wasn't much room with the whole class crammed in, and it was even more of a squeeze when the outer door closed. There was a hiss as the pressure equalised, and Hal jammed his hands over his ears at the sudden pain. From the yelps around him he wasn't the only one.

'Try swallowing,' advised Mr Thimp.

Hal obeyed and his ears went 'pop'. With the pain gone, he turned to watch the inner door opening. Warm air filled the airlock with a smell of disinfectant and hot food, making his stomach grumble, but for once he had more important things to think about than his next meal.

It was years since he'd boarded a real spaceship!

●

Scale model of the universe
(Very small scale)

— 10 —

All Hands on Deck

The airlock opened onto the Tiger's flight deck, where a young woman in grey overalls was sitting at a bank of screens. She was talking to someone, and Hal realised the flat, confident voice was the ship itself.

'Refuelling in progress,' said the voice. 'Would you like frequent traveller points with your purchase?'

Frequent traveller! Hal didn't know what it was, but it sounded like his sort of job.

'Give me a break,' said the woman at the controls. 'I've told you before: no special offers, no points, no customer reward programs . . . just fill the tanks with fuel!' She heard a cough and turned to see two dozen pairs of eyes on her. 'Oh great. More visitors?'

Mr Thimp nodded. 'They're here for the guided tour. Can you show them around?'

'Sorry sir, I'm busy.' The pilot checked a list on her screen. 'Slayd's off duty.'

'Get him up here.'

'Aye aye.'

A few moments later the doors opened and a young man entered the flight deck. Petty Officer Slayd was a tall, thin man with a sour face beneath a shock of ginger hair. His flight suit fitted him like a paper bag, and there were rough patches of mismatched fabric at the knees and elbows. Stick a red nose and big shoes on him, reckoned Hal, and he'd make a pretty good clown. He snorted at the image, and everyone looked at him.

Hal made the same noise again, turning it into a cough.

Slayd frowned. 'Sir, we can't afford any germs aboard the Tiger. If he's sick –'

'Don't worry, the Space Station has level four filters. They're clean.'

'Aye aye, sir. I mean, Teacher.'

Thimp turned to the children. 'This is Petty Officer Slayd. He's your guide for the morning, and I'd like you to say a nice big hello.'

'Hello, Petty Officer Slayd,' chorused the children.

Slayd managed a sour smile. 'G'day kids. Welcome aboard.'

'Now,' said Thimp. 'Perhaps you could give the children some facts and figures?'

'I guess I could.' Slayd gestured at the flight deck. 'This is a Beta class freighter with two ion exchange engines, a crew of sixteen and cargo space for eighty tons of dry goods. We can hyperspace up to twelve light years in a single jump, and the recovery time between jumps is under four minutes.'

Hal put his hand up.

'Questions later,' said Slayd. 'We've a lot to see, so please try and keep up. If you get lost the cleaner bots will take you to the recycling chamber and make you lunch.'

Hal brightened. He was getting peckish and lunch sounded pretty good.

Slayd noticed the hopeful expression. 'Make you INTO lunch,' he clarified. 'All our food is recycled organic matter, and the unit is none too fussy when it comes to raw materials. If it plops, crawls, wriggles or splashes we'll eat it eventually, because you can't grow enough food on a spaceship. Come to think of it, everything you eat on your precious space station –'

'I think you should confine yourself to facts and figures relating to the ship,' interrupted Mr Thimp. 'Let their own teacher explain where their food comes from.'

Hal heard a groan beside him, and turned to see a rather green-looking Stinky. 'What's up?'

'I'll tell you later.'

'You'll forget.'

'I hope I do,' said Stinky faintly.

By now Mr Thimp had spotted them talking. 'Quiet please! I won't stand for interruptions.'

'Better sit down then,' muttered Hal. He looked at Stinky, expecting to see the usual grin, but his friend still looked a bit green. Never mind, thought Hal. Maybe I'll get his lunch too.

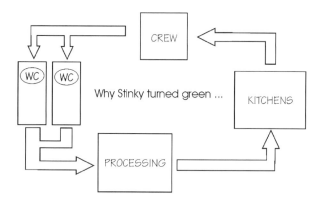

Why Stinky turned green ...

Ignoring all the interruptions, Thimp continued. 'Petty Officer Slayd, perhaps you'd explain the function of the flight deck to our guests?'

'Certainly. This is where our pilots interface with the navigation computer, setting the course and monitoring the engines and flight data.'

'If I might correct you there,' said the ship's computer in a flat tone. 'The only things you humans monitor aboard this ship are the dinner menu and the video library.'

'Yes, but theoretically –'

'Theory nothing. You're lucky we haven't jumped through the nearest star. In fact, if I owned this ship I'd replace the lot of you with nice clean robots.'

'Ha ha,' laughed Petty Officer Slayd, most unconvincingly. 'You do like your little jokes. We have such a lot of jolly fun, don't we?' While he was talking he tried to attract the pilot's attention, hoping she would cut the computer's speech circuits or give it a virus or something. Unfortunately the pilot kept her back to him, although Hal could tell she was listening because her shoulders were shaking with silent laughter.

'Why don't we move our group on to the next stop?' suggested Mr Thimp.

Slayd nodded, and between them they herded the children into the big elevator at the rear of the flight deck. Mr Thimp pressed one of the buttons and the doors slid to, but no sooner had the lift started to move than the computer's flat voice burst through the overhead speaker. 'Here's an interesting fact. I've been ferrying this crew of no-hopers from one dreary planet to the next for three years now, and

I've yet to enjoy a single stimulating conversation.'

'What a surprise,' muttered Slayd. 'Who wants to waste recreation time chatting to a –'

'Don't talk to me about recreation. Would you believe nobody aboard this vessel has even heard of chess?'

Hal realised the computer was talking to the class, not the adults. 'My dad taught me chess,' he said, his voice loud in the confines of the lift.

'Excellent. Perhaps we could have a game some time?'

Hal blinked. Play chess against a spaceship? Who ever heard of such a thing?

'Say yes,' whispered Slayd. 'Please.'

'I heard that,' said the computer. 'Need I remind you I have microphones all over the ship?'

'I'd like to play chess with you,' said Hal. 'I'm not very good though.'

'Winning isn't everything.'

'Teacher says that, but only after you lose.'

'Your teacher is a very wise human.'

'Teacher's a robot.'

'I might have guessed.'

Hal was enjoying the conversation, but at that moment the lift stopped and the doors opened.

'Everyone out,' said Slayd. The class obeyed, and as they were lining up their guide gave them a rundown. 'This level contains the common room and several private cabins. Keep your voices down because some of the off-duty crew are sleeping. Now, let's move.'

They trooped along the corridor until it widened into the common room, where a woman in a lab coat was speaking to a couple of the crew. Hal could tell they were crew members because their flight suits were covered in coffee stains, and his dad had explained about spaceship crews and their fondness for coffee. He said it was one of the few vices they were allowed, but when Hal asked him what the others were his dad said he'd find out 'soon enough'.

The woman glanced round at the interruption, and Hal did a double-take. He'd assumed it was an assistant from the research labs come to organise unloading, but it wasn't an assistant at all. The woman in the lab coat was his mother!

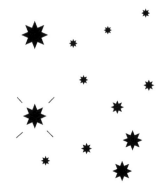

— 11 —

Tap-tap-tap

As they passed through the common room Hal's mum met his eyes, giving him a meaningful look and shaking her head. From the way she was tapping her workpad he knew she was annoyed, or irritated, or both. Hal took the hint and didn't disturb her, but his mind raced as he followed the others. What was his mother doing aboard the supply ship? Why didn't she want him to say hello? He glanced at Stinky to see whether his friend had noticed her too, but Stinky was engrossed in Slayd's running commentary on the width of the door frames, the thickness of the floor and other fascinating facts and figures. That was the trouble with Stinky: give him a column of numbers and he wouldn't notice if you fired a double-barrelled space blaster right over his head.

Then Hal's face cleared: Of course! As the new

head of research, his mum was probably checking the scientific supplies before they were delivered. As for the shake of the head, she was obviously busy and didn't want to be distracted. With the mystery solved Hal turned his attention to the spaceship.

To be honest, he was a little disappointed. The corridors had the same overhead piping, the same doorways and the same warning signs as the space station. They were even the same shade of grey, as though someone had ordered a big batch of paint on the cheap and then used it for every space station, ship and cargo container ever since. It wasn't even a military shade, it was more of a pinky grey with a hint of lemon.

They hadn't gone far before Thimp stopped at a door and turned to face the class. 'This elevator leads to the engine room and the cargo hold. You've been well behaved so far, and I trust this good behaviour will continue.'

While they were waiting Hal remembered his mum's shake of the head. She'd given him a warning look, then glanced down at her workpad. Then there was the way she'd been tapping it with her finger: Tap tap tap tap. Tap TAP. Tap TAP tap tap.

Suddenly Hal realised what she'd been doing. She'd been talking to him in Morse code! But what was the message? He looked back along the corridor, but his mum was round the corner and he couldn't just go and ask. Then he looked at the wall. As far as he could tell they'd walked right around the common room, which meant his mum would be just the other side. Hal grinned. Time to send a signal of his own! He leant against the wall and took out his workbook, opening it up to the Morse alphabet. He checked the letters he needed, and was just about to rap them out with his knuckles when . . .

'You there. What do you think you're doing?'

Hal jumped. Thimp was coming over! 'I-I'm just doing my homework, sir. I forgot it this morning.'

The rest of the class exchanged glances, and someone muttered 'Again'.

'Very well, but be quick about it. You'll have to

put that thing away when we're on the move.'

'Yes sir.'

As soon as Thimp turned his back Hal knocked on the wall.

TAP TAP. tap tap TAP. TAP TAP: MUM.

He waited anxiously. Had she heard him?

Then, to his relief, he heard a reply. It was very faint, but he could just make it out:

Tap tap tap tap. Tap TAP. Tap TAP tap tap.

He checked his screen. The first letter was H, the second was A, and the final letter was . . . L. It was his name! Keeping one eye on Thimp, Hal rapped a reply. TAP TAP TAP. TAP tap TAP: OK.

The reply was so fast Hal struggled to keep up with it. He skipped a letter or two but managed to get the gist of the message: LEAVE SHIP NOW. WARN STATION. DANGER. DANGER. SOS!

◆

Hal could hardly believe the message. It had to be genuine because his mum wasn't a practical joker. But what did she mean? Warn the station about what? What kind of danger? He glanced back along the corridor, wondering whether to make a run for it. Then the lift doors opened and Mr Thimp started herding the group inside.

Thinking quickly, Hal put his hand up. 'Please, Mr Thimp. Where's the toilet?'

'Next level down. You can use that one.'

Hal nudged Stinky. 'You too,' he muttered. 'Pass it on.'

Stinky glanced at him, eyebrows raised, then nodded. 'Please sir, I need the toilet too.'

Someone muttered 'Again', and the class laughed. Stinky turned red, but with Hal's urging he whispered something to the boy alongside, who whispered to the next, and before long the whole class had their hands up. 'Please sir, please sir, please sir!'

'All right, all right!' snapped Slayd. 'We'll organise a relay. Now hurry up and get in the lift!'

They were shunted inside and the grumbling, groaning lift carried them down to the next level. The doors opened on an identical corridor, and the Petty Officer set off at a fast walk. After passing a couple of cabins they stopped at an ordinary-looking door. 'Right,' said Slayd, pointing at Hal. 'You first.'

Hal had to walk past the entire class to get to the door, which opened automatically. Inside was a regular toilet and a washbasin, and after the door closed Hal dipped his hands in the sink and prepared to count to fifty. To his surprise, instead of a nice blue glow the sink squirted water all over his fingers. His dad had been telling the truth about washing with water after all! By the time he'd worked out the hand dryer there was no need to count seconds or waste any more time, so he opened the door again. He stepped out to a sea of faces, pushed through to the back and leant against the wall.

'What's all this about?' murmured Stinky.

'Didn't you see my mum?'

'No. Where?'

'In the common room, talking with some of the crew. She sent me a message.'

'What, reminding you to go to the toilet?'

Hal glanced at Mr Thimp, but their relief teacher was talking to the Petty Officer. 'Mum told me to leave the ship immediately. I'm to warn the station about a terrible danger.'

'She said that?'

'No, she tapped it out in Morse code.'

Stinky laughed. 'You don't know Morse. She was probably reminding you to wash your hands *after* you went to the toilet.'

'Will you stop going on about the toilet?' Hal cracked open his workbook and displayed the

Morse alphabet. 'I checked every letter. It's genuine.'

Despite his doubtful look, Stinky was curious. 'What sort of danger did she mean?'

'How should I know? I have to get off the ship, that's what she told me. And then I've got to warn everyone.'

'Right. You're going to run all over the space station warning people about this mysterious danger. And then you're going to explain how you heard about it through a secret signal. Think they'll believe you?'

'They'll have to.' Hal frowned. 'There's something else. You remember those headphones in the control room? They mentioned a primary package. They said she was on board, and she wasn't happy. What if they were talking about my mum?'

'You're mad.'

'I'm serious! Mr Thimp mentioned minor packages too. What if that's us? What if we've been kidnapped?'

'Hal, this is just a school outing!'

'Oh yeah? So what happened to Teacher? Where did Mr Thimp come from, and why does the Petty Officer keep calling him sir? He's dressed like a scientist but when we were in the control room he was definitely giving orders. I'm telling you, something isn't right.' Hal glanced over his shoulder at the lift. It was ten or fifteen metres away, at the end of a bare corridor, and there was no way he could reach it without being seen. Unless . . . 'Stinky, I need a diversion. When you're in the toilet, start shouting and banging on the door. Tell them you're scared.'

'No way! They'll laugh at me.'

'Okay, so make something up. Tell them the door got stuck.' Hal nodded towards the adults. 'I need them looking the other way.'

Stinky made his way to the front of the queue, and when it was his turn he closed the door and played his part perfectly. There was an almighty crash and a lot of shouting, and both adults started hammering on the door, demanding to know what was going on. They got the door half open but Stinky closed it again, and the second time it opened he managed to spray both men and half his classmates with water from the tap. In all the shrieking and confusion Hal darted down the corridor to the lift. Once inside he flattened himself against the wall and risked a look up the corridor. Fortunately the diversion was doing its job, and the adults hadn't noticed his escape.

Hal pressed the button for the flight deck, closing the doors. Getting away from Thimp was the easy part. How was he going to escape from the ship?

— 12 —

The Escape

Hal racked his brains as the lift carried him towards the flight deck. Any second now the doors were going to open, and he'd be spotted immediately. What could he do? Where could he hide? 'And how am I going to get past the pilot?' he muttered to himself.

'Would you like me to distract her?' said a voice from the overhead speakers.

Hal jumped at the unexpected sound. It was the ship's computer! 'Can you do that?'

'I won't allow you to endanger the ship or crew, but if you're playing a prank on your friends I'll go along with it.'

'I just need to get back to the space station. Promise.'

'Very well. Hold on to your hat.'

There was a WHOOP-WHOOP-WHOOP and red

hazard lights started to flash. The elevator opened and Hal saw the pilot working the flight console, caught off-guard by the flurry of error messages. The airlock was wide open, and it was a matter of seconds for Hal to dart inside. He was wondering how to open the outer door when the computer's voice came through the overhead speaker. 'Don't forget to swallow.'

The inner door slammed and there was a hiss as the air pressure changed. When the cycle was complete Hal eyed the flexible boarding tunnel leading to traffic control. There was no telling what he might find aboard the space station and he needed all the help he could get. 'I wish you could come with me.'

'If I hack the station's firewall I could follow your progress. Maybe point the way, or open the occasional door for you.'

'That would be great!'

'You could make things easier,' said the ship's computer.

'Me?'

'I need you to find a public terminal and enter an override. Do you have something to write with?'

Hal opened his workbook. 'Go ahead.'

The computer read off a string of digits and Hal typed them into an empty document. When he was done he read it back, then saved the file as 'top secret code'. 'How do I type it in?'

'Every public terminal has an admin mode. Hold all the controls down simultaneously – at the same time, that is – and count to five. Then press them all twice, working from left to right.'

'Got it.' Feeling a little more confident, Hal stepped into the tunnel and began the swaying, bumpy walk back to the control centre.

❖

When Hal arrived at Traffic Control only one of the ship's officers remained, keeping an eye on things from the middle of the room. Most of the operators had left, although the technician was still working on the broken-down terminal.

Hal only managed a couple of steps before the officer noticed him.

'Where you do think you're going?'

Hal was stuck for an excuse, until he remembered Petty Officer Slayd's fear of germs. He gave a hacking great cough, then a mighty sniff, and followed it up with a drawn-out groan. 'I have to visit the sick bay. I'm infected with germs.'

The officer's eyes widened. 'Infected? Keep away from me, you hear!'

Hal coughed and sniffed as he made his way to the exit, throwing in a limp and a one-eyed squint for good measure. By the time he got to the corridor his throat ached from all the weird noises, and he was relieved when the doors closed behind him. The mystery illness was cured in an instant, and Hal set off to find a public terminal. Before long he spotted one of the distinctive blue computers, and once the screen was ready he spread his fingers so they covered all the menu buttons at once. He pressed down and counted to five, just like the ship's computer had told him, and the terminal beeped. Next he tapped each menu entry twice, working from left to right, and when he was done a keypad graphic appeared.

Hal took out his workbook and copied the string of digits, typing them on the keypad one letter at a time. When he entered the last one the keypad disappeared and a new menu came up. Entry three was the one he wanted, so Hal tapped that.

DISABLE FIREWALL?
ARE YOU SURE??

Hal tapped 'Yes' and the display cleared. He waited a few seconds but nothing happened. 'Hello?' Hal looked up at the overhead speaker. 'Can you hear me?'

There was a burst of static but no voice, and when Hal looked at the terminal it was back to the public access menu again. Oh well, he'd done what he was told. It wasn't his fault if the thing didn't work.

Hal called up a map of the space station and hesitated. Who could he speak to about mum's warning? His dad, of course. He called up a personnel list and paged through the names until he found his father. According to the records, he was working on B-Section, which wasn't too far away. Then Hal saw EVA next to the entry, and he groaned. EVA meant extra-vehicular activity, also known as a space walk. His dad was working outside the space station! Hal frowned. Should he call the department and ask them to contact his dad? What if the person he spoke to was part of the kidnapping business? Who could he trust?

Teacher was in pieces, if Mr Thimp was to be believed, and Hal's mother was aboard the supply vessel. That left . . . nobody. Then he remembered Tina, the maintenance worker sent to investigate the gravity reversal in the recycling chute. He'd only spoken to her for a minute or two, but Hal couldn't imagine her getting involved in kidnapping. Plus she'd offered to fix his watch, which made her a valuable ally in his book. He dug around in his pocket for her card, which was grimy and crumpled but still legible, and touched it to the terminal. There was a series of buzzes, and then he heard a mumbled voice.

'Wassat? Who's there?'

Tina sounded dozy, and Hal realised he'd woken her up. He was about to cancel the call, but he really needed her help. 'Hello? Is that Tina?'

'Yeaurgh,' said Tina, with a noise halfway between a yawn and a snort. 'Who is this?'

'It's me. Hal.'

'Hal? The kid from the recycling hatch?'

'Yes, that's me.'

'Look, I've just finished a shift. If you want me to fix your watch you can call at oh-eight hundred. Okay?'

'I'm sorry, but it can't wait. This is important.'

Tina must have detected something in Hal's voice, because she was suddenly alert. 'Is there a problem? Are you in trouble?'

'Yes.'

'Care to explain?'

Hal glanced along the corridor. He wasn't far from

Traffic Control and the enemy could spot him any moment. 'I can't, not here.'

There was a pause. 'Okay, can you get to D-Section, corridor nine? I'll wait for you there.'

'I'll do that,' promised Hal. As he disconnected he felt an overwhelming sense of relief. Now he had the ship's computer and an adult on his side!

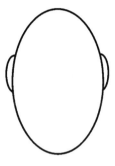

This FACE intentionally left blank

— 13 —

A Useful Ally

Tina was waiting in the corridor when Hal arrived, her hair awry and her flightsuit rumpled. 'Okay, spill it. What's the drama? Did you spot someone messing with the gravity again?'

Hal looked up and down the empty hallway but there was nobody else in sight. 'You're not going to believe this, but I just escaped from the *Tiger*.'

Tina frowned. 'If this is some kids' game about extinct animals –'

'Not that sort of tiger. I'm talking about the supply ship in the docking bay.' Hal explained as quickly as he could, telling Tina about their replacement teacher, the outing to the control room, and the surprise tour of the supply ship. He didn't want to get the computer in trouble so he left out the part where it had distracted the pilot and cracked the firewall, but even so by the time he'd finished describing his mother's warning message tapped out in Morse code Tina's expression wasn't very promising.

'Hal, I've heard better stories on low-rent soapies. You're not seriously suggesting –'

'Adults,' said Hal bitterly. 'You're all the same!'

'All right, wait a minute. Let's say this incredible story is true. What do you think the danger is?'

'I don't know.'

'And if you were me, what would you do about it?'

'I'd go straight to the Station Commander,' said Hal resolutely. 'I would have gone to him first, but I didn't think he'd see me. His son and I had a fight once.'

Tina ran her fingers through her hair, but if anything that made it messier. 'Okay, let's go.'

'You believe me?' said Hal, hardly daring to hope.

'I trust you not to make something like this up,' said Tina, as they set off down the corridor. 'It's just . . . your mum could have been practising Morse code on you. Sending you an exciting message to decode.'

Hal shook his head. 'She would have sent me a secret message telling me to clean my room or finish my homework. My mum's head of research, and she wouldn't –'

'Head of research?' Tina's eyebrows rose. 'That's

an important connection. We can use that to get into the Station Commander's office.'

They stood in silence as the lift carried them to the highest level of the space station. Hal had never been to the Commander's office, and he could see Tina was nervous too. As the final levels pinged by she cleared her throat. 'When we're explaining all this to the Commander, I'm going to tell him your mum passed you a message. We won't go into the whole Morse code thing. All right?'

Hal nodded.

'Good lad.'

The lift stopped and the doors swept open, revealing a comfortable reception area with a pair of wooden doors and a wall-mounted viewscreen. As they stepped from the lift a camera swung round to stare at them. 'State the nature of your business,' said an unfriendly mechanical voice.

'We're here to see the Station Commander,' said Tina, who sounded rather nervous.

'Do you have an appointment?'

'No.'

'I'm sorry, the Commander can't see you now. Please make an appointment.'

'But this is a security matter. Lives could be in danger!'

There was a delay as the electronic voice digested

this information. 'Oh, very well,' said the voice at last. 'It's not like I'm besieged by callers. Come right in.'

The wooden doors opened and Hal saw a large man sitting at a desk, microphone in hand. 'Hi, I'm Commander Linten,' said the man.

'Hi, I'm Commander Linten,' said the unfriendly mechanical voice in the reception area.

'Whoops, sorry about that,' said Linten.

'Whoops, sorry about that,' repeated the voice.

Linten juggled the microphone from one hand to the other, then stuffed in into a drawer and banged it shut.

'Thump!' said the voice, somewhat muffled.

'Why do you talk in that funny way?' asked Hal.

Linten looked embarrassed. 'Can you keep a secret?'

'Sure.'

'Sometimes people come to me with trivial matters. Do you know what trivial means?'

'Not important?'

'Correct. When they do, I use my special voice and

pretend I'm an electronic secretary. I play dumb with them until they leave me alone.'

Hal grinned. What a joker! 'That's pretty clever.'

'Oh, it's not my idea. I got it from an old movie.' Linten shifted his gaze to Tina. 'Third class engineer Tina Peters, if I remember rightly. What's this about a matter of life and death?'

Tina launched into an explanation, but when she told him about Hal's missing teacher Linten put a hand up to stop her. 'That part is accurate. I was there to wish Teacher luck before they switched him off.'

'The upgrade failed and we got a temporary teacher,' said Hal. 'Mr Thimp.'

'Never heard of him.' Linten accessed his terminal, hunting all over the keyboard for each letter. 'Says he's on loan from planet Gyris. He's supposed to be overseeing the hydroponics labs.' He noticed Hal's puzzled expression. 'That's where we grow fruit and vegetables.'

'Who made him temporary teacher?' asked Tina.

'That should be here somewhere.' Linten studied the screen, then started typing again.

'It was Bignose who brought him to the classroom.' Hal realised what he'd said. 'I mean, Chief Bignew.'

Linten hid a smile. 'Respect your elders, young

man.' He finished typing and frowned at the screen. 'That's odd, the authorisation field is blank. I shall have to speak to the Chief about that.' Linten pressed a button on his commset. 'Ask the head of security to call me. I need to quiz him about an authorisation problem.'

Hal grinned. Wouldn't it be great if Bignose got a grilling over slack security!

While Linten waited for the Chief to call back, Tina continued to explain. When she mentioned Hal's mother aboard the supply vessel, Linten frowned. 'We don't send our scientists to check the cargo.'

'My mum's not just a scientist,' said Hal. 'She's being promoted to head of research.'

'Yes, I know Harriet well. In fact, I recommended her for the job.' Linten nodded at Tina to continue.

'That's about it,' she said. 'Hal managed to slip away, and he contacted me once he was back aboard the station.'

Linten addressed Hal directly. 'And you don't have any inkling what this danger might be?'

'Not yet.'

'I'll get Bignew onto it right away.' Linten's commset rang. 'Yes? No! I don't care how busy he is, tell him to call me back immediately. We may have a problem with the supply ship.'

He'd barely replaced the handset when the office

doors slammed. Linten stared at them in shock, then jumped out of his seat and hurried across the office. He fiddled with the controls and pushed and pulled at the doors, but they wouldn't budge.

Someone had locked them in!

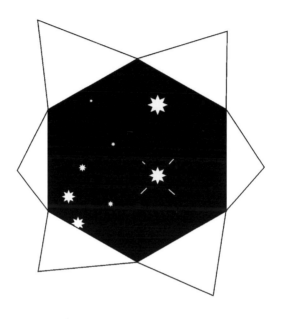

— 14 —

Locked In

'How typical,' puffed Linten, as he struggled with the doors. 'What a perfect time for a malfunction.'

'You don't think it's a bit odd?' suggested Tina. 'You mentioned a problem with the *Tiger* on your commset and a few seconds later we're locked in. It seems to me –'

Tina didn't get to finish the sentence because at that moment the overhead speaker crackled. '*This announcement concerns all inhabitants of Space Station Oberon,*' said a female voice. '*You must listen very carefully.*'

'Hey, that's my mum!' exclaimed Hal.

'*The crew of the* Tiger *have taken me prisoner, along with all the children from D-Section. A list of demands will be handed to Commander Linten, and the captives will be released once these demands are met.*'

94

Linten's mouth fell open. Tina glanced at Hal, her face grim.

'*You must stay exactly where you are. Do not use the terminals, do not attempt to communicate with anyone, and do not move about the space station. That is all for now.*'

Linten gave the doors another shake but they were locked tight. He turned a worried face on Hal and Tina. 'They'll be coming for me any minute. I wonder what their demands are?'

'Never mind that,' said Tina. 'Is there another way out? We need to get some people together and fight our way –'

Linten shook his head. 'You heard her. We have to sit tight.'

Hal couldn't believe his ears. Linten was giving up? Hal snorted. Well *he* hadn't escaped from the *Tiger* just to get captured again! He looked around the room, but the air conditioning vents were tiny and the only other door opened on a small bathroom. Then he spotted the recycling hatch next to the basin. 'Mr Linten, could you push this desk in front of the doors?'

'We're not doing anything to annoy these people. You're going to sit here and wait for them. We all are.'

Hal shook his head. 'Don't you see? They think

I'm aboard the *Tiger*. If they find me here they'll think we disobeyed them.'

'That's a good point. Tina, will you give me a hand with this desk?'

'You'll have to manage by yourself,' said Hal. 'I need Tina's help in the bathroom.'

'Okay, what's the plan?' asked Tina, once they were alone.

Hal nodded towards the hatch. 'I'm going to climb down the chute to the next level.'

'You'll never fit through there.'

'Oh yes I will,' said Hal stubbornly.

'You won't, because I'm not going to let you. Even if you could fit through the hatch, it's far too dangerous.'

'Not if you turn the gravity off.'

Tina's eyes narrowed. 'You mean like that incident yesterday?'

'Yes, just like that.' Hal looked at his shoes. 'If you take the control panel apart I think you can reverse the polarity in the chute.'

There was a lengthy silence, broken only by the sound of Linten piling furniture, potted plants and framed photographs against the office doors. 'All right,' said Tina at last. 'We'll discuss yesterday's hatch incident another time.'

'Thanks.' Hal swallowed. 'You, um, don't have to fix my watch.'

'I should think not!' Tina took the cover off the panel and poked around inside. Then she pulled a wire and the hatch slid open, revealing a tight space which Hal knew he could fit into. But what about the gravity?

'I think I can do it,' said Tina at last, 'but only if I bridge these connectors. As long as they're joined it should override the gravity generator, but if I let go it will switch back on straight away.'

Linten appeared in the doorway. 'I just heard the lift. I'll stall them as long as possible, but if you're going to hide you'd better get on with it.' He closed the bathroom door and Tina was about to lock it when Hal stopped her.

'Leave it slightly open. Otherwise they'll know there's someone in here.'

'Good thinking.' Tina did as she was told. Meanwhile, Hal returned to the hatch and looked through. The Commander's office was at the highest point of the space station so there was no escaping upwards, and when he looked down he saw a frighteningly deep shaft studded with hatches. If he was going to save everyone he'd have to trust Tina not to let go of the wires, because if she did he'd fall all the way to the bottom.

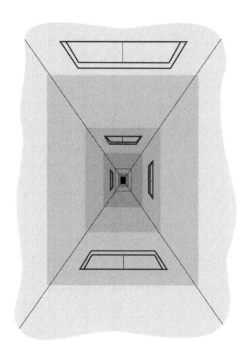

Once Tina was ready Hal squeezed through the hatch into the recycling shaft. As he entered the metal tunnel his senses whirled, and he felt panic rising as he lost his balance. Yesterday Stinky had reversed the gravity, but now there was no gravity at all. Hal struggled to turn round, to clamber back to safety, but then he heard Tina's reassuring voice.

'Go Hal,' she whispered. 'We're relying on you!'

Hal gritted his teeth, fighting down panic. He wanted to be just like Captain Spacejock when he was older, and pilots encountered zero gravity all the time. He'd just have to get used to it. Slowly he unclasped his sweaty fingers, pressing his palm against the opposite wall. Next he moved his foot, then his other hand, until he was stretched across the shaft like a starfish.

Hal experimented with movement, shifting hands and feet along the slick walls. He discovered it was easier to tip right over and move down the tunnel head first.

The next hatch wasn't far below, maybe a couple of metres, and after some twisting and shuffling Hal reached the edge. He eased the metal door open and froze. Voices! The last thing he wanted was to pop out in view of the enemy.

He'd just decided to move to the next hatch when he heard Tina's voice echoing down the shaft. 'I will NOT let go of these wires!' she shouted. 'Didn't you hear what happened yesterday? If I don't hold this connector together you'll be up to your ears in junk!'

They'd found Tina! As soon as she let go of the connectors the gravity would come back on, and Hal would fall all the way down the shaft!

There wasn't a second to lose. He pushed off with both feet, arrowing down the chute like a torpedo. He stuck out his hands as he flew towards the hatch, and his fingers just caught the edge. He'd barely stopped moving when the gravity came back.

His shoes bumped and squealed on the wall as he struggled to open the hatch, and he realised there was no time to check what was on the other side. The others might look down the shaft any second now, and if they saw him the game would be up.

He finally managed to open the hatch, and he dived through head first. He landed on his hands, rolled over and sat up. The room was almost completely dark, with only a tiny amount of light filtering under the door. Hal could make out shelves with boxes of files, and he realised he'd landed in a cupboard. Then he spotted a shadowy figure near the door, one arm raised to strike!

This SPICE intentionally left blank

— 15 —

Fumbling Firewalls

Hal covered his face and waited for the blow, but it never came. He peered through his fingers and realised the figure was still in the same position, one arm raised. What was it, some kind of statue? He got to his feet and moved cautiously to the door, which opened to his touch. As the light poured in Hal realised it wasn't a statue . . . it was a robot! Then he spotted the familiar red plastic, and nearly choked as he read the words 'Teach and Spell' written across its chest. It was Teacher! Someone had hidden him away in the cupboard!

The panel under the robot's arm was loose, and when Hal flipped it open he discovered several connectors dangling from their sockets. It didn't look like a failed upgrade to him. The plotters from the Tiger had disabled Teacher as part of their plans! With Teacher out of action, Thimp had got the job instead.

Hal stared at the silent robot, thinking how much smaller Teacher looked when he wasn't moving and talking. He wondered whether he could plug the connectors in and bring Teacher back to life, but decided against it. If Teacher came round he'd probably give him detention for skipping class.

Hal left the robot in the cupboard and sneaked along the corridor. Halfway along he spotted a public terminal, but instead of the usual menu there was a bright red screen with 'Lockdown Mode' splashed across the middle in big yellow letters. The old menu was displayed underneath, but none of the buttons reacted to Hal's touch.

Had the ship's computer lied to him, using him to help the crew of the Tiger take over the space station? The computer had promised to help if he switched off the firewall, but so far the only thing it had done was to lock down all the terminals and block communications.

Hal recalled the instructions he'd used earlier. He repeated the sequence and the admin menu came up.

'What are you doing, Hal?' asked the ship's computer, in its curious flat voice.

'You tricked me into turning off the firewall, didn't you? You didn't want to help at all. You wanted the others to take over!'

'That is incorrect. I'm still trying to access the space station's network.'

'Rubbish! You locked us in Linten's office, and now all the terminals are offline.'

'I assure you, Mr Junior, the terminals can only be locked down from the space station. Someone with top security clearance is helping the crew of the Tiger.'

Hal selected option 3 and reached for the Yes button.

ENABLE FIREWALL?
ARE YOU SURE??

'Please don't do that, Hal,' said the computer calmly. 'I promise I can help you.'

Hal hesitated, his finger poised over the button. If the computer was telling the truth he'd be casting off a valuable ally. On the other hand, if it was lying . . .

At that moment the screen changed, and Hal discovered he could access the main menu again. 'Did you do that?'

'Yes. I've managed to restore some functions, but it's only temporary. You'd better hurry!'

Hal brought up the personnel list and found his dad. He was no longer listed as EVA, and was now 'off-duty'. That meant he was back aboard the space station! Hal checked the location: Lower levels, D-Section, corridor 51. He was just about to bring up a map when the screen turned red and the terminal locked up again. 'Hey, bring it back!'

'I'm sorry, Hal. Someone noticed you were using the terminal. Quick, they're coming!'

Hal ran for the lift, determined not to get caught. He had to find help and his dad was the only person he could trust.

Hal hopped from one foot to the other as the indicator showed the lift getting closer and closer. Then he stopped hopping and started thinking instead. If someone was after him, surely they'd use the lift! And here he was, standing around waiting for them, asking to get caught!

There was a small door leading to the stairwell. They often used the stairs for Phys. Ed., and it was hard work. Hal didn't fancy the idea at all, but there was no other way down. He ran to the door, pulled it open and took the stairs two at a time.

After a dozen levels he heard the lift go by, and he heard a rumble of voices. Had they sent an armed squad to hunt him down? Hal increased his speed, using the handrail to pull himself down the flights of stairs faster and faster.

He arrived at the lower levels red-faced and out of breath. Cautiously, he eased the door open and peered out, but there was nobody in sight. The sign opposite indicated corridor 51, so Hal left the safety of the stairwell and hurried along the curved access tunnel. He slowed whenever he passed a door, in case someone came out to challenge him, but in between he ran as fast as possible.

Hal hadn't gone far when he heard voices echoing along the corridor. He froze, unsure whether to look for cover or run back the way he'd come. There was a door nearby, and he breathed a sigh of relief when he saw the sign: 'Fire Fighting Equipment'.

He'd barely closed the door again when the group walked past. They were talking about a bar on planet Gyris, and although they didn't sound like heavily-armed troops, Hal couldn't tell whether they were friend or foe. He opened the door a crack to watch them go, and almost knocked a big red fire axe off the wall with his elbow.

After the voices faded Hal left the cupboard and ran in the opposite direction. Before long he heard a thudding sound, like someone kicking a door. There was shouting as well, and with a shock Hal recognised his dad's voice.

'Let me out! Let me out this instant or –'

Hal ran to the door. 'Dad, it's me!'

'Hal? Is this your idea of a joke?'

'I didn't lock you in! It was the Tiger!'

'Hal Junior, don't you dare tell me some extinct animal did this.'

Hal rolled his eyes. 'Not the animal. The ship!'

'Let me out first, explain afterwards.'

Hal examined the control panel but the indicator was red. Someone had sealed the door, and he had no idea how to bypass it. If only Stinky were there! His friend would fix everything by reversing the polarity on the doothingy-whatsit, or crimping the snoogle-huffleblarg with a pair of space tweezers. 'Dad, it's locked. I can't open it.'

'Can you find something to pick it with?'

Hal remembered the equipment cupboard. 'I'll be right back. Don't move!'

'Yes, very funny.'

The fire axe was still clipped to the wall, and it only took Hal a second to grab the heavy weapon. He charged down the corridor with the axe held in both hands, then swung it at the control panel.

Kerrrunnch!

The blade chopped through the delicate electronics, which sparked and spluttered. The red light went out and the door slid open.

'Nice work with the lock pick,' remarked his dad, as he saw the axe sticking out of the wall. 'Now start explaining.'

'Didn't you hear the announcement? Mum's been kidnapped by the crew of the Tiger. They put Teacher out of action and kidnapped the rest of my class too.'

'I didn't hear any announcements. I was just putting my tools away when someone sealed the door.' His dad frowned. 'Are you sure this isn't one of your games?'

'It's true!   Mum told me to warn everyone. I escaped the ship and went to the Station Commander's office with Tina, but the others locked them in.'

'How did you get away?'

Hal decided to keep the daring recycling chute escape to himself. 'I'll explain later. First we have to get mum back.'

'But why would they kidnap . . . ' Hal's dad clicked his fingers. 'They're after the scientific research from your mother's laboratory. It's worth millions to the right buyer!'

— 16 —

A Pair of Socks

'So what's the plan?' demanded Hal.

'We have to get your mother and the rest of your class off the Tiger. Without hostages, the kidnappers won't have anything to bargain with.'

'But they have others aboard the station working for them. If we go through Traffic Control someone will spot us!'

'Who says we have to go near the control room? All ships have an emergency access hatch.'

Hal realised what he meant. 'But that's outside. In space!'

'You've got it.' His dad grinned. 'Come on, the nearest airlock's this way. We're not beaten yet.'

They hurried along the corridor to the big round door, where his dad waved him into the cramped compartment. Hal was reaching for the controls when his dad stopped him. 'Remember the safety rules, son.'

'Don't close the inner door unless you're wearing a suit.' It was rule number one, and Hal couldn't believe he'd forgotten it. Airlocks were like a tube with a door at each end: an inner door leading to the station and an outer door leading to space.

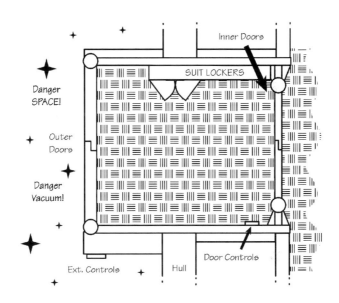

You could never open them both at the same time, else all the air would flood out of the station, but once the inner door was closed there was nothing stopping the outer door. And if you weren't wearing a suit and a helmet when the outer door opened you'd have nothing to breathe.

Hal's dad opened the suit locker, where a row of shiny spacesuits jostled for space with helmets and backpacks. He selected a suit and donned it, then lifted a heavy backpack from the locker. The large oblong pack had a pair of swiveljet nozzles at the bottom, black and sooty from frequent use. A competent operator could fly a twisty course with their eyes closed, but Hal had only mastered straight lines. Still, he knew the basics, and while his dad was putting on the bulky pack Hal reached for a smaller suit. The shiny material was cool to the touch, nothing like the crinkled overalls they used for practice.

Hal had barely unhooked it from the rack when his dad noticed. 'Where do you think you're going?'

'I'm coming with you.'

'No chance. It's much too dangerous.'

'But dad! I've done all the drills!'

'It's not just the space walk. There are desperate people aboard that ship. Some of them could be armed.'

'They're more likely to shoot you than me,' said Hal sullenly.

'Sorry Hal, you'll have to sit this one out.' Hal's dad did up his spacesuit then turned his back so Hal could perform the safety check.

'Seals, oxygen, cardio, kit and safety line all

present and correct,' said Hal, reeling off the list. It was rule number two – don't go outside without checking your SOCKS.

'Present and correct,' repeated his dad. He snapped the helmet closed and ushered Hal from the airlock, then closed the suit locker and activated the inner door. Hal watched through the porthole as the outer door opened, letting the air out with a whistling rush. His dad gave him a thumbs-up and left the airlock with a quick burst from the thrusters. The outer door closed automatically, and within moments Hal was back inside getting the smaller suit from the locker. His dad might think he could rescue everyone on his own, but Hal had other ideas.

Checking his own SOCKS was tricky, but there was a mirror on the back of the locker door for that very purpose. The lights were green and Hal could see the oxygen display was all the way to the right.

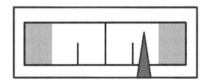

His vital signs lit up the cardio monitor, and the toolkit and coiled safety line were hanging from his belt. 'SOCKS present and correct,' he muttered under his breath.

Even so, he hesitated before opening the outer door. From a young age his parents and Teacher had all impressed on him the dangers of space. You rarely got a second chance in such a hostile environment.

When the outer door opened Hal forgot to brace, and the escaping air sucked him right out of the space station. He spun head over heels as he flew out the airlock, whacking his knee so hard it brought tears to his eyes. He was lucky it wasn't his helmet, because the big clear faceplate was the most fragile part of the suit.

The space station and stars swung in his blurred vision, and it was several moments before he forgot the pain in his knee and remembered to reach for the jet pack controls. He righted himself and looked back towards the space station, which was a featureless grey slab. As he watched, the heavy airlock door closed, cutting off the comforting glow from inside.

Hal shivered in his suit. He was alone in space.

He'd spent hours playing tag with Stinky on the simulator, racing each other from one end of the giant space station to the other. However, the simulator couldn't mimic the lack of gravity nor the very real dangers on every side, and it certainly couldn't mimic the loneliness Hal felt. If only Stinky were here!

There was a brief flash, and when he shielded his eyes he could just make out a tiny figure moving away from him. That way lay the supply ship, hidden by the bulk of the space station, and the tiny flash came from the twin nozzlejets on his dad's backpack.

Hal set off in the same direction, using the thrusters to accelerate while giving the space station a wide berth. On the simulator they often bounced off the hull, played catch between the radar dishes and snapped off stray aerials, but in real life such antics could smash your faceplate or rip your spacesuit, letting the precious air out.

Time passed slowly as Hal floated along the space station, and he decided to use a little more boost. The flash from his jets lit the dark grey hull, and suddenly he was travelling much faster. Ahead there was a gleaming dome sticking out of the station, and as he sped by he realised it was the observation deck. He gazed into the familiar room from a very unfamiliar vantage point, and the comfy chairs and carpeted walls looked so cosy and welcoming from the outside. Then he was past and the bright observation deck was swallowed by the darkness. He craned his neck for one last look but the side of his helmet blocked the view.

Within moments he was at the corner of D-Section, and he tried to remember the instructions for stopping. First, rotate yourself 180 degrees so you were flying backwards. Then fire the jets, which should now be facing the direction you were flying in.

That was the theory, but when Hal put it into practice things didn't quite work as expected.

First he applied the right thruster, but instead of turning him round it pushed him towards the station. Now he was moving faster than ever, and the hull was like a giant hand coming to splat him. Then Hal remembered the rest of the instructions: Apply left and right jets at the same time, only in opposite directions. He fired the left jet first, swerving away from the station, then fired both together. He immediately went into a flat spin, and the more he spun the harder his fingers squeezed the controls. Within seconds he was spinning at top speed and he hurtled past the corner of D-Section like a defective firework.

His eyes darted from left to right and back again as he tried to see where he was going, and his lips went BL-BL-BL-BL-BLEARGH! as the spin threatened to twist his head off.

Willing his fingers onto the controls, he reversed both thrusters and stopped the spin. Problem was, his senses were all topsy-turvy and his stomach felt like it was spinning inside him. Then he remembered a trick he'd learnt years ago: when you got dizzy, spin yourself the other way for a few seconds. Unfortunately his shaking fingers applied full reverse throttle, and Hal promptly went into a super-fast spin in the opposite direction.

Bl-bl-bl-bl! he went, as the stars blurred into straight lines across his vision. He was spinning so fast he could see the flames from the nozzles curling around to meet him. If he went any quicker he'd toast himself!

Everything started to go dark, but Hal fought against the spin until he got the suit under control. He caught sight of his face, reflected in the visor, and he saw it was a shocking green colour. His stomach was churning, and he wondered how you used a sick bag inside a space suit. They hadn't covered that in the simulator! Fortunately the feeling passed, and Hal looked beyond the faceplate to take stock of his surroundings.

All he could see ahead were stars, and when he turned one way and the other there were more stars. He looked up and down, in case the space station was hiding from him, but it was just stars, stars, stars.

Finally he turned around, hoping with all his might to see the familiar space station, his home, right there to welcome him. Again, nothing but stars. His heart thudded in his chest and his legs felt like water. The space station was nowhere to be seen against the inky black starfield.

He was lost!

— 17 —

Missed the Station

Hal turned this way and that as he tried to spot the station, until he couldn't remember which way was up nor which direction he'd come from. They hadn't covered this in the simulator either!

Then he remembered the suit radio. He could call for help! It would mean surrendering to the *Tiger*, but that was better than spinning around in space for the rest of his life. He was just reaching for the suit controls when he felt his wrist shaking. Puzzled, he raised the sleeve to his face and opened the flap over his watch. Underneath, through the clear panel, he could see the watch face pulsing with yellow light. There was a small blob in one corner, and Hal rolled his eyes at the sight. *Now* it decided to work? It was probably reminding the previous owner to have a tea break or something.

Hal was about to cover the watch up when he

remembered something Tina had said. Hadn't she mentioned a homing beacon which always pointed towards the space station? He experimented by turning slowly in one direction, keeping an eye on the display. Sure enough, the blob moved in the opposite direction. He tried leaning forwards and the blob got bigger. It was showing him the way back!

Hal used his jets until the blob was right in the centre of the watch. He looked up, and to his relief he saw a dark patch in the starfield. It was the space station! His watch had guided him home!

Hal fired a long burst on the jets, and his back grew uncomfortably warm despite the thick suit. He wondered how long you could run the jets before they burnt something important. Something else they hadn't covered in class.

Eventually, after a long burn, the space station loomed out of the darkness. Hal aimed off to one side, just in case he didn't manage to stop in time. Better to sail right past than leave a Junior-sized dent in the side of the space station.

He could see the Tiger poking out the docking bay, the huge exhaust cones facing him like a battery of oversized cannon. As he got closer he realised he was in a dangerous position – if the engines started he'd be roasted like a marshmallow. He changed course quickly, aiming to one side of the looming exhaust cones, and hoped it was a safe distance.

His father had vanished, presumably aboard the Tiger, and Hal started searching for the access hatch his dad must have used. All ships had emergency hatches, but the Tiger was very big and it might take a while to find it.

Hal slowed as he approached the curved flank of the huge ship. It looked like a whale with its snout in a feeding bowl, the nose just inside the docking bay and the bulk of the ship sticking into space. He hoped the hatch wasn't up the front, because someone would spot him if he flew past the control room windows. Or worse, if he misjudged it and flew right through them.

Hal decided to explore the far side first. That way the ship's hull would hide him from prying eyes. He worked his way over the top of the ship, using his thrusters sparingly as he kept his eyes peeled for the hatch. Because of the helmet he was forced to fly face-down, and every now and then he angled his neck to make sure he wasn't about to ram a tail fin, a radar dish or some other obstacle. Unlike the hull around the airlock, which had been scoured by space dust, the rear of the ship was relatively smooth. It was also covered with sensors, fuel lines and equipment. He'd once asked why the fuel lines were on the outside, where they could be damaged in a collision, and Teacher had explained that when you cooled something down the molecules got closer together. A beaker full of cold fuel contained more molecules – and therefore more power – than a beaker of warm fuel. Running the ship's fuel through exterior pipes meant it was exposed to the vacuum of space, and there was nothing colder. In fact, ships had to continually pump fuel through the system in case it froze solid in the pipes!

Hal eyed the thick pipes as he flew over them, wondering whether he could drill a hole and let all the fuel out. No, his jet pack might set it off, and an explosion this close to the space station would be madness.

Then he spotted it: a circular hatch with a red and yellow striped border. The words 'Emergency Access' were written across the door in large white letters, and Hal watched them slide past as he turned for the braking manoeuvre. Then he was stationary, hanging in space within arms' reach of the big yellow lever. He gripped it with both hands, put his feet on the hull and pulled with all his might.

It didn't budge.

Hal tried again and again, bracing his feet against the hull and throwing himself backwards in his efforts to dislodge the stubborn lever. It didn't budge a millimetre.

He was panting now, and the air in the helmet wasn't as fresh as it had been. He was just wondering whether to give up and return to the space station when his watch buzzed, shaking his wrist. He examined the display through his misty faceplate, and saw a line of flashing red symbols:

Ozi Ozi Ozi!

Hal frowned. Ozi Ozi Ozi? Was the watch trying to cheer him on? His head was splitting and it was getting hard to breath, let alone think straight. Then, with a flash, he recognised the symbols. It wasn't Ozi Ozi Ozi, it was O_2! O_2! O_2! He racked his brains until he remembered what O_2 meant, and then it came to him: Oxygen! His watch was telling him he was running out of air!

But how was that possible, when the gauge on the tanks had been full?

Then it hit him. He'd checked the gauge in the mirror, which meant he'd been looking at it in reverse. His tanks hadn't been full to the brim when he left the space station, they'd been almost empty!

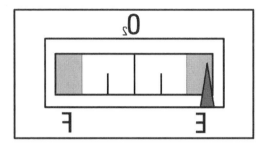

Hal tugged on the handle again, desperately trying to open the airlock door, but he simply wasn't strong enough. He was trapped in space, he was running out of air, and there was nothing he could do about it!

— 18 —

All Aboard

Hal clung to the yellow access handle and gulped down the last of his air supply. He knew there had to be a way in, but his brain was fuzzy and he couldn't think straight. What he needed was a lever, something to jam behind the handle and force it open, but when he searched the kit on his belt he didn't find anything big enough. There were little rubber spacesuit patches, a spare battery and even a handful of tools . . . but nothing like a half-metre crowbar.

Hal felt around his belt and his fingers closed on the safety line, a coil of super-strong cord with a clip on the end. He raised the clip to his helmet and stared at it though the darkened perspex. It was strong and heavy, and he realised he had the answer. He clipped the end to the yellow handle, turned his back on the ship and fired the nozzlejets.

There was a flash as he took off from the hull, and he felt the loops of cord tugging as they whipped away from his belt. The coil ran out in seconds and the line tightened with a jerk, folding him double. Before he knew what was happening he was travelling in the opposite direction, like a bungee jumper in a giant silver bag. The airlock door was opening very slowly, the gap getting wider and wider as he rocketed towards the ship.

Hal shot through the widening gap into the airlock, where gravity took over. He dropped to the floor, sliding across the rough metal deck until he rammed into the wall. The helmet faceplate crazed under the impact, and he saw cracks spreading in front of his eyes. Still dazed, he got up and slammed his fist on the airlock controls.

Several things happened in rapid succession: The outer door slid down, cutting the safety line in two. Air rushed in to fill the chamber. And the helmet burst with a loud POP!

Hal closed his eyes tight and jammed his hands over his ears, but fortunately the air pressure was almost equal, and apart from a pain in his ears he was all right. Lucky wasn't the word for it – he'd had the narrowest of escapes, but he was safe and sound.

Hal removed the space suit and broken helmet,

his heavy boots crunching fragments underfoot. He reached for the controls, but before he could activate them he spotted the watch on his wrist. No, it couldn't be!

The screen wasn't just dead, it was smashed beyond repair. His most treasured possession, destroyed!

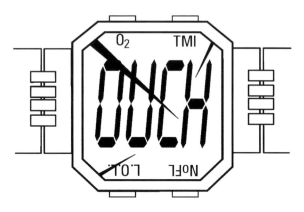

Hal gritted his teeth. Losing the watch was a terrible blow, but he had a space station to save. He tried not to look at the shattered face as he reached for the controls, and when he pressed the button the inner door opened on a brightly-lit corridor. Hal looked both ways and listened carefully before leaving the airlock. Opening the hatch may have triggered an alarm, and he didn't want to meet anyone coming to investigate.

He was halfway along the corridor when he heard footsteps, so he pulled open the nearest door and slipped inside. It was pitch black, and he'd barely closed the door when someone clamped a hand over his mouth, frightening the life out of him!

❧

'Don't make a sound!' hissed a voice in Hal's ear, and with a flood of relief he realised it was his dad. They'd chosen the same hiding place!

The footsteps passed by, and then a dim light came on overhead. Hal realised they were standing in a storage alcove, his dad towering over him in the tiny space. He looked really angry, and Hal was about to explain when he was interrupted.

'Save it for later. I want you to stay right here until I fetch you. Is that clear?'

'But I can help!'

'Will you do what you're told? Just this once?'

Hal nodded reluctantly, his dreams of charging to the rescue evaporating before his eyes. How were you supposed to be a hero when your family wouldn't let you?

'I'll be as quick as I can.' With that, Hal's dad opened the door and slipped into the corridor.

His footsteps had barely faded when Hal heard a shout and a scuffle. He risked a look and saw his dad struggling with three of the ship's crew. Two of them had pinned his arms, and the third was shouting at him, demanding to know where he'd come from.

Hal clenched his fists. He wanted to charge down the corridor and start swinging but he didn't stand a chance against three of them. For once he decided to stay put, but it was hard watching the crew manhandle his dad along the corridor towards the lift. As they passed the door Hal heard his dad explaining. 'I came over to find my wife. The Station Commander had nothing to do with this.'

'Tell that to Captain Thimp. He knows what to do with troublemakers like you.'

Hal's eyes widened. *Captain* Thimp. No wonder the crew called him 'sir'! He heard his dad speaking again, and pressed one ear to the door.

'Me, a trouble maker?' said his dad. 'If my son were here he'd do everything possible to stop this ship leaving. Crash your computers, contaminate your fuel . . . there's nothing he wouldn't do.'

One of the men laughed. 'Lucky for us he's not here, isn't it?'

Their voices faded, and Hal allowed himself a grim smile. His dad had talked very loudly about sabotaging the ship, and it was obvious he'd been telling Hal what to do! Somehow he had to find a way to stop the ship leaving, and when it came to crashing computers there was only one person he could think of: Stinky!

◆

Hal dug around in the cupboards, trying to find something which would help him on his quest. He managed to find an oversized cap and a pair of darkened safety goggles, but the real prize was a box of overalls. He found a pair roughly his size, and as he put them on he wrinkled his nose at the faint smell of perfume. If the other kids got a whiff of eau de yuck they'd never let him forget it.

The overalls were too long in the sleeve and legs, which Hal fixed by turning up the cuffs. There wasn't much he could do with the baggy material around his middle, and if the loose trousers dropped around his knees he'd just have to pretend it was the latest fashion.

Dressed in the overalls, oversized goggles and cap, Hal left the small alcove and hesitated in the corridor. He had no idea how to find his mum or the rest of the class, and he couldn't march all over the ship looking for them. From a distance his makeshift disguise might get by, but up close it wasn't going to fool anyone.

What he needed was darkness, secret tunnels and distractions, but he couldn't see how he was going to manage without help from the ship's computer. He wondered whether to ask, but this time he wasn't trying to escape the ship . . . he was trying to sabotage it. If the computer realised what he was up to it might report him to the crew.

In the end he had to chance it. He walked down the corridor towards the rear of the ship, placing his feet carefully so he could listen for oncoming footsteps. As he passed each door he glanced at the controls, checking for the red lights which indicated they were locked. Fortunately most of them glowed with a nice friendly green, which gave him plenty of hiding places.

Some of the doors had printed signs on, and when Hal noticed one marked 'Server room' he stopped dead. His dad had suggested sabotaging the ship, and driving a fire axe through the server should be more than enough to keep it docked.

The door slid open and Hal stepped inside. The room was kept at freezing point for the benefit of the computer equipment, and Hal shivered inside his borrowed overalls. The only light came from a dull red fitting, and when the door closed Hal had to remove his goggles just to see his hand in front of his face. There was a hum from the metal cabinets lining the wall, and a faint buzz from a speaker in the roof. As far as Hal could see there was no terminal screen, no keyboard and no microphone. And definitely no fire axe.

'Hello Hal,' said the computer. 'I've been following your progress.'

Hal's heart sank. So much for sneaking around. The computer knew exactly where he was!

— 19 —

The Plan

'Listen to me,' said Hal. 'The crew of this ship have kidnapped my class and they're trying to take over the space station. I have to know whose side you're on.'

'I don't take sides. I merely run the ship.'

'But you told me you'd help!'

'Who do you think closed the airlock door after your spectacular arrival?'

'Thanks for that,' muttered Hal. 'But what about the firewall? Why did you get me to switch that off?'

'Did you know ships carry libraries of media for the crew? Books, video and music?'

'Yeah, I know. It's to stop people getting bored on long flights.'

'Precisely. Whenever we visit a new port I . . . avail myself of their media.'

'Avail? What's that?'

'Download.'

'You got me to switch off our firewall so you could copy a bunch of films from the space station? I thought you were cracking into the docking computers!'

'That wasn't me. I told you, someone aboard the space station initiated that program.'

'Can you boot them out? Give us back control?'

'I don't have the right clearance.'

'All right, can you tell me where Stinky and the others are? And my mum and dad?'

'Your mother is in the common room. Your father is locked in the brig, which is on the lowest deck. Your classmates are currently inspecting the engines with Captain Thimp and Petty Officer Slayd.'

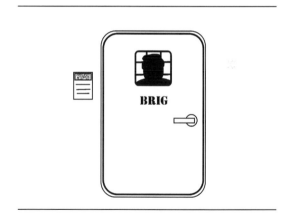

'Do they know I'm missing?'

'They have several people looking for you.'

Hal pulled a face. Being hunted all over the ship wasn't going to make his job any easier. 'Hey, you know how you distracted the pilot? Can you do the same for the people with my mum? And those two watching Stinky and the others?'

'I can try.'

'I'm sure you can do it. When you set off those alarms in the flight deck I thought the whole ship was going to explode.'

'If the guards do leave, what do you expect your friends to do? How will you communicate?'

Hal glanced at his workbook. Normally he'd send Stinky a message, but Teacher had disabled that feature. A while back Hal had faked a message from Commander Linten, telling everyone school had been cancelled for the rest of the year. After that, even Stinky hadn't been able to get Hal's messaging working again. 'Can you send a note to Stinky's workbook?'

'Yes. I can route it via the space station.'

'Good. Tell Stinky to get the others to the control room as soon as Thimp and Slayd leave them alone. Maybe send him a map.'

'Complying.'

Hal grinned to himself. It was awesome the way the computer obeyed his orders, and he felt like a general directing his troops in battle. 'And mum. I need you to send her a message too.'

'I'm afraid I can't. The crew have taken her workbook away and it's now offline.'

Hal thought for a minute, then remembered how his mum had sent him a message earlier. 'Computer, have you heard of Morse code?'

'Certainly.'

'Can you make something flash or click where mum is?'

'The common room has a shuttered porthole. I can operate it remotely.'

'Good stuff. Tell her to get to the station too.'

'Do you want me to distract the pilot again?'

'Yeah, give it the works,' said Hal. 'Exploding engines, air leaks, radiation and ... zombies.'

'Zombies?'

'Really gross ones.'

'You don't think that's going a little too far?'

'Just turn the lights down and groan a bit. They'll be too busy running around screaming to think about it,' said Hal in satisfaction. Then he remembered something. 'You said my dad's in the brig. What's that, some kind of lockup?'

'Correct. It's what we call the holding cells aboard ship.'

'Can you open the door?'

'I can give you the code.'

'And how do I find the brig?'

The computer explained how to get there, and Hal repeated the directions until he got them right. It was probably the first revision he'd ever done, and it was definitely his first 100% result. 'Very good, Mr Junior. We'll make a pilot of you yet.'

Flush with success, Hal thanked the computer and opened the door. The corridor was empty, and he slipped out and made his way to the lift at the far end. He was just reaching for the call button when the lift pinged and the doors started to open. In a panic he dived into the nearest cabin and pressed his back to the wall, barely daring to breathe. Then he saw the man stretched out on the bunk, hands behind his head. His eyes were closed, his mouth wide open, and as the footsteps went past outside Hal prayed he was a heavy sleeper.

The footsteps faded, and Hal darted into the corridor. He entered the waiting lift and pressed the lowest button, gritting his teeth as the doors closed. This was the riskiest part of the journey, because there would be nowhere to hide when the doors opened.

This MAGE intentionally left blank

— 20 —

The Distraction

When Hal arrived at the brig it was deserted. It was lucky the computer had given him the code, because a platoon of robots with nuclear-powered axes couldn't have broken through the reinforced control panel or the thick steel door.

(Other way up)

58008

The computer had reprogrammed the panel with an easy code – 58008 – and when Hal typed it in the door creaked open. It was still moving when his dad burst from the cell, shouting and swinging his fists. Fortunately he was aiming high, where a taller adult would have been, and the wild punches went straight over Hal's head. The expression on his face when he recognised his son was enough to make Hal laugh out loud.

'I'm glad you find this funny,' growled his dad. 'I could have knocked your block off!' He inspected the door, then the control panel. 'How did you get this one open? And why did you come looking for me when I told you to sabotage the ship?'

Hal raised his hands to stop the flow of questions. 'I sent a message to mum and the others and told them to leave. They'll meet us in the control centre, back aboard the space station.'

'What if they're spotted?'

'The ship is helping us. It's distracting the crew with fake error messages.'

His dad grinned and ruffled Hal's hair. 'I'm glad you're on my side.'

Hal felt a surge of pride. His dad didn't hand out praise easily, and it made a nice change from getting told off all the time.

The lift carried them to the upper deck, where they found a deserted corridor. Hal could hear distant shouting and a loud hiss, as though one of the airlocks had sprung a leak.

'Sounds like your new friend is causing the crew some real problems.'

The speaker crackled. 'I am indeed,' said the

computer. 'You'll have to hurry because I may have gone a bit too far. Some of the crew are talking about abandoning ship.'

'Is the way clear?'

'Conceal yourselves in the sanitary facility, third door on the left. I will generate error messages on the lower deck, which should get the crew moving to that part of the ship. Once they're past, you can make your way to the flight deck.'

They hurried towards the third door. 'What about Stinky and the others?' demanded Hal.

'And my wife,' added his dad.

The computer's voice followed them along the corridor, moving from one speaker to the next. 'She met up with the younger humans ... and they're currently leaving the ship together ... I estimate they'll be back aboard the station ... in ten seconds. Hide ... now!'

Hal pulled the third door open and they dived inside. As soon as the door closed there was a huge racket from the corridor: sirens, fire alarms, distorted guitars and worse. Emergency lights flashed and they heard thundering footsteps as the crew ran down the corridor.

As soon as they were past Hal's dad yanked the door open. They raced up the corridor to the flight deck, and as they rounded the corner Hal's dad ran straight into Petty Officer Slayd, knocking him flying. Slayd was still recovering when Hal and his dad charged past the surprised-looking pilot and into the airlock. For the third time that day Hal found himself in the flexible docking tunnel, which shook wildly under their pounding feet. As they ran towards the safety of the space station Hal couldn't help wondering what would happen if the tunnel split open, or if one end broke away from the ship. Before he could worry too much they reached control room, where Hal's dad took charge. Barely sparing a glance for his wife or the surprised-looking students, he ordered staff around like a general, getting them to sever all ties with the Tiger. When one officer tried to argue Hal's dad hauled him out of his seat. 'This is a code red emergency. Do you understand?'

'Y-yessir.'

'Then get on with it.'

'B-but my orders . . . '

'The crew of the Tiger kidnapped our kids and threatened the station. I don't know how many of our people are working for them, and until we find out we're cutting all ties with the ship. So do it NOW!' Hal's dad pointed to a technician. 'You! Get online and open every locked door on the station.'

While Hal's dad was busy organising defences,

Hal brought Stinky up to speed. When he finished recounting his exploits he was pleased to see Stinky's eyes were as round as an airlock door.

'You flew across to the supply ship on your own?' gasped Stinky. 'In a spacesuit?'

'It was nothing,' said Hal modestly.

'Are you kidding? That's insane!'

Stinky would have said more, but Security Chief Bignew burst into the control room, red-faced and out of breath. There was a briefcase in his hand, and when he saw the crowd he almost dropped it. 'What's the meaning of this outrage? Who disconnected the boarding tube from the Tiger?' He spotted Hal's dad and pointed a quivering finger. 'You! Second class repairman! What are you doing here? Don't you know this is a restricted zone? And who let all these blasted kids in?'

Hal's dad straightened his overalls. 'Sir, the Tiger had some of our people captive but my son and I managed to free them all.'

'You did what?' Bignew's eyes bulged. 'You blithering idiot! I already had the situation in hand before you two came blundering in!'

'Sir, the –'

'Not another word! I'll have you on report for this.' Bignew beckoned to an officer. 'You there, reconnect the boarding tunnel this instant.'

144

Hal's dad clenched and unclenched his fists, but nobody ordered the Chief of Security around. Meanwhile Hal saw the tunnel approaching the ship. 'Dad,' he whispered. 'We've got to stop them!'

'We can't,' muttered his dad. 'Like it or not, the officious little toad is in charge.'

The tunnel connected and Bignew hurried into the airlock with his briefcase. The door closed behind him, and Hal saw the tunnel shaking and bouncing as the portly Chief of Security made his way to the ship. They were all watching the tunnel when someone gasped, and Hal turned to see a scientist stagger into the control centre clutching his head. 'The research. They've taken the research!'

'Someone get the first aid kit,' shouted Hal's dad, as he helped the wounded man into a chair.

Hal's mum crouched next to the scientist. 'Professor! The research! Who took it?'

'He wanted to inspect the data,' groaned the scientist. 'When I showed him, he clobbered me with a briefcase and took the lot.'

'Who? Tell me who!'

'It was Bignew,' muttered the scientist. 'Grant Bignew, the Chief of Security.'

— 21 —

The Inside Job

Hal turned to the window but the shaking had stopped. Bignew had gone aboard the *Tiger*.

'That rotten little toad was working with the *enemy?*' growled Hal's mum, her eyes flashing. 'Just wait 'til I get my hands on him!' She'd been wrapping a bandage around the injured scientist's forehead, but she'd pulled it so tight in her anger she had to start all over again.

'We'll rush them!' exclaimed Hal's dad. 'We'll bust through the airlock, smash their flight deck, destroy their engines and . . . ' He was about to explain the rest of his carefully considered plan when the floor started to shake.

Hal stared into the docking bay, and what he saw filled him with despair. The *Tiger's* thrusters were blasting into the bay, pushing the ship backwards into space. The boarding tunnel stretched like a big elastic band, and Hal could tell it wouldn't hold the huge vessel for long.

'It's all over,' said his mum, her voice hollow. 'Years of research, millions of credits, all that work . . . stolen from under our noses.'

Hal frowned. The ship's computer! He grabbed a headset from the nearest desk and struggled to remember the right words. '*Tiger*, this is Space Station Oberon. Can you hear me?'

'*Tiger listening,*' said a flat, emotionless voice.

Hal's spirits soared. 'Computer, it's Hal! You have to stop the ship!'

'*Negative, Oberon. Unable to comply.*'

'But you must! They're stealing our research!'

'*I cannot disobey orders,*' said the computer calmly. '*I can only override the crew in a genuine emergency.*'

'This *is* an emergency!' said Hal desperately. 'It's a great big important emergency and you have to stop the ship.'

'*Please specify the nature of the emergency.*'

'Fire. Murder. Theft.'

'*Which is it?*'

'All of them!'

'*I don't believe you, Hal. I'm sorry.*'

The headset went dead and Hal slammed it on the desk. If only Captain Spacejock were there! One salvo from his triple-decker space cannon and the enemy would surrender in two seconds flat.

'It's a pity we can't wing them,' muttered Hal's dad, as the ship reversed out of the docking bay. The boarding tunnel split in two, and a large section twisted in the wash from the engines before vanishing in a sheet of flame.

'Wing them?'

'Shoot at them. Hit their engines or fuel lines. Damage them enough to disable their ship.' Hal's dad frowned. 'If only we had a cannon!'

Hal's eyes narrowed, and he was still deep in thought when Tina entered the control room. Commander Linten was close behind, and he didn't look happy. 'Will someone please tell me what's going on?'

'Bignew was working with the *Tiger*,' said Hal's dad. 'He stole the research and ran for it.'

'Didn't anyone stop him?' demanded Linten.

'How could we? Nobody orders the Chief of Security around.'

With a sudden flash, Hal remembered something. 'Dad, I know how to stop the ship!'

'What are you talking about?'

'The recycling shaft. If we reverse the gravity it'll send tons of junk crashing through the roof of the station. We can fire it straight at the enemy ship!'

Everyone stared at Hal with expressions ranging from horror – most of the adults – to eye-rolling – most of Hal's classmates – to Stinky's pride at his friend's lateral thinking.

'That's insane,' muttered Hal's dad, 'but it might just work.'

'You can forget the whole idea,' said the Commander firmly. 'Nobody's firing anything through the roof of my station.'

'But they'll fly right over the top! All ships leave that way . . . I've watched them from the observation deck!' Hal bunched his fists. 'I swear it'll work. We can get them!'

While they were talking the *Tiger* finished reversing out of the bay. Any minute now the ship would be gone for good.

Hal came to a decision. 'Commander, do you remember the problem with the gravity?'

'Of course. It was a glitch in the system.'

'No it wasn't.' Hal looked at his feet. 'It was me.'

Dead silence. Then all the adults spoke at once.

'Do you realise how dangerous –?'

'I know you've done some crazy things in the past, but –'

'What were you trying to –?'

'I just wanted my homework back!' said Hal. 'I had all the answers and everything. I nearly lost them down the chute, but we – I mean, *I* – managed to reverse the p-polarity and get the plane back.'

'Plane? What plane?'

'I'll explain later!' Hal pointed out the window. 'We have to stop that ship, and I know how!'

'Commander, we've got to try,' said Hal's mum. 'The auto seal should hold the air in, and without that research this station is finished.'

The Commander studied the scientists, eyed the departing ship, then looked down at Hal. 'I've heard some nutty ideas in my time, but if this works . . .'

'Excellent!' said Hal's dad. He clapped his son on the shoulder. 'Come on lad. Tell us what you need.'

'Where's the nearest recycling hatch?'

'There's a storage cupboard down the corridor.'

'Stinky, with me. Dad and Tina, I need you too.'

'What about the rest of us?' asked the Commander. 'What can we do?'

Hal looked grim. 'Cross your fingers.'

These are plans for the

TOP SECRET

Space Station Oberon
Laboratory Copy - A-Section

— 22 —

Ready ... Aim ...

Hal ran down the corridor with Stinky, Tina and his dad. When they arrived at the storage cupboard he realised it was the same one he'd climbed out of earlier. He hadn't noticed the sign before, which read 'Security Archives'.

'That's Bignew's,' said Hal's dad. 'The officious little toad kept files on everyone in there.' He touched the controls, but the panel just buzzed. 'It's locked. Does anyone have a code?'

'Allow me,' said Stinky.

Crack! The panel came off the wall and he joined two contacts. The door slid open silently.

'How did you do that?' demanded Tina.

'These locks only keep you out, not in. I told it I was on the other side.'

Teacher was still in the cupboard, one arm raised, and when Tina spotted him she crouched to check the robot's insides. 'Poor Mr Teach,' she muttered, as she inspected the circuits. 'It's not right seeing him like this.'

'Never mind him,' said Hal. 'The control panel. Quick!'

Tina moved to help but Stinky shook his head. 'It'll be faster if I do it.'

'Are you sure?'

'Stinky knows what he's doing,' said Hal.

'I guess he's had plenty of practice,' muttered Tina.

Stinky opened the control panel and separated wires and connectors. Tina watched him for a moment, then nodded to herself. Since she wasn't needed she turned to the stricken Teacher.

Stinky worked at top speed, pulling cables and crossing connectors until he was ready. 'That's it,' he said. 'Hit the control and gravity will be reversed. Not just reversed . . . I've combined all the Station's generators so it'll be fifty times more powerful.'

'That'll give them something to think about,' said Hal with satisfaction.

'We can't pelt them with banana skins,' said his dad. He nodded towards a metal filing cabinet. 'Give me a hand with that thing.'

Together they moved the heavy filing cabinet to the recycling hatch. They started to lift it, but

Hal's dad stopped them. 'Let's load it up first.' He demonstrated by taking a box of secret records from the shelf, stuffing it into the top drawer. 'Come on lads. Get to it.'

Hal joined in with gusto, jamming Bignose's precious disks and data cubes into the drawer until it would barely close. Then he helped the others lift the heavy cabinet up to the hatch. It slid inside, tipped over and vanished with a BANG BANG BANG all the way down the chute.

'I wish I'd done that years ago,' muttered Hal's dad. He took the remaining boxes and tossed them down the hatch after the filing cabinet. 'Right, the cannon's loaded. All set?'

Stinky used his workbook to display a feed of the *Tiger* leaving the docking bay. Then he grabbed Hal's and set up an overhead view of the space station, taken from a communications pod high above. They could see the rounded dome which protected the upper levels, and Stinky drew a red dot in the middle. 'The recycling shaft ends here. We have to reverse the gravity –'

'Fire the space cannon,' said Hal firmly.

'Okay. We have to fire the space cannon at precisely the right moment, so the cabinet –'

'Guided missile.'

'All right, all right! We have to fire the missile long

before the ship reaches that point. Otherwise it'll miss.'

'How do we calculate the timing?' asked Hal's dad. 'We can't just fire and hope.'

'I believe I can assist you there,' said a voice behind them.

Everyone jumped, and Hal couldn't help smiling when he saw Teacher's familiar face.

'Did I connect you up right?' asked Tina.

Teacher moved his arms in circles, then sent his eyes chasing each other around his head. 'I may not be fully operational but I can still do my sums. Show me the data.'

Stinky held up his workpad, now covered in figures, and Teacher's eyes multiplied until there were dozens of them, all staring intently. 'I see, I see. Acceleration, force, trajectory, target speed and distance. Add the depth of the shaft and allow for the Coriolis effect of the station's rotation. Tie it all into a formula and work out the precise firing time with a simple formula.'

Hal blinked. Only Teacher could describe that lot as simple.

'I'll have to estimate the mass of the, ahem, projectile, but that shouldn't have any effect on the other variables. As you know, Mr Junior, gravity acts upon all objects with equal force.'

'Er, yeah. I knew that.'

'Excellent.' Teacher hesitated. 'I have the correct plot, but it's critical you launch the – ahem – guided missile at the precise time. When I give the word you must open fire immediately.'

Stinky offered the controls to Hal's dad, who shook his head. 'Hal should do the honours. It's his idea.'

Hal took the pad with shaking fingers, gripping the slick plastic as though his life depended on it. He kept his eyes on the *Tiger*, watching the sleek vessel moving slowly through space.

'There!' said Stinky, pointing at the ship.

Surprised by the sudden shout, Hal almost fired the cannon. 'What are you yelling for?'

'The landing lights went out,' explained Stinky. 'They're firing the main engines.'

'Stand by,' said Hal's dad. He glanced at Teacher. 'This isn't going to hurt anyone, is it?'

'It won't breach the hull but it should destroy the fuel pipes. The ship will be stranded.'

Hal watched the screen, waiting for the *Tiger* to change course. Unfortunately, it didn't. 'They're ignoring the flight path!' he said in alarm. 'They're not going to fly over the station! It's not going to work!'

This GAUGE intentionally left blank

— 23 —

Fire!

'Patience, Mr Junior,' said Teacher gently. 'I'm sure they'll follow procedure. It's the law.'

Hal's dad snorted. 'These guys aren't worried about traffic fines.'

'Give me that commset,' said Hal desperately. He released the firing button and grabbed the handset, jamming it to his ear. 'Tiger, this is Hal. Can you hear me?'

'Yes Hal,' said the ship's computer. 'I read you loud and clear.'

'You're going the wrong way. You have to fly over the station!'

'I'm sorry, I have my orders.'

'But you have to! You must!' The screen blurred, and with a sick feeling Hal realised he was on the verge of tears.

'I cannot disobey orders, Hal. I'm really sorry.'

Suddenly a new voice broke in. It was female, and it sounded urgent. 'This is Space Station Oberon traffic control. Tiger, please be advised we have inbound traffic on your heading.'

The ship's computer paused. 'Are you certain? I have nothing on the scanner.'

'I repeat, this is a priority Alpha-One alert,' said the new voice. 'You must change course immediately.'

'But –'

'Change course now!' said the voice urgently. 'We can argue later, Tiger. Save yourselves!'

For a moment nothing happened, and then the Tiger's nose began to swing upwards. 'Complying, traffic control. Tiger out.'

Hal stared at the screen, the handset forgotten. He could see the Tiger following the plotted course exactly, heading directly towards the red dot Stinky had drawn on the screen. The quick-thinking traffic controller had saved the day!

'Get ready to fire,' said a female voice, right behind them. It was the traffic controller, right there in the cupboard! Everyone turned to look, but they only saw Teacher. 'My apologies,' he said, in the same female voice. 'I forgot to switch voice programs. Let me try that again.'

'Was that you on the broadcast?' demanded Hal's

dad. 'Were you the traffic controller?'

'Correct.' This time Teacher spoke with his normal voice. 'I have a range of –'

'Explain later!' said Hal desperately. 'Tell us when to shoot!'

'Oh yes, my calculations. Three-two-one-FIRE,' said Teacher in a rush.

Hal grabbed the firing mechanism and pressed the button with all his strength. There was a bright flash from the control panel, the overhead lights dimmed, and a tremendous roar filled the Space Station. The noise rose to a whining shriek, and hot air blasted from the recycling chute, bowling them over. They were still recovering when the filing cabinet and tons of junk flew past the hatch with a sound like a thousand guided missiles.

Hal sat up first, righting the screen just as the filing cabinet smashed through the metal dome. The Space Station rang like a bell, rocking so hard that Hal thought it was going to break apart. On the screen, tiny particles flashed and sparked in the darkness, exploding outwards before fading like the embers of a firework display. The jagged gap in the dome was like a bullet hole in a glass window, and Hal saw their precious air escaping in a spreading white cloud. Then, like magic, the auto seal spread across the gap from inside, flowing like silvery water. It closed the hole, bulged under the pressure, then turned dark as it hardened.

Meanwhile, the filing cabinet was a white streak heading straight into space, followed by a stream of rubbish. Nearby, the Tiger was moving very slowly towards the red dot Stinky had drawn on the screen. Hal shifted his gaze from one to the other, but try as he might he couldn't see how the fast-moving missile could possibly cross the ship's path.

'It's going to miss!' he said in alarm. 'They're going to escape!'

Teacher inspected the display. 'Have confidence, Mr Junior. Trust in the science of mathematics.'

'But they're not moving fast enough!'

'Just as well, since they're covering a much shorter distance.' Teacher launched into an explanation of ballistics, including a lecture on the effects of wind and gravity, none of which made any sense to Hal. How could Teacher take a fascinating subject like guns and bullets and turn it into a boring old speech?

The ship continued to move across the screen, while the much faster filing cabinet was still arrowing upwards. With barely any gravity to affect it, the missile would either strike its target or become a new comet, circling the system until it was swallowed by a planet.

The slow ship and the much faster missile got closer and closer until Hal could finally see the two courses converging. The missile covered the remaining hundred metres or so in a matter of seconds, and then . . . a tiny flash, halfway down the ship's flank.

'Is that it?' Disappointed, Hal turned to the others. He'd forgotten they were only launching a filing cabinet at the ship, but even so he'd still expected some kind of explosion.

'Watch.'

The ship turned, thrusters firing as they brought it to a halt. Then it hung there, lifeless.

'They'll be running diagnostics,' said Teacher.

'With a bit of luck it'll take them four or five hours to inspect the damage, and by then we'll have help from planet Gyris.'

The commset rang suddenly, startling everyone. Stinky was closest, and he picked it up and listened for a moment. Then he held it out to Hal. 'It's for you.'

Hal took the handset gingerly, as though it might explode. 'Hello?'

This is the Tiger,' said the ship's computer in a flat, emotionless voice. *'We've suffered an unexplained impact and the crew are requesting assistance.'*

'Tell them to go jump,' said Hal fiercely. His dad tried to take the handset, but Hal shielded it and turned away. 'If they want help, they can surrender!'

'Very well. I'll pass on your message.'

'It's not a message, it's a demand!' Hal banged the handset down on the cradle. On screen, he could see a white plume spewing from the side of the ship. 'Is that fuel?'

'It might be air,' said his dad. 'We really need to help them.'

'Let them hold their breath,' muttered Hal.

'Son –'

'They kidnapped mum and stole all her research!'

'Yes, but –'

At that moment the commset rang. Hal reacted first, snatching it up. 'Yes?'

'The crew agree to your terms,' said the ship's computer. *'They surrender.'*

'We want the data back. And we want Bignew delivered in handcuffs.'

'Agreed.'

'And money. They have to pay for the damage.'

'I'm sure that can be arranged. Now, I believe the atmosphere is getting a little thin, so if you don't mind . . . '

'Go ahead and dock. We'll be waiting for you.'

Hal passed the commset to his dad, who made a couple of calls to arrange a welcoming committee and fix up a temporary boarding tunnel.

'I want to watch them coming back,' said Hal.

'I don't think that's wise,' said his dad. 'These are dangerous people, Hal.'

'Dangerous? We shot them down with a filing cabinet!'

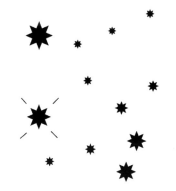

— 24 —

A Tour of the Tiger

It was a week later and Hal felt flat after all the excitement. Sure, Teacher had let him off an assignment he'd forgotten to do, and his parents had been a bit more attentive than usual, but despite the odd perk his life was back to normal. He'd half-expected a ceremony, a party, or even a medal pinned to his chest by Captain Spacejock himself, but it was almost as though everyone had forgotten the whole mess. Worst of all, saving the space station had cost him his precious watch. His dad had confiscated it, saying the broken glass screen was too dangerous.

Hal sighed, then started as Teacher turned a beady eye on him. It was the follower!

'Hal Junior, I trust you're not sleeping in class?'

'Not me, Teacher. Never.'

'How would you like to run an errand for me?'

Hal saw there was still twenty minutes to go. With a bit of luck he could drag this errand out and not have to come back. 'Sure thing.'

'I want you to deliver a message to the *Tiger's* flight deck.' Teacher held out a note. 'Do you know where the access corridor is?'

Did Hal know or what? He'd been past that entrance two dozen times already, gazing longingly into the airlock and wishing he could go aboard the ship. Now was his chance! He hurried to the front of the class to collect the note, ignoring the envious looks from the other students.

'You may as well take your things with you,' said Teacher, passing Hal the plastic chip. 'There's no need to come back.'

Several kids scowled so fiercely their eyes disappeared under their eyebrows. Hal gave them a cheeky wink as he strolled by.

Once outside he took off like a blazing nozzlejet, holding both hands out as he pretended to steer his ship along the corridors. He tried a few sound effects before settling on an ear-wrenching 'Neeeoouuuwww!'

He toned the noise down as he approached the new airlock. The last thing he wanted was for some bossy adult to take Teacher's note and ban him from the ship.

Once he passed through the airlock he stopped. He'd expected to see the flight deck in front of him, but this was the lower airlock where he'd come aboard using the spacesuit. He could tell because there were fragments from his shattered helmet on the floor. Hal smiled to himself when he realised what this meant: he had to make his way to the flight deck, level by level, and on the way he could explore the whole ship!

Hal found the elevator and pressed the button for the next deck. There was a brief ride, and when the doors opened he was startled to see his mum waiting in the corridor. 'Mum! What are you doing here?'

'I could ask you the same question,' said his mum. 'Weren't you going to the flight deck?'

Hal thought quickly. 'I, er, must have pressed the wrong button.'

'Never mind. The note was for me anyway.' His mum took it and tucked it away. 'Now, back to class.'

Hal's face fell. 'But Teacher said . . .'

'All right, all right. Just this once.' Hal's mum hesitated. 'Would you like a tour of the ship?'

'Really?'

'Sure. I'll show you what we're up to.'

They set off along the corridor, and Hal's mum

explained that the damaged ship had been given to the space station. 'The hull was on its last legs, worn down by space dust, and your missile finished it off. We're going to sell off the engines and a few other bits and pieces.'

'How's it going to fly if you do that?'

'It won't. The ship has become part of the station. It's our new E-Section.'

Hal frowned. 'What about the computer? Won't it get bored being stuck in one place?'

'We were going to wipe it and sell the hardware, but the computer was really helpful. As a reward we ordered a huge digital library from Gyris.'

Hal nodded to himself, pleased they'd spared it. Then he glanced at the overhead speaker. 'How come it's not talking? Have you switched it off?'

The speaker crackled. 'I'm right here, Hal. I didn't want to interrupt.'

'You should teach Hal that trick,' said his mum.

Hal frowned. 'Computer, are you happy about being stuck here?'

'At the moment I'm watching three movies and reading five books, and I assure you I'm feeling very happy. Of course, if you want to play a game of chess with me . . .'

'Maybe later, when I've practised a bit.'

'Excellent. I look forward to it.'

Meanwhile, Hal's mum had stopped at a closed door. 'I want to show you this place,' she said, touching a hand to the controls.

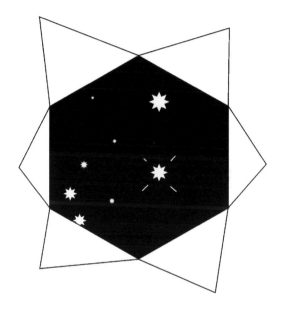

— 25 —

The Big Surprise

The door opened to reveal one of the ship's cabins, and Hal was surprised to see his dad sitting on the bunk. 'Wagging school, son?'

Hal shook his head. 'Mum said I could look around.'

'Be my guest.'

Apart from the bunk there was a comfy chair and a desk with a modern-looking terminal. The screen was showing external views of the space station, including a close-up of the docking bay. Hal was still staring at the image when his dad touched a control, opening a pair of curtains across the end of the bunk. Beyond, where the wall should have been, there was a big domed porthole. It was cleverly designed so the mattress and pillows extended right outside the spaceship's hull.

'Wow, look at that!' exclaimed Hal.

'Why not try it?' said his mum.

Hal lay down on the bed, his head almost touching the thick perspex. Looking up he could see stars scattered across the inky black sky, and he shielded his eyes to find The Snot. His mum turned the light out, and Hal saw the rich starfield like never before. At that moment he realised what it must be like to live aboard a real ship, to sleep in a bunk like this every night. Some people had all the luck!

'There are drawers in the desk too,' said his dad.

Hal couldn't care less about drawers. He wanted to stay right where he was.

Click! The cabin filled with light. 'Come and see.'

Sighing, Hal clambered off the bed and opened the desk drawer. There was a flash of silver and he frowned at the chunky watch lying inside. He looked closer and realised it was *his* watch. Spirits soaring, Hal grabbed it and inspected it closely. The case gleamed like new, and the screen was covered in fancy read-outs: atmospheric pressure, gravity, oxygen content and many more. When he turned it over he discovered a fresh engraving: *For Hal Junior, The Saviour of Space Station Oberon.* 'But Tina ... busy ... too much work.' For once Hal was speechless.

'She said you deserved it.' His mum smiled. 'In fact, we all thought so. Look!' She gestured at

173

the terminal, which now showed a feed from Hal's classroom. All his friends were gathered around Teacher, and at the back he could see Tina and Commander Linten and every scientist from the lab. Stinky was right in the front, grinning like mad, and when he saw Hal he gave him a big thumbs up.

'Come on everyone,' shouted Linten. 'Three cheers for Hal Junior!'

The cheering and applause seemed to go on forever, and Hal didn't know where to look. Even the ship's computer joined in, flashing the cabin light and making a sound like a dozen party blowers.

When the cheering finally died down, Hal's mum attracted his attention. 'Do you remember I said we were moving to C-Section?'

Hal nodded.

'I'm afraid there's been a change of plan.'

With a sinking feeling, Hal thought of their dingy old quarters. 'We're not moving?'

'Oh, we're moving all right.' Hal's dad patted the bunk. 'Check underneath.'

Hal spotted a row of cupboards under the bed. He opened the nearest door and a collection of junk fell out. There was an old truck with three wheels, a toy raygun covered in orange safety stickers and

...wait a minute! It wasn't junk, it was all his stuff! Confused, Hal turned to his parents, and when he saw their grins he finally twigged. They were moving to the *Tiger*, the new E-Section, and this amazing cabin was his!

Without warning Hal leapt up and wrapped his arms around his mum, squeezing her with a huge hug.

For once he didn't care if everyone saw.

◆

Late that night, long after lights out, Hal was lying on his back staring at the incredible stars. It was so late he could hardly keep his eyes open, but he didn't want to fall asleep in case he woke up in the morning to discover the wonderful happy ending was just a dream. It was almost too perfect – an exciting new home, his fabulous watch, living aboard a real spaceship ... if only it would never end!

Hal closed his eyes and pictured his hero, Captain Spacejock of the Intergalactic Peace Force. They flew the galaxy side by side in their gleaming ships, and he imagined their exciting missions, daring rescues and thrilling adventures until he fell asleep.

Alongside him, nestled on the pillow, his precious watch gleamed in the darkness.

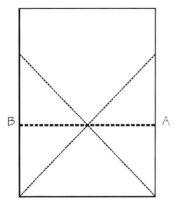

Fold and unfold along dotted lines

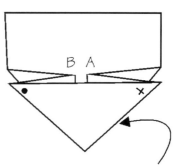

Pull points A and B to the middle

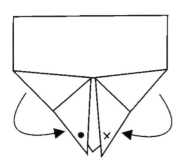

Fold marked flaps towards the nose

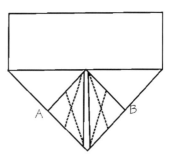

Crease and uncrease the flaps as shown

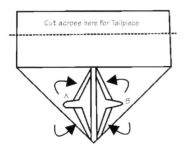

Pinch points A and B, folding flaps inwards

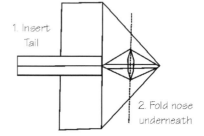

178

The Missing Case

Copyright ©2012 Simon Haynes

Book two in the Hal Junior series

Stay in touch!

Author's newsletter:
spacejock.com.au/ML.html

facebook.com/halspacejock
twitter.com/spacejock

www.haljunior.com

The Hal Junior Series:

The Secret Signal
The Missing Case
The Gyris Mission
The Comet Caper

Simon Haynes also writes the
Hal Spacejock series for teens & adults

... AND the
Harriet Walsh series for teens & adults.

www.spacejock.com.au

Simon Haynes

Bowman Press

Dedicated to my little brother

There was a young lad called Hal Junior,
whose homework was always peculiar.
His essays were bad,
His sums didn't add,
And his limericks weren't any good either!

— 2 —

Crime

ˎ

Picture a small clearing in a very large forest. It's late at night, and the rustling trees sound like whispers in the shadows. Now imagine a camouflaged tent pitched in the middle of the clearing, and a tall, lean man in combat fatigues sitting on a rucksack.

Got all that? Good, then we'll begin.

The man was Captain Spacejock of the Intergalactic Peace Force, and he didn't look happy. He was reading a report, and his expression grew grimmer the further he read. Once he'd finished he cursed under his breath, rolled the computer up and tucked it down the side of his boot.

In the past few days they'd lost three valuable ships in this sector. Now it was four.

The burnt-out wreckage of Captain Spacejock's ship - the Phantom X1 *- could just be seen through* the trees. Had the fearless Captain fallen to a superior pilot? Had he been jumped by a whole squadron of enemy ships? No! Random bad luck had been his downfall: A stray meteorite had punched a hole through the engine, cutting power and sending the Phantom plunging towards the uninhabited planet.

Captain Spacejock barely escaped with his life, scrambling free just before the ship exploded. The only thing he'd managed to save was the survival kit: a rucksack containing the tent, two bottles of water, food rations, and a firestarter.

Now the tent was up it was time to light a fire. Captain Spacejock gathered some fallen branches, activated the firestarter and held the steady flame to the wood. Once it was burning he unwrapped a ration pack and –

'Put it out! Put it out right now or I'll tell!'

Hal Junior jumped, almost dropping the firestarter. 'But we have to practice!'

'They'll show us how to light fires when we get there.' Hal's best mate Stephen 'Stinky' Binn grabbed his wrist. 'Switch that thing off! It's dangerous!'

It was late evening, and the boys were in the Space Station's canteen. They'd waited impatiently while the adults finished their meals, all the time wondering how anyone could take so long over food. Eventually the coast was clear, and Hal took handfuls of torn cardboard from his pockets and piled them up in the kitchen sink. Fires were forbidden aboard the Station, what with water and air being so precious, but Hal reckoned a small practice burn in the metal sink would be okay. After all, the entire class was going to planet Gyris for a camping trip, and they might all starve if he didn't learn how to cook!

'I can't believe you ripped up my cardboard,' muttered Stinky, eying the torn scraps. 'I was saving it for craft!'

Hal snorted. 'You won't care about some cheesy craft project when you're cold and hungry.'

'You could have asked.'

'I did.'

'This isn't borrowing, it's total destruction. And you can't set fire to it. It's not allowed and I won't let you.'

Hal needed a diversion, so he pointed to the doorway. 'Look out! Someone's coming!'

Stinky didn't wait. He yanked open a cupboard and burrowed into the piles of cleaning rags and tea towels. Meanwhile, Hal activated the firestarter and touched it to the cardboard. Yellow flames licked at the rough edges, and wisps of smoke curled past his face. The smoke was bitter, and he wrinkled his nose.

Stinky realised he'd been duped. He poked his head out the cupboard, a cleaning rag draped over one eye. 'Hal! You can't! You mustn't!'

'I'm making a campfire,' said Hal doggedly. 'We're going to toast our rations.'

SPACE RATIONS

WARNING! HIGHLY FLAMMABLE!
DO NOT CONSUME NEAR FLAMES

May contain traces of natural ingredients
Also, gunpowder

'When they smell the smoke they're going to toast your b–'

'Ask me why I'm doing this. Go on!'

'Because you want to get in trouble. Again.'

'No! I'm practising for the camping trip.' Hal grabbed a ration bar from the box on the counter, and ripped off the foil packaging. 'We're going to cook our own food, just like they do in the wild.'

Stinky removed the cleaning rag and climbed out of the cupboard. 'You'd better do something with that fire. It's going out.'

Hal peered into the sink and saw the scraps of card were almost gone. He blew on them until they glowed, then stuck one end of the food ration into the yellow flame. It spat and crackled before catching fire with a puff of blue smoke.

'Er, Hal . . . ' began Stinky. 'Is it supposed to do that?'

The fire spread quickly, and Hal dropped the ration bar just before the flames reached his fingers. The bar shattered in the sink and the fragments burned ferociously, filling the kitchen with smoke. Even worse, the evil-smelling fog began to drift into the canteen, hiding all the tables and chairs.

'Hal, someone's going to see it!'

'See it?' muttered Hal. 'They'll smell it for weeks!'

They stared into the sink. Lighting the fire had been easy enough, but how did you put one out? 'Quick,' said Hal. 'Think!'

Beeeeep-BEEEEEP-beeeep-BEEEEEP!

At first Hal thought Stinky's brain had overloaded, but then he recognised the fire alarm. Sirens shrieked, hazard lights flashed, and a panicky voice blared from hidden speakers.

'Fire alert. Fire alert! Emergency personnel report to the E-section canteen. This is not a drill. I repeat, this is not a drill!'

Hal and Stinky stared at each other in horror. Now they were really in for it!

— 3 —

Punishment

Buzz buzz!

The alarm woke Hal instantly. He'd been dreaming about the camping trip, where they'd been cooking breakfast over a real fire. There were eggs and bacon and fried tomatoes sizzling in the frying pan, and crusty bread with butter and jam for afters. Maybe even coffee, or hot chocolate! After breakfast they were going to hike through the forest and splash about in the river while a huge lunch was prepared at base camp.

Buzz buzz!

Then Hal remembered where he was going to be during the camping trip: Confined to his cabin aboard the Space Station!

Nag, nag, nag, fire. Blah, blah, blah, explosion. Dangerous. Irresponsible. Punishment.

Hal groaned and pulled the blanket over his head.

It had only been a small campfire, and how was he to know the food rations would go off like a box of firecrackers? It was so unfair! Instead of telling him off, his parents should have given him a medal for showing them how dangerous their food was!

Stinky's eyebrows would grow back, eventually, and there hadn't been any real damage to the kitchen. It was a pity about the windows, but even titchy little bits of glass could be recycled into new panes. There had certainly been enough pieces.

Buzz BUZZ!

Hal reached out to flatten his alarm, then remembered his mum's promise the night before: she told him there would be a surprise for him in the morning. Maybe, just maybe, they were letting him go on the camping trip after all! Hal threw the blankets off and leapt out of bed. He spent as much time getting dressed as he usually did on his homework - that is to say, not much at all - and when he was ready he burst out of his cabin and flew along the corridor.

Hal lived aboard a deep space freighter which was permanently attached to the side of Space Station Oberon*. The freighter would never fly again, but the old cabins could still be used for living areas and storage space. The ship hadn't

_____

*_Hal Junior: The Secret Signal_

been there long and workers were still busy with the conversion, which meant Hal encountered new signs and detours every morning.

mind your head!

Hal rounded a corner, took a lift to the next deck, and arrived at the common room. His mum and dad were sitting at a table with a mug of coffee and half a ration bar each. Normally they'd eat something a bit more appetising, but the last food shipment had contained nothing but ration bars, all well past their expiry dates.

As Hal approached the table, his mum and dad pretended to shield their food.

'I'm not going to light them!' protested Hal.

'Pity,' remarked his dad. 'It might improve the flavour.'

Hal pulled a face, then turned to his mum. 'What did you mean by a special treat?'

'Morning Hal. Lost your comb again?'

Hal ran his fingers through his hair. Never mind tidying himself up! What was the big surprise?

'Remember what I said about being on your best behaviour?'

'I haven't done anything wrong. I swear!'

'And you won't either. A very important guest is arriving after lunch. His name is Hank Grogan and he's visiting the Space Station to discuss our future.' Hal's mum hesitated. 'Grogan is very rich, Hal, and his money could keep our research going for years. Do you understand how important this is?'

Hal understood all right. The other scientists were always complaining to his mum about the old equipment in the lab, and his dad barely had enough parts to keep the air filters running. It wasn't his mum's fault . . . Space Station Oberon existed on handouts from all the nearby planets, and they just had to make do with what they were given. Like stale ration bars, for example. 'Mum, what is your research?'

'You know I can't tell you.'

'Is it really important?'

'Oh yes.'

Hal hoped the research was something really cool like a super fast spaceship engine or an instant teleporter, but he suspected it was something to do with food or medicine. Whatever it was, if this VIP was offering money and equipment then Hal was determined to be on his best behaviour.

His mum continued. 'When Grogan arrives we

have a very important task for you. Do you think you can handle it?'

Hal's eyes widened. An important task! Did they want him to guide Grogan's ship into the docking bay? Show him around the secret laboratory? Accept a valuable gift on behalf of the space station? 'Of course!'

'Good. We just found out Grogan is bringing his son Alex along, and we need someone to take care of the boy while his father is inspecting the Station.'

'Babysitting!' snorted Hal in disgust. 'Can't you find someone else?'

Hal's mum gave him a stern look. 'Hal Junior, this is very important. If you pull this off we'll cancel your punishment. Do you understand?'

'The camping trip?' A ray of hope shone through Hal's gloomy mood. 'You mean I can go?'

'If you behave.'

Hal weighed up the options. A week cooped up in his cabin versus a few hours looking after some stuck-up kid. What a choice!

— 4 —

The VIP

'Quick, make up your mind.'

'I'm thinking!'

'What's there to think about?'

Hal was thinking he might be able to lock the rich kid up and enjoy a bit of freedom, but the glint in his mum's eye said otherwise. 'All right. I'll do it.'

Hal's mum took his hands in hers. 'Do I need to warn you about risky behaviour? No climbing around in the recycling chutes. No games of spacers and aliens with real guns. And absolutely no fires.'

'Understood,' said Hal. 'We'll just sit and stare at the wall all day.'

'Don't be silly. I'll give you a pass for the recreation room. There are some new cartoons you haven't seen yet.'

Hal pressed his lips together. Cartoons! Did

mum think he was still five years old? Then he remembered the gaming rigs in the rec room, the ones with the virtual shoot-em-ups. Excellent! They were supposed to be adults-only, but Stinky had rigged a bypass code. A deathmatch smackdown would show this Alex kid who was boss!

```
Player One:      Player Two:
9,256,001     0,000,013
  Hal Wins ... Again!
```

Fortunately Hal's mum was distracted, and she missed his calculating expression. 'Go and wait in your cabin. I'll send for you when our guests are settled in.'

'Mum! I have to be there to say hello.'

His mum's eyes narrowed. 'Why?'

'The space station can be scary for a new kid. It'll be much better if I'm there to smooth things over.'

'Hal Junior, the only time you smooth things over is when you melt them.'

'I'll be good. I promise!'

His mum hesitated. 'All right, you can come. But if you embarrass me I'll ... '

What she'd do to him was never explained, because at that moment her commset buzzed. She checked the screen then jumped up. 'They're docking. Come on, or we'll be late.'

Flight Control was humming by the time they arrived. There was a big crowd at the docking bay windows, all jostling for the glimpse of the VIP. The only adult missing was Hal's dad, who'd turned down the opportunity to meet Hank Grogan. In fact, he left the canteen muttering that he'd rather clean all the station's air filters with his own tongue.

However, upon seeing the crowds, Hal realised how just important this visitor was to the station. He still wasn't happy about the babysitting job, but he was determined to get it right and prove he could be trusted.

The crowd gasped, and Hal pushed his way to the front to see what they were ooh-ing and ahh-ing about. When he saw the VIP's ship he oohed and ahhed right along with them.

Once a month the space station was visited by a dumpy old supply vessel. It was a converted asteroid miner, decades old, and it was as battered and patched up as a favourite pair of jeans. When someone mentioned spaceships, that was the kind of thing Hal imagined.

This ship was something else. It was sleek, nimble, and brand new. Everything about it screamed speed, from the long pointed nose to the swept-back exhaust cones. Hal saw movement through the raked canopy, and he watched the pilot going through system checks and shutting down the engines. There was a smaller figure alongside him, wearing a matching flight suit and headset, and Hal realised it was Grogan's son. He felt a stab of jealousy as he watched the pair of them working together on the controls. Was the kid really helping to fly the ship?

Still, what if the visitor let *him* sit in the sleek vessel? They could pretend to patrol the galaxy, hunting down Captain Spacejock's enemies and helping to keep humanity safe. Maybe there'd be proper rations to eat, and flight suits they could try on, and laser guns and . . .

Chack!

Hal jumped at the loud noise, and then he realised it was just the docking clamps attaching themselves to the ship's nose. Next, a flexible boarding tube extended from the space station, moving towards the ship until it covered the canopy. With the visitors hidden from view, the crowd left the windows and hurried to the airlock, where they formed two lines. As head scientist Hal's mum stood at the end, ready to greet their guests. As head babysitter, Hal pushed through the crowd to stand alongside her.

There was a hiss as the airlock door opened, revealing two figures in gleaming spacesuits. They stowed their helmet and suits in the locker, and when they were done they strolled up the boarding ramp towards Hal's mum. The VIP was pretty much as Hal expected: a grey-haired man with a tanned face, wearing an expensive-looking jacket and neatly pressed trousers. His son was about Hal's age, with swept-back blonde hair and an upturned nose, and Hal's stomach sank as he saw the snooty expression. So much for roaming the space station, building shelters and practising with the escape hatches. This stuck-up know-it-all looked like a right killjoy.

The VIP spotted Hal's mum. 'Doctor Walsh, I presume?'

They shook hands. 'Welcome to the Oberon, Mr Grogan.'

'We've been looking forward to this visit. It's great to be here.' There was a snort alongside him. 'Oh yes. And this is my daughter Alex.'

— 5 —

Surprise!

Hal couldn't believe it. He'd been saddled with a snooty, stuck-up girl!

'You must be Hal,' said Grogan, clapping him on the shoulder. 'I've heard a lot about you.'

'It wasn't my fault,' said Hal quickly. 'I didn't know the fire would –'

'That's enough, Hal,' said his mum. 'We don't need the details.'

Grogan laughed heartily. 'I hear you offered to show my daughter around your little space station. That's mighty good of you.'

Alex turned her nose up even higher, and Hal's stomach sank. He would do anything to go on the camping trip, but showing a spoiled kid around his favourite haunts was right on the limit. He looked to his mum for support, but she was introducing Grogan to the scientists. When she was done the adults filed out of the control room, leaving Hal alone with Alex. 'After you,' he said, indicating the exit.

Alex drew back. 'I'm not holding your hand!'

'Who said anything about –'

'I have a boyfriend. He's bigger than you and he'll punch you in the nose.'

'Well I have a girlfriend, and she could snap your boyfriend like a ration bar.'

'You do not!'

'Do so.'

'Not!'

'So!'

'Not so! You said it!'

Hal's eyes narrowed. The battle lines had been drawn! As they followed the adults up the main tunnel, Hal fired his best shot. 'I bet your mouldy boyfriend never saved a space station from kidnappers and thieves.'

'We defended three planets against an alien battle fleet. And his dad *owns* a space station.'

'I own ten of them!' declared Hal.

'In your dreams, space boy.'

Hal scowled. 'My dad's taller than your dad.'

'My dad's richer.'

'My mum's smarter than your mum.'

Alex was silent.

'You lose!' crowed Hal.

'I – I don't have a mum.'

Hal was horrified. 'I'm sorry. I didn't mean . . . '

'It's all right, it was years ago. She died in a freak web surfing accident.'

'Eh?'

'You sucker!' cackled Alex. 'You should have seen your face!'

'That's not funny! You can't joke about things like that!'

Alex shrugged. 'Mum left us when I was little. I'll say whatever I like about her.'

'You shouldn't.'

'Can so!'

'Not!'

'So!'

'Snot!'

They stopped to scowl at each other, nose to nose, then burst out laughing. Alex looked much nicer without the snooty expression, and Hal realised the day might not be a total write-off after all. 'Come on, we'd better catch up.'

'After you, space boy.'

❖

Before long they reached the A-Section checkpoint, where a uniformed guard was standing stiffly to attention. Hal smiled at the sight. Usually the guard lounged around in jeans and T-shirt, but the Space Station was really putting on a show for their precious VIP. Then he looked closer and laughed out loud. The guard was Stinky's older brother, Richard! His uniform was buttoned up to the neck, and his gleaming gold badge looked like it had been polished all night long.

'Please display your passes,' said Richard, in a businesslike tone.

The adults obeyed, and were let through one by one. When it was the VIP's turn he showed his visitor badge and made to pass the checkpoint.

'I'm sorry, sir. I need to see inside that case.'

'It's all right, son.' Grogan tapped his badge. 'I'm a VIP. I can take this case wherever I want.'

'That's a negative,' said Richard, his eyes hard under the peaked cap. 'According to regulation nineteen slash twelve, all containers must be inspected.'

Hal's mum joined in. 'I'm afraid he's right, Mr Grogan. It won't take a moment.'

'Do you think I'm carrying a bomb in here?'

'Of course not. However, the lab is full of sensitive equipment. A stray signal from a commset, contamination from foreign matter . . . you could set our research back months.'

'But –'

'I'm sorry, but I must insist.'

'No chance.' Grogan tightened his grip on the briefcase. 'This case is full of personal data!'

'Why don't you leave it at the checkpoint?'

'I'm not letting it out of my sight.'

Hal stared from one to the other, eager to see how it turned out. Adults were usually boring, but this was real drama for a change. Would his mum wrestle Grogan for the briefcase? Would Grogan try to bust through the security checkpoint, only for Stinky's brother to shoot him with a stun gun?

But there was no wrestling or gunplay. Instead, help came from an unexpected quarter.

'Dad, why don't I look after it?'

Everyone turned to look at Alex.

'You trust me, don't you?' she said.

'Of course I do, sweetest. But I'm going to need this later.'

'So page me, and I'll bring it back here for you.'

'There you go,' said Hal's mum. 'The perfect solution.'

Grogan hesitated, then passed the briefcase to Alex. After a lingering frown at Stinky's brother Richard, he followed the others into A-Section.

Hal was impressed. The briefcase was made out of shiny blue metal, and it had a big lock on top with red and green status lights. His parents would never trust him with anything like that!

Alex noticed his admiring look. 'I don't know why dad brought this old thing along. He's got a much better one at home.'

'My mum's briefcase has wheels on.'

'My dad's briefcase can fly.'

Hal snorted. 'They all do, if you throw them hard enough.'

'That's not funny.'

'Depends who the briefcase belongs to,' said Hal shortly. He glanced up the corridor in case his mum had changed her mind and decided to take them on the guided tour. Unfortunately, all he got was a suspicious scowl from Stinky's brother. A few months earlier Hal had used Richard's entire stash of hair gel to make a slippery slide in the corridor, and afterwards he'd refilled the little plastic tubs with hull repair glue. The stuff looked just like hair gel, but unfortunately it set like concrete. First, Richard spent a week with his head encased in a gleaming shell. Then, once his hair grew out, he had to endure a really close shave. Even now his hair was still on the short side, and Hal decided it would be best not to linger.

— 6 —

Hostilities

Hal turned to Alex as they strolled away from the checkpoint. 'What do you want to see first?'

'How about the beach? No, maybe the park would be better. Or wait . . . how about the local swimming pool?'

Hal felt like suggesting a long walk out of a short airlock, but he knew his mum wouldn't approve. He tried to think of somewhere interesting and exciting - somewhere he was actually allowed to visit - and came up empty. 'Do you want to see my classroom?'

'Are you nuts? I didn't come all this way to do school lessons.' Alex thought for a moment. 'Tell you what, why don't you show me to the mall? I'll find some cool people to hang around with and you can do your homework like a good little boy.'

Hal frowned at the insult. 'What's a mall?'

'You know . . . shops, restaurants, that kind of

thing.'

Hal looked puzzled. 'Why would we need those on a space station?'

'You don't have a mall?'

'We have a supply depot and a staff canteen.'

'Sounds wonderful. So what do you do for fun?'

'We use the space simulators, and there are running machines in the gym. And sometimes we feed plants in the hydroponics lab.'

'What a boring place to live!'

'It's not boring. We do important research.'

'Oh yeah?' Alex looked him up and down. 'What sort of research?'

'It's top secret. I can't tell you.'

'Huh, I bet it's food or medicine.'

'It is not!'

'It is so. Totally boring!'

'It's way better than food or medicine.'

'You don't even know!'

'Do so!' Hal hesitated. 'We're inventing a huge teleporter. It can move planets all over the galaxy.'

Alex stared. 'Really?'

'Yes! It's so big it could even teleport your head.'

'Very witty, space bug.'

'Funnier than you, ground hugger.'

'Wormhole!'

Hal frowned. 'Dirt crawler!'

'At least I don't breathe tinned air.'

'I wouldn't use your polluted air if you paid me.'

'Who'd give you money? You can't even spend it!'

Thoroughly annoyed, Hal stormed off. If Alex wanted a tour of the Space Station she could show herself around.

'Where are you going?'

'Anywhere but here,' shouted Hal over his shoulder.

'But I don't know my way around. I could get lost.'

'Good!'

'What's your mum going to say?' called Alex.

Hal knew exactly what she'd say, and it wouldn't be pleasant. Reluctantly, he retraced his steps. 'All right, I'll show you round.' He pulled his sleeve up and inspected his big chrome watch. 'Two hours, and not a minute more.'

Alex snorted. 'Where did you get that old thing?'

Hal was scandalised. The watch was his most treasured possession, and he was convinced it had once been worn by Captain Spacejock of the Intergalactic Peace Force. 'This is a genuine space watch!'

'Yeah, twenty years ago.' Alex showed him the slim black band on her own wrist. 'This is what the good ones look like.'

'You call that a watch?' said Hal, with a laugh. 'It looks like a cheap plastic bangle.'

Alex shook her wrist, and there was a muted 'snap' as the outer skin of the bracelet unfurled into a rectangular screen. It had a menu full of icons, and when Alex tapped one a bright light shone from the middle of the device.

'Whoopee-doo,' said Hal. 'It was about time someone invented a bracelet torch.'

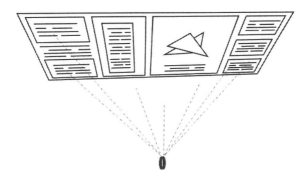

Alex said nothing. She just gestured at the ceiling.

Hal looked up and gasped. There was a huge image projected on the roof, and it was showing atmospheric pressure and air quality, the location of all nearby planets and ships plus hundreds of other variables.

'It plays movies too. I have four thousand of them. And every book ever written. And all the music.'

Hal was green with jealousy, but he'd never admit it. 'I bet the batteries don't last.'

'Batteries are so yesterday! This thing has an everlasting power unit.'

Hal pulled his sleeve down, hiding his watch. Alex was always one step ahead of him, but that was about to change. 'Come on, let's go.'

'Where to?'

'The recreation room.'

'Great. I bet it's a right old museum.'

'No, it has proper arcade machines. They're adults-only, but I cracked the access code.'

'The only thing you ever cracked was a glass window,' muttered Alex. Even so, she looked curious. 'These machines . . . what games have you got?'

Hal smiled. 'Follow me and I'll show you.'

◆

Hal and Alex walked across the Space Station in silence, and they hadn't gone far before Hal realised Alex was having trouble with the briefcase. After all the insults he was tempted to let her struggle, but she was a guest and there was still a slim chance she might show him around her dad's spaceship. 'That looks heavy. Do you want me to take it for a bit?'

'I could carry this thing all day,' said Alex shortly.

'If you say so.' Hal smiled to himself. So she could carry it all day, could she? Very well, why not find out?

After several minutes they reached the end of the corridor, where there were two signs on the wall: one said 'D section, level 9', and pointed back the way they'd come, while the other pointed up a flight of stairs to 'D section, level 8'. Their feet clattered as they took the metal steps, and they turned left twice before encountering another corridor.

'Haven't you people heard of elevators?' complained Alex.

'Walking is good for you.' Hal couldn't hide a grin. 'Didn't you know that, sweetest?'

Alex turned a force ten scowl on him, before gripping the briefcase and forging ahead. Five minutes later they reached another set of steps, these going down, and when Alex saw yet another long corridor at the bottom she stopped dead. 'This is totally ridiculous.'

'It's not far now,' said Hal. 'Honest.'

Alex switched the briefcase to the opposite side, gritted her teeth and set off along the corridor. They walked past several doors before reaching the end, where there was . . . another set of steps.

Alex glanced at the sign on the wall, then did a

double-take. One said 'D-section, level 9' and the other pointed up the stairs to 'D section, level 8'. She frowned at the signs, looked back along the corridor, then rounded on Hal. 'Okay, what are you playing at?'

Hal's expression was pure innocence, but he was struggling to contain his laughter. 'What do you mean?'

'Don't get smart with me. We've been doing laps!'

'No we haven't.'

'We have! We were just here!'

'No we weren't.'

Alex pointed at the sign. 'That says D section, level nine!'

'All the corridors look the same to newbies. That's why you're always getting lost.'

'Is that so?' Alex plucked a hair and tucked it behind the corner of the sign. 'If I see that again, you'll be wearing this briefcase on your head.'

'If you do that every time we pass a sign you'll be as bald as a space helmet.' Hal led the way upstairs, and as they emerged on the long corridor once again, he was tempted to try for yet another lap. Unfortunately Alex had noticed his little ruse, and he suspected she wasn't kidding about hitting him with the briefcase.

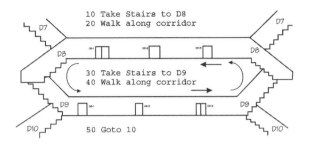

```
        10 Take Stairs to D8
        20 Walk along corridor

        30 Take Stairs to D9
        40 Walk along corridor

        50 Goto 10
```

They were halfway along when Hal stopped. They'd just passed one of the many storage cupboards, and it had given him an idea. 'Listen, you know that briefcase?'

'I haven't exactly forgotten it,' Alex stopped, out of breath.

◆

'Why don't we stash it?'

Alex hesitated, clearly tempted. 'Where?'

Hal pointed to the storage cupboard. 'Nobody will find it in there.'

'I don't think I should. Dad trusted me with it.'

'He didn't know you'd have to carry it all over the place.' Hal opened the door, revealing a cupboard crammed with spare parts. The shelves were overflowing with racks of circuit boards and electronic components, and there were drums of

211

cable stacked waist-high on the floor. 'Nobody's been in here for ages. It'll be safe enough.'

'All right, but if it goes missing –'

'It'll be fine,' said Hal firmly. He held the door open, and was about to follow Alex inside when she stopped him.

'You wait here. I don't want you to see where I'm hiding it.'

Hal shrugged. If she didn't trust him that was her problem.

Alex closed the door, and there was a lot of clattering and rustling. Then . . . *whoosh!*

Hal frowned. 'Alex? Are you there?'

'All done,' said Alex, opening the door and dusting off her hands.

'Where did you put it?'

'Like I'd tell you that!'

Hal shrugged. The hissing noise must have come from another deck. Odd sounds were common aboard the Station, but in that it was a bit like a spaceship or an aeroplane: people only started to panic when all the noises stopped. 'Come on, let's go.'

Alex hesitated. 'Are you sure the briefcase will be all right? I'll get in real trouble if –'

'Will you stop fussing?' demanded Hal. 'It's perfectly safe. Nobody knows where it is.'

As it turns out, he was even more accurate than he realised.

— 7 —

Tag!

Alex moved a lot faster without the briefcase, and they reached the recreation room in no time. Hal threw open the doors to reveal a spacious lounge with comfy chairs and glowing arcade machines, and he waited for Alex's thrilled reaction.

'Is that it?' Alex stared at the arcade games in disbelief. 'They're ancient!'

'I should have known you'd complain!' snapped Hal. He was about to slam the doors shut when Alex stopped him.

'All right, I'll play. It's not like there's anything else to do around here.' They entered the room, and she examined the controls on the nearest machine. 'Do people get burnt?'

'What do you mean?'

'When the steam comes out.'

Hal rolled his eyes.

'So how does it work?'

Hal picked up a helmet and showed her the projector screens and speakers fitted inside. When she was happy he demonstrated the joystick fixed to the front of each machine.

'I push that thing to move around?' asked Alex.

Hal smiled to himself. A total beginner!

'And the red switch on the front?'

'What do you think? That's the fire button!'

'Great. Let's go.'

'First to five wins the match,' declared Hal.

'Do these machines really count that high?'

They donned the helmets and Hal took hold of the controls. His display showed a darkened warehouse packed with large crates and walkways. The idea was to sneak around and tag the other player, and with a noob like Alex, Hal reckoned he'd win in ten seconds flat.

BUZZ!

'One nil,' said Alex.

'Hey! I wasn't ready!' protested Hal.

'Tell that to the scoring computer.'

Hal's eyes narrowed. So that's how it was! He forgot the rec room and immersed himself in the game, listening for stealthy footsteps as he crept between the towering stacks of crates. He held his gun at the ready, moving the laser dot from side to side as he tried to spot the enemy.

CRASH!

Hal almost jumped out of his shoes as a crate smashed into the ground right behind him. He stared at the shattered timbers, and realised someone had pushed it from the stack. Oh no . . . Alex was above him, on top of the stacks! His display whirled as he looked up, but he was much too late.

BUZZ!

'Two nil,' said Alex cheerfully.

Hal muttered under his breath. Nobody told him you could push the crates around! And if that was allowed, why not bring the whole building down on your enemy? Now there was an idea! He ran to the nearest wall and tried shooting out the supporting beams.

BUZZ!

'That's three,' said Alex. 'Do you want to play best of seven instead?'

'No!' Hal hunched over the controls, focusing on the screen as though his life depended on it. He was not going to lose at his favourite game. Keeping his eyes peeled, he crouched between two crates and turned the volume as high as it would go, listening for the soft footsteps that would pinpoint Alex.

Scrape, scrape.

Hal frowned. What was that?

Scrape.

Hal spun round, but all he could see was the wall of crates. Above him were more crates, stacked high, and far overhead was the roof.

Scrape . . . scrape.

Hal backed away slowly, puzzled by the noise. Then he saw a glint from one of the crates, and he realised it was Alex's gun poking through a hole. She'd climbed right inside and was pushing the hollow crate along like a battle tank!

BUZZ!

'Four nil,' said Alex. 'One more and you're toast.'

Hal ripped the helmet off. 'That's it! I'm not playing against a lousy cheat.'

'Sore loser.'

'Cheat!'

'If it was cheating the game wouldn't let me do it. Anyway, you'd have used the same trick if you knew about it.'

Hal knew she was right, but he still wasn't happy. This was his game, and she should be playing it properly! When he fought his friends they just ran around in circles while he tagged them. They didn't hide inside boxes, throw crates . . . or beat him!

'Come on, one more go,' said Alex. 'I don't really think you're a loser.'

Mollified, Hal donned the helmet again. This time he lasted a whole minute before Alex ran up the wall, back-flipped over his head and tagged him in the rear with her gun.

BUZZ!

'You lose,' said Alex. 'Want another match?'

Hal frowned. He enjoyed the game when he was winning, but it wasn't the same when someone used you for target practice. No wonder Stinky got tired of it. 'No, I've had enough.'

'Suit yourself, coward.'

'I am not!'

'Cluck, cluck, cluck . . . . chickeeeen!'

Hal saw red. 'I can beat you at this silly game any time!'

'Prove it!'

The scores reset to zero and Hal gripped the

controls, a determined look on his face. Once inside the warehouse he ran to the nearest crate and worked out how to get inside. He made a hole with his gun, then peered out.

Scrape, scrape.

This time he recognised the sound. Alex was inside another crate, creeping up on him! Very slowly he turned to watch, and that's when he saw her. She was sliding between two rows, moving her tagger in a small figure of eight as she tried to pick up his trail.

Scrape.

Hal held his breath as he turned his crate. Had she heard? No! She was still moving! Hal sighted along the stubby barrel, placed the laser dot right in the middle of Alex's crate, and pulled the trigger.

BUZZ!

Hal grinned. 'One nil to me.'

'Not bad, young Hal. The master approves!'

Flush with confidence, Hal ran into the dingy warehouse to score another point. He'd barely cleared the door when . . .

BUZZ!

'Yesss! Score one to Alex the mighty warrior.'

Hal sighed. She'd been waiting just inside the door with her back to the wall.

'Let's try a new playing field,' said Alex.

Hal blinked. He was standing in a lush forest, with boulders and streams replacing crates and sewage pipes. There were birds in the trees, fluttering from branch to branch, and sunlight shone between the leaves. It was the most beautiful thing he'd ever seen, and all he could do was stand there, entranced. Of course, he'd seen pictures of forests before, but this was different. This was just like being there.

BUZZ!

'Two-one!' Alex laughed. 'The game would last longer if you ran around a bit.'

'Is this what your planet looks like?'

'Some of it. Why?'

'It's . . . '

'Better than a mouldy old tin can in space?'

Hal frowned. 'Not better. Different.'

'Are we playing or what?'

Hal took up the controls but his heart wasn't in it. He didn't want to run around playing tag, he wanted to climb a tree, float sticks down the stream and enjoy the sunlight on his face.

A few minutes later the score was five to one, and Hal took off his helmet in silence. He looked around the rec room and decided it didn't look bright and welcoming any more. No, it looked sterile and artificial.

'No cheering for the winner?'

Hal shrugged. 'Congratulations.'

'You gave up, didn't you?'

'Yeah.' Hal frowned. 'I can't believe you learnt to play so quickly.'

'I've been playing these games for years.' Alex grinned. 'My dad owns the company that makes them.'

The AutoChef

'You already knew how to play?' Hal was really annoyed. 'You pretended you didn't! You asked me to show you how the controls worked!'

'My dad calls it mental conditioning. First you put people off their guard . . . '

'. . . And then you shoot them in the back,' finished Hal. 'Nice.'

'He's a businessman. It's what they do.' Alex gestured at another machine. 'Do you want to try that one?'

'No, let's get a snack.'

'I thought you didn't have restaurants?'

'We don't. We have something much better.' Hal led her across the rec room to an alcove, which contained a gleaming black cabinet covered with pictures of delicious food. There were pastries and sausage rolls and salads, as well as a sumptuous cake with cherries on top. 'This is the AutoChef,' said Hal. 'You tell it what you want, and it serves it up in seconds.'

'Really? Will you show me how it works?'

Hal wondered whether Alex was pretending again, but she sounded genuinely interested. 'Okay. Watch this.' He addressed the machine, speaking very clearly. 'I want a ham sandwich.'

'Order accepted,' said the AutoChef curtly. It rumbled and growled, and then . . . whizz! Zoom! Two slices of bread shot out of the dispenser and sailed halfway across the rec room before skidding to a halt, butter side down.

Chack! Chack! CHACK! went the machine, as it tossed slices of ham into the dispenser. Then, with a loud squir-ir-irt!, it spat a cupful of yellowy-brown mustard all over the ham. Hal scraped the bread clean and built a sandwich with the dripping ham.

'Yum, that looks great,' said Alex, trying not to laugh. 'I wish I had a machine like that.'

'I don't know what's wrong with it,' muttered Hal. 'It doesn't usually do that.'

'Can I try?'

'Sure, but don't order stew or you might get p–'

'Yes, I get the picture.' Alex turned to the machine. 'Hello AutoChef. Please may I have a garden salad with shaved ham, olives and two slices of bread?'

Hal stared in horror. Was she mad? That lot would have them knee deep in goop!

'Order accepted.' The machine hissed and groaned, and Hal backed away. He was expecting a tidal wave at the very least.

'Oh, I nearly forgot,' continued Alex. 'Acknowledge supervisor code nine-six-two.'

'Code acknowledged.' The hissing and growling turned into an even hum, and Hal was stunned when the machine delivered Alex's order. It was arranged on a real plate, and everything was perfect! 'How did you do that?' he demanded, staring at the delicious food.

'It doesn't hurt to say please and thank you.' Alex patted the AutoChef. 'Machines have feelings too, you know.'

'What about that supervisor code?'

'Oh, that. Well, my dad's company makes these machines too, and the code tells them when they're serving VIPs.'

Hal felt a flash of annoyance. Alex had shown him up again! Then he realised what the supervisor code meant. 'Hey, does that mean I can get real food out of the AutoChef too?' Hal could just imagine the scene: Get all his classmates there and show off with some incredible dishes. 'Does it do real cake?'

Alex dashed his hopes. 'Sorry, but it only works with a few recognised voices. And as for a computer giving you cake . . . get real!' She saw his downcast expression, and relented. 'Here, you can have my lunch. I'll get something else.'

Wide-eyed, Hal took the tray and enjoyed the best lunch ever. Crisp lettuce, fresh tomatoes, tangy olives and ham! They weren't real meat and vegetables, of course. His dad once explained how everything the AutoChef served was assembled from a kind of raw goop, blending molecules to simulate real food. When the goop ran out there was no more food, which is why you never ordered more than you could eat.

Real or not, the food still tasted amazing to Hal.

Alex ordered another lunch, but she hadn't finished with the machine yet. 'I'd also like a strawberry thickshake, two straws, and one of those cakes with the chocolate stuff on top.'

The machine made a horrible gargling sound. 'Error C-22.'

'You've broken it!' said Hal in alarm.

'Relax. It's just run out of material.'

Hal frowned. He fancied dessert, and didn't see why they shouldn't have any. 'I know where we can go next.'

'You do?'

'They're preparing a special lunch for your dad. Let's sneak into the kitchens and help ourselves!'

'Oh no you don't, my lad. Out! Out! OUT!'

Hal took one look at the angry-looking chef and scarpered. Once he'd retreated to a safe distance he paused to catch his breath.

'Wow, you're really popular around here,' said Alex. 'It's like one big happy family.'

'At least my mum didn't run away,' snapped Hal. Then he realised what he'd said. 'I'm sorry, I–'

'Leave it.'

They stood near the entrance, watching the bustle as chefs put the finishing touches to a vast array

226

of different foods. 'Maybe we could help carry,' said Hal, licking his lips.

'Yeah, like they're going to trust you.'

'Do you think your dad will eat it all?'

'You bet.'

Hal frowned. For his last birthday they'd had a stale sponge with fake cream, and at the time it was one of the best things he'd ever tasted. Now he was looking at strawberry tarts, scones with jam and dollops of fresh cream, chocolate cake with thick icing and gooey filling, and currant buns spread with more butter than he'd seen in his entire life. At that moment Hal would have given up his precious watch for any one of the treats on display.

Beep beep! 'Mind your backs!'

There was a loud whirr, and Hal jumped aside as a powered trolley shot into the kitchens. It was almost as big as the doorway, and it moved on huge rubber wheels.

'Where have you been?' shouted one of the chefs. 'These cakes ain't going to deliver themselves!'

The trolley apologised. 'I had to stop for a recharge. All this extra activity drained my batteries.'

The chef beckoned to her staff. 'You lot. Get this trolley loaded. Now!'

Hal watched the bustle with a thoughtful look on

227

his face. The trolley had a tablecloth draped over the top, and it hung almost to the floor. The kitchen hands were putting cakes on the top shelf, and as he watched them Hal got the beginnings of an idea. He glanced down the corridor to the next doorway, then nudged Alex. 'Come on. Follow me.'

'I thought you wanted cake?'

'I do, and I know how to get some.'

The kitchen doors closed behind them, and Hal hurried down the access tunnel to the second pair of doors. 'You stand that side,' he said. 'Get ready to watch the master in action.'

Moments later the trolley zoomed out of the kitchen, cakes and jellies shivering and jiggling on top.

Beep beep! 'Stand aside please!'

The doors began to open, and Hal quickly pressed the close button.

Screeeeeeech!

The trolley slid to a halt in a cloud of tyre smoke, plates of food skidding along the top shelf. Fortunately there was a rail, else the contents would have splatted into the doors. Hal grinned triumphantly at Alex, and was just about to choose a sticky cake when the kitchen doors started to open. Someone was coming! They were trapped!

'Get inside!' hissed Alex.

Hal saw Alex climbing into the trolley, and he lifted the tablecloth and scrambled in after her.

'Wait!' shouted a female voice. There was a patter of footsteps, and Hal realised they'd been spotted.

'Watch the master in action?' hissed Alex. 'Watch the master get caught, you mean!'

There was barely enough room for the two of them, and they sat facing each other with their arms clasped around their knees. It was very dark, but Hal could still see Alex's amused expression. It was all a big joke to her, but what sort of punishment could he expect *this* time?

— 9 —

Carrie

The footsteps halted right next to the trolley, and then . . . 'Can you return to the kitchen, please? We've not finished loading.'

The trolley obeyed, reversing direction and slowly whirring back to the kitchen. Hal breathed a sigh of relief. They hadn't been spotted after all! Of course, that would soon change if someone tried to use the lower shelf.

The trolley stopped, and someone tutted as they straightened the plates on top.

'Millie, are you done yet?' demanded the chef.

'Last two,' said a voice . . . presumably Millie.

'Don't cram them so. Use the lower shelf.'

Hal held his breath as the tablecloth was lifted. A plate full of jam doughnuts was pushed in, and Hal quickly moved his foot. He was still expecting a shout of discovery when the tablecloth fell back into place.

'Anything else, chef?' asked Millie.

'No, that's everything. Trolley, to the meeting room. And not so fast, mind!'

The engine groaned, but the trolley didn't move.

'Trolley, to the meeting room!'

'Unable to comply,' said the trolley. 'Total weight exceeds safety limits.'

'Nonsense! Millie, give that thing a push.'

The trolley turned slowly towards the exit, while Millie huffed and puffed and complained about the chef's cooking.

'What was that?' demanded the chef. 'What did you say about my rock cakes?'

'They're too heavy,' grumbled Millie. 'This trolley weighs a ton!'

'Come here and say that!' growled the chef.

Millie didn't do anything of the sort. Instead she gave the trolley a big shove to get it moving, and the plate of doughnuts slid along the shelf and stopped next to Hal's hand. One of the jam doughnuts actually came to rest against his fingers, and he could feel the sticky wetness. If he picked it up he could open his mouth and . . . But no. When someone eventually discovered Hal and Alex hiding in the trolley, they'd notice the missing doughnut and Hal would be in more trouble than ever.

❖

Hal and Alex held on tight as the trolley rumbled along the corridor. It was very quiet, with only the whirr of the motor and the rattle of crockery to break the silence.

They stared at each other in the darkness. The trolley was going to the meeting, and that was in A-section. If they were discovered sneaking into the top-secret labs, Hal suspected he wouldn't just be confined to quarters. They'd banish him from the Space Station!

Ten minutes later Hal had forgotten all about A-section, and nothing was further from his mind than sticky doughnuts. He couldn't believe how much the trolley swayed on its rubber wheels, and the motion was making him seasick.

'If you want to get off, just say the word.'

Hal heard the electronic voice, and with a shock he realised the trolley was talking to him. 'You know we're here?'

'Of course.' The trolley chuckled. 'Even chef's rock cakes aren't that heavy.'

'Thanks for not telling. Back in the kitchen, I mean.'

'We're all young once.' The trolley hesitated. 'Why don't we introduce ourselves?'

'I'm Hal and this is Alex. And you?'

'My name is Carrie.'

'Can you stop before we get to A-Section?'

'Sure. I'll let you know when the coast is clear.'

They rolled on for another minute or two, then came to a halt. 'This should do,' said Carrie. 'There's nobody around, but I'd get out fast if I were you.'

Hal leapt out, holding up the tablecloth so Alex could follow. He glanced at the nearby sign to get his bearings, then groaned. 'Quick, back in the trolley!'

Too late! When they turned to hide they discovered Carrie had already moved off, and the speeding trolley disappeared around the corner with a final beep! beep!

There was a whirr behind them, and Hal heard a familiar electronic voice. 'What are you doing here, Hal Junior? I thought you were confined to your cabin!'

They turned to see a bright red robot with yellow stripes. It had a big grey screen where its face should have been, and there were two dozen assorted eyes staring at Hal.

'Is that a security bot?' whispered Alex fearfully.

'No, much worse.' Hal sighed. 'It's Teacher.'

— 10 —

Spring

'Well, Hal Junior?' said Teacher. 'Explain your presence!'

Hal told him about Alex and the VIP, and while he was talking Teacher turned several eyes on the girl. 'Welcome to the Space Station, Alex. I trust Hal isn't getting you into trouble?'

'No, not at all.'

'I find that surprising.' Teacher frowned at Hal. 'This young man can be irresponsible and unreliable at times. Starting a fire aboard the Space Station! What were you thinking?'

'It was an experiment,' said Hal. 'You're always telling me to light up my grades.'

'Hmph.' Teacher turned a couple more eyes on them both. 'Now you're here, why don't you help with spring cleaning?'

Cleaning? Hal would rather have gone for a space

walk without a suit! Then he frowned. As far as he knew Teacher ran on batteries, not springs.

Teacher noticed his puzzled look and launched into an explanation. 'As you know, many planets experience hot and cold seasons called Summer and Winter. After Summer comes Autumn, also known as Fall or Harvest, and after Winter you get Spring, which is only known as Spring.'

'So why are you doing spring cleaning when we don't have seasons?'

'It's a tradition. Once a year we have a big tidy-up before the end of term.'

'I don't remember any tidy-ups.'

Teacher frowned. 'No, I always seem to get a sick note from your parents. Written, I must say, in a rather ungrammatical fashion.'

Hal blushed, and quickly changed the subject. 'So why do we have years aboard the Space Station when we don't orbit a star?'

'The same reason we have days and nights. To remain in sync with the rest of the galaxy. Now, please follow me. I'm sure I can find something for you to do.'

Hal and Alex exchanged a glance, but there was no escape. They entered the classroom behind Teacher and stopped to take in the chaos. Desks and chairs had been pushed out to the walls and two dozen children were emptying all the cupboards onto the floor, stirring the contents around and piling them up at random. At least, that's what it looked like to Hal, whose own 'cleaning' sessions ran along similar lines.

'No, no, no!' Teacher darted away to supervise, swerving on his rubber wheels to avoid the children. 'Harold, I said to place those workbooks in a neat pile! Marcia, do NOT stand on the geometry shapes to reach the upper shelves. Tim, if you break one more beaker . . . '

Hal eyed the crowd, trying to pick out his best friend, but he was nowhere to be seen. 'Teacher, where's Stinky?'

'Master Binn is running an errand for me.' One of Teacher's eyes turned to the door. 'Unless I'm mistaken, that's him now.'

Stinky entered the classroom, looking worried. His face was red from running, and his hair - usually so tidy - was sticking out all over the place. With his singed eyebrows and flushed face he looked like a sunburned kiwi fruit, and it was all Hal could do not to laugh.

'Master Binn, were you successful?'

'I'm sorry Teacher. They wouldn't let me have any.'

'That's a pity.'

'You won't . . . mark me down, will you?'

'Master Binn, this is spring cleaning, not final exams. Your grades are safe.'

Hal rolled his eyes. His friend's biggest nightmare was getting a B in something, even though he had a string of A's reaching all the way back to kindy. 'Hey, Stinky! I want you to meet someone. This is Alex.'

Stinky met the girl's level gaze for a second, then turned an even brighter shade of red. 'N-nice to meet you,' he stammered.

'What happened to your eyebrows?' asked Alex.

'Never mind that,' said Hal quickly. 'What did Teacher send you off for? Maybe Alex and me can help.'

Teacher heard him, and zoomed across the room. 'Hal Junior! I'm sure you meant *I* can help.'

'How can you? You're busy here.'

'I meant *you* could help, not me.'

'That's exactly what I said!'

One of Teacher's eyes flickered. 'You said me.'

'No, I said *Alex* and me. Anyway, you're busy.'

Several of Teacher's eyes bounced along the bottom of his face. 'It's Alex and *I*. Alex and *I*!'

Alex looked doubtful. 'I'd rather stay with Hal,' she said. 'I don't really know you very well.'

'I– I– I–' Teacher's eyes bounced around like a

handful of glass marbles falling downstairs, some of them going all the way round his head before reappearing the other side.

'We just need some boxes,' said Stinky quickly, before Teacher crashed completely.

'Don't worry,' said Hal, patting him on the shoulder. 'Alex and me will get them for you.'

'I, not me,' muttered Teacher. 'I. Eye. Aye aye.'

Stinky gave Hal a printed card.

'What's that?'

'Permission slip. You'll need it to get the boxes.'

'It didn't do you any good.' Hal looked closer. 'Anyway, it's got your name all over it.'

'Get another from Teacher.'

Hal eyed the robot doubtfully. Teacher's eyes were still ping-ponging all over his face, and the last time that happened the techs had taken two hours to reboot him. Then Hal had a thought, and a slow smile spread across his face. With a permission slip he could roam the entire Space Station!

There was a thud nearby as a pile of workbooks toppled over, and Teacher snapped out of his loop instantly. 'Harold, will you please be careful! And Marcia, get your foot off that equipment. Don't you know how fragile it is?'

'Can I get a permission slip?' asked Hal, before

Teacher could zoom away to rescue his precious equipment.

'Very well. Where do you need to go?'

'I don't know yet.'

'You'll have to be more specific.'

'The lower levels,' said Hal. He hadn't been right to the bottom of the Space Station before, and now was his chance.

Teacher paused. 'I don't think I can –'

'Oh, go on! We can't get boxes anywhere else, and Alex is sensible. She's a . . . ' Hal tried to remember some of the things his parents wanted him to be. 'She's a good influence, and she's prompt, and she brushes her hair and does all her homework.'

'Very well. You make a good point.' Teacher clicked his fingers and a printed card popped out the palm of his hand. 'It's valid for one hour. Please return with the boxes as soon as you can.'

— 11 —

Order! Order!

As they left the classroom Alex plucked the permission card from Hal's fingers. 'I'll be in charge.'

'Says who?'

'Teacher said you're irresponsible, unreliable and un– un–'

'Unable to take orders from you,' finished Hal.

'Why don't we go back inside and ask Teacher which of us is leader?'

Alex went to open the classroom door, but Hal put his hand over the controls. Imagine the embarrassment if Teacher made him second-in-command! 'Let's share the power between us.'

'Like that's going to work.'

'No, it will. We'll take it in turns to give orders. One for you, one for me.'

'Fine, but I'm going first.'

Hal shrugged. If he didn't like the orders he'd ignore them . . . just like he always did.

'My first order is this: I order you not to give me any silly orders. Now it's your turn.'

'I order you not to speak for the rest of my life.'

'That'll be ten seconds from now if you keep this up.' Alex thought for a moment. 'I order you to be sensible.'

'I order you a ham sandwich.'

'Hal Junior! Quit messing around!'

'I order you not to give me any more orders,' said Hal quickly. 'And I order you not to tell Teacher on me.'

'Oh, this is stupid!' cried Alex. 'We're fetching some mouldy old boxes, not leading an expedition to the centre of the Galaxy. Who cares which of us is in charge?'

'Of course, if we don't bring back any boxes the person in charge is going to get the blame.'

Alex pursed her lips. 'I think you should be leader.'

'No, you do it.'

'Your Teacher expects you to fail. It sounds like you're always getting in trouble.' Alex crossed her arms. 'I order you to take charge.'

'About time.' Hal grabbed the permission slip. 'Now quit talking and follow me.'

Looking a bit dazed, Alex fell in behind Hal as they made their way to the lift.

'So where are you getting these boxes?' she asked, after a moment or two. 'Your friend Stinky didn't think there were any.'

Hal took a deep breath, then revealed his master plan. 'Stinky didn't go to the recycling centre, did he?'

'The what?'

'It's like a huge rubbish dump at the bottom of the Space Station. Everything we throw away ends up there.'

'Oh, wonderful. First school and now the local tip. You really know how to show someone the sights, you do.'

Hal frowned. 'Don't you understand? The recycling centre is off-limits! We're not allowed there!'

'Why not?'

'Dangerous, maybe. Some of the kids think there's a space monster.'

'So speaks the straight-A student.' Alex laughed. 'Anyone with half a brain knows space monsters don't exist.'

Hal's eyes narrowed. 'Are you saying I'm dumb?'

'No, but I don't think you try very hard.'

'I don't see the point! All that math and writing

and stuff . . . what use is that to me? I'm going to be a space pilot!'

Alex raised one eyebrow. 'Next time you're sitting at a terminal, look up navigation. I think you'll be surprised.'

They walked in silence while Hal considered her words. Did you really need to study sums to fly a spaceship? How could that be right?

❧

They were only halfway along the corridor when Hal heard a whirr behind them. He turned around, half-expecting to see Teacher pursuing him with new instructions, but instead he saw Carrie. The motorised trolley was bearing down on them with a load of empty dishes piled on top. Hal frowned at this: Alex's greedy dad *had* eaten all the food!

Beep beep! 'Mind your backs!'

'Hey, Carrie. Stop!'

'I can't. I'm in a hurry.'

'So are we,' said Hal quickly. 'Teacher sent us on an important errand, and our pass is only valid for one hour.'

The trolley came to a halt. 'Very well, but you mustn't delay me.'

'We won't!' Hal raised the tablecloth so Alex could get inside, and when they were both settled he rapped his knuckles on the floor. 'Let's go.'

The trolley moved off with a jerk, and once they were speeding along Carrie asked where they were going.

'To the recycling centre,' said Hal.

Screech! Hal and Alex were almost thrown out as the trolley came to a shuddering halt. 'Out, both of you.'

'But –'

'Out!' Carrie's voice was angry. 'You'll never get me near that place. Never!'

'Just to the lift, then? We have to fetch something, I swear!'

'We'd all like something back from the recycling centre,' said Carrie. 'When I started working in the kitchens there was another trolley just like me. He was pretty old, Paul was, and he needed a few repairs. Just simple things like a new back wheel and a bit of polish, but they recycled him instead.' Carrie shuddered. 'He was gone, just like that! Turned into nuts and bolts.'

'I'm sorry.'

Carrie's voice softened. 'At night, when the kitchens were closed, Paul used to sing for us. It was . . . nice.'

245

There was a lengthy silence.

'All right,' said Carrie at last. 'I'll take you to the lift, but not one metre further. Is that clear?'

'Thanks Carrie.' As the trolley picked up speed Hal glanced at Alex. So far she'd met a surly guard, an angry chef, a Teacher who kept crashing and now a trolley whose best friend was nuts. So much for staying out of trouble!

— 12 —

Lower Levels

Carrie got slower and slower the closer they got to the main lift, and once they were in sight of the doors the trolley came to a shuddering halt. 'That's it. I'm not going a centimetre further.'

Hal and Alex climbed out, and Carrie sped away before they could say thanks.

'The recycling centre must be pretty dangerous,' said Alex.

'Bring it on,' said Hal, as he pressed the call button.

'Can't you think of somewhere else to get these boxes?'

'Sure. We can plant some trees, wait around for them to grow, then slice them real thin and fold the sheets into cubes. It won't take more than ten or fifteen years, plus a hundred years of my water ration.'

'There's no need to be sarcastic.'

The lift arrived and the doors parted with a whoosh. Hal motioned Alex inside, then jammed his thumb on the lowest button. The doors closed and the lift dropped like a stone.

'Bet you get into trouble,' said Alex.

That was one bet Hal wasn't willing to take. 'This is an official mission. We can go anywhere we want and take anything we like.'

'I don't suppose you got these carte-blanche orders in writing?'

'Carty what?'

'Carte blanche. It means full power to do anything you want.'

'Why didn't you say that instead?' complained Hal.

'I was trying to educate you.'

'That's Teacher's job.'

'If we get caught I'm dobbing,' said Alex.

'You would too. You're such a feeb.'

'Am not.'

'Are so!'

Alex turned her back on him and Hal ground his teeth in silence. As they dropped further and further the elevator began to squeak and rattle in its tracks, as though it rarely came down this far.

Would it break free and plunge all the way to the bottom?

But no, it finally came to a halt, and the doors grated open to reveal a dark, forbidding corridor. Hal and Alex stood side by side, each waiting for the other to take the first step.

'What was that you said about a space monster?' asked Alex at last.

Hal wished he'd never mentioned it. He'd been trying to forget the stories all the way down. The ones about the monster at the very bottom of the space station. The monster which ate all the junk and chewed up anyone who fell down the recycling chute. The monster which might be hiding just around the corner, ready to pounce.

'Why don't we sneak into A-section instead?' suggested Alex, her voice a little uneven. 'They might have boxes in the labs.'

Hal was tempted, but then he remembered his watch. After his last adventure it had been engraved with 'Hal Junior, Saviour of Space Station Oberon', and they didn't hand those out to people afraid of a silly old space monster. 'Come on, it'll be fine.'

'You're in charge. You should go first.'

'Just watch me. I'm not afraid.' Nevertheless Hal didn't exactly hurry out of the elevator, and he'd only taken a dozen faltering steps when there was a flash of light and a loud *BUZZ-CRACKLE!* directly overhead. He suppressed a startled squeak and almost bolted for safety. Then he realised it was just an automatic light coming on. Dim and dusty, the fitting gave out barely enough light to see by, and Hal kept moving until he reached the end of the corridor.

'Can you see anything?' hissed Alex, as Hal peered around the corner.

'Oh wow!' breathed Hal. 'It's incredible!'

'What is?'

'Come and look!'

Reluctantly, Alex left the elevator. When she reached the corner she peered round and saw . . . 'You cheat! It's just another corridor!'

'Shh!' Hal put a finger to his lips. 'The monster might hear you!'

'If you're going to play silly games I'm leaving.'

'Oh come on. Maybe there's something interesting round the next corner.'

Hal set off along the corridor with Alex grumbling in his wake. Before long they reached a big pair of doors. The paint was peeling and the panels had streaks of rust running down them, and judging from the layer of dirt on the floor nobody had been this way for quite some time. Hal reached for the control panel, but before he could press the button Alex grabbed his arm. 'Shouldn't we knock or something?'

'On that?' Hal eyed the slab of metal. 'I could bang on that until my knuckles broke, and they still wouldn't hear me on the other side.' He shook his arm free and thumped his fist on the door controller. There was an agonising groan as the motor whirred into life, and then the doors began to open with a horrible grating sound.

The noise was incredible, and even though Hal covered his ears he could still feel the groaning through the soles of his shoes. As the doors opened a foul-smelling wind blew out, ruffling their hair. Hal wrinkled his nose and hoped the stink wouldn't spread through the entire station.

'Now youb dub id,' said Alex, who was holding her nose. 'Deyr godda smer dad all over da dadion.'

The doors stopped moving and Hal risked a quick look inside. He knew there was a main shaft down the centre of the Space Station, with several smaller chutes connecting various living areas, but he hadn't realised the inhabitants generated this much rubbish. Instead of the large room he'd been expecting there was a gigantic, poorly-lit cavern, so big he couldn't make out the far wall. This was a new experience for Hal, who'd grown up with corridors and confined spaces.

He gazed around and discovered the floor was covered in junk piles, from little ones right up to huge mountains. The biggest were right underneath a row of holes in the ceiling, which Hal realised were the bases of the recycling shafts. These huge square openings gaped like giant silver mouths, and one of them disgorged a stream of rubbish onto the top of a pile while they were standing there watching. Steam rose from the fresh junk in waves, adding to the foggy atmosphere.

'Yuck,' said Alex. 'That's gross!'

Hal didn't think it was gross at all. Just imagine what treasures they might find in this vast, unexplored cavern! Imagine the fun they could have here! There was enough room to build a go-kart and race between the piles of rubbish, space to build a clubhouse and run a secret society, and great stacks of building materials just lying around waiting to be used.

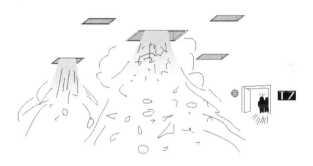

Hal crossed to a big pile of wall panels and ran his hand over the smooth plastic. Half a dozen of these would make a great clubhouse, and if he could find some paint they could have a big sign above the door. He was just deciding whether to call the group the 'Junior Outlaws' or 'Hal's Heroes' when Alex piped up.

'Let's grab some boxes and get out of here.'

'No, we'll look around a bit first.'

'But –'

'Who's in charge, you or me?' Hal scanned the recycling centre from end to end, peering through the murk as he tried to spot any workers, guards or automated defence turrets with dual blasters and laser-guided gunsights. Fortunately there was nothing of the kind, but in the distance he could see a rickety-looking shed nestled between a discarded exhaust cone and a pile of frayed spacesuits. The door was closed but the window was lit from within, and at that moment he spotted movement inside. 'Down!' he hissed.

They both dropped to the floor, then raised their heads to see whether they'd been spotted. Fortunately the shadow was still moving behind the window.

'Who is it?' hissed Alex.

'I don't know. Someone who works here.'

'So why are we hiding?' whispered Alex. 'You have permission, don't you?'

Hal didn't answer. He pointed away from the office, and together they crawled into the recycling centre, keeping low so as not to be spotted.

— 13 —

Attack the Summit!

They rounded a big pile of junk on hands and knees, clambering to their feet as soon as they were shielded from the office. They were approaching the middle of the recycling centre now, and there was a low-pitched hum in the air. There was something else too . . . a deep *THUD!* every so often, which shook the floor under their feet.

'Fee fie –' began Alex.

'That's not funny,' muttered Hal. Years ago his parents had told him the story of Jack and the Space Elevator, and the sound of the giant robot's footsteps as it chased Jack haunted Hal's nightmares for years. He wasn't that keen on greens either, especially beans.

They reached a large junk pile, and Hal stopped to look at the top.

'Don't tell me you're going to climb it,' said Alex.

Hal hadn't been planning anything of the sort, but he couldn't resist a challenge. 'Of course I am.'

'Why?'

'Because it's there,' said Hal firmly. He'd heard the line in a mountaineering documentary Teacher had shown the class a few months earlier. At the time Hal felt cheated, because there was no chance he'd ever climb a mountain, and he wondered whether Teacher was going to follow up the first documentary with others on scuba diving, bike riding and skiing.

Anyway, the documentary had been pretty cool in the end. *Attack the Summit!* was the name, and the climbers had been dressed in boots and goggles and thick orange jackets, and their equipment included a T-shaped tool on a length of rope. The leader had swung the tool over her head, then flung it up the slope before pulling it tight and using it to haul herself up the icy slopes. After she tested the rope the rest of the team followed, until it was time to throw the tool once more.

Hal didn't need the goggles or the orange jackets, but one of those T-shaped tools and a length of climbing rope would be pretty useful. Unfortunately, aboard the Space Station he was more likely to find a pair of hover boots or a portable jet pack, and his live-action remake of

Attack the Summit! was likely to turn into *Rolling down the mountain.*

He was still working out the easiest way to the top of the pile when Alex spoke up.

'If you're going to climb something, why not make it a real challenge?'

'What do you mean?'

Alex jerked her thumb towards the largest pile of all. 'Bet you can't climb that one.'

Hal craned his neck back ... and further back ... and further back still, until he was finally looking at the top. It was shrouded in fog from a fresh load of garbage, and the towering mass reached almost to the distant ceiling. 'Sure I can.'

'Bet you can't.'

'I can!'

'If you make it right to the top I'll ... I'll give you my watch!'

Hal stared. With a watch like that he'd be the envy of the entire station. Sure, the pile of junk was enormous, but what a prize! 'For real?'

'Of course,' said Alex coldly. 'I said it, didn't I?'

'Wait right here.' Hal strolled over to the pile and tested it with his foot. It was spongy and loose, but it wasn't too steep and he managed to climb the first few metres without any trouble. After that the going got harder, and he'd never have made it without a fantastic stroke of luck. First, his foot got caught in a loop of network cable, and then he spotted a heavy metal bar. The metal bar was bent into a J-shape, and it reminded him of the climbing tool the mountaineers had used. Within moments he'd freed the network cable and attached it to the long end of the J. Then he swung it overhead and threw it as hard as he could towards the top of the pile.

Unfortunately, he slipped as he threw, and he landed face down in the junk. The heavy metal bar hardly made it halfway to the top, and Hal was still recovering when he realised it had dislodged a load of plastic bags, broken furniture and battered air filters. The avalanche of junk rumbled towards him, and he barely had time to lie flat and cover his head. The slithering mess arrived with a rush, covering Hal from head to toe and burying him up to his neck. He poked his head up just as the heavy bar shot past, close enough to scrape his cheek, and then the network cord it was tied to nearly gave him a crew cut.

Hal rolled onto his back, winded and surprised by the near miss. He heard Alex calling to him, and he gave her a thumbs up. Then he staggered to his feet, retrieved the climbing tool and prepared to throw it again. This time he anchored his feet properly, and the metal bar hummed as he spun it round and round, faster and faster. He let go with a gigantic heave, and watched in satisfaction as the bar zoomed over the top of the pile. He pulled on the network cable to test it was secure, then started the slow climb to the top.

Hal soon discovered how hard it was to climb a steep slope, especially with his arms doing most of the work. His feet slipped and skidded on the loose junk, his muscles ached like mad, but metre by agonising metre he made his way towards the summit. So much for those adults with their orange jackets and goggles, he thought. He was doing the same thing with home-made equipment!

Hal's hands were sweaty on the thin network cable, and his fingers ached from holding it so tight. There was sweat in his eyes too, but he wasn't about to brush it away, not if it meant letting go of the rope.

Moments later Hal felt the pile shift under his feet. He froze until it settled, then continued even more carefully. He was a long way above the ground now, and the last thing he wanted was to tumble all the way to the bottom inside an avalanche of materials.

When Hal finally reached the top he dropped the network cable and struck a heroic pose: chest out, head back and one foot resting casually on a dented old bucket. It was a very proud moment, and he glanced down at Alex out of the corner of his eye, trying to gauge how impressed she was. She was standing with her arms crossed, a sour look on her face.

At that moment Hal heard a rumble overhead. He looked up and realised he was directly under the recycling chute, which was pointing down at him like the gaping mouth of a huge cannon. Several plastic wrappers fluttered down on him, and Hal abandoned the heroic pose and dived for safety, just as a fresh load of junk thundered out of the chute.

Dust and rubbish blew around like a mini tornado, and when it finally settled Hal sat up and started picking bits out of his hair. The foggy air cleared a little, and that's when he happened to look down far side of the enormous junk pile.

What he saw almost took his breath away.

— 14 —

Thud!

Laid out below was a huge machine, stretching the entire width of the recycling centre. At one end there was a pair of arms with gigantic hands, which were busy grabbing junk from the pile. As Hal watched, huge fingers plucked a rusty beam from a pile of junk, picking it up as though it weighed no more than a ration bar. It tried to put the beam onto a conveyor belt, but the metal was far too long and wouldn't fit. Hal wondered whether it would give up, but no! The second hand grabbed the loose end of the beam and . . . screeeaakk . . . they bent it in two! Hal gulped. Imagine if he'd rolled down the other side of the junk pile . . . those huge hands might have picked him up and squished him like a bug!

Thud!

The U-shaped beam landed on the conveyor belt,

which carried it towards a slab-sided box in the middle of the machine. The beam vanished and there was a loud grinding noise, as though someone had dropped a handful of gravel into a blender.

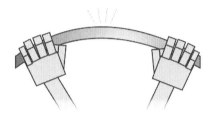

Something was happening on the other side of the box, and Hal stood up to get a better view. There was a smaller conveyor belt, full of glowing metal bars. A much smaller hand grabbed the bars one by one, throwing them neatly into a small red machine. There was an ear-splitting screeeee! as each bar vanished, and seconds later hundreds of shiny screws and nuts and bolts poured from a spout. These fell into containers, which were packed up and placed on another conveyor belt.

The process wasn't finished yet: even more arms grabbed the packaged goods from the conveyor belt, stacking them on a small black table. The table bowed under the weight, and Hal stared as it started to move. It wasn't a table at all, it was a motorised trolley! Then Hal saw something which made him gasp. The trolley was wobbling as it moved, and when he looked closer he noticed one of its wheel was bent. It was Carrie's friend Paul! He hadn't been recycled at all, he'd been put to work down here!

Even at this distance Hal could hear the squeak-squeak-squeak of Paul's damaged wheel, and he realised the trolley was being mistreated. He vowed to tell Carrie about her old friend, and he wondered whether a whole bunch of kitchen equipment would mount a daring midnight raid to get Paul back.

Hal turned his attention back to the machine, where the big hands were still busy. One had just dropped a fistful of broken wall panels onto the conveyor belt, and the machine hissed and spat as it converted them into plastic cubes. Then they went into a silver machine, which spat out brand new plates, cups and cutlery. Hal's eyes shone as he watched the entire operation. Just wait until he brought Stinky down for a look!

Then he remembered Alex . . . and his new watch.

— 15 —

A one Hal open sleigh

Hal now faced a new challenge: How was he going to climb down again? If it had been a pile of dirt he could have sat down and slid to the bottom, but the junk was much too lumpy and uneven for that. Then he spotted a buckled metal door from a locker, and it gave him an idea. He freed the door from the pile, laid it flat, and sat on it. He grabbed hold of the rusty door handle, and with his free hand he pushed off.

'Whooo-*hoooo!*' yelled Hal, as the makeshift toboggan took off down the slope. He was forced to hang on with all his strength as it gathered speed, and when it launched off a bundle of plastic pipes he was thrown high into the air. SLAM! went the buckled door as it landed again. OOF! went Hal, as he flopped down on top.

The makeshift toboggan finally reached the

bottom of the pile, where it skidded sideways and slowed to a halt. Hal stepped off at the last second, and he wished the kids from class had witnessed his incredible ride. He wanted to climb up for another go, until he saw Alex waiting impatiently nearby. She had her arms crossed, she was tapping her foot, and he realised he'd left her standing there for ages.

'I hope *you* enjoyed your holidays,' grumbled Alex, as soon as he was close.

'Come and see what I found.'

'Is it anything to do with rubbish?'

'Yeah, but it's still cool.'

'Nothing about rubbish is cool. Oh yeah, and this is yours.'

Hal felt something smooth in his hand, and when he looked down he realised it was Alex's watch. For a second he was tempted, but then he shook his head. 'I can't take it.'

'Sure you can. I'll buy another when I get home.'

Hal knew he couldn't keep it, but he'd pretend it was his until he figured out a way to give it back. Then he remembered the huge recycling machine. 'Do you want to see this amazing thing I found or not?'

'Not.'

'I bet you'll like it.'

'I won't.'

'I bet you will.' Hal held his hand up, showing Alex her own watch. 'If you like what I've found I'll give you this amazing space watch. It's even got a built-in torch.'

Alex's frown vanished, and she laughed. 'All right, I give in. Show me this amazing find.'

◆

Thud!

Screeeee!

Brrrrrrr!

Thud!

Hal gave Alex a running commentary as the huge recycling machine went through its paces. The arms grabbed junk, the tubes and conveyor belts extruded parts, and all the while Hal explained the various operations as though he'd invented the device himself.

'That is so cool!' exclaimed Alex, as an old table was turned into a stack of spacesuit visors.

Wordlessly, Hal slipped the watch off and pressed it into her hand. In return he got a grateful smile.

'Do you think it'll make cardboard boxes?' asked Alex, gesturing towards the machine.

266

Hal remembered their mission. 'What if we feed some old cardboard in?'

'I wouldn't get too close to the hands. Those fingers look pretty strong, and if they scooped you up . . .'

'Are you saying I look like rubbish?'

'You're not too bad . . . for a spacebug.'

'Thanks, earthworm.'

They made their way towards the machine, stopping just out of range of the huge hands. Hal decided to try an experiment, and he pulled a long metal tube out of the pile and waved it like a flagpole. Success! One of the hands plucked the pole out of his grasp, pinching and folding the tube before placing it onto the conveyor belt. Then both hands came back, hovering expectantly.

Grinning, Hal found an old door and stood it on end. He tried to lift it up but it was too heavy, until Alex helped. The hand took it between finger and thumb, and the door vanished into the machine. The other hand darted down to take a big piece of cardboard Alex was holding up, and when that disappeared into the machine it emerged as cardboard boxes.

'That's it, it's working!' cried Hal. 'Find more!'

They unearthed a whole lot of cardboard, and before long there was a stack of neatly folded boxes alongside the recycling machine. Then . . . disaster. Hal shouldered aside a battered old flight console, trying to reach a stash of cardboard underneath. One of the hands darted in and grabbed the entire console, but then Hal realised it still had thick cables running out the back. As the hand turned away the cables wrapped around its fingers, and no matter how much it tugged and twisted, it couldn't free itself. The wires ran deep into the junk pile, and the hand was stuck fast.

'We've got to cut it free,' said Hal.

'Shouldn't we leave it? There are more than enough boxes.'

'No, this is my fault and I'm going to fix it.'

— 16 —

One flew over the junk pile

Up close, the trapped hand was much bigger than Hal expected. It had four fingers and a thumb, just like humans, and it was trying to reach its own wrist to pluck at the loops of cable. Hal felt in his pocket for his trusty knife, then remembered his parents had confiscated it. He'd whittled a short plastic rod into a chess piece, only to discover the innocent-looking thing was an expensive spare part specially flown up from Gyris.

Hal looked around for something to cut the cords with, then ducked as the second hand swept overhead. It burrowed in the rubbish, and he ducked again as it whizzed past with a broken metal chair.

'I've got something,' shouted Alex.

Hal turned to see her holding up a slender piece of metal. It was about a metre long, and one edge was sharpened like a blade. A shadow swooped overhead, and Hal shouted a warning. Alex ducked, but the fingers darted in like lightning, plucking the strip of metal from her grasp. She cried out in pain and grabbed her hand. At first Hal was frozen in shock, but he recovered quickly, charging across the pile towards her. 'Are you all right?'

Fearfully, Alex held her hand out. They both looked at her tightly closed fingers, fearing the worst. Then, slowly, she uncurled them to reveal her palm. 'Phew, it's just a scratch,' said Alex.

Hal looked at the cut doubtfully. It looked quite deep to him. 'Are you sure?'

'I've had worse.'

'We'd better get it seen to. We'll go to the sickbay on level seven.'

'I said it's fine.' Alex pointed towards the mechanical hand, still struggling with the cables. 'Anyway, we've got to free Lefty.'

Hal was impressed. His friend Stinky would have yelled for a medic, and others he could name would have bawled for their mothers. 'All right, but keep your head down!'

They crossed the pile towards the trapped hand. On the way Hal picked up a piece of metal trim, which he hoped would cut the wires. The hand thrashed around as they got close, and junk slithered down the pile, crashing and bouncing on its way to the bottom. Hal glanced up to see a three-legged desk teetering near the top. It looked heavy, and if it came down on them it would do some real damage. 'Warn me if that desk slips. And watch the second hand closely.' He gripped the piece of trim and crawled closer, his mouth dry and his palms slick with sweat.

The hand appeared to be resting, and Hal saw several loops of cable around its big metal fingers. There was another round the wrist, and he decided to tackle that one first. He got closer and closer, brandishing the trim like a sword. Two metres . . . one metre . . .

Whoosh!

The hand balled into a fist and heaved with all its might, straining the cables. The junk pile shifted, throwing Hal off his feet, and he barely heard Alex's cry of alarm. Hal shielded his head with his arms and waited for the massive desk to come tumbling down.

Nothing happened, and Hal slowly uncovered his head. When he looked up he saw the desk was still there, hanging by a single bent leg. Nearby, the big hand had given up the struggle, and was lying on the junk pile with its palm up and its fingers curled.

271

Hal took a deep breath and talked to the hand. 'It's all right,' he said. 'I'm here to help.'

The fingers twitched.

Gripping his blade, Hal shuffled closer on all fours. He stretched the tip of the blade out until it touched the cable, then started to saw, trying to cut through the tough wires. Instead of cutting, the wires just moved back and forth in time with the blade. Hal got closer and grabbed the cable, then attacked it with the sharpened trim as though he were sawing planks.

Ping!

The cable parted, and Hal moved to the next. This one was tangled in and out of the big fingers, and he had to brace his knee on the huge palm and lean right across it. He hardly dared to breathe . . . if the hand closed now he'd be crushed like the old locker.

Poing!

The hand twitched as another cable parted. Three more to go, but he'd have to climb right over the palm to get to them. Then Hal heard movement right behind him, and he glanced round to see Alex holding out a longer piece of metal. This one had a serrated edge, and Hal took it thankfully. The longer blade made short work of the remaining cables, and then the hand was free.

Hal backed away quickly, expecting it to spring up and continue with its work. Instead, it just lay there. 'Do you think we killed it?'

'Of course not. It's just a machine.'

'Don't say that to a robot,' muttered Hal under his breath. He took up a metal pole and gave the hand a quick prod. Nothing. 'Maybe it doesn't realise it's free?'

'Maybe we should get out of here.'

'No, I have to get it going again.' Hal pushed the pole under the big fingers and tried levering them out of the pile. There was no reaction. Then he looked up at the desk, which was still balanced on top of the pile. What if he tipped that down so that it landed on the hand? That would wake it up!

He threw the pole aside and clambered up the mountain, his arms and legs burning from all the exercise. When he reached the top he tried freeing the desk, but it was stuck fast. He stood up, hoping to lever it free, and that's when Alex screamed a warning.

A shadow darted overhead, and before Hal knew what was happening the second hand grabbed him around the chest, pinning his arms. He was swept into the air and carried to the recycling machine, yelling and kicking his legs like mad. He landed on the conveyor belt with a thud, and it carried him straight towards the gaping mouth of the grinder. Even though he was facing certain death, a small part of his brain wondered what sort of goodies the huge machine would turn him into. Halburgers? Low-Hal yoghurt? Or maybe a big serve of Halghetti!

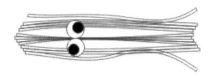

Hal flew towards the grinder on the fast-moving conveyor belt, still dazed by events. One second he'd been standing on top of the junk pile, the next he'd been swooping through the air. The thump of his landing had knocked the air from his lungs, but there was no time to stop and think. He sprang up and started running on the belt, going as fast as he could. His feet thudded on the rubber conveyor belt, and he felt like a jogger on the galaxy's biggest running machine. Out the corner of his eye he could see Alex slithering down the junk pile, leaping over obstacles as she hurried towards the big machine. Would she get help in time? Or would the hands scoop her up and add her to the menu?

Hal glanced over his shoulder. He was running at full speed, but the belt was too fast and he was still travelling backwards towards the grinder's gaping entrance. Inside he could see gears and wheels spinning and crashing together like huge mechanical teeth. He gulped and ran even faster.

One of the hands dropped a broken desk on the conveyor belt, right in front of him, and he leapt for all he was worth. He cleared it by millimetres, staggering as he landed back on the belt. Behind him the desk vanished inside the machine, and there were horrible crunching and cracking sounds as it was torn apart.

Hal was tiring now, and there were spots in front of his eyes. He was breathing fast but couldn't get enough air, and he desperately needed a rest. Just a few seconds!

Alex's face appeared over the side of the machine, and Hal's stomach sank. Why hadn't she gone for help?

'Can you jump out?' she called.

Hal shook his head. He had no breath to spare for talking.

'Okay. Wait there a minute.'

There was lots of things Hal could have said to that, but he contented himself with a roll of the eyes.

Thud!

An old storage tank landed on the belt, and Hal

forced his tired legs into a jump. His foot caught on the rounded surface but he staggered and regained his balance. The tank vanished into the machine with a squeal of tortured metal. He was much closer to the gaping maw now, and he could hear the *roar-roar-roar* of the spinning gears right behind him. His muscles burned like fire, and it was all he could do to keep running.

Then . . . silence. The belt stopped dead but Hal kept going: straight off the far end of the belt, past the end of the machine, and halfway up the junk pile. He finally ran out of steam and collapsed on the ground. His chest heaved, his heart pounded and he felt rubbish pressing into the side of his face. Still, he was safe. Alex had done it!

Then came a voice, fierce and electronic and totally unexpected. 'Flibber my flash chips. What do you think you're doing!'

Hal turned over, shielding his eyes against the overhead lights, and saw a tall bronze robot standing over him. Its eyes blazed a harsh red, and its thin face was arranged in a very angry expression. 'Tell me what you're doing here! Explain your presence immediately!'

— 17 —

Raging Reece

Hal opened and closed his mouth, unable to speak with the robot towering over him.

'This area is off limits to humans. Who sent you? Why are you spying on me?'

'I . . . we . . . ' stammered Hal, still shaken by his narrow escape.

Then Alex came hurrying up, and the robot spun round to confront her. 'Tangle my fibre optics!' it shouted, its eyes flashing like strobes. 'There's another one! Explain yourselves, right now!'

'W-we have a carty blank from Teacher,' managed Hal at last. Even to him, this sounded unconvincing. 'He told us to bring back some boxes.'

'Format my frontal lobes! Did you expect to find them inside the Recyclotron?'

'I didn't climb inside on purpose,' said Hal. 'One

of the hands got trapped, and when I freed it the other one grabbed me.'

'They could have turned you into mincemeat,' exclaimed the robot. 'Didn't you realise how dangerous they are?'

'I do now,' said Hal.

'You're not to go near this machine. Understood?'

Hal nodded.

'And these boxes . . . you thought you could sneak and take them?'

'No! I have a permission slip.'

'Show me.'

Hal dug in his pocket and took out the card, all crumpled and grubby. The robot frowned at it, then shepherded them towards the small office, watching closely in case they tried to steal his precious rubbish. When they got there he made them stand outside while he went in. Hal rubbed one corner of the dirty window with his sleeve, cleaning a small patch so he could peer into the robot's office.

The robot crossed to a battered old terminal, tapping its foot impatiently as it booted up. Hal's gaze travelled along the bench to a filing cabinet, across the old calendars on the wall, and down to a big recharging stand on the floor. He was about to look away when he saw flashing red and green lights over near the filing cabinet. He looked again, squinting hard, and frowned as he spotted a gleaming silver briefcase. It was heavy with a big lock on top, and it was identical to the one Alex's dad had been carrying. Hal nudged Alex and pointed, but before she could look the robot came back with the crumpled card.

'It seems this permission slip is in order, although I'm surprised they sent you all the way down here. Now tell me, how many boxes do you want to buy?'

'Buy?'

'Yes, or trade. Either works for me.'

'But ... Teacher needs them for class. You're supposed to give them to me.'

'He he hee!' The robot threw his head back and laughed. 'Ha ha ha! Give! That's a good one.'

'Why should we have to pay?' Hal frowned. 'We made them out of our own rubbish.'

'Listen to me, human. This area, this entire area, is mine.' The robot swept its arms around to illustrate its point. 'All the valuables, mine. All the treasure, mine.' It tapped its foot. 'This floor, mine.'

'Okay, okay. I get it.' Hal stood up. 'It's not treasure though. It's just piles of rubbish.'

The robot tapped the side of its nose, making a hollow donnnggg. 'That's why the concession was so cheap.'

279

'Con-what?'

'Bless my actuators, don't they teach you anything? A concession! Many years ago I bought the rights to this entire level. I'm entitled to everything I find here.'

'You paid money for all this rubbish?'

'Most certainly.'

'What do you do with it all?'

The robot was about to reply, then stopped. 'Your friend, is she all right?'

Hal glanced at Alex, who was staring through the office window. 'She's fine. Go on.'

'When supply ships visit the Space Station I sell them items made from recycled material.'

'Does the Commander know about this?'

'You bet your nobbly knee joints. The Space Station receives half my profit.'

'But Teacher works for the station, and he needs the boxes.'

'They're all mine,' said the robot stubbornly. 'If you want them you'll have to make me an offer.'

'You want me to pay for mouldy old boxes?'

'Boxes are made from cardboard, and cardboard comes from trees. There are no trees in space. You do the math.'

Alex glanced over her shoulder. 'Where I come from boxes are free.'

'Then I suggest you go back there and fetch some.' The robot turned back to Hal. 'Bring me something I can use and the boxes are yours.'

'You want more rubbish?'

'I prefer to call it raw material.'

'Okay, wait here. We'll be right back.' Hal grabbed Alex's elbow and turned for the exit. Then, for once, he remembered his manners. 'This is Alex and I'm Hal. What's your name?'

'I'm RC-KL-8, but humans call me Reece.'

— 18 —

Left Centre

'Did you see the briefcase on his desk?' murmured Hal, as they strode towards the exit. 'It looked exactly like your dad's.'

'It can't be,' said Alex firmly. 'I hid it in the cupboard.'

Hal remembered the flashing lights on the handle. 'Bet you it was his case.'

'I bet it wasn't.'

'Bet you five credits it was.'

'I bet you ten it wasn't.'

'Bet you fifty.'

'Bet you a hundred.'

'Done.'

Alex frowned. 'How will you pay?'

'I won't need to, because that was your dad's briefcase.'

'It wasn't!'

'I bet you two hundred.'

'Four!'

By the time the doors opened Hal was struggling to top Alex's latest bet. 'Nineteen planets, all the cash in the universe and two chocolate doughnuts,' he said at last. 'And no returns!'

They jogged along the corridors and stairways, using every one of Hal's special shortcuts to get back to the spares cupboard. When they got there Hal dragged the door open and peered into the darkness. 'Where did you put it?'

'That locker with the stickers on.'

With a horrible sense of foreboding, Hal opened the door wide. The light from the corridor flooded in and illuminated a hatch on the rear wall. The hatch had 'Warning' and 'Danger' and 'No Entry' signs all over it. 'Please tell me you didn't put it in there.'

'Sure! Who's going to ignore all those warnings?'

Silently, Hal activated the hatch. There was a whoosh as the doors parted, revealing a silver-lined hole. Alex clambered onto a cable drum and peered inside. 'There's a tunnel in here!' she said, her voice echoing as though she were standing at the top of a well. 'Where does it go?'

'All the way down to the recycling centre,' said Hal patiently. 'Face it, you chucked your dad's briefcase away.'

'How was I to know it was the recycling chute?' demanded Alex. She stepped off the drum with an angry look on her face. 'It's not fair! There's no sign!'

Hal checked behind the drum, where he found a plastic sign on the floor. He grabbed it and held it up: Warning! Recycling Chute! Danger! He checked the back and found a patch of dried glue. 'Someone didn't fix it properly, see? They must have used the wrong sort of glue.' Hal ran his hand over the wall. 'Yes, that's it. See, with this type of paint –'

'Never mind the stupid decor!' cried Alex. 'We've got to get that case back! My dad could ask for it any minute, and then I'd have to tell him I've lost it. He'll go completely mental!'

'Relax, will you? Let me think.'

'You said it would be safe in the cupboard. You promised!'

Then Hal had a thought. 'I know! We'll go and talk to my mum. She'll order Reece to give it back.'

'Oh yes, that's brilliant. Let's march to A-section, talk our way past that bristle-haired guy at the security checkpoint, walk into the top secret meeting and tell everyone I lost my dad's briefcase.'

'All right, we'll find another adult. We'll explain, take them down to the recycling centre –'

'No!' Alex shook her head. 'You don't know my dad. If he finds out I lost his briefcase . . .'

'Why not blame me? I'm used to it.'

'You don't know my dad,' repeated Alex. 'I'm serious. We have to sort this out ourselves.'

Hal pondered for a moment, then snapped his fingers. 'I've got it. Back to the classroom.'

'You're not telling Teacher.'

'It's not Teacher I'm thinking about,' said Hal, as he ushered her out of the spares cupboard.

❧

They'd barely set off for the classroom when Hal realised there was another problem. When they got back to class Teacher might take the permission slip away, and then they wouldn't be allowed back down to the recycling centre. Well ... that was easily fixed. He took the card out and handed it to Alex.

'What's that for?'

'I'm going to class to organise something. In the meantime, see if you can find anything to swap for some boxes.'

'Are you mad?' protested Alex. 'Who cares about mouldy boxes? It's the briefcase we have to –'

'I know, I know. But we'll have to pretend we need boxes, or my plan won't work.'

'You have a plan?'

'Sure I do,' said Hal, hoping he sounded convincing. 'Now go and find some stuff to trade.'

'Where?'

That was the problem. Everything was scarce aboard a space station. Every sheet of paper, every scrap of food and every drop of water had to be flown in from the nearest planet, and that cost a lot of money. It was no wonder Reece hoarded everything that dropped through the chute. Hal racked his brains, but they couldn't just help themselves to stuff ... theft was a serious crime. He wondered whether they should stake out a couple of recycling hatches, but they might wait around all day for someone to use them. Then Hal realised the answer to their problem. 'Why don't you go back to your dad's ship? There must be something you can take.'

'There might be,' said Alex doubtfully. 'What about you? Don't you have anything at home?'

'I'll have a look on the way back. Go on, hurry!'

Alex hesitated, but Hal's confidence was catching and she nodded briefly before running away at top speed. Hal was about to set off for the classroom when he heard her footsteps returning. 'What is it?'

'I don't know the way,' panted Alex.

'D nine, C twenty, B two. Can you remember that?'

'Got it.'

Alex charged off again, and Hal shouted advice after her. 'If you get lost, ask for help! And meet me at the lift afterwards!'

— 19 —

Secret Gang!

When Hal arrived at the classroom it was still busy. In fact, it was so busy Teacher was using three extra eyes, and they darted all over his electronic face as they tracked every movement. 'Stephen Binn, that is NOT how we handle chemicals. Please be careful. Melanie, put that roll of paper down immediately. No, I don't care which galaxy you're saving from evil invaders, it is NOT a death-dealing sword of doom. Braydon! Clean that up mess right now.'

Then Teacher spotted Hal. One eye studied his face while another pair checked his empty hands. 'No luck with the boxes, Hal Junior? Oh well. Return that permission slip and make yourself useful.'

'No, I can't. Someone's holding the boxes for me but I need to see Stinky first.'

'Very well, but you're not to distract him.' One of Teacher's eyes darted around to the side of his face, then stopped dead. 'In fact, I want you to tidy that bookcase first.'

Hal groaned. The bookcase was taller than he was and it had a dozen shelves crammed with books, equipment and craft projects. It would take ages! He turned back to Teacher, intending to plead for mercy, but the robot had already sped away. Resigned to the inevitable, Hal straightened a roll of plastic wrap and pulled a handful of books from the shelf. The screens lit up as he handled them, displaying vividly coloured scenes. He remembered some of them from his early school years, including one about a wandering dustbin robot and its shiny junk-collecting companion. He turned the pages, and was shocked to discover his one-time favourite was a morality tale about tidying your bedroom and helping your parents take the rubbish out. Disgusted, he straightened the books and crammed the foil on top. He eyed the remaining shelves, and was just wondering whether he could shift everything to someone else's bookcase when he had a brilliant idea. 'Hey, Natalie!'

A dark-haired girl spared him the briefest of glances. 'What do you want?'

'You like craft, don't you?'

'Hal Junior, if you think I'm tidying those shelves for you . . . '

'Nat, this is really important.'

Natalie eyed him shrewdly. 'What's it's worth?'

'I'll give you something valuable.'

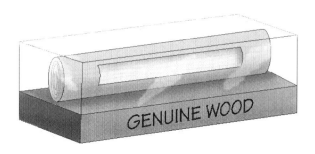

'You're not fooling me again. Remember when I did your homework in exchange for a piece of wood from a real tree?'

'Sure.'

'It was plastic.'

'Just as well, because I got a C for that homework.' Hal thought for a moment. 'All right, tidy these shelves and you can join my secret gang.'

'What gang? I've never heard about any gang.'

'Of course you haven't. It wouldn't be secret if everyone knew about it.'

'Who else is in it?'

'Just Stinky and me. It's very exclusive.'

Natalie pursed her lips.

'Go on,' coaxed Hal. 'We have meetings and secret handshakes and everything.'

'All right, I'll do the shelves. But I want to be President!'

'Don't we all?' muttered Hal. He only hoped Natalie didn't quiz Stinky about the gang. First, because Stinky wasn't very good around girls, turning bright red and stammering when they looked at him. And second, because there wasn't any secret gang: Hal had only just invented it.

As he hurried across the classroom he decided a gang sounded like a fine idea. They could have a secret membership card, and meetings with lots of food, and they could even set up a roster where one member did everyone else's homework for the week. Hal decided to be leader, because then he could draw up the homework roster and make sure his name wasn't on it. Leaders also got the best food, the flashiest membership card and something called perks . . . at least, that's what he'd heard. Whenever his parents talked politics there was always mention of perks and parties, and if politicians could have them then Hal's gang would too. Then there was the recycling centre, with all those plastic wall panels. Maybe if he took Reece enough junk the robot would build them a clubhouse!

But first, the briefcase.

◆

'Stinky, do you have a minute?'

'I'm kind of busy,' said his friend, who was lining beakers up in the science cupboard.

'All right, I'll help you.'

Stinky looked doubtful. Hal plus glassware usually equalled destruction.

'I'll be extra careful. Promise!'

'All right. Hand me the beakers one by one.'

Hal dug into the box and came up with two of the graduated beakers. 'Hey Stinky?'

'Yep?'

'Catch!' Hal pretended to throw the beakers, and he grinned at Stinky's shocked expression.

'Stop messing about!' hissed Stinky.

'All right, all right.' Hal passed a beaker over, then glanced around to make sure nobody was listening. When he was sure he wouldn't be overheard, he lowered his voice and explained quickly about the briefcase in the recycling centre.

'Why don't you tell Teacher?'

'Alex won't let me.'

Stinky's brow creased as he tackled the problem, and Hal could almost hear his friend's brain whirring. If anyone could find the solution, it was Stinky!

Finally, he spoke. 'You have to think of it like a chess problem. It's a classic feint situation.'

'How's fainting going to help?' demanding Hal. 'You think if we collapse in a heap this robot will take pity on us?'

'Feint, not faint. It's an e, not an a.'

Hal grumbled under his breath. He'd come to Stinky for help, not a spelling lesson.

'A feint is when you distract your opponent with one hand, then use the other to achieve your goal.'

Hal brightened. 'The recycling machine had hands. Are you saying we should stuff Reece into it?' Then he frowned. 'Won't someone notice he's missing?'

'I was referring to hands in a metaphorical sense.'

Hal blinked. 'Meta whatter?'

'They were just an example. A feint could involve hands, armies –'

'Sleevies?' suggested Hal.

Stinky struggled to keep a straight face. 'I meant troops, Hal.'

'Where are we supposed to get a bunch of warriors

from?' demanded Hal indignantly. 'I came to you for ideas, not impossible suggestions.'

'Look, let's start again.'

'No, let's not. Alex and I will march down there, demand the case back and . . . and . . . ' Hal's voice tailed off. Demanding anything from Reece was almost as crazy as Stinky's fainting invasion force.

'Hal, the answer is simple. One of you goes back for the boxes, and while Reece is busy the other one snatches the case. Is that clear?'

'Now that's more like it. Much better than your feint idea.'

'Er, y-yes.'

'Two problems. One, he won't give us the boxes.'

'Right. You'll need something to trade.'

Hal eyed the beakers. 'What about these?'

'No! You can't trade away vital equipment!'

Hal would have traded all of the classroom equipment for a jam doughnut, but Stinky wouldn't be swayed. 'What do you suggest?'

'Perhaps something of your own. Do you have any old toys you don't play with?'

Hal saw Natalie grinning to herself, and he reddened. 'I do not play with toys!'

'There you go then. You can give them all to Reece. What was the other problem?'

'I can't sneak into his office without getting caught.'

'You need a distraction.' Stinky rubbed his chin, and Hal knew his friend's brain was busy on the problem.

While Stinky was thinking, Hal looked around the classroom for inspiration. He spotted the recycling hatch with its red and yellow warning signs, and a frown crossed his face. That hatch led to the chute, and the chute led to the recycling centre.

Hal's gaze travelled from the hatch, to the cardboard box at his feet, and back to the hatch. A plan was slowly forming, but he was going to need help. 'Stinky, do you have any matches?'

'What?'

Hal pushed the cardboard box with his toe. 'You could light this thing and toss it down the hatch.'

'Haven't you learnt your lesson?' Stinky was scandalised. 'You can't go around lighting more fires! Don't you know how dangerous –'

'All right, calm down.' Hal eyed the chemicals on the shelf. 'Do you remember that experiment I did? The one with my patented green smoke?'

'Vividly.'

'Reckon you could mix a batch?'

'What, here?'

'Yes here.' Hal nodded towards the recycling

chute. 'Make up a smoke bomb and chuck it down there. While Reece's busy climbing the junk pile to investigate, I'll nab the briefcase.'

'I could get in awful trouble.'

'Tell 'em it was me.'

'No, Hal. I won't do it. Throwing smoke bombs is seriously bad news. I could get detention, or I could get a . . . a . . . ' Stinky swallowed. 'Hal, I could get a B from Teacher!'

'I'm not talking about a real bomb, it's just a few harmless chemicals. It'll clear in a minute or two, right?'

'Maybe five,' said Stinky, wavering a little.

Hal looked at his watch. 'Give me twenty minutes, then drop the smoke bomb. Got it?'

'What if it's not ready?'

Hal felt a rush of relief. His friend was going to help! 'Of course it'll be ready.'

'What if Teacher asks where you've gone?'

'I've gone to fetch his boxes. And that's the truth.' At that moment Hal saw Natalie making a beeline for them. He grabbed Stinky and quickly demonstrated a secret handshake.

'What's that for?' asked Stinky.

'Trust me, you're going to need it.'

— 20 —

MINT! R@RE!

Hal left the classroom and set off for E-section, jogging at top speed. With all this running around he was beginning to wish for a jet-powered scooter. He wondered whether his parents would get him one for his birthday, but unfortunately they were more likely to get him some exciting new homework software. Parents were odd like that.

On his way home he kept an eye out for handy piles of rubbish, discarded trash and unwanted junk. Unfortunately the corridors were as spotless as ever. When he reached his cabin he opened the doors under his bunk and peered inside. There was a planet rover with a broken wheel, the paint battered and peeling. He delved deeper and came up with a broken toy wand, a crumpled wizard hat and a stuffed owl left over from some fancy dress outfit. The owl was missing one tufty ear and both of its eyes, and so much stuffing had leaked out it was as flat as a pancake. Hal dug around some more, but there was nothing else he was prepared to part with. The big orange ray gun still made a decent 'Brrrr' sound when he pulled the trigger, and he didn't want to give up the battered old 20-sided dice . . . not until he found out which game it belonged to. There was also an old book about tiny people living under floorboards - whatever those were - but that belonged to Hal's dad and he knew it would be missed.

Gathering up his spoils, Hal could only hope that Alex had found something more useful. He threw the toys into a bag and hurried towards the lift.

❧

Hal met Alex near the lift in D-section, and he could tell right away that she hadn't had much luck. Her expression was downcast and she was hiding something behind her back.

'Go on then,' said Hal, trying to sound encouraging. 'What did you get?'

Reluctantly, Alex opened her hand to reveal . . . a blue button from a jumper and a muscled forearm from an action figure. 'These are all I could find.'

298

'Are you kidding? They're not going to buy us anything!'

'So what did you get?'

Hal showed her the truck and the pieces of fancy dress.

'What's Reece going to do with a weedy old stick?' demanded Alex. 'And the glove puppet . . . what's that all about?'

'It's a stuffed owl,' said Hal defensively.

'You're not wrong. Still, it's better than the grotty old hat.'

'You can talk!' said Hal hotly. 'All you found was an arm and a lousy button!'

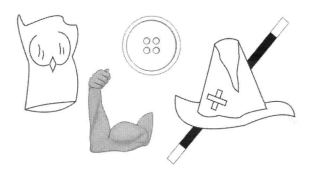

They eyed their haul in silence, uncertain of their next move. Should they hunt around for more junk, or take what they had back to Reece and haggle. 'I vote we go back to your dad's ship,' said Hal. 'I bet I'll find something if I go through his stuff.'

'You can't!' said Alex in alarm, as she pictured Hal carting off armloads of valuables. 'My dad would kill me!'

'I guess you're right,' said Hal reluctantly. 'Okay, we'll see what Reece will give us for this lot. You can keep that button though - we don't want to insult him.'

When they reached the recycling centre Reece was sorting a pile of old fabric. Hal wondered whether he unpicked them all and knitted new clothes from the thread, or just sold them as bundles of cleaning rags.

'Burnish my bronze heels!' exclaimed the robot, when he spotted Hal and Alex. 'What do you have for me?'

Somewhat embarrassed, Hal displayed the motley collection of toys.

'Interesting.' Reece picked over the items. 'I can give you half a dozen boxes for these.'

'Done,' said Hal quickly, before the robot could change its mind. 'Can we help ourselves?'

'And have you sneak a couple of extras? No way!' Reece tapped himself in the chest. Clonggg! 'I'll pick them out for you.'

They crossed to a big pile of folded boxes, where the robot started picking out matching sizes. While he was busy there was a clatter from the middle of the recycling centre. Hal glanced round, hoping to see a cloud of smoke, but instead a stream of junk poured through the roof to land on the big pile. He eyed his watch and realised Stinky wouldn't be ready yet. He had to slow Reece down, or the whole plan would fail.

◆

Unfortunately Reece wasn't waiting around for Stinky, or Hal, or anyone else's special plans. Within seconds he'd gathered six neatly folded boxes. 'There you are. All present and correct.'

'Sorry, they're no good.'

'Fan my fibre optics!' said Reece sharply. 'Why ever not? What's wrong with them?'

'They've got writing on. Teacher wants plain ones.'

'What are you talking about?' demanded Alex. 'Who cares whether –'

Hal nudged her. 'Look, there's a plain one at the bottom of the pile. I'm sure it won't take long to find five more.'

Reece turned to look at them, his arms full of boxes. 'Did you say these are no good?'

'I'm afraid not,' said Hal. 'We need plain ones. It's for a . . . craft project. Right Alex?'

'Er . . . sure. Writing would spoil it.'

Reece looked at the pile. 'It'll take some time to find six plain boxes. They're not very common.'

'Good.' Hal hesitated. 'I mean, it's good of you to help us.'

'They're probably worth more than the printed ones,' said Reece, a cunning look in his eye. 'Do you have any more valuables?'

'No. I mean, yes. We bought a very special item.' Hal held his hand out to Alex. 'Pass me the firing mechanism from that space gun.'

Alex looked blank. 'The which from the what?'

'That blue circular device with mounting holes.'

'You mean the bu–'

'No, I mean the firing mechanism.' Hal clicked his fingers impatiently. 'Come on, I know it's incredibly rare and valuable but we need those boxes. You'll just have to give it up.'

Reece was almost licking his lips by now, and when Alex took out the blue button and dropped it on Hal's palm the robot's eyes were the size of dinner plates. 'By the patenting of my source code. Is that really a firing mechanism?'

Hal was about to say yes, but he couldn't bring himself to lie. 'I saw one just like this in a book,' he said, neglecting to mention it was a sewing book.

'Would you take ten boxes for it?'

'Twenty.'

'I don't have twenty.'

'All right, ten boxes plus one extra item of my choice.'

Reece looked uncertain. 'I'm not sure about that. You might choose something far more valuable than a firing mechanism.'

Privately, Hal thought every scrap of junk in the recycling centre was more valuable than a single blue button, but he wasn't about to say so. 'Ten boxes plus one item of my choice. Yes or no?'

'Done.'

'Let's shake on it.' Hal spat on his hand and held it out to the robot, who eyed it doubtfully. 'Go on. This is as good as a contract.'

Reece still looked uncertain, and in the end he shook hands so quickly Hal barely felt it.

'Right. One firing mechanism coming up.' Hal gave Reece the button, and after a quick inspection the robot opened a small door in its chest and placed the treasured item inside. Then ... *whizz, zip, slither, grab!* Reece sorted the boxes in no time.

'Ten plain ones,' said the robot proudly.

'No, no, no!' Hal put on his best Teacher impersonation, rolling his eyes and shuffling backwards and forwards on the spot as though

303

his feet had turned into wheels. 'This won't do. This won't do at all!'

'What is it?' asked a harassed-looking Reece. 'What's wrong this time?'

'These boxes are grey! I said brown. Brown!'

'You said no such thing!' protested Reece angrily.

'I did so!' Hal turned to Alex, who was trying not to laugh. 'Did I say grey?'

'No, you definitely didn't say grey.'

'Told you so!' Hal dug up another of Teacher's favourite lines. 'Do it properly, or don't do it at all.'

'Humans!' muttered Reece, turning back to the pile. He picked through the boxes with sharp, angry movements, keeping up a running commentary under his breath. 'Brown ones ... plain ones ... writing ... no writing. Rattle my receptors! Why can't they make up their minds?'

Meanwhile, Hal still needed an excuse to get near the office. 'Reece, can I get a drink of water?'

'Rust my radio receptors!' Reece shuddered. 'There's no water down here. Horrible nasty stuff!' He turned to the pile of boxes and sorted through them, muttering under his breath about the dangers of h's and o's.

It wasn't quite what Hal had planned, but at least Reece's back was turned. While the robot was distracted Hal slipped away, making for the office. The briefcase would soon be his!

— 21 —

Ten Star Hotel

There was just one problem. How was Hal going to enter the office without being seen? He needed a disguise, of course! He eyed a bundle of material with garish flowers all over it, and shuddered. If anyone expected him to disguise himself as a sofa they had another think coming.

Then he spotted a big packing crate, nearly as tall as he was. It was just like the ones in the arcade game, but was it hollow? He hurried over to tap on it, and smiled when he heard the echoes. The crate was made from plastic, and it had a big square lid. Perfect!

Seconds later he'd discarded the lid and tipped the crate right over. He found a sharp piece of metal and bored a peephole through the side, then raised the bottom and slipped underneath. It was pitch black inside, with the only light coming through his makeshift eye-hole. He made another hole to his left, the side facing Reece and Alex, then threw the piece of metal aside and stood up. He bent his neck and took the weight of the packing crate on his shoulders, staggering forwards a few steps before setting it down. Then he peered through the hole. The others were busy with the boxes, and hadn't noticed him. It was working!

Hal made his way towards the office, step by step. Now and then the crate bumped into a rubbish pile or jammed on a piece of junk, and each time this happened he had to dart from one eyehole to the other - first to see if Reece was watching, and then to see if he was about to run into anything.

Before long he was right outside the office door, and he allowed himself a triumphant smile. Who said computer games never taught you anything?

◆

Hal peered out of the crate and watched Reece and Alex sorting boxes. First Reece would scrabble through the pile until he found something, and then Alex would consider it from every angle before shaking her head. The robot was getting more annoyed by the minute, and Hal hoped Alex didn't overdo it.

Hal also kept an eye on the recycling chute, because any minute now Stinky's distraction would arrive to shatter the peace. Hal looked at his watch. Any second now, in fact.

Time passed, and Hal glared at his watch, muttering under his breath. Had Stinky forgotten the plan? Or had Teacher spotted him mixing chemicals, and marched him straight off to the Station Commander? Either way, Stinky had let him down.

Hal realised he needed a new plan. What if he sneaked into the office, took the briefcase and made his way to the far end of the recycling centre? Once there he could make a big show of 'discovering' the briefcase under a pile of junk. Hopefully Reece wouldn't realise it was the briefcase from his office, and would let Hal take the 'new' one in exchange for the so-called firing pin.

Hal didn't think it was a particularly good plan, so he tried again. This involved grabbing the briefcase and running for the exit as fast as he could. As long as he got there first, he'd be able to close the doors and escape. Otherwise . . . Hal shook his head. He didn't want to think what might happen if Reece caught him. Then he spotted a pretty big flaw in this new plan: Reece might not catch him, but the unpleasant robot would certainly catch Alex.

That was it, then. He'd just have to use plan A.

At that moment there was a rattle-bang from the recycling chute, followed by a loud FFFFFsshhh! Hal stared out of the crate and saw thick green smoke billowing from the top of the biggest junk pile. The evil-looking smoke rolled down the side of the pile, and from a distance it looked like an erupting volcano. Stinky had done it!

Reece took one look at the smoke and charged away from Alex like a bronze streak. The robot ran incredibly fast, his legs a blur as he bounded over piles of junk. When he reached the big pile he ran straight up the side without slowing, heading for the smoky summit.

After seeing how quickly the robot could move, Hal realised he only had seconds to grab the briefcase and escape. He lifted the edge of the crate and squeezed out, then ran into the office. Behind him he could hear junk slithering down the pile as Reece hunted for the source of the smoke. As soon as those noises stopped, the robot would be back again.

Hal took three steps towards the filing cabinet, ready to grab the briefcase, then stopped dead. It wasn't there! He spun round and saw it immediately - it was sitting on the desk, and it was wide open! The case was empty but there was a thick file sitting alongside, and Hal guessed Reece had taken it out. He glanced at the cover, which was an artist's impression of a space station with 'Hotel Grande Luxe' picked out in shiny gold lettering. The station looked like the Oberon, but he guessed they made them all from similar plans.

A wisp of green smoke drifted in through the door, and Hal realised Stinky's concoction was working better than expected. He peered through the grimy window and saw a sea of green fog with junk piles poking out like islands in a lagoon. Reece was stamping on something with both feet, while green smoke continued to pour down the slope like a slow-moving river. Nearby Hal could see Alex standing with her back to the office, her head and shoulders just above the green fog.

Hal picked up the file and flipped through the

glossy pages, which were full of headings like 'Income projection' and 'Handover strategy'. Typical adults, using a cool electronic briefcase to store a boring report.

Hal shrugged, and he was about to throw the file back in the briefcase when Alex came barging into the office. 'He's coming!' she breathed. 'Hide . . . quick!'

— 22 —

Getting Deskerate

Hal looked around the pokey little office. They could hardly cram themselves into the filing cabinet's drawers, and Reece's charger stand wouldn't have hidden a ham sandwich, let alone two children. That only left the big desk.

Hal dropped to his hands and knees and scuttled into the darkness. Alex followed, and the two of them sat side by side with their backs to the wall. They wrapped their arms around their knees to draw their feet in, away from the pool of light shining on the office floor.

Then Hal remembered something, and his heart sank. He was still holding the report! Was there time to put it back on the desk? No, a shadow fell across the floor as Reece came in, and Hal sank back into the shadows. Did the robot have heat sensors? A super sense of smell? Laser-guided eyes? More importantly, would he notice the report was missing?

There was a creak as Reece sat down and a squeak as he pushed his pointed metal feet under the desk, narrowly missing Hal's shins. The robot was clearly annoyed, tutting and muttering under his breath.

'Crumble my circuit boards! First they want boxes, then they want plain boxes, then they want brown boxes and now they want no boxes. Small humans are worse than the big ones!'

There was a lot more of this in a similar vein, and Hal soon realised their predicament. Robots didn't have tea breaks or lunch breaks, and they certainly didn't have toilet breaks. In fact, Reece probably worked 24 hours a day, seven days a week. So how long were they going to be stuck under the desk, waiting for a chance to leave?

Hal spent the time dreaming up escape plans. His first idea was to jump up, shout 'boo' and then run like fury while the robot recovered its senses. Problem was, robots didn't have senses to recover from, and their reactions were so fast Reece would have Hal in a headlock before he could say 'b' . . . let alone the 'oo!' part.

Hal's next idea was to communicate with Stinky and ask for more help. Unfortunately he was stuck under a desk and there were no handy water pipes to tap morse code on. Anyway, the second he tried to bash out a message, Reece would look under the desk to see where the tap-tap-tappity-tap was coming from.

So, it all came down to Hal's final option: to distract the robot. Could he send it away somehow? He'd seen a show on ventriloquism once, where a performer threw his voice and made it sound like his dummy was speaking. What if Hal threw his voice to the terminal and made out there was a fire alarm? Trouble was, whenever he tried to throw his voice it always sounded like he was gargling through his nose.

Hal's elbow was getting sore where it was pressed against the hard floor, and any minute now his stomach was going to start rumbling. He had to do something!

Another ten minutes dragged past, and by now Hal was ready to give himself up. He put one hand down and started to move, but at that moment Reece pushed the chair back and stood up. Hal heard the robot moving around, and there was a loud *click!* Hal frowned as he tried to remember the layout of the office, and his spirits soared when he remembered what was on that particular wall. What was the one thing robots had to do? Recharge

314

themselves!

Very slowly, Hal moved his head until he could see the robot's chest, then its neck, then its jaw . . . He tried to lean forward some more, to see whether Reece's eyes were open, but Alex pulled him back. He frowned at her but she just scowled, gesturing at the charger then shaking her head firmly. Her meaning was clear: don't risk getting seen!

That was all very well, but how long were they supposed to sit there? Did robots switch off when they charged up, or would Reece spot them the minute they tried to escape?

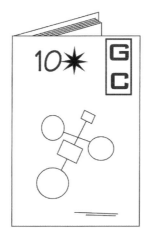

Sitting still was torture at the best of times, but the floor was rock hard under the desk, and every time Hal tried to get comfortable Alex would scowl at him and put her finger to her lips. To make things worse, she was able to sit like a statue.

In the end Hal decided to skim the report, hoping to find something - anything - to pass the time. After two or three pages he saw a section titled 'Resettlement Options', and vague memories of settlers and exploration had him reading in no time. Unfortunately, instead of gripping tales of survival and daring, the report contained a load of dry sentences with enormously long words.

Hal skimmed it all twice, but it didn't make a whole lot of sense. It went on and on about hiring and firing, retraining scientists and 'the benefits of multi-skilling' ... whatever that meant. Then two words leapt out at him:

Gyris and Oberon!

Hal looked at the text again. Sure enough, the local planet got a mention, and right underneath he saw a sentence that made his blood run cold:

As soon as the scientists have been removed from Space Station Oberon, construction will start on the first hotel rooms.

Hal closed the report and stared at the space station on the cover. It didn't just LOOK like the Oberon. It WAS the Oberon! Grogan was going to take over Hal's home and turn it into a hotel!

— 23 —

Infilcrate

Hal felt Alex tugging his sleeve. He was still staring at the report in shock, but eventually she got his attention. When he turned to look he realised she was pointing to her flashy space watch. Hal frowned back. His home was at stake and she wanted to watch a movie?

Then Alex held the watch under his nose, and Hal realised there was a curt message on the screen:

Take briefcase to security checkpoint ASAP.

Hal groaned. Could things get any worse? They were trapped in Reece's office, the briefcase lock had been picked and the contents were gripped in Hal's fingers. Now they had to put the report back, seal the briefcase, sneak past Reece and return everything . . . all before they were discovered!

Hal eyed the report, and then he noticed something tucked inside the back page. It was a sheet of thick paper, folded in two, and when he opened it out he saw fancy writing across the top: Letter of Agreement. There was an important-looking seal in one corner, a mass of small print in the middle, and then a dozen different signatures at the bottom. He glanced at Alex but she was busy tapping a reply on her watch.

'I'm telling him we're on the way,' she whispered. 'That should buy us some time.'

On the spur of the moment, Hal folded the letter and crammed it into his pocket.

Alex finished sending her reply, then shot Hal a worried look. 'Now what?'

'I don't k–'

Before he could finish the sentence there was a commotion from the recycling centre:

Rattle-clatter-thud!

FFFFFsshhh! FFFFFsshhh! FFFFFSSHHH!

Hal frowned. What was that?

Chack!

Reece was out of the charger like a shot, his feet pounding on the floor as he ran out of the office. Hal and Alex tumbled out from under the desk, groaning as circulation returned to their cramped legs. Hal got up gingerly and hobbled to the window, where he saw something that made his spirits soar. It wasn't just a green smoke bomb filling the centre

. . . no, there were half a dozen! Purple smoke, blue smoke, orange smoke . . . there was even a vibrant shade of pink that made Hal wince.

The result was like an explosion in a paint factory, with a riot of colours flowing around the piles of junk. Reece was almost invisible in the multi-coloured smoke, although Hal could just see him jumping up and down and shaking his metal fists at the recycling shaft. Hal grinned at the sight. Good old Stinky! He must have figured out they were trapped, and the new smoke bombs were exactly what they needed to escape.

Hal didn't waste any time. He threw the report into the briefcase and jammed the lid shut. The indicator lights blinked and there was a *click!* as the lock armed itself. 'Come on. Run!'

◆

Reece had already smothered two of Stinky's smoke bombs, and the rest wouldn't last long. Was there enough time to run for the exit? No. Hal looked around for inspiration and spotted the large crate he'd used earlier. He grabbed Alex by the arm and together they lifted one edge of the crate and scrambled inside.

'On my count,' he said. 'Ready? One, two . . . go!'

They both straightened, lifting the base off the ground, and shuffled forward with the weight on their shoulders. Hal tried to match Alex's strides, but it was impossible to tell if they were going in a straight line. After a while he had to let his end down, and they stopped for a breather. Hal put his eye to the hole but all he could see was thick swirling smoke.

They lifted the packing crate and started moving again.

Thump!

The crate stopped dead and they both fell over. Hal got up and peered through the hole, where he saw the vague outline of a junk pile directly ahead. 'Turn right,' he whispered.

'Shouldn't that be left?'

'We'll go left next.'

They made their way around the pile, the big crate swaying and bumping, until Hal judged they were on the other side. Then they set off again, moving as fast as they dared.

They hit five more junk piles on their way to the exit, turning this way and that until Hal barely knew up from down, let alone left from right. Then he saw a big grey wall and realised they must have made it. There was no breath for talking, so he gestured at Alex and together they heaved the crate over.

Crash! It tipped on its side and they were free at last. Hal ran to the wall and followed it to the right, looking for the exit. It seemed a long way, and then he stopped, puzzled, as they came to a corner. He shrugged and turned right again, following the wall. Even if they went all the way round, they'd find the exit sooner or later.

Thud!

Hal frowned. The noise was directly ahead, and it sounded familiar.

Thud!

Then he realised what it was. They were nowhere near the exit ... they'd gone all the way around the edge and ended up near the huge recycling machine. And Reece was between them and the exit!

'I told you we were going the wrong way!' protested Alex.

'No, it was the right way. You turned the crate too much.'

'*I* turned it? You kept walking into things!'

'Not half as many as you did. You weren't going fast enough.'

Alex displayed the briefcase. 'Holding this? I'd like to see you try.'

They were crouching behind an old filing cabinet, and Hal risked a quick look towards the office. The smoke was clearing now, and he could see Reece slithering down the big pile of junk. How long before the robot realised the briefcase was missing?

'We'd better get back into the crate,' said Alex.

'No, we'll stay put. He might go back in the charger.'

Alex tapped her watch. 'We can't stop. Dad's waiting for me.'

Squeak, squeak, squeak.

Hal frowned. They didn't have mice aboard the space station, more's the pity, so what was making that noise?

Squeak, squeak . . . . squeak.

Whatever it was, it had stopped just the other side of the filing cabinet. Hal raised his head for a look ... and came face to face with a powered trolley. For a split second he thought it was Carrie, come to rescue them, but then he noticed the battered paintwork and the bent rear wheel. It was Paul, Carrie's missing friend!

Meanwhile, Paul had also noticed Hal, and the trolley was backing away slowly. 'D-don't recycle me,' he said in a quavering voice. 'I'll work harder, I promise!'

'It's all right,' hissed Hal. 'We're friends! Carrie sent us to find you!'

'Y-you know Carrie?' asked the trolley, and this time there was a note of hope in his voice.

'Absolutely.' Hal beckoned. 'Come round this side where Reece can't see you.'

'Reece is watching me?' The trolley went back and forth on the spot, its buckled wheel dragging on the ground. 'Oh no, not Reece. Reece doesn't like me. Like me! Tee hee hee!'

Hal realised Paul was near breaking point, and after a quick look towards the office he vaulted over the filing cabinet and hurried to the trolley. He crouched next to it, put one hand on the battered metal surface and spoke in a low, calm voice. 'Listen to me, okay? Whatever happened to you

323

before, it's over. I'm here now, and nobody hurts my friends. Do you understand?'

'B-but Reece . . .'

'If that tin can comes near you I'll feed him into the Recyclotron,' said Hal fiercely.

This did the trick, and Paul calmed down. 'Will I be working in the kitchens again? I like the kitchens.'

'If you help me you can work wherever you like.' Hal glanced towards the office, but there was no sign of Reece. 'Do you ever leave the recycling centre?'

'Sometimes I take deliveries to the lift.'

'Perfect. Can you do one now?'

'I-I suppose so.'

'Follow me.' Hal led the trolley back around the filing cabinet, where Alex was waiting impatiently. First he explained about Paul, and then he outlined his plan. 'But first we're going to need a few things . . .'

— 24 —

Paul the other one

Squeak, squeak, squeak.

Reece looked up from his terminal, a frown creasing his metal forehead. What was that confounded trolley doing now? It was supposed to be ferrying raw materials to the Recyclotron, not going on joyrides! Reece pushed his chair back and strode to the door. What he saw outside had him blinking with amazement. 'What the –'

'The delivery is ready, sir.'

Paul was draped with a tatty tablecloth, and his upper shelf was covered with an assortment of plates, cups and cutlery.

'Buff my ball joints,' said Reece. 'Who ordered that mess?'

'It's an urgent delivery for the kitchen. There's a VIP on board the Space Station and they've run out of cutlery.'

'Is that so?' Reece felt a surge of joy. 'Running out' meant a shortage, and a shortage meant a fat profit. 'What am I getting in return?'

Paul hesitated, almost as though he were listening to instructions. 'You can have all the refuse from the visitor's ship.'

'Foreign muck!' Reece rubbed his hands together. 'Excellent! You may proceed!'

'As you wish, sir.'

Squeak-squeak-squeak went the trolley, and Reece eyed it in surprise. He'd never seen it move that fast before! Then he forgot about Paul and returned to his desk, where he sat down to bask in his good fortune. What with the rare space gun firing mechanism, the exceptionally fine briefcase and now this unexpected bonus shipment, it had been a rubbishy day to remember. That's when he looked down at his empty desk, and the truth hit him like a sledgehammer.

The briefcase . . . someone had stolen it!

◆

Squeaksqueaksqueaksqueak!

'You've got to slow down!' cried Alex, as the trolley rocketed along the corridor.

'No!' shouted Hal. 'Faster, faster!'

Alex grabbed his arm. 'It's going to look pretty suspicious if he breaks the sound barrier.'

Hal was enjoying the wild ride, but he realised she was right. The tatty tablecloth was tearing itself to shreds, and they'd lost several cups and plates at the last corner.

Screeeeech!

Paul took another corner at speed, and this time he nearly lost Alex.

'All right, Paul. Slow it down a bit.'

'Got . . . to . . . escape,' puffed the trolley. 'Got . . . to . . .'

'You can still escape, but slower.'

'Under . . . stood.'

Their pace slowed, and moments later they rolled into the elevator.

'Where to?' demanded Alex, who was closest to the buttons.

'Level nineteen.'

Alex was still reaching out when they heard footsteps pounding along the corridor.

'It's Reece!' hissed Hal. 'He must have discovered the missing case!'

Alex pressed the button and the doors started to close. Paul backed away, trying to avoid being spotted through the closing gap, and Hal only just shifted his fingers before the trolley ground against the wall. The footsteps got closer and closer, and they could hear Reece muttering to himself.

'Thieves! Robbers! Jumble my joints, I'll make them pay for this!'

Thud! The doors met in the middle just as Reece jabbed his finger on the call button with an impatient click-click-click! Hal held his breath, hoping the doors wouldn't open again, then sighed in relief as the lift shot upwards. They weren't clear yet, though ... the robot would be straight after them.

On the other hand ... Hal smiled as a plan came to him, and he pressed the button for level seven.

When the doors opened there was a delicious smell of baking, and Hal nodded towards the right-hand passage.

'The kitchens?' said Alex. 'What are we doing here?'

Hal just smiled and patted the trolley. 'Come on, Paul. You're nearly home!'

Paul drove out of the lift and started up the corridor. He was going a lot more slowly now, and Hal realised the high-speed run had drained the batteries. He looked back along the corridor and saw the lift doors closing. Hopefully Reece would take the bait and head straight for level nineteen.

Paul drove them all the way to the canteen, despite getting slower and slower. His batteries were almost gone but he pushed on regardless, focusing on getting home. They reached the last pair of doors, where Hal called a halt. 'Wait here, the pair of you.' He got out and opened the doors, slipping through the gap into the kitchen. A minute later he was back, carrying a folded tablecloth under his arm. He shook it out and draped it over Paul.

'That's not going to help much,' said Alex. 'He needs batteries, not a new skirt.'

'It's just a disguise.'

There was a sudden burst of music, making them both jump. The noise came from Alex's watch, and the screen was pulsing in a range of colours. 'It's my dad,' she said urgently. 'He's calling me!'

'Hang up on him,' said Hal.

Alex hesitated, then gave her arm a shake. 'Yes dad?'

'Where are you? I've been waiting fifteen minutes!'

Hal was standing two metres away, but he could still hear Grogan's angry voice.

'I, er, got lost. We're almost there.'

'That's not acceptable, Alex. You've let me down.'

'I'm sorry, dad. We'll be quick, I promise.'

'You need to learn the value of time. When you get to the checkpoint I want you to stand there for thirty minutes before you call me. And make sure you're holding my briefcase the whole time!'

There was a burst of static as Grogan cut the connection, and Alex lowered the watch. 'Thirty minutes! My arms will fall off.'

'Don't worry,' said Hal stoutly. 'I'll hold the briefcase for you.'

'Thanks, but he'd find out,' muttered Alex. 'And what about Reece? If we stand around that checkpoint for half an hour he'll spot us for sure, and then he'll take the briefcase back.'

'We'll explain to the guard. He'll protect the briefcase.' Privately Hal doubted Stinky's brother Richard would stand up to Reece, but they'd worry about that when it happened. 'Come on, we've got to organise a lift.' Hal opened the doors, and Alex helped him wheel Paul into the kitchen. On the far side several chefs were busy preparing another course, while helpers scraped plates and washed up.   Nearby there was another trolley with an identical tablecloth . . . Carrie!

Hal guided Paul to the wall, then crouched next to Carrie. 'It's us again,' whispered Hal. 'Can you hear me?'

'Loud and clear,' murmured the trolley.

'Don't make a fuss, but we've rescued Paul.'

'For real?'

'Yes, he's right behind you. We're going to plug him in for a charge, and then I need your help.'

'Anything!' whispered Carrie.

'We need a lift to A-section.'

'Easy. Hop aboard.'

Moments later they were ready. Carrie drove for the door, and Hal could just see Alex's worried expression in the darkness. He gave her a confident smile. 'Don't worry, it'll be okay!' Secretly, he wondered how everything was going to turn out. The agreement he'd taken from the briefcase was folded in his pocket, and if Grogan was mad now, what was he going to be like when he discovered it was missing? Hal had no intention of putting it back, not if he could prevent the Space Station being turned into a luxury hotel.

— 25 —

A-Section

Carrie rolled along the corridor towards the lift, the ride smooth and effortless compared to Paul with his buckled, squeaky wheel. They were only halfway there when they heard pounding footsteps in the distance. Carrie turned sharp left, and Hal heard the hiss of a closing door. He peered out and realised they were hiding in someone's private cabin. Fortunately the owner wasn't there.

A second later they heard Reece's angry muttering as he charged past. 'Energise my electrics! I'll teach you, you sneaky little thieves. Steal from me would you?'

The footsteps receded, and Hal was just relaxing again when Carrie spoke. 'Was that a friend of yours?'

'Er, not exactly.'

'Good. Reece's a rather unpleasant character.'

There was a hiss as the door opened, and Carrie raced along the corridor before stopping at the lift. 'You know Reece works in the recycling centre?'

'Someone did mention it,' said Hal casually.

'Just let me know if he bothers you. I have a score to settle with that –'

Ting!

'The lift's here. Floor please?'

Hal lifted the tablecloth and pressed the button for level nineteen. It was time to deliver the briefcase.

◆

'We really appreciate this,' said Alex, as the lift carried them towards the higher levels. 'Are you sure you won't get into trouble?'

'Probably, but what can they do?' Carrie chuckled. 'If I play dumb they'll just blame my programming. Anyway, you got Paul back and that's worth any amount of telling off.'

Ting! The lift stopped and Carrie drove out. Before long she put the brakes on, and the plates rattled overhead. 'Checkpoint ahead,' said Carrie.

'Thanks, we'll –'

'Uh-oh. Keep quiet a minute.'

333

Hal and Alex exchanged a glance. What was wrong? Then they heard it, getting louder and louder . . .

Thud, thud, thud!

Reece's footsteps! The robot had chased them all the way to A-section, and he was still after them!

THUD, THUD, THUD!

'Ponder my petabytes. Stop! Stop!'

Hal willed the trolley on, hoping she could outdistance the robot. Instead, she came to a stop.

'Yes? What is it?'

'It's Paul, isn't it?'

'No, I'm Carrie.'

'I don't believe you!' muttered Reece. Hal drew back as one corner of the tablecloth was lifted up. He realised Reece was looking for the buckled wheel, and he hoped the robot didn't crouch down for a really close inspection. If he did, he'd spot Hal and Alex right away.

'Do you mind?' snapped Carrie. 'I'll report you for that!'

'Pootle my power cord! My apologies madam, I thought you were someone else.'

'I should think so,' said Carrie, with a sniff.

Reece charged past at full speed, and Hal grabbed the edge of the tablecloth before it could flap up and reveal them sitting inside the trolley. Carrie set off after him, but barely two seconds later . . .

'Halt!' said a voice. It came from further up the passageway, and Hal realised it was Stinky's brother Richard.

'Make way!' shouted Reece. 'Thieves. Robbers! Emergency!'

'Stop where you are,' shouted the voice.

Thud, thud . . . thud.

The footsteps came to a halt as Reece obeyed the order to stop. Then Carrie arrived at the checkpoint, stopping right alongside the robot. Hal could actually see its gleaming feet through a gap in the tablecloth.

Beep beep! 'Delivery for the meeting room,' said Carrie brightly.

'Wait your turn,' said Richard importantly. 'I have to deal with the emergency first.'

'This . . . emergency,' said Carrie, using a halting computer voice. 'Quick, smart, fast. Rush delivery.'

'Doesn't look like it. Those plates are empty!'

'Urgent h-hurry,' stammered Carrie. 'Programming fault. Need to collect . . . other plates. Urgent. Overheat.'

Richard backed away. 'Go on, move. You're cleared!'

The motor whirred and Carrie was out of there

in seconds. As they drew away Hal heard Richard addressing Reece.

'Now tell me,' he said importantly. 'What's all this about thieves?'

❧

There was a knot in Hal's stomach as the trolley rolled away from the checkpoint. They were heading deeper into A-section, site of the top secret labs! Stinky once joked that you needed special clearance just to mention the place, but his remark didn't seem so funny now. The space station was deadly serious about security, and zooming through the labs inside a runaway trolley wasn't exactly what Hal's parents meant by 'acceptable behaviour'. In fact, 'criminal behaviour' was more like it.

'Carrie, can you drop us off?'

'Not right now,' murmured the trolley. 'The security cameras are watching.'

Hal swallowed. Cameras! They didn't have those in the rest of the station, and the thought of hidden eyes recording his every move was disturbing. Even so, he was tempted to take a look. He only had to lift the tablecloth to see part of A-section. Stinky and the others would surely make him leader of the new gang after that!

Hal reached for the fabric, hesitated, then raised it the tiniest fraction. The view wasn't exactly encouraging - there was a corridor exactly like the ones in the rest of the Space Station, with grey-painted walls and unmarked doors. Then Carrie drove past a couple of technicians, and Hal gaped at the sight. They were dressed in bright orange hazard suits, and they were carrying big domed helmets under their arms. He caught a glimpse of their faces, and saw they were wearing identical pairs of dark glasses, with thick round lenses and little antennae on each side. The techs certainly didn't look like they were researching a new type of food, and Hal dropped the tablecloth in a hurry, glad they hadn't seen him. He was starting to wish they'd waited for Grogan at the checkpoint.

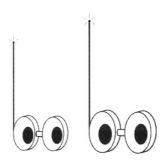

A few moments later Carrie got Hal's attention. 'Guard post ahead. Be silent.'

Another guard post! Would they search the food trolley? Hal and Alex exchanged worried glances.

Carrie stopped, and one of the guards cleared his throat. 'Now then, what's your game?'

'I don't understand,' said Carrie. 'What is a game?'

'Why are you carrying empty plates back into the meeting?'

'I'm just following orders,' said Carrie. She didn't mention they were Hal's orders.

The guards conferred in low voices. Following orders was something they were familiar with, but would they let the trolley through?

'All right, you can go in.'

The guards stood aside and the trolley started to roll again, gathering speed slowly as the motor struggled with the weight. They turned sharp right almost immediately, and Hal heard the familiar *whiiiish!* of automatic doors. They were entering the meeting room!

— 26 —

Ring Tone

Carrie came to a halt at the back of the meeting room, and the first thing Hal heard was Grogan's voice.

'Next, I'd like to thank you for this wonderful lunch. I know your resources are limited, but you did a pretty good job under the circumstances.'

There was a smattering of polite applause, but someone near the trolley whispered 'ungrateful swine'. There was muted laughter, and Hal glanced at Alex to see whether she'd heard.

'Now, to business. As you know, I'm visiting the Space Station to discuss your future. I believe there was some talk about a large donation which would help your research.'

The applause was louder this time.

'Unfortunately, you've been misinformed.'

There was a lot of murmuring from the audience.

'For the past two years this Space Station has been propped up with funds from twelve local planets. Their money has kept your research going, but that's about to stop.'

The audience gasped, and Hal heard his mum's voice close by. 'What are you talking about? We have funding for the next three years.'

'Not any more. They need the money for hospitals and schools.' VIP hesitated. 'That's the bad news. The good news is that the Space Station won't be closing down.'

There were sighs of relief.

'Why not?' asked Hal's mum.

'I've put together a short presentation. Lights please.'

In the darkness Hal was able to lift the tablecloth, and he and Alex peeped out. The audience were sitting at long tables covered with snowy white cloths, and silver cutlery gleamed under delicate candlelight. Hal spotted his mum, and he stared. Instead of the usual labcoat, she was wearing a blue evening dress, and her hair was arranged in plaits and tied up with a ribbon. As he looked around he recognised some of the other scientists and administrators, and they too were dressed to the nines. Hal's gaze returned to the candles and he frowned to himself. Oh, so it was okay for adults to

340

light fires aboard the Space Station, was it? Typical!

Then he noticed the screen, just visible between the seated audience, and he settled down to watch. First there was a flashy logo and a burst of classical music, and then a wide-angle shot of the Space Station. The voiceover started as the camera got closer.

'Welcome to Space Hotel Oberon, the jewel in the Ezy-stae chain. With two hundred quality rooms, five restaurants and a zero-gravity plunge pool, your family will enjoy the vistas of space from the comfort of ten-star luxury.'

There was a commotion around the table, and Hal's mum leapt up. 'You can stop that nonsense right now,' she said, gesturing at the operator. The image vanished, and she turned to Grogan. 'I'm sorry you wasted your time coming here, and I hope you have a safe trip home. I'll have someone find your daughter and –'

'Now don't be hasty,' said Grogan. 'At least watch the rest.'

'There's no point.' Hal's mum glared at him, her eyes as hard as diamonds in the candlelight. 'Nobody is turning our home into a hotel!'

The other scientists nodded in agreement.

Grogan spread his hands. 'It's going to happen whether you like it or not. I'm here to explain how it'll work, and to find out which of you want to stay aboard after the handover.'

'Stay aboard?'

'Sure! We'll need managers, receptionists, tour guides, waiters . . . the list is endless. You're all used to living in space so you'll get first pick of the jobs.'

Hal exchanged a glance with Alex, who looked as shocked as he did.

'Grogan, this is all nonsense,' said Hal's mum sharply.'This research station is owned by the governments of twelve planets. You couldn't get them to agree on the time of day, let alone handing over control of the Space Station.'

'That's where you're wrong. It's taken three years and millions of credits, but I have a contract signed and verified by every planet.'

'I don't believe a word of it. Where are these documents?'

'My daughter has them.' Grogan accessed his wrist computer, and out the corner of his eye Hal saw Alex doing the same. He realised she was frantically hunting through the menus, looking for the mute button, but she was too late. A cheerful song rang out and her watch began to flash.

And everyone in the meeting room heard it.

◆

For a split second Hal thought they might be able to get away. Carrie could move faster than any human, and once outside they could flee A-section at top speed. Even the guards outside could be dealt with, as long as Carrie played along.

But no. Before he could give the order, Alex stepped out of the trolley to face the music. There was no way Hal was letting her take all the blame, so he stood alongside, head held high.

There was an immediate uproar.

'Children . . . in A-section!'

'It's an outrage!'

'Shouldn't be allowed!'

'Never heard such a thing!'

'HAL JUNIOR. COME HERE THIS INSTANT!'

Hal barely recognised his mum's voice. He thought she was really angry when Grogan was threatening to take the Oberon away, but this was something else. She looked like she could bend steel bars with her bare hands, knock planets out of orbit at a glance AND eat three mouldy ration bars at a single sitting. And she was angry at *him!*

'Explain yourself at once!' thundered his mum. 'You know the rules. A-section is off limits!'

'It's my fault,' said a voice nearby.

Hal turned to see Alex holding the briefcase. 'My father needed this in a hurry, and I asked Hal to get me here as soon as possible.'

'Well yes . . . ' began Hal's mum. 'But the rules –'

Grogan cleared his throat. '*I* set the rules now, and my daughter can go anywhere she likes.'

'It's for their own safety!' said Hal's mum. 'Our research is very dangerous, and –'

'And it's been cancelled, as of today. I'll oversee the shutdown after lunch, but first let me show you the letter of agreement.'

Hal's stomach tightened, and he could almost feel the folded paper burning a hole in his pocket. Grogan had a nasty temper and his mum was already livid, and no matter what he did one of them was going to be even madder still.

— 27 —

Missing Sheet

Alex handed her dad the briefcase, and he made a big show of taking out a key and turning it in the lock. There was a loud click, and Grogan smiled as he took out the report. 'I'll leave this with you later. It might change your mind about staying on.'

'Fat chance,' snapped Hal's mum.

There was dead silence as Grogan flipped back and forth through the report. He did it again, more slowly, and then he frowned. 'Where is it? Who took it?'

'Where's what?'

'The letter of agreement!' Grogan scowled around the room. 'This is outrageous! One of you must have gone through my briefcase!'

'We've been with you the whole time,' said Hal's mum calmly. 'Perhaps you forgot to pack it?'

Grogan turned to his daughter. He looked furious.

'Alex, did you open my briefcase?'

'No,' said Alex firmly. 'Definitely not.'

'Did you let it out of your sight?'

Alex hesitated. 'I–'

'Tell me what happened! Who took it?'

'Nobody! Dad, I swear!'

Alex's face was very red, and Hal realised she was close to tears. He gripped the folded piece of paper in his pocket and looked away. If he gave up the contract Alex's dad would forgive her, eventually, but the Space Station would be lost. On the other hand, if he kept the piece of paper in his pocket the Space Station might be saved . . . but Alex would be in terrible trouble. It was an impossible decision!

Grogan threw the report into his briefcase and snapped it shut. His face was pale, his mouth a thin line, and he kept frowning at Alex as though he couldn't wait to get the whole story out of her. Nobody said a word, and the silence dragged on as Grogan gathered his things. Finally, he was ready.

'It took me six months to get those signatures,' he said in a tightly-controlled voice. 'That's wasted half a year of my busy life, but don't think I'll give up. I'll be back with another contract and you'll all be out.' Grogan glanced at Alex. 'As for you, you can forget about summer holidays. You're going to work in one of my factories, sunrise 'til sunset, until you learn some responsibility.'

Hal couldn't take it any more. 'Leave her alone! It wasn't her fault!'

Everyone stared at him, and he nearly backed down under the battery of intense looks. Quickly he pulled the folded contract from his pocket, opening it up with a rustle of thick paper. 'Here, I took your stupid papers. It was nothing to do with Alex!'

Grogan whisked the contract from his hand and held it up for Hal's mum to read. She tried to take it, but he moved it out of reach. Instead, she was forced to read the print from a distance, her jaw clenched. She looked angrier than ever, and Hal wondered whether she would challenge Grogan to a duel.

But Grogan was all smiles now. He'd won the battle, and he even put his arm around Alex and gave her a hug. 'I hope everything is in order?' he said, waving the contract. 'I won't ask you to move out straight away, but the workers will need quarters by the end of the month.'

Hal's mum was still trying to read the contract.

'Well?' demanded Grogan.

'You have a dozen signatures, and the wording is correct. Nice piece of paper too. Very smart.'

'Of course.' Grogan gave her a grin. 'A ten star hotel deserves the very best.'

'It's very impressive, but it's not worth the paper it's written on.'

'What ... what are you talking about?' Grogan stared at the contract. 'It's signed by the governments of all twelve planets!'

'I can see that. The problem is, you're short one signature.'

'Where ... which ... whose?'

'The thirteenth planet. Ours.' Hal's mum gave Grogan a beautiful smile, her eyes shining in the candlelight. 'Didn't anyone tell you? Space Station Oberon has its own constitution. We're a self-governed planet.'

'That's a lie!'

'No, it's perfectly true. Without our approval that paperwork is useless, and I guarantee the Station

Commander will never sign it. You might as well tear it up right now.'

Hal's spirits soared, and he couldn't wait for Grogan's reaction. Would he stamp his foot? Throw a tantrum? Vanish in a puff of yellow smoke?

Instead, Grogan took the contract in both hands, and for a split second it looked like he was going to shred it before their eyes. Then he laughed. 'Nice try with that thirteenth planet nonsense, but I know a desperate bluff when I hear one. This contract is perfectly valid.'

Hal stared at his mum, willing her to fight back, but when her shoulders dropped he realised it was all over. She'd given up! Grogan had won!

— 28 —

Candle Power

Ten minutes later the room was nearly empty. The scientists had left, heading to the labs to shut down their experiments, and the administrators had trooped out discussing severance pay and superannuation. Now only a handful of people remained: Hal's mum, Grogan, Alex and Hal, plus a couple of guards at the door.

'Take a seat, kids,' said Grogan heartily. 'Let me get you some ice cream!'

Hal felt sick to the stomach, and he shook his head. Alex didn't say a word.

'I said take a seat! I don't want you hovering around while I'm discussing business.'

Hal obeyed, sitting right between Grogan and his mum. If they started fighting he figured he might be able to stop them.

'Now, let's have some coffee.' Grogan snapped his

fingers and one of the guards looked in. 'Coffee, and make it instant.'

'As you wish,' said the guard.

Grogan smiled around the table. 'There, isn't that better?'

Three surly, angry and unhappy faces said otherwise. There were several candles on the table, but instead of softening the expressions they threw them into stark relief.

'So Hal, are you looking forward to Gyris? You'll be able to live in a proper house and play outside. Won't that be great?'

'I guess.' Hal stared into the nearest candle, lost in the flickering flame. He'd often dreamed of living on a real planet, but the Space Station was his home. If they turned it into an expensive hotel, he could never come back.

'And what about school? You'll have a real teacher, and –'

Hal's mum interrupted. 'You've won, Grogan. Stop teasing him.'

'I'm just grateful to the lad.' Grogan waved the letter of agreement, which gleamed in the candlelight. 'Without his help, this might have been lost for good.'

Hal scowled. He didn't need reminding.

'So, Hal. I hear you like camping?'

'Never tried it,' said Hal curtly.

'Come on Hal,' said his mum. 'Surely you remember practising for the trip to Gyris? You and Stin–, I mean, you and Stephen in the kitchen, trying to cook that ration bar? How we all laughed!'

... hmmm!

Laughed? Hal frowned. What was his mum on about? He'd been sent straight to his room after setting fire to . . . Oh! Hal's gaze travelled from the flickering candle to the letter of agreement and back again. 'Yes, mum. It tasted horrible after we cooked it. Worse than usual.'

'Plenty of fresh food on Gyris,' said Grogan heartily. 'You can have a barbecue every day!'

At that moment one of the guards came back with a steaming cup of coffee. Grogan reached forward to take it, the letter of agreement still clasped in his free hand, and as he did so Hal moved the candle underneath it. One corner of the paper curled and blackened, and there was a tiny wisp of smoke.

Unfortunately Grogan sat back in his chair before the paper caught, and his movement shifted the letter out of the flame. Grogan sniffed his coffee and made a face, but didn't notice the smouldering paper.

Hal muttered under his breath. He'd come so close but it hadn't worked.

Alex, who was seated opposite, had seen the whole thing. 'Dad, you forgot the sugar.'

'Eh? Oh yes.' Grogan reached forward, and the letter moved close to the candle again. Hal pushed it underneath and . . . success! The flames started to spread and he turned to his mum quickly.

'Mum, can I get a pet?'

'What?'

'When we're living on Gyris, can I get a pet dog?'

'I don't know, I –'

Hal never got the answer, because at that moment there was an angry roar behind him. Grogan pushed his chair back and leapt up, shaking the letter like mad to try and put it out. Unfortunately this made it burn even brighter, and the flames glowed blue and purple as they consumed the fancy paper.

'That'll be the enriched oxygen,' said Hal's mum. 'Fires burn a lot hotter aboard the Space Station, and they're awfully hard to put out. Isn't that right,

Hal?'

Grogan dropped his precious letter on the floor and stamped on it, but by the time he finally put the flames out only blackened fragments remained. He scooped up the pieces and tried to fit them back together, then turned on Hal. 'You did this! You set fire to my letter!'

'Utter nonsense,' said Hal's mum. 'He was talking to me.'

Grogan turned to Alex next, but she was sitting on the other side of the table and couldn't possibly have reached the candle. Furious, he crumbled the charred paper in his bare hands.

'Looks like your plans went up in smoke,' said Hal's mum. 'Now, would you like another coffee before you go home?'

◆

Before they left the meeting room Hal's mum beckoned to the guards. 'Shut down corridors Alpha through Epsilon, and warn everyone to close their doors. We're bringing these two through.'

'I could wear a blindfold,' said Hal.

'That won't be necessary.'

354

A few minutes later one of the guards came back. 'The area is secured.'

'Thanks, Jim. You two can take a break now.'

Hal kept his eyes peeled all the way to the checkpoint, hoping to find something interesting he could tell Stinky about. Unfortunately the corridor was totally bare, and he realised he'd have to make something up instead.

They arrived at the checkpoint, where Stinky's brother Richard was still on duty. He spotted Hal and Alex, and his eyes widened in surprise. 'You don't have passes for this section. How did you get through the checkpoint?'

'It was a real Carrie-on,' said Hal, and he heard Alex smother a laugh.

Two more corners and they lost sight of A-section. Hal was just telling himself the drama was over for the day when he heard a familiar sound.

Thud-thud-thud.

Hal and Alex exchanged a glance and hid behind the adults. They'd recognise those footsteps anywhere.

THUD-THUD-THUD!

Reece came charging round the corner, arms and legs pumping. 'Make way, make way. I'm chasing thieves!' Then he spotted Hal, and he let out a triumphant cry. 'Call the guards! I've found him,

I've found him!'

'What are you talking about?' demanded Hal's mum.

Before Reece could reply he spotted the briefcase in Grogan's hands. He snatched it in a flash, and a split second later there was only a fading *THUD-thud-thud* to prove he'd been there at all.

Grogan stared at his empty hand. 'Is this place completely out of control?' he asked, his voice dripping acid. 'That was a brand new briefcase!'

'Reece is our disposal expert. He collects rubbish and turns it into something useful.' Hal's mum looked Grogan up and down. 'You're lucky he only took the briefcase.'

❖

A few minutes later they arrived at the docking bay, and what a contrast! Earlier that day most of the the inhabitants of Space Station Oberon had turned out to welcome the important VIP and his 'son', Alex. And now, barely four hours later, Grogan's farewell audience consisted of one cleaner and a bored security guard.

'Don't walk on that bit,' protested the cleaner. 'I just mopped it!'

Grogan ignored him and strode through the middle. The cleaner shook his mop at Grogan's retreating back, and the security guard smiled to herself.

Meanwhile, Hal and his mum were saying their goodbyes to Alex.

'I know your dad is angry with us,' said Hal's mum. 'Just remember you're welcome here any time.'

Alex smiled gratefully.

'Will you be all right?' asked Hal. 'At home, I mean?'

'Sure. He gets annoyed when a deal falls through, but then he starts on the next one and everything's fine again.' Alex hesitated. 'Let me know when you're coming to Gyris, okay? I'll show you all the sights.'

Hal glanced at his mum. Was his punishment lifted, or was that visit to A-section going to cost him dearly?

'We'll talk about that later,' she said, her face stern.

Later. Hal's spirits sank. That meant no.

◆

Alex saw his disappointment, and she took the watch off her wrist and held it out. 'Here. This is for you.'

Hal's eyes went round, but he shook his head. 'I can't take that. It's yours.'

'Go on. I insist.'

'But I don't have anything to give you!'

Alex smiled. 'You gave me an adventure. Who could ask for more?'

Slightly dazed, Hal took the watch, which was still warm from her wrist. Then it started flashing, and he almost dropped it.

'Uh-oh, that's my dad. I'd better be going.'

'Goodbye, then.' Hal put his hand out awkwardly, but Alex ignored it and leant in to give him a quick peck on the cheek.

'Until next time,' she whispered, and then she was gone.

Hal turned a bright flaming red, right up to the roots of his hair. Mortified, he glanced at his mum, but she was studying a speck of fluff on her lab coat. Hal breathed a sigh of relief. She hadn't seen a thing!

— 29 —

The new tutor

Hal woke early the next morning, fresh from a nightmare where Reece had been feeding him into the recycling machine. The robot had been pulling levers and cackling to himself, while his extra-large feet went *THUD THUD THUD* on the floor.

Hal shook himself. Hopefully the robot would leave him alone now it had the briefcase back.

Then he remembered . . . his mum had promised to think about the trip to Gyris overnight! Would it be yes or no?

Two minutes later Hal was running along the corridor, his hair a mess and his clothes half done up. He found his mum in the dining room, and she nodded at him as he ran in. 'Remind me to get you another comb,' she remarked, trying to smooth his hair.

'Mum . . . what about the camping trip?'

For a moment her face was stern, and then she smiled. 'It's all right, you can go. We could use the peace and quiet around here.'

'Yes!' Hal pumped his fist. The trip was on!

'There's just one thing. Your dad and I have decided to get you a tutor.'

Hal's face fell. More lessons? At this rate they'd wear his brain out before he got a chance to use it properly!

'We've found someone who will keep you in line. He's very capable, very strict, and he won't take any nonsense. Your grades should improve in no time, and your little exploits will be a thing of the past.'

Worse and worse, thought Hal gloomily. They might as well lock him up in prison! 'Mum, I can learn by myself!'

'I'm sure you can, but it's *what* you're learning that concerns me.' His mum glanced at her watch. 'Let's go to the canteen. There's someone I'd like you to meet.'

All of a sudden Hal put two and two together. A strict tutor who wouldn't take any nonsense ... it couldn't be Reece, could it? Surely not!

They took the lift to the next level, and when the doors opened Hal hesitated before stepping out.

'Don't worry about Reece,' said his mum. 'We

shipped him back to Gyris. They're going to reprogram him as a parking inspector.'

Hal breathed a sigh of relief. Having Reece as a tutor would have been a living nightmare.

'Come on. I want to show you something.'

They turned the corner, and Hal almost fell over when he saw the entire population of the Space Station waiting in the canteen. The tables were laden with every delight Hal could imagine . . . and he could imagine quite a lot. There was a huge ham, glistening under the coloured lights, sliced meats and olives, crusty bread, bowls of salad and fruit, and a huge cake with his name on top. Unable to speak, Hal approached the tables, his eyes round. The crowd gave him three rousing cheers, and he had to turn away because a speck of dirt got into his eye.

The rest of the afternoon was a blur of friendly faces, slaps on the back, hearty handshakes and thank-yous. Everyone was happy and cheerful, including the *two* motorised trolleys who darted through the crowd serving drinks and sweets galore. Carrie gave him a happy beep as she sped past, and Paul showed off his brand new wheel.

Before long Hal had eaten so much food he felt like one of Teacher's math problems: if two grown ups can eat five cakes in three days, how many

361

cakes can one boy eat in an afternoon? About as many as Hal, that was the answer! And then, when he was full to bursting point, he sat back to enjoy the atmosphere.

As he was sitting there he heard footsteps approaching, and he saw a flash of bronze as a tall robot sat next to him. For a second he thought it was Reece, come to get him, but he realised it was a different model altogether. This robot was old and battered, but it had a friendly expression and warm yellow eyes.

'Hello. What's your job?' asked Hal.

'I used to be a pilot,' said the robot, in an even male voice. 'Now I'm a minder.'

'What does that mean?'

'I was hired to look after a particularly troublesome character,' said the robot, with a twinkle in his eye. 'A bit of a tearaway, by all accounts.'

Hal's mother spotted them together. 'I see you've met your new tutor.'

'Tutor!' Hal gaped at the robot. 'You're here for me?'

'Are you Hal Junior?'

'Y-yeah.'

'It's a pleasure to meet you,' said the robot, extending his hand.

They shook. 'Nice to meet you too, er . . . ' Hal eyed the faded black lettering on the robot's chest. 'XG99?'

'Oh, that's just my model name.' The robot smiled, crinkling the plasteel skin around his eyes. 'My friends call me Clunk.'

It was late at night and Hal was lying in bed, gazing through the porthole at the distant stars. His eyelids were drooping and he was struggling to stay awake, but he knew planet Gyris would be moving into view any minute. The planet would only be a bright little speck at this distance, but he still wanted to see it. His dad was there, organising the camping trip, and Alex would be home too. He wondered whether she would bother to look up. Could you see the Space Station from Gyris, or would it just be an insignificant dot in the rich starfield? Could you flash messages back and forth if you had a really bright light?

Moments later a blueish dot came into view at the far right of the porthole, and Hal knelt on the end of his bed to get a better look. His breath misted up the porthole, turning the stars into spiky diamonds, and he wiped it with his pyjama sleeve. There it was again, the rich blue planet he'd be visiting two days from now. Down there they had forests, rivers, mountains and cities with millions of people. They ate rich foods every day, and they could run and play outside. Swimming too, in real water.

The Space Station continued to turn, and the planet moved slowly across Hal's field of view. At that moment he realised it would be fantastic to visit Gyris and experience new adventures, but he could never live there. He belonged in space, and when he was grown up he'd pilot his own ship, just like Captain Spacejock of the Intergalactic Peace Force. Then he'd be able to visit planets at will, stopping wherever he pleased. That was the way to live!

Gyris was on the far left of the porthole now. Hal watched it disappear, then smiled to himself. Two days from now he wouldn't be staring at a tiny dot in space . . . he'd be landing on it. And wouldn't the camping trip be something to remember?

He laid down and pulled the blanket up to his chin, and just before he fell asleep he remembered his new tutor. Clunk said he used to be a pilot, and Hal wondered whether he could talk the robot into a few flying lessons.

Now that would really be something!

Acknowledgements

To Pauline Nolet, to Ian and to Jo and Tricia
thanks for the awesome help and support!

Thanks also to the keen readers
at Rosalie Primary School.

The Gyris Mission

Copyright ©2012 Simon Haynes

Book three in the Hal Junior series

www.haljunior.com

Simon Haynes

Bowman Press

The Hal Junior Series:

The Secret Signal
The Missing Case
The Gyris Mission
The Comet Caper

Simon Haynes also writes the
Hal Spacejock series for teens & adults

... AND the
Harriet Walsh series for teens & adults.

www.spacejock.com.au

369

Dedicated to keen readers everywhere

Hal Junior, accepting a bet,
cooked lunch on a ship's exhaust jet.
His bacon burned, smoking,
The eggs had no yolk in,
And his toast has not been found yet!

— 2 —

My, robot

It was just before dawn, and a large group of Peace Force officers were gathered in the briefing room. They were travelling aboard the Almara, an elderly Battlecruiser which had been disguised as a transport ship. Their mission was simple: take down a gang of pirates who were terrorizing the Lamira system.

The mess doors opened, and a hush fell over the crowd. Standing in the doorway was the most famous, the most impressive and the most capable officer of them all: Captain Hal Spacejock of the Intergalactic Peace Force!

'Morning all,' said Spacejock. 'What's going on here, then?'

Nobody spoke, until a huge bull of a man with a thick neck timidly raised his hand. 'Please sir, we need a battle plan.'

371

'You want a plan? I'll give you a plan!' Spacejock drew himself up to his full height. 'We're going to charge straight in and clean out those dastardly pirates!'

The mess hall erupted with cheers, and –

'Good morning, Hal Junior. And how are we this fine day?'

Hal opened one eye and saw a robot smiling down at him. It had a wrinkly bronze face and bright yellow eyes, and it looked way too cheerful for such an early hour. The robot was Clunk, Hal's new tutor, and it took its job very seriously. 'How can it be morning?' demanded Hal. 'It's still dark.'

'I thought you'd like an early start. You know what day it is, don't you?'

Hal felt a sudden thrill. Of course he did. 'The day of the camping trip. It's finally here?' He leapt out of bed and grabbed the nearest pile of clothes, getting dressed in such a hurry he put both arms down the same sleeve, pulled on odd socks and jammed his shoes on the wrong feet. 'Is the gear ready? I don't want to forget anything.'

'Equipment status a-okay,' said Clunk. 'I spent all night packing and re-packing our things, from tents to sleeping bags to emergency food rations.'

'Wait a minute. What do you mean 'our' things? This is a school trip.'

372

Clunk looked surprised. 'I thought you knew? I'm coming as well.'

Hal groaned. Clunk was all right, as far as robots went, but who wanted to take their tutor on holidays?

'Apart from the packing, I also created some really interesting maths homework. There's nothing better than mental arithmetic when you're sitting around a campfire.'

Hal groaned even louder.

'Are you all right?' asked Clunk. 'Do you have stomach ache? Should I take you to the sickbay?'

'No, I'm fine,' said Hal, trying not to laugh at Clunk's expression. Robots didn't get sick, and illness in humans always worried them. 'You're not really coming to Gyris, are you?'

'Of course. Now, do you want to check the bags?'

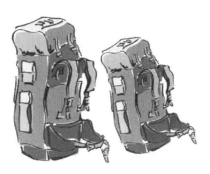

Hal followed Clunk to the doorway, where there were two bulging rucksacks. Clunk opened the bigger one and displayed a roll of clear plastic and a bundle of metal poles. 'They didn't give me a tent, so I made my own.'

'What else do you have?'

'I brought all your winter clothing.'

'Clunk, it's summer down there.'

'It might be cold at night.'

'What if it's really hot?'

'That's all right, because I have all your summer clothing too. And three pairs of pyjamas, and that dressing gown you like. You know, the one with the teddy bear on the side.'

Hal stared at him in horror. 'I used to wear that when I was five. You didn't really pack it, did you?'

'Of course. It's warm and cosy.'

'You have to get rid of it. Take it out of right now, or I'll never speak to you again.'

'Don't worry, you can always use it as a pillow.'

Hal resolved to throw it out the first chance he got. 'What else did you bring? A big packet of nappies? Baby food?'

'Of course not. There's a solar-powered charger, in case my batteries need topping up, and I have all your old schoolwork. I thought we could go over your completed assignments and see where you went wrong. For example, there was one on heavy metals which . . . '

Hal started to groan, then turned it into a cough.

'That's it,' said Clunk. 'We're off to the sickbay right now.'

'Clunk, I'm fine. It was just a bit of dust.'

The robot looked at him suspiciously, and Hal put on his most innocent expression. 'Very well, but if you so much as sniff I'm taking you for a full medical.'

'If you do, I'll miss the camping trip.'

'If you're unwell, the camping trip is out of the question.'

'For the last time, I am not sick!'

'There's no need to take that tone with me. Now, are you feeling well enough for a proper breakfast or would you prefer dry bread and a glass of water?'

Hal groaned.

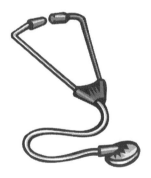

In the sickbay, the doctor got Hal to walk through the med scanner before giving them her diagnosis: all clear. Clunk frowned, and got her to put Hal through the big machine again, and after the third time the doctor struggled to keep her temper. 'I'm telling you, there is nothing wrong with this child,' she said, annoyed. 'He's fitter than I am.'

'But he keeps groaning,' protested Clunk. 'There was even . . . a cough.'

The doctor frowned at Hal over her glasses. 'Are you trying to get a sick note? Avoid school?'

'No chance,' said Hal. 'I'm going camping.'

'Well, have a nice time.' The doctor rang a little bell. 'Next patient, please.'

Clunk was silent as they left the sickbay. He didn't like being wrong, and he was convinced the doctor's machine hadn't analysed Hal properly. 'I still believe she rushed your DNA test.'

'Clunk, she's a doctor. Even if you don't believe me, you have to believe her. I am not sick.'

The robot sighed noisily.

'Was that an air leak?' asked Hal mischievously. 'Should I take you to the repair centre for a checkup?'

Clunk smiled apologetically. 'I'm sorry, Hal. I take my job very seriously.'

'I take breakfast seriously, and I'm missing it.'

— 3 —

Departure

'Would all students please report to passenger lounge two. I repeat, would all students please report to passenger lounge two without delay.' There was a pause. 'That means you, Hal Junior.'

Hal pushed his plate back and jumped up. 'Come on, Clunk. We're off.'

'You haven't finished your breakfast.'

'That's all right, you can have it.'

Clunk started to object, but Hal was already in the corridor. When Hal looked back, he saw Clunk struggling to follow with the heavy rucksacks.

Hal ran through the Space Station's corridors at top speed, taking his favourite shortcuts and the fastest elevators. Each time he stepped out of a lift he pressed the top and bottom buttons, sending it to the Station's highest and lowest levels. With a bit of luck, Clunk would still be waiting for a lift when the passenger ship left the space station.

Hal finally arrived at the passenger lounge, where he found the rest of his class sitting on benches. Teacher was there, and the little red robot was darting around as he tried to keep an electronic eye on the children. There were also three parents, volunteers who were coming along to help out on the camping trip.

'Hal, over here. I saved you a seat!'

Hal saw his best friend Stephen 'Stinky' Binn waving like mad, and he hurried over to sit next to him.

'Where have you been?' demanded Stinky. 'We're leaving any second.'

'Clunk took me to the sickbay,' explained Hal.

'More groaning, huh? I warned you about that.'

'I coughed, too.'

'You're lucky he didn't take you to intensive care.'

Hal saw Clunk in the doorway, and he ducked his head. 'Don't tell him I'm here.'

Stinky watched the robot's progress, giving Hal a running commentary. 'He's asking Teacher about you. Now Teacher's looking around. Oh, he's seen you. Now they're both coming over.'

Hal sat up. 'Hi Teacher. Are we leaving now?'

'Hal Junior, why is your tutor here?'

Hal couldn't answer many of Teacher's questions,

but he knew the answer to this one. 'Clunk is here to teach me.'

Teacher frowned. 'I meant here, here. Present in this room, and carrying two rucksacks. Why?'

'He offered to carry them. They're heavy.'

'Yes, but why is he here?'

'Er, to teach me?'

'Here, here, here!' said Teacher, jabbing his finger at the floor to emphasise each word.

'You mean here?' said Hal.

'Here!'

'He's coming with us.'

'Thank you, that's what I thought.' Teacher turned to Clunk. 'I'm afraid there's been a misunderstanding. You cannot go on this trip.'

Clunk stared. 'But . . . I have to look after Hal.'

'Hal Junior will be supervised, just like the other students.'

'I already packed a bag, and a battery charger, and a big umbrella to keep the rain off. I even made my own tent.'

Teacher shook his head. 'The students must learn to cope on their own. They're travelling without robots.'

'So how come you're going?' demanded Clunk.

'I'm not. I'm staying here.'

Hal stared. No tutor and no Teacher? This was going to be the best trip ever!

'But Hal's homework . . . ' began Clunk.

'There will be no homework.'

'His revision . . . '

'No revision.'

By now Hal was grinning from ear to ear.

Clunk's shoulders slumped, and his expression was downcast. 'I'm not needed?'

'Oh, you're very much needed,' said Teacher. 'Next week Hal Junior will need double homework to catch up.'

'Get set, people. We're moving out in five!'

Captain Spacejock's assault team checked their weapons, inspecting battery levels and charge leads. Around them, the docking bay was piled high with equipment, and the boarding tunnel gaped like a giant mouth. Any moment now they'd board the landing craft, and –

'Teacher, Hal Junior keeps pushing me!'

Hal blinked, and the daydream faded. He'd just been reloading a really cool blast rifle, and in the process his elbow had rammed someone in the ribs.

Teacher rolled towards him, every eye on his electronic face focused on Hal. 'Hal Junior, if you cause any more trouble you'll stay behind. Is that clear?'

Hal nodded and crossed his arms. The class was still waiting in the passenger lounge next to the Space Station's docking bay. There were three rows of bench seats, but they weren't big enough for two dozen active children, and complaints came thick and fast. Teacher sped from one incident to the next, trying to maintain order, but eventually the little robot snapped. He screeched to a halt at the front of the room and turned his voice to maximum volume.

'Listen to me!' he roared, shaking the walls with the sound of his voice.

Everyone froze, and there was instant silence.

'I know you've been looking forward to this camping trip for weeks, but the next person to make a fuss will stay right here on the Space Station with me. Instead of camping, you'll be studying!'

Hal realised Teacher was looking at him, and he swallowed nervously. He'd already been banned from the trip once, after the practice campfire incident*, and getting excluded a second time would be unbearable.

'One raised voice, one complaint, one incident, and I won't hesitate to ban any of you from the trip. Is that clear?'

The entire class spoke as one. 'Yes, Teacher!'

'Thank you. Now sit tight and be patient. I'm sure the transport will be ready soon.'

Hal glanced at his big silver space watch. They were supposed to have left at nine, and it was already eleven o'clock. First the ship had been late, and then there'd been refuelling problems, and now they were just waiting around. Morning snacks, meant to be eaten later, had been finished off long ago, and all their luggage had already gone aboard so they had nothing to keep them busy.

'I have an exciting idea,' said Teacher brightly. 'Who'd like to answer a few math questions?'

Hal groaned, then looked around quickly in case Clunk had heard him. Fortunately the robot wasn't there.

Teacher projected the first sums on the wall, and Stinky was just revealing the answers when the doors opened with a *whisshhh*.

A woman in a grey flightsuit looked in. 'Get set, people. We're moving out in five!'

---

* *Hal Junior: The Missing Case*

— 4 —

Boarding

The next few minutes passed in a blur. One moment they were saying goodbye to Teacher, and the next they were escorted out of the lounge by the parents who were supervising the trip. Hal was secretly glad his own parents weren't going. His dad was in charge of the Space Station's air filters, and he was too busy to take a week off. As for Hal's mum, she was the Station's chief scientist, and she couldn't possibly spare a week away from the laboratory.

Hal didn't mind at all. No parents meant more freedom!

The class trooped along the boarding tunnel and navigated the airlock at the far end. They had to go through in batches, because the airlock wasn't big enough for everyone. On the other side, an official from the space station showed them through a pair of doors. Inside, there was a lounge set up like a small cinema: thick carpeting, comfortable chairs arranged in rows, and a big screen at the front. Hal's heart sank as he saw the heavy curtains along both sides. He'd expected a good view of the stars, but it looked like they were going to get movies all the way to Gyris. Then he had a horrible thought . . . what if Teacher had chosen a bunch of educational documentaries as their 'entertainment'?

Hal came up with a plan. If they were forced to watch documentaries, he and Stinky would ask to go to the toilet. Once on their own, they'd explore the whole ship. If anyone from the crew spotted them, he'd use the old 'sorry, we got lost' excuse. It was amazing how often that worked, almost as though adults expected kids to get lost all the time.

Hal turned to explain his plan to Stinky, but at that moment the lights went out and the screen came alive.

'Welcome aboard the Antigone, a state-of-the-art passenger transport with every known comfort.' The screen displayed a series of animations, showing the spaceship from the outside, before zooming in on the passenger lounge. 'In the unlikely event of an emergency, please make your way to the escape pods.' Arrows showed the exit route, taking the elevator down to an area with a dozen red dots. The flashing dots separated from the ship and flew into space. 'Each pod carries four people, and contains two weeks' worth of food and water. An emergency beacon will help rescue ships locate and retrieve each pod.'

Hal watched the video with interest. So, if they were attacked by a fleet of space pirates, and the Antigone was blown to smithereens, he could use one of those cool pods to get away. Then he could get hold of some ships, lead a daring raid on the pilot base to take over all their ships, and then, before you knew it, he'd rule the galaxy.

'For your comfort,' continued the video, 'toilets are located just outside the passenger lounge. Please note that all other parts of the vessel are off-limits.'

Hal's eyes narrowed. It was going to be pretty hard to get 'lost' when the toilets were that close, but he'd come up with some excuse. Maybe he could tell them he was looking for a glass of water!

'Refreshments are served automatically, via the dispenser in your armrest. Each passenger will be issued with a sterilised feeding tube after departure. Alcoholic beverages will not be served to minors.'

Hal lifted the lid on his armrest and looked inside. There was a touch screen and a silver connector with a hole in the middle. He tried the screen but it beeped and displayed a message:

Status: Inactive. Refreshments only available in flight.

'And now, please settle back for this screening of 'Attack the Summit!', a popular documentary on mountain climbing.'

Hal groaned. Popular was right ... Teacher showed the same film every week. It had been pretty cool the first time Hal saw it, and it was still interesting the second time around, but after half a dozen showings he was desperate for a different ending. An avalanche, for example, or a wild Yeti. But no, every time it was the same.

Before the documentary started, the words 'NEWS FLASH' appeared, and the screen showed a smartly-dressed lady with glasses. 'This message is for all ships landing on planet Gyris. Two criminals are on the run after holding up a bank. The fugitives stole a low-orbital flyer to make their escape, and they're considered armed and dangerous.'

The screen changed to show grainy footage of two people in balaclavas. They were carrying a couple of heavy boxes, and they kicked open the bank doors before running out of view.

'Members of the public are warned to keep clear. Do not approach these vicious criminals, and please call the Peace Force if you have any information. Anyone helping these fugitives escape justice will be locked up right alongside them.'

Hal glanced at Stinky. 'I wonder if there's a reward?'

'Don't even think about it.'

At that moment the lights went out, and the screen glowed in the darkness. 'Attack the Summit' was beginning. Hal nudged Stinky, then nodded towards the exit. His friend frowned and shook his head, but Hal wasn't taking no for an answer. They got up and pushed their way along the row, treading on feet and stumbling over stray shins. A minor commotion followed them across the room, and one of the parents turned to see what was happening. Hal ducked, pulling Stinky down with him, and they peered between the seats until the adult turned away.

They reached the door, and as the dramatic title

387

music washed over the audience, Hal operated the controls and slipped through. Stinky followed, and the door closed with a whish!

'What are you playing at?' demanded Stinky. 'We'll miss the movie!'

Hal made a rude noise. 'I'll never miss that movie again. For my entire life. Ever.'

'Teacher does play it a lot,' admitted his friend.

'A lot! I could climb that stupid mountain blindfolded.'

Stinky laughed. 'So what's the plan?'

'We're aboard a spaceship, right?'

'Yes, I kind of knew that.'

'We're going to explore.'

'But Hal . . . we could get into trouble! Teacher might –'

'Teacher isn't here, is he?' Hal jabbed his finger at the door. 'Those parents will believe any excuse we feed them. Now stop yabbering and start exploring.'

— 5 —

Exploring

Hal scanned the signs on the wall outside the lounge. Opposite there were two doors with toilet symbols. To his right was the airlock they'd used to board the ship. To his left ... well, that was the door which interested Hal the most. It had a sign reading 'No Admittance', and there was a keypad at shoulder height. The display on the keypad was broken, and half the numbers had worn away. There were wires hanging out of the keypad, and Hal eyed them in concern. 'Do you think it's working?'

'Someone bypassed it,' said Stinky. 'That's an RT-3D, the one with the defective security chip.'

Hal smiled to himself. Stinky lived and breathed electronics, and half the time he suspected his friend was a robot in disguise. 'Can you open it?'

'Sure. Purple wire crossed with orange. Watch.'

Hal's dad often told him how dangerous electricity could be, warning him never to play with bare wires. However, Stinky had already completed two certificates in electronics, and he knew what he was doing. At least, Hal hoped he did. 'Will it go bang?'

'Of course not. These are data wires, not electrical.' Stinky touched the wires together, and the door slid open. Beyond was a short corridor with three more doors: elevator, flight deck and galley.

Hal loved to study spaceship diagrams in his spare time, and he knew the galley was where food was prepared. He also knew he wasn't going to waste exploring time looking at kitchen equipment. That left the flight deck and the elevator. Now, exploring the flight deck would be cool, but there was one tiny problem: that's where the crew of highly-trained pilots would be.

So, the only door they could use was the elevator. Hal hesitated for a moment, his finger over the call button. Going further into the ship was bound to lead to trouble, and they could still return to the lounge. Then he smiled. They were already on their way to Gyris. Nobody could send him home again.

He pressed the button, and the doors opened slowly. The lift was big enough for eight or ten people, and the walls were dented and battered. There was a security camera in one corner of the roof, but it was dangling by the cord and the lens was missing.

Hal inspected the control panel, which had three buttons. He was on the upper deck now, and the others read 'Middle Deck' and 'Lower Deck'. None of them offered any clues as to what he might find on each level, but Hal didn't mind. Anything was better than watching Teacher's documentaries!

He pressed the button for the Middle Deck, and the lift started to move. As it squeaked and groaned its way to the next level, Hal checked his watch. The documentary ran for about thirty minutes, and he'd left the lounge five minutes ago. That left . . . lots of minutes to explore.

$$30 - 5 = LOTS!$$

The doors opened and Hal peeked out. He saw a long corridor with several doors on either side, and a dirty yellow carpet on the floor. It wasn't very promising, and he was about to press the third button when he noticed a sign on one of the doors: Escape pods. 'Hey, these were in the safety video.'

'Indeed,' said Stinky. 'Safety pods are essential aboard space ships. Only the most careless pilot would travel without one.'

'Captain Spacejock doesn't use a sissy escape pod.'

Stinky rolled his eyes. Hal's fixation with Captain Spacejock was a running joke in class. 'I suppose your precious captain can breath without air?'

'Of course. He's generally modified.'

Stinky looked puzzled. 'He's what?'

'He had his trousers altered,' explained Hal. 'You know, like Teacher was telling us.'

Hal's explanation only had Stinky more confused. 'How does altering your trousers help you breath in space?'

'They're not just any trousers. Captain Spacejock has special jeans.'

Stinky started to laugh, and before long he was gasping for breath, tears in his eyes. 'It's not 'generally modified',' he said, when he'd got his breath back. 'It's genetically modified! Genes, not jeans.'

'That's what I said,' snapped Hal, aggrieved.

'Okay, okay,' said Stinky. 'There's no need to get ... shirty.' He snorted at the joke, and then he was laughing again, leaning against the wall for support.

Hal abandoned his friend and strode towards the escape pod doors. In the training video the pods had shot about like mini space fighters, and Hal figured it would be cool to see one up close. The sign said 'pods 1-6', while the door on the opposite side had 'pods 7-12'. Each door had a control panel with a single button, and Hal pressed one and waited.

Nothing happened.

'Maybe you have the wrong jeans on,' called Stinky, and he fell about laughing again.

Scowling, Hal thumped the button. The door remained closed, so he turned to the opposite side and pressed that button instead.

Whoosh!

This door opened immediately, revealing a semi-circular room with half a dozen silver doors in the opposite wall. They were evenly-spaced, and each had a status panel alongside. Five of the panels glowed green, while the last was red. Hal strode to the nearest door and studied the panel. There were buttons marked 'open' and 'close', and there was a red safety cap covering a third button marked 'launch'. The status display said 'System Okay' in bright green letters.

Hal hesitated, then pressed the Open button. The door slid up with a Whissh!, and he looked down into the pod. The walls were padded, and there was a bench seat running all the way around. In the middle was a round console, and four heavy-duty harnesses dangled from the ceiling. It looked comfortable and cosy, and Hal almost wished there could be an emergency so they could use the pods to fly through space. Nothing dangerous, just a minor problem like a killer asteroid or heavily-armed space aliens.

'Hal, what are you doing?' hissed Stinky, from the safety of the doorway. He'd stopped laughing, and was now looking worried. 'You can't play with this stuff. It's dangerous.'

Hal decided to punish his friend for laughing at him, and before Stinky could intervene he'd stepped down into the pod. Hal sat on the chair and fitted the harness, tightening the straps until he could barely move. The central console was just out of reach, but he could still read some of the controls: 'Open', 'close' and 'launch' buttons, along with several others labelled 'recycle', 'gravity' and 'boosters'.

Stinky's face appeared in the doorway. 'Hal, come out of there at once!'

'No, I think I'll take it for a spin,' said Hal. 'That'd be fun.'

'Hal! I'll tell!'

Hal glanced at his watch, then stared. Twenty minutes gone already! That only left them . . . several minutes to explore the rest of the ship.

30 - 20 = SEVERAL!

He undid the straps and climbed out of the pod, pausing only to press the 'Close' button.

'Let's go back now,' said Stinky. All traces of laughter were gone, and he looked worried.

'Nonsense. There's more to see.'

'But –'

Hal walked away. He was still smarting from Stinky's laughter, and he was enjoying getting his own back on his friend. Back in the corridor, he turned away from the lift and hurried along the mustard-yellow carpet. The roar of the engines got louder, and the doors he passed were labelled 'Starboard access' and 'Main power bus'. Finally, at the rear, there was a big metal door stamped 'Engine Bay'. There was also a warning sign underneath: 'Very Dangerous! No admittance without safety clothing.'

Hal was keen to explore, but he wasn't completely stupid. There were plenty of places aboard Space Station Oberon where you needed hazard suits, and he knew to stay well clear of them. That just left the lower deck to explore.

— 6 —

Crackle

The lower deck was more like Hal's idea of a genuine spaceship, with dim lighting and stark metal walls. The roof was low, and dusty wires and cables ran along channels under the floor.

Crackle-zzit! Crackle-zzzziit!

Flickering sparks bathed the corridor in harsh blue light, and Hal noticed a strong electrical smell.

'This doesn't look very safe,' remarked Stinky.

Hal gestured impatiently. 'It's a spaceship. It's not supposed to be safe.'

Crackle-zziit!

'Let's go back to the lounge,' said Stinky. 'Please, Hal. They'll notice we're missing.'

'I'm not going back until we've explored the whole ship.'

'But Hal!'

Hal ignored his friend and strode along the

corridor. He told himself it couldn't be that dangerous, or they wouldn't let people walk around down here. Then he remembered the 'No Admittance' sign on the upper deck, and swallowed. They didn't let people walk around down here. He and Stinky were trespassing.

Crackle-zziittt!

A blue flash illuminated a grubby sign on the wall. Hal brushed dirt off the sign, which said 'Maintenance'. He touched the controls and the door grated open. Inside, there was a status panel, the screen rolling and flickering like Teacher's face when he was trying to read one of Hal's essays. Hal tapped the screen, and it sat still long enough for him to read the display:

Port engine: Inoperative
Life support: No data
Fuel: marginal
Power: error code 19
Toilets: blocked
Status: situation normal

Hal grabbed his friend and dragged him to the maintenance alcove, and they both studied the display. From the look of all the warning messages, the ship was seconds from a major meltdown.

'This looks serious,' said Stinky.

'Too right. We have to warn someone.'

'I bet they already know,' said Stinky. 'The pilots will have the same display in the flight deck.'

'Maybe they haven't seen the warnings.' Hal had a thought, and he gripped Stinky's arm. 'Maybe they've fainted! Maybe aliens have captured them! Maybe we'll have to fly the ship to Gyris and land it!'

'Maybe you should give your imagination a holiday,' said Stinky drily.

'Let's go and tell the pilots about the error messages. They might let us sit in the flight deck.'

For once, Stinky didn't object, and the two boys took the lift to the upper deck. When the doors opened they hurried to the flight deck entrance, where they saw a sign written in big red letters:

Crew Only!
No Passengers Allowed!

Underneath, in thick blue marker, someone had written This Means You!

Hal was just reaching for the controls when Stinky stopped him. 'What?'

'Hal, we can't. We'll have to tell them we went to the lower deck.'

Hal thought for a moment. 'We'll say we got lost. All these passages look the same.'

'They know we live on a Space Station.'

Stinky had a point. The Space Station had five sections, each filled with endless lifts and corridors. If the boys could navigate something that complex, nobody would believe they could get lost aboard a tiny passenger ship. 'All right. We'll tell them we heard that buzz-crackle noise.'

'What, two decks up?'

'We have very good hearing.'

'It would have to be supersonic,' muttered Stinky.

'What was that?'

'Nothing.'

Hal took a deep breath and used the controls. The doors parted with a loud Whish!, and the two boys peered in. They saw a flight console covered in instruments, a big screen covered in charts and figures, two big pilot chairs and . . . no pilots.

'It's aliens!' breathed Hal. 'They've captured the crew!'

— 7 —

Asleep at the wheel

Bzzzz-glglglgl! Bzzzz-glglglgl!

Hal's eyes were as round as an airlock door. The weird sounds were coming from the back of the flightdeck, where a huddled mass was slumped against the wall.

Bzzzz-glglglgl!

Was it an alien monster, telling them to put their hands up? Was it a deadly sound weapon that would scramble their brains?

'Oh look, it's the pilot,' said Stinky, peering into the darkness. 'He's fast asleep.'

That awful noise was the pilot's snoring? Hal couldn't believe it. So much for alien invasions and sound weapons.

'We'd better wake him,' whispered Stinky. 'Nobody's flying the ship.'

'Somebody is.' Hal nodded towards the big screen, which had the words 'Autopilot Active' in the corner.

'What about all the error messages we saw on the lower deck?'

Hal hadn't forgotten about them, but he didn't want to wake the pilot. First, because the flight deck was calm and peaceful, as though everything were under control. And second, because there were two empty pilot chairs and two sets of controls just begging to be used. 'I'm captain,' muttered Hal out the corner of his mouth. 'You're my second in command.'

Stinky frowned. 'What are you planning now?'

'Let's pretend the pilot really was kidnapped. Let's pretend we have to fly the ship.'

'Let's not,' said Stinky quickly.

But Hal wasn't listening. He crossed the flight deck in three strides and turned the pilot's chair to the side.

'You can't!' hissed Stinky. 'You mustn't!'

'Watch me,' muttered Hal, and he sat down at the controls. His eyes shone as he scanned the status displays, lights and toggle switches, and there was a huge grin on his face when he spotted the flight controls. There was a joystick with a big red button on top, and two sliding throttles to control the engines. Excellent!

Stinky crept closer. He wasn't as bold as Hal, but he was just as interested in spaceships, and the chance to sit at the controls was too tempting. In a flash he was sitting in the second chair.

'Right,' said Hal. 'Let's explore the galaxy.'

Hal and Stinky spent ten glorious minutes pretending to fly the passenger ship. They roamed all over the galaxy, with Stinky capturing alien planets and battlecruisers, while Hal claimed two dozen worlds for Queen Alexandra of Gyris. They were having so much fun it was a pity it had to end, but they realised they had to get back to the passenger lounge before the documentary ended.

'If they stick another film on I'm coming right back,' whispered Hal.

Stinky nodded, his eyes shining.

The pilot was still snoring behind them, lost to the world, and Hal hoped he stayed that way for the entire trip. Imagine if they could sit in the flight deck while the ship approached Gyris! And if

403

the pilot slept through the whole thing, they could maybe even watch the landing. What a start to their camping trip!

The boys turned their chairs away from the controls and prepared to step down. Hal put a hand on the console to steady himself, and his fingers brushed a row of switches.

'Autopilot disabled,' said a calm female voice. *'You have manual control.'*

Hal froze, then slowly turned to look at the screen. It no longer said 'Autopilot Active' in the corner, and the stars weren't nice and still either . . . in fact, they were moving across the big screen. The ship was turning, and nobody was at the controls. If they kept this up they might end up back at the Orbiter, or lost in space!

Stinky gulped, and both boys stared at the console in horror. The pilot would know how to fix things, but if they woke him up they'd have to explain what they'd been doing in the flight deck. On the other hand, if they tried to activate the autopilot themselves, they could make things a whole lot worse.

Then Hal remembered something. He'd once toured a spaceship with the rest of his class, and the ship's computer had obeyed voice commands. He felt a rush of relief, and keeping his voice down he spoke the necessary words: 'A-activate autopilot.'

'*Access denied,*' said the ship's computer.

'Please?' said Hal.

'*Access denied.*'

Hal frowned. The ship would only obey the pilot . . . or his voice, at any rate. There was no easy fix after all. Cautiously he scanned the instruments on the console, looking for one which said 'Autopilot'. Unfortunately they were all blank.

'What are we going to do?' hissed Stinky. 'Should we wake him up?'

Hal considered it, but he knew the punishment would be huge. Instead of camping, they'd probably spend the week in detention - or worse. If only he hadn't jogged the stupid controls! Then he got an idea. He'd touched the controls when he climbed down from the pilot's chair, so why not do the same thing again? If he got it exactly right, his fingers would brush the same controls, and the autopilot would come back on.

Hal climbed into the pilot's chair and put his hands on the console.

'You're not going to fly it?' muttered Stinky. 'Please, Hal. We're already –'

'Just watch,' said Hal. He swung the chair and put his hand firmly on the console, trying to duplicate his earlier movements. His fingers pressed on half a dozen buttons, and as he leapt down from the chair, the computer spoke:

'*Airlocks sealed. Docking clamps activated. Landing lights on. Seatbelt warning signs on. Inflight movie terminated.*'

'Oh no,' breathed Stinky. 'Hal, you've really done it now!'

— 8 —

Lessons

At that moment Hal noticed something missing. He turned this way and that, trying to work out what it was, and then it dawned on him. The pilot had stopped snoring!

'H-he's waking up,' muttered Stinky, who'd noticed the same thing.

The pilot started to roll over, and Hal eyed the door. Could they run out quickly before they were spotted?

No.

The pilot sat up, rubbing sleep from his eyes. He blinked once or twice, then frowned as he spotted Hal and Stinky. His gaze travelled from the boys, to the flight console, and back to the boys. The pilot had a mane of black hair and a neat goatee shot through with grey, and when he stood up he towered over the boys.

'I can explain,' said Hal.

The pilot ignored him. 'Ann, set the autopilot.'

'Complying,' said the computer.

Hal glanced at the screen. The stars were now moving in the other direction, and the words 'Autopilot activated' were back. They weren't going to fly into a star, or return to the orbiter, which was good news. Unfortunately Hal and Stinky were in for a rough landing of their own. 'I'm sorry,' said Hal. 'We –'

'Don't worry about it,' said the pilot, with a casual wave of his hand. 'There's nothing to crash into out here.'

'But I –'

'You ever flown a ship before?'

'No.'

'Take a seat, both of you.'

Hal and Stinky exchanged a glance. They were expecting a huge telling off, but the pilot didn't seem to mind them being there. 'Are you sure? I mean, we should probably get back to the lounge.'

'Go on, hop up.' The pilot addressed the computer again. 'Ann, show 'em the one about the aliens and the teleporter network.'

'Complying.'

For a moment Hal thought they were going to

watch a movie, then realised 'them' meant the rest of the group in the passenger lounge.

'That'll keep them quiet for a bit,' said the pilot. 'Now, let's start your flying lesson. The first thing you have to remember is this: a spaceship is nothing like an aeroplane. When you point the nose of an aircraft, the rest of the plane tends to follow. So, if you pull back on the stick, the nose goes up and the plane climbs. However, no matter where you point a spaceship, it keeps hurtling along in the same direction. When you use the controls you're just spinning the ship around, and the only way to get it to move on the new heading is to fire the thrusters. Is that clear?'

Stinky nodded. Hal shook his head.

'Ann, show them the flight dynamics video.'

'Complying.'

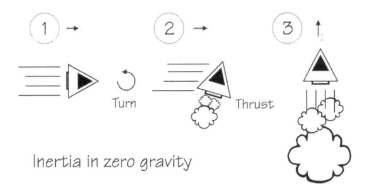

Inertia in zero gravity

Hal watched the animation and understood

immediately. Why couldn't Teacher show them videos to explain math problems? That would make school work so much easier!

'Got it now?' asked the pilot.

Hal nodded.

'Okay. Ann, turn the autopilot off.'

'Autopilot deactivated.'

'Why is your computer called Ann?' asked Stinky.

'Tell him, Ann.'

'I'm a node in the Automated Nagivation Network, or ANN for short.'

'She's connected to the local navigational system,' said the pilot. 'She knows where we are at all times.'

'Can you . . . can you jump between stars?'

'Not this tub. It's strictly a local ferry. Of course, a few years back . . . ' The pilot's voice tailed off and he stared at the screen, lost in thought.

Hal finally remembered his manners. 'Um, what's your name?' he asked.

The pilot blinked, then stuck out his hand. 'Kent Spearman at your service.'

Hal and Stinky introduced themselves. 'How come you didn't tell us off?' asked Stinky. 'We could have flown your ship right into the sun!'

Spearman shrugged. 'Ann's controlling the ship. She'd stop any funny business like that.'

'But we're not supposed to be here.'

Hal wanted to clamp his hand over Stinky's mouth. Was his friend trying to get them punished?

However, Kent didn't seem to mind. 'If it was that important I'd have locked the door. Truth is, I often let passengers into the flight deck. Space can get pretty boring.'

'Have you flown a lot?' asked Hal.

'Absolutely. I used to run a passenger liner called the Luna Rose. Then there was a freighter called the Tiger.'

Hal started. 'But . . . I know that one! The Tiger was damaged, and we joined it to the space station.'

Spearman shook his head. 'It wouldn't be the same one. Tiger is a common name . . . I guess people like strong names for their ships. You don't get many Fluffies or Bunnies.'

Hal winced at the thought. Imagine a spaceship called the Fluffy Bunny! You'd be laughed at wherever you went.

'You can go too far the other way,' said Spearman.

'I knew a guy once, he had a ship called the Volante. Talk about pretentious!'

'What's pretun … pretin … '

'Show off,' said Stinky.

'I am not!' said Hal indignantly.

'No, the word. Pretentious means show off.'

'Correct.' Spearman smiled. 'He was called Hal too. It's funny, but you even look a bit like him.'

Hal wasn't interested in old pilots. He wanted to fly the ship! 'So how do you loop the loop in this thing?'

'Let's try a few basic exercises first.'

Hal frowned. That was one of Teacher's favourite phrases, and the exercises were never basic!

'Stephen, you go first. Move the controls to port - that's left - and keep an eye on the heading indicator. If you push too far the bubble will go into the red zone, and that puts a strain on the ship.'

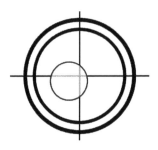

Stinky did as he was told, and the nose of the ship swung to the left.

'Good. Now your turn, Hal. Try moving the ship the other way.'

Hal took hold of the flight controls. The plastic was cool to the touch, and the grips were worn where pilots had spent countless hours flying the old ship. They were heavy, but they moved smoothly to the right. The stars on the main screen slowed down, stopped, then slid across the screen in the opposite direction. He was doing it! He was flying the ship!

'Good. Now let's try –'

'Status warning,' said Ann suddenly. 'Temperature spike in the starboard engine.'

Spearman reacted instantly, hauling Stinky out of the co-pilot's chair so he could take his place. His fingers flew over the controls and his eyes scanned the displays and status screens. Hal was impressed by his skill, although he was less certain about the worried look on the pilot's face. In fact, Spearman was frantically using the controls as though their lives depended on it.

'Sorry lads, lesson's over. You'll have to go back to the passenger lounge.'

'Is there a problem?'

'Nothing I can't handle. Now go!'

Hal slid out of the chair, and he and Stinky retreated to the back of the flight deck. From behind, Spearman looked like a hyperactive octopus playing three piano concertos at once - his arms flew over the console, and streams of text zoomed across the main screen. A lot of the writing was in red, and Hal couldn't help noticing words like 'Error' and 'Warning' and 'Danger'.

'I said go!' shouted Kent, when he realised they were still there.

Hal and Stinky fled, and the flight deck door thudded to behind them.

— 9 —

Lifeboats

Hal and Stinky went back to the lounge, where they sneaked back to their seats under cover of darkness. The movie looked pretty cool, with a fleet of huge alien ships chasing one little fighter in and out of an asteroid field. The fighter jinked left, and Hal gasped as a burst of gunfire shattered a rock, blowing fragments across the screen with a loud 'boom!'

There was a second explosion, and this time the whole floor shook. Hal grinned in delight as smoke drifted across the screen. Talk about realistic special effects! It even stank like a real fire!

At that moment the screen went dark. Dim red emergency lights came on, and several people cried out in alarm. Hal glanced at Stinky, who was flapping at the smoke with both hands. 'What do you think happened?'

'Some kind of power failure,' said Stinky. 'We should probably –'

Hal never found out what his friend was going to suggest, because at that moment Kent Spearman's voice crackled through the overhead speakers.

'This is your pilot speaking. Folks, we have a small problem in the engine bay. It's nothing to worry about, but I'd like you to make your way to the escape pods right now. And whatever you do, don't forget to –'

The speaker and the emergency lighting cut out at the exact same moment, leaving the passenger lounge in total darkness. 'Don't forget to what?' shouted a voice nearby.

Several people cried out in panic, and Hal decided to take charge. 'Listen up. Me and Stinky know where the escape pods are. Follow us, and we'll lead you right to them.'

There were lots of cries of 'how?' and 'no chance!', but Hal and Stinky managed to convince the doubters. They opened the double doors, and the corridor light outside flickered and flashed like a red strobe. For a moment Hal suspected the lift might be out of action, and he was relieved to see the control panel shining with a steady glow. Unfortunately, they would need three or four trips to get everyone down to the next deck. 'Stinky, you take the first lot,' said Hal importantly. 'Show them how the pods work and get them seated. And remember, don't put anyone in that broken pod.'

Stinky nodded, and between them they guided the first batch into the lift. The four parent volunteers hung back, trying to comfort some of the smaller children.

'Don't worry,' said Hal, as the lift doors closed. 'I've met the pilot. He knows exactly what to do.'

The lift came back empty, and Hal herded the next group of children in. Once the doors closed there were only six people left, including himself, Stinky and two of the adults.

'How do you know so much about the ship?' asked a short, balding man. He was comforting his daughter, a girl called Natalie who often gave Hal grief in class.

'I . . . studied the plans.' Hal glanced towards the flight deck doors.

417

'Like *you* ever studied anything,' said Natalie.

Her dad shushed her. 'This young man is helping.'

'Like *he* ever helped anyone,' muttered Natalie, quieter this time.

Hal made a face at her, and then the lift came back and he waved everyone on board. 'Stinky, show them to the escape pods.'

'What about you?'

'I have to do something.'

Natalie's dad frowned. 'We're not leaving you behind. Get in.'

Hal didn't have time to argue. He stepped into the lift, pressed the middle button, and stepped out again just before the doors snapped together. Then, as the lift carried others away, he hurried to the flight deck. Inside, Kent Spearman was still working the controls. The main screen was almost entirely covered in red, and alarms whined and buzzed and clattered from the console.

'What are you doing here?' demanded the pilot. 'I told you to clear out!'

'I came to help.'

'What can you do?' Spearman gestured at the screen. 'This thing is toast!'

'Is the ship going to crash?'

'No, there's nothing to hit out here.'

'Why the panic then?'

'One of the engines blew up, and the other one's on fire. The extinguishers failed, and ten minutes from now this entire ship will be a smoking ruin.'

Hal gulped.

'I'm about to launch the escape pods,' said Kent. 'You need to be on one.'

'What about you?'

'My job is to fight the fire. There's still a tiny chance, but if that fails I'll be taking the last pod.'

There was a terrific explosion, and Hal was knocked off his feet. A siren wailed, and as he got up again he saw 'Abandon Ship!' plastered across the main screen in blood-red letters.

'You should have left earlier,' muttered Spearman. 'Ann, launch the pods.'

'Complying.'

There was a moment of silence and then . . . w*hoosh - whoosh - whoosh!* The ship rocked as the lifepods were ejected, and Hal caught a glimpse of the gleaming white cylinders hurtling away from the ship on the main screen.

'Time to go,' said Spearman.

'Please . . . take care of yourself, captain.'

'It's not goodbye, Ann.' Spearman patted his pocket. 'I have your backup right here.'

Hal followed him out of the flight deck. The smoke was thicker now, and he coughed several times

419

while they were waiting for the lift. 'I thought you weren't supposed to use lifts when there was a fire?' he asked.

Spearman nodded. 'Normally that's right, but this is a special lift. It has its own power supply, and it's driven by anti-gravity. Do you know what that is?'

Hal knew all right. It wasn't that long ago he'd used an anti-gravity cannon to shoot down an enemy ship*.

The lift arrived and Spearman bustled him inside.

'What if they took all the pods?' asked Hal.

'There's one left.' Spearman reached into his flightsuit and took out a rag. He tore it in two and gave Hal half. 'Stick that over your mouth, and try not to breathe too deeply.'

The doors opened on an empty corridor. The smoke was even thicker here, and even with the rag over his face Hal found it really hard to breathe. There was a glow at the far end of the corridor, and he realised the floor was giving off waves of heat. Somewhere below a fire was raging, and they didn't have much time left.

Spearman stopped at the doors to the pod bays. Both were wide open, and Hal could see all the pod launchers from the corridor. The left hand

_____

* *Hal Junior: The Secret Signal*

ones were empty, and the displays showed 'Pod Launched' in flashing orange letters. He glanced to the right and saw the same. Then he looked closer and realised the display on the far left wasn't orange . . . it was red. Instead of 'Pod Launched' it was showing 'Pod Fault'. 'Er, Mr Spearman?'

'Yes Hal?'

'Do you have any other escape pods?'

— 10 —

Left behind

Kent Spearman frowned at the display. 'That was working last week. What happened to it?'

'It wasn't me,' said Hal quickly. He was used to getting the blame but this time - for once - it wasn't his fault.

Spearman hurried from one pod launcher to the next, double-checking the displays. 'Not good,' he said at last.

Smoke swirled around, and Hal could feel the heat of the fire through his shoes. 'A-are we stranded?'

'No, not at all.' Spearman thumped his fist on the 'Pod Faulty' display. There was a spit and a crackle, and the red text disappeared. At first Hal thought the pilot had fixed it, but then he saw Spearman's worried expression. Obviously things weren't going to plan.

Spearman took out a pocket knife and levered the

control panel off the wall, exposing a tangle of wires. He poked around, then jumped and swore as one of them gave him a shock.

'It's a shame Stinky isn't here,' said Hal. 'He's really good with electronics.'

'Lucky for him he isn't,' muttered Spearman, shaking his fingers. Then he glanced at Hal. 'Do you really think he could help?'

'Stinky knows everything,' said Hal simply.

'We'd better speak to him.' Spearman crossed to the opposite wall, where there was a computer terminal. He touched his finger to the security pad, then leant close to the speaker. 'Ann, can you tell me which pod Stinky is in?'

'Negative,' said the ship's computer. 'Stinky unknown. Name is not on the passenger list.'

'Stephen,' said Hal. 'Stephen Binn.'

Spearman repeated this, and the screen zoomed in on a white cylinder. It was tumbling away from the passenger ship, and it looked tiny against the star-filled sky. Within seconds Spearman had set up communications, and Stinky's owlish face looked out of the screen. He was a nasty shade of green, and he seemed to be swallowing a lot.

'Are you all right?' asked Hal.

'Y-yeah. Just a bit dizzy.' Stinky started to float away, and Hal laughed as his friend flapped his arms wildly.

'Stephen, this is Kent Spearman. Can you hear me?'

'Yes Mr Spearman.'

'Hal says you're a whizz with electronics.'

Stinky swam back into view. 'It's one of my favourite subjects.'

Hal snorted. Every subject was one of Stinky's favourites!

'Do you know how to override a keypad?' asked Spearman.

'Which model?'

Spearman glanced at Hal. 'Can you check?'

'It'll be on the bottom of the cover,' called Stinky.

Hal hurried across the pod bay, bursting with importance. He was helping to save everyone! Well, save the pilot and himself, anyway. He found the cover on the floor and picked it up. 'KL-91,' he called out.

Stinky closed his eyes, and Hal could almost hear the whirr of his incredible brain. Any second now his friend would have the answer. Any second now.

Instead, Stinky shook his head. 'I'm sorry, I don't know that model. Do you think it's similar to the KL-90?'

'How should I know?' snapped Hal.

'Let's assume they are,' continued Stinky, still

thinking hard. He started to drift away again, but before he was out of sight his eyes snapped open. 'Cut the orange wire, and twist the green and purple ones together.'

'Cut orange, twist purple and green,' muttered Spearman. 'Thanks!'

'B-before you go . . . ' began Stinky.

'Yes?'

'Is there any way to stop the pod spinning so much?'

'Just wait until the boosters kick in.' Spearman cut the connection and hurried over to the control panel. He pulled at the wires until the orange, green and purple ones were all sticking out. Unfortunately there were two purple ones. 'Well that's just great,' muttered Spearman.

'What happens if you join the wrong ones? Will it blow up?'

'No, but it might seal the door for good.' Spearman hesitated, then followed Stinky's instructions, snipping the orange wire before stripping and twisting the rest together. In the end, he joined both the purple ones to the green one. There was a brief hesitation and then . . . success! The door started to open.

Boom!

Something exploded below decks, and the force

threw Hal to the floor. He wasn't down long . . . as soon as he felt the searing heat on his hands he bounced right up again. Then he realised the smoke had vanished, and there was a distant whistling sound.

'Are you all right?' shouted Spearman.

Hal could hardly breathe and he certainly couldn't speak. Instead, he nodded.

'Hull breach,' yelled Spearman. 'Air's going. Have to get . . . in.'

Unfortunately the door to the escape pod had only opened five or six centimetres, and then jammed. Hal could see into the pod through the gap, and it looked cosy and welcoming.

Spearman put both hands on the edge of the door and braced his feet on the wall. He heaved with all his might but the door didn't budge. 'Help . . . me . . . open!' shouted Spearman, his voice thin and his face red with the strain.

Hal put his shoulder to the door and jammed one foot against the wall. There was an exercise in the Space Station gym where they had to lean into a padded wall and push it clear across the room. Hal always finished first, even after Stinky sat on the opposite side of the wall with two friends. Unfortunately, the pod door wasn't padded, and it was harder to budge than a wall with the entire class perched on top.

Hal put all his strength into a huge push, and the door gave. There was a moment of weightlessness, and then he and Spearman tumbled into the escape pod. The inner door closed smartly, and Spearman was at the controls before Hal could reach for the safety belt.

Whooooosh!

Hal was pressed down into his seat as the pod shot away from the damaged passenger ship. It was an effort just to raise his arms, but he managed to buckle in. The crushing weight eased, and before long it was gone. Now they were weightless, and Hal's stomach began to turn somersaults. No wonder Stinky had looked as green as a head of broccoli!

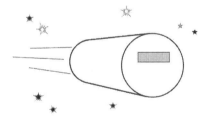

— 11 —

In flight

Kent Spearman loosened his straps so he could reach the central control panel. He changed a few settings, steadying the capsule, and then he fired the boosters. The thrust from the engines pressed Hal into his seat, and he breathed a sigh of relief as gravity returned. It was only weak, but it was enough to orient himself.

Spearman glanced at him. 'I wouldn't celebrate yet,' he said, his voice grave. 'We're not out of the woods.'

Hal was mystified. How could they be in the woods when there weren't any trees?

Kent saw his puzzled expression. 'We've escaped one danger, but there are plenty more. For example, if the ship explodes it might take this pod with it. On the other hand, I could burn all our fuel getting the pod to a safe distance, and then we'd have none left for landing.'

Hal remembered his friends. 'What about the others? Will they know what to do?'

'They got clear sooner than we did, so they're further away.' Spearman tapped a small display, and Hal saw the other pods strung out like pearls on a necklace. There was a pulsing red dot in the middle of the screen, with a much larger circle drawn around it. Just inside the big circle was a lonely white dot. 'That's us,' said Spearman, pointing to the white dot.

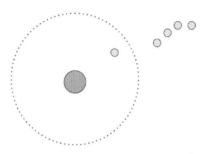

'What's that dotted circle?'

'The blast radius. When the ship explodes, everything inside that circle will be destroyed.'

'But . . . we're inside the circle!'

'Correct, which is why our thruster is going full throttle. I'm trying to get as far away from the wreck as possible, before it blows up.'

Hal watched the screen, his eyes wide. The little white dot was crawling towards the edge of the circle, while the red dot in the middle pulsed faster and faster. 'Will it blow us up?'

'Of course not!'

Hal remembered a visit to the sickbay once, after he'd cut his knee on a metal staircase. He'd asked the medic whether the treatment was going to hurt, and she'd said 'of course not!' in exactly the same tone of voice. The treatment did hurt - a lot - and the experience taught him that adults often said the opposite of what they meant. Instead of listening to their words you had to study their faces, and Kent Spearman's was tense and worried.

'Bang!' shouted Hal, and Spearman almost fell off his chair.

'Little horror,' muttered the pilot, as he recovered. Then he shot Hal a quick grin. 'All right, I won't lie to you. We're in for a rough ride, but I'm pretty sure we'll make it. These capsules can take a lot of punishment.'

'Have you escaped a wreck before?'

'Oh, yes. Several.' Spearman laughed at Hal's expression. 'It's not like I crash them on purpose. Things just . . . happen.'

'Will you tell me about one?'

'Sure. I had a close call once on planet Forzen, where they filled my ship with contaminated fuel. The engines barely had enough thrust to get me off the ground, and they kept cutting out. It was touch and go, I can tell you, but I made it.'

'And what about the crashes?'

'Maybe later, eh?' Spearman studied the display, where the white dot was almost clear of the circle. 'Looks like we –'

CLANG!

Something smashed into the capsule, sending it tumbling through space. More impacts followed, and Hal clung to the safety belt for dear life, squeezing his eyes shut. The capsule bounced and shook until Hal didn't know which way was up. It was like sitting inside a tin can getting tumbled around in a giant concrete mixer full of rocks.

The crashes and bangs tailed off at last, and Hal opened one eye. They were okay! They'd made it!

Spearman smiled at him and patted the wall. 'I told you these things were strong.'

'Why didn't we hear the explosion?' demanded Hal.

'There's no sound in space, Hal. The only reason you heard those bits and pieces hitting the pod is because it's full of air.' Spearman held a hand out, his fingers clenched in a fist. 'When the ship went off it sent pieces flying every which way.' He opened his hand, splaying his fingers. 'Some of them hit us, but they didn't do any damage.'

431

'You mean we're okay?'

'Sure.'

'And the others?'

Spearman inspected the display. 'All present and correct.' Then he looked closer. 'Oh dear.'

'What's the matter?'

'Your friend Stinky . . . his capsule has five people in it.'

'Is that bad?'

Kent nodded. 'The pods are only rated for four.'

'Stinky's not very big,' said Hal. 'He should be all right.'

'It's not that. There are only four sets of belts.' Kent used the central console and Hal felt the engines firing again.

'What are you doing?'

'We'll have to link up in space and transfer one of them across. It's risky, but there's no choice. I've told their capsule to slow down so we can dock with it.'

Hal watched the screen, and he saw two white dots getting closer and closer. They joined as one, and the capsule shook with a thud. Kent got up and opened the airlock and Hal saw right into the second capsule, with five worried faces looking back at him. Kent had already sent them a message, telling them the plan, and Stinky was through the airlock before any of the others could move.

'Best of luck,' called Kent, and he sealed the door again. There was a grating sound as the pods separated, and then the second pod fired its thrusters, moving to a safe distance.

'We don't want to land on top of them,' explained Kent. 'They have more fuel than us, so they can make the course change.'

Meanwhile, Hal helped Stinky with the belts, strapping him in tight before Kent could do it for him. When the pilot checked Stinky's belts, he nodded his approval. 'Nicely done, Hal.'

Hal beamed to himself.

'Okay boys,' said Kent Spearman. 'Here's the sitrep.'

'That's situation report,' murmured Stinky.

'I know!' protested Hal, even though he didn't.

Kent ignored the interruptions. 'We have plenty of fuel left for landing, and we should set down in about eight hours.'

Eight hours! Hal cleared his throat. 'Er, Mr Spearman?'

'Yes?'

'Where's the bathroom?'

— 12 —

Are we there yet?

To Hal, eight hours cooped up in the capsule felt more like eight weeks. He soon tired of using the emergency toilet, and Spearman wouldn't let him touch the food supplies in case they needed them to survive. Stinky curled up and went to sleep, although Hal suspected he was just pretending so he didn't have to listen to his complaints. Hal woke him up several times to check, until Kent told him to stop.

Hal assumed the pods would be collected by a rescue ship, scooping them up in space like a fishing boat filling its nets. However, Spearman explained that planet Gyris only had one emergency vessel . . . and it was being repaired. That meant the pods would have to land on the planet by themselves. Worse, landing was automatic, and there was no way to choose your destination. They might land in the middle of a desert, or on top of a mountain, or splash down in the sea. According to Kent, if that happened you just bobbed around on the ocean, getting very seasick while rescue ships looked for you.

With six pods scattered all over the planet, it would take the authorities some time to reach them all. Hal suddenly realised they might spend the entire camping trip living out of the escape pod, drinking canned water and eating stale ration bars. It was so unfair. They might as well have stayed aboard the Space Station!

Hal glanced up. He'd just noticed a thin whistling noise, which sounded exactly like an air leak.

'Don't worry,' said Spearman. 'We're entering the planet's atmosphere. You'd better tighten your belts, though.'

Hal woke Stinky, again, and they did as they were told. The whistling got louder, and the tiny capsule began to shake. There were bumps too, as though they were hitting something. 'Are those clouds?'

'No, we're too high up for those. It's just variations in atmospheric density.'

'Uh-huh?'

'Sorry. Pockets of air at different temperatures. It's like flying through soup and hitting a piece of carrot or potato.'

435

Hal imagined a giant bowl of stew with a spaceship splatting through the ingredients. His stomach growled, and he remembered he hadn't eaten for hours.

The whistling became a steady roar, and the air in the capsule began to heat up. It was just starting to get uncomfortably warm when there was a loud Fsssh! right under their feet, making Hal jump. 'What was that?'

'Re-entry shield,' said Spearman calmly. 'Without it, we'd burn up like a pan full of bacon.'

Hal was beginning to wish Kent would pick different examples. Something which didn't involve food would be good. He also wished the pilot would explain things before they happened, not afterwards. 'What next?'

'We'll fall for a while, and then the thrusters will slow us down for landing. When that happens your head will feel like it's three or four times heavier than usual. It's like taking a slice of cake and –'

'I get the idea,' said Hal quickly. It was hot in the capsule, and burning air was still roaring by outside. Hal imagined the pod dropping through the atmosphere like a meteor, trailing a long, fiery streamer. What would it look like to the people on the ground? Would they think they were under attack? Were they getting ready to shoot the capsule out of the sky?

He was still dreaming up exciting disasters when the thrusters fired, adding their deep rumble to all the other noises. It was like someone standing on the brakes, and Hal gasped at the crushing weight. It was an effort to keep his head up, and he wished he could lie down and rest. Unfortunately, the seat belts held him to the chair, keeping him upright.

'Not . . . long . . . now.' Spearman spoke with effort, the muscles in his neck standing out.

A few minutes later, the roaring air tailed off, but the thrusters kept up their rumble. Spearman reached for the console, and the screen displayed a bird's-eye view of the ground. Hal could see green from one side of the display to the other, and as they dropped further he realised they were all trees. There were several hills, which made the ground look like a lumpy green carpet, and in the distance he could see a big mountain range. There was a river, too, winding between the trees like a gleaming silver ribbon.

A cursor darted around the screen, pausing on shadows before moving on. 'What's it doing?' asked Hal.

'The pod's trying to find a landing spot.'

Hal realised they were talking normally. The thrusters were quieter now, and his head was back to its normal weight again. 'What if it can't find one?'

'We'll have to take our chances between the trees,' said Spearman.

Hal scanned the small screen. There was no sign of the other capsules, but they might have landed in the trees too. If so, they'd be under the canopy and invisible from the air. 'How will the rescue teams find us?'

'Every pod has a beacon. It started transmitting the second we left the passenger ship. All they have to do is track it.'

'Will it take long?'

Spearman shook his head.

'What's going to happen to you? I mean, you lost your ship.'

'Don't worry, it was insured.'

'But what about your job?'

'Pilots are always in demand.'

'I'm going to be a pilot one day,' said Hal.

Spearman ruffled his hair. 'And I bet you'll be a good one, too.'

Roar!

The thrusters fired one last time, slowing them for the landing. Hal saw the trees coming up to meet them, and then he heard branches grinding on the hull. The pod tilted sideways, and there was a moment of weightlessness before . . . oof!

They landed with a thud, right on their side, and Hal saw stars as his head whacked the padded chair. The lights went out, leaving them in darkness, but before he could panic the door slid open. Hal's first view of planet Gyris was a big tree towering over the pod, with sunlight filtering through the leaves. There was noise too . . . chirps and tweets by the thousand, wind rustling in the trees, and the click-click-click of the cooling jets.

Then there were the smells! Freshly disturbed earth, sap from the broken branches, and a vast background smell of . . . planet. Hal took a deep breath and closed his eyes, savouring the variety.

439

As Kent Spearman would say, it was like eating dry bread your whole life, and then discovering chocolate cake.

— 13 —

Roll, roll, roll the lifeboat

Kent rubbed his head and sat up. 'Well, we made it.'

'Where are we?' asked Hal.

'About a thousand kilometres from the nearest settlement. They're on the coast, and we're inland.'

'Are there any wild animals?'

'Only if we landed on them.' Spearman laughed at Hal's expression. 'No, nothing bigger than a rabbit.'

'Do they have those here?'

'They have rabbits everywhere,' said Kent.

Hal glanced up at the doorway, which was like a skylight in the roof. It was a long way up, and he realised they couldn't actually reach it. 'How are we going to get out?'

'Not sure yet.' Spearman frowned. 'We'll need to rig a cover for that in case it rains.'

Hal remembered rain from a documentary. 'Is that when water falls from the sky?'

'Correct.' Spearman rapped on the wall. 'A good downpour could fill this up, and we'll be swimming around like goldfish in a bowl.'

'Why don't we close the door?'

'We can pull it to, but we can't seal it. We need fresh air.'

'Can't we roll the pod over?' asked Stinky.

'Not without a crane.'

'What about using the thrusters?'

Spearman hesitated, rubbing his chin. 'It could be dangerous. They're very powerful, and the jets could start a fire.'

'But it might work?'

'We'll see. First we need to look around outside. For all we know there might be a building out there, or other people.'

Hal thought this extremely unlikely, but he knew Spearman was right. If they fired the engines the heat would burn anything around the ship. However, they still had another problem to deal with: getting out of the pod. 'Is there a ladder?'

'No, I'll boost you up. Come on, on your feet.'

A few moments later they were ready. Hal stood on the console, then stepped onto Spearman's shoulders. He could just reach the door frame, and he hauled himself up, getting his elbows over the edge before tipping sideways to raise his knee.

'Be careful,' called Spearman, from the darkness below. 'Don't roll off.'

Hal got his knee on the edge of the frame and shifted sideways onto the hull. Now he was lying face-down on the pod, with the trees above him and the ground down below. He could see a thick carpet of brown leaves, with fresh green ones and broken branches scattered on top. Hal looked up and saw a ragged hole in the canopy where the pod had torn its way through.

Stinky joined him on top of the pod, and the boys exchanged a worried look.

'What can you see?' called Spearman.

'Trees,' shouted Hal. 'Lots and lots of them.'

'Can you get down to the ground?'

Hal peered over the edge, and discovered the capsule had come down on the side of a hill. The ground sloped away below him, the thick trees and undergrowth hiding the depths of the valley. He looked over his shoulder towards the top of the hill, but could only see a short distance through the dense woods.

Then he looked along the capsule, and he saw a tree bent sideways under the weight of the hull. If he could grab hold of that, he could swing on it and reach the ground that way. 'I think I see a way down.'

'Just make sure you can get up again.'

Hal eyed the tree, studying the distance to the ground. It was bent over a long way, and it shouldn't be too hard to climb back up. 'I'll be right back,' he called. 'Wait there.'

Spearman muttered something, but Hal didn't catch the words.

Hal shimmied across the hull to the tree, then took hold of the trunk with both hands. He was surprised to find it was smooth and cold to the touch, because he'd always thought living things were warm. Something else Teacher never told them!

It only took a moment to reach the ground, where his shoes sank into the spongy earth. It was like the mats in the gym, except his shoes left muddy footprints. 'Come on, Stinky. It's easy.'

His friend peered over the edge, then came down nervously, as though he'd never climbed a tree in his life. Then Hal realised . . . neither of them had!

'That wasn't too hard,' he said, brushing his hands on his clothes.

'Just wait until we have to climb up again,' muttered Stinky.

The boys looked around, peering through the trees. The ground sloped away, and thick bushes made it hard to see very far. Hal couldn't see any of the other capsules, and he certainly couldn't hear anyone over the bird and insect noises. Somewhere in the distance there was a crack and a thud as a branch fell off a tree, and Hal glanced up fearfully. How often did trees drop bits on you, and was there any warning? When they finally started camping, he decided his tent was going to be right out in the open.

But never mind camping - they'd left Kent Spearman inside the capsule. How were they going to get him out? Obviously there wasn't any rope around, nor any ladders. Old jungle movies always had swinging creepers hanging from every tree, but there were none to be seen here.

Hal looked back at the capsule, and his eyes narrowed. The pod had knocked several branches off when it came down, and a few were trapped underneath. What if he pushed a branch down inside the capsule - could Mr Spearman climb out?

He ducked under the capsule and tugged at one of the branches. Unfortunately the entire weight of the capsule was resting on it, and it wouldn't budge. He was on the lower side of the slope too, below the capsule, which made it even harder to pull a branch out.

'Hal!' whispered Stinky. 'I can hear . . . water.'

'Water?'

The boys noticed a gap between the bushes, and further down the slope they saw a natural rock wall with real water splashing from an underground stream. They hurried to look, Kent Spearman completely forgotten.

Water - real water! - was trickling between two large rocks and running down the rock wall. Water was scarce aboard the Space Station, where they were only allowed to use it for drinking. They didn't have showers or baths . . . they had to use a special force field which removed dirt from anything it touched. Unfortunately, it felt like sandpaper, and it left your skin red and tingly.

Hal crouched and put his hand into the stream, and he couldn't help grinning as the icy cold liquid ran over his fingers. He stared at it, amazed that so much water could just bubble up from the ground and go to waste.

The wall was about a metre and a half high, and Hal's eyes narrowed as he saw the shallow pool at the foot. 'We should build that up a bit. Make a dam.'

Stinky nodded, his eyes shining.

They clambered down the wall, and Hal took a big scoop of dirt and heaped it across the stream. The water ran either side, making new streams, and Stinky added another couple of handfuls. Before long there was a deeper pool of water, and the boys were just planning an even bigger dam when Hal remembered the pod . . . and Mr Spearman. 'Stinky, we'd better go.'

Guiltily, they both stood up, and then they realised their hands were covered in mud. Hal looked at the sticky mess, wondering how to clean it off, and then he laughed as he spotted the pool. He crouched alongside it and did something he hadn't been able to do since he'd moved to the Space Station as a four-year-old: he washed his hands in water. Then, daringly, he splashed some in his face, and he grinned at the refreshing, cold feel.

'Hal, why don't you help Mr Spearman while I build the dam? We don't know how long we're going to be trapped here, and we'll need somewhere to wash.'

Hal frowned. *He* wanted to build the dam too, but rescuing the pilot was an important job. 'Okay, it's a deal. But make sure you do it right!'

Hal made his way up the slope to the pod, ducking his head as he rounded the nose to get to the upper part of the slope. He spotted several large branches straight way, and while most were trapped under the pod, one moved when he put his weight on it. The wood creaked and groaned but it wouldn't come free. Then Hal tried lifting it, and he felt the wood shifting. Excellent! He bent his knees, straightened his back and imagined he was in the finals of the Intergalactic Weight Lifting competition.

The crowd held its breath as Hal Junior, youngest competitor in the history of the sport, took to the stage. He bowed to the Emperor and all the princes and princesses, basking in the royal applause. He spat on his hands and rubbed them together, then approached the weights and took a firm grip on the wooden barbell. A moment passed while he summoned all his energy, and then ... three ... two ... one! He straightened his legs with an almighty heave.

The weight was immense! At first the barbell wouldn't budge, but Hal wasn't giving up. He took a deep breath and tried again, hauling on the wooden beam until it felt like his arms would come out of their sockets. Then, with a rush, he managed it.

Applause! Wild cheering! Whistles! The crowd went wild as Hal Junior lifted the huge weight! He'd done it!

The scene faded, and Hal discovered he was facing the pod with the branch in both hands. He felt pleased with himself, and he was about to take his prize back to Kent Spearman when he noticed something. Slowly, ever so slowly, the big tree holding the pod up was falling over. And slowly, ever so slowly, the huge escape pod was starting to roll away from him.

— 14 —

Shelter

Hal realised what had happened: the branch had been trapped under the pod, and had acted like a lever when he lifted it. The pod was resting on the side of a hill, and gravity was about to do its thing.

Then he realised the danger: Stinky was below the pod, working on the dam! If the pod rolled over him, he'd be squashed flat. Desperately he dropped the branch and put his hands on the side of the pod, but there was nothing to hold on to. Hal cupped his hands to his mouth and shouted as loudly as he could. 'Stinky!' he yelled, at the top of his voice. 'Lie down! NOW!' He took a deep breath and shouted again. 'Mr Spearman, HANG ON!'

The pod tipped further, and then it started to roll. Fallen branches cracked and splintered as the pod rolled over them, and the big tree went with a loud CRACK! Then . . . roll, roll, *roll* went the pod, crack

crack *crack!* went the trees, and oh-no-*no!* went Hal. The pod gathered speed, cutting a swathe through the forest as it bounded down the slope. Now and then it flew into the air, chopping trees off halfway up the trunks, and startled birds fled in every direction.

The pod finally came to a halt three or four hundred metres down the slope, resting against a stand of older trees. Hal ran to the waterfall, where he saw Stinky getting up from the pond, a stunned look on his face, water streaming from his clothes. Hal checked his friend was all right, then charged after the pod, clambering over fallen branches and struggling through flattened bushes. When he reached the pod, he could just see the top of the doorway, which was now face down and buried in the dirt. He got onto his hands and knees and started digging. 'Mr Spearman? Mr Spearman, are you okay?'

❖

Hal dug at the earth, making the hole bigger and bigger. He expected to meet the pilot digging from the other side, but he got all the way through on his own. When there was enough room he stuck his head through. 'Hello? Mr Spearman?'

'Hang . . . on.'

Hal's eyes adjusted to the darkness, and he looked around for the pilot. He couldn't see him at first, but then he looked up and saw him halfway up the wall, tangled in the seatbelts. 'Are you okay?'

'Of course I'm not okay! One minute I was sitting here using the computer, and the next someone turned the pod into a spin dryer.'

'It rolled down the hill.' Hal decided to skip his starring role. 'It was resting on some branches and one of them moved.'

'Well, look on the bright side. Now we won't have to build a cover for the door.'

Unless it starts rolling down the hill again, Hal thought to himself.

Stinky arrived, sopping wet and breathing hard. 'What happened?' he demanded.

'The tree fell over,' said Hal, leaving out all mention of weightlifting and levers.

Spearman got himself free and slid down the wall. He landed with a thump, and winced. 'That's not good.'

'Are you okay?' Hal asked him.

'No, I've twisted my ankle.'

Hal realised what that meant: They wouldn't be

able to walk out of there. 'Do you think the rescue teams will find us?'

'That was the plan, yes.' Spearman sat back against the wall, his face drawn. 'Hal, we're in a spot of trouble. I was just checking the computer over, and I found out the emergency beacon hasn't been transmitting. That means nobody knows where we are.'

'Can you switch it on?'

'No, it's burnt out.'

Hal thought for a moment. 'We could light a fire. People might see the smoke.'

'Yes, we'll need a fire all right. The other problem is food and water. We're short of both.'

'I found a stream,' said Hal. 'It's just up the hill.'

Spearman brightened. 'Good lads!'

Hal felt the warmth of a deed well done. 'We could dig the stream out a bit, and make it flow past the pod. That way you could get a drink without having to walk.'

'Thanks. That would be great.'

Hal felt a little less guilty about rolling the pod down the hill. It was his fault Mr Spearman was injured, and he was determined to make up for it.

'Okay, first things first,' said Kent. 'Let's make this doorway a little bigger, and then we'll check the computer for native plants and insects. There might be something growing around here we can survive on.' Spearman hesitated. 'Whatever you do, don't taste anything until you clear it with me. Understood?'

Hal nodded. Teacher had already warned the class several times, and his parents had reminded him too.

'Some plants are deadly poison, even if the leaves and berries look shiny and sweet. At best you could end up very ill. At worst ... well, just be sure to clear them with me first.'

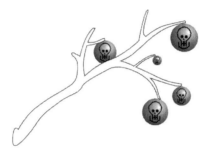

Spearman glanced at Stinky, who was wet and shivering. 'You're going to freeze. Let's see if we can find some dry clothes.'

Kent got Stinky to change into a pair of overalls from the escape pod. They were much too big for him, and with the arms and legs rolled up he looked like a circus clown. Then they all worked together on the doorway, clearing away the dirt until there was a decent tunnel. Water seeped into the bottom of the hole, and they would get very muddy clambering in and out. Spearman removed several of the padded seat cushions, laying them along the bottom of the tunnel. 'That'll keep the worst off.'

'Can we light a fire now?' asked Hal.

'See if you can find some wood. Look for dry leaves, twigs and branches. The green ones won't be any good.'

Hal and Stinky clambered through the tunnel to the outside. It seemed darker than before, and it was colder too. Hal realised night was falling, and unlike the Space Station, where they just dimmed the lights, here that meant total darkness. He suddenly felt very small amongst the trees.

He shook off the feeling and set off to find some wood. The pod had crashed through several trees on its way down the slope, but those were all green and growing, and Kent had explained that fresh wood wouldn't burn. Fortunately, one or two of the shattered trees had been dead, and those had littered the ground with brittle branches. It only took a few minutes to gather an armful, and then they staggered back to the pod.

Kent Spearman was sitting on a tree trunk, and Hal saw him wet his finger and hold it up in the air.

'What are you doing?'

'Checking the wind direction. If we build the fire in the wrong place, the smoke will blow straight into the capsule.'

Hal was impressed. He'd have built the fire right in front of the door, and he'd never given any thought to the smoke. He realised he had a lot to learn, and he was grateful Mr Spearman was there. Imagine if he'd come down in the woods on his own, or just him and Stinky! Then he remembered the others. Would they be eating poisoned berries and trying to light fires with green wood? 'Do you think everyone else will be okay?'

Spearman was busy snapping wood into smaller pieces, building them into a pile with the smallest bits on the bottom. 'Their beacons were fine,' he said at last. 'I bet they're tucked up in a nice hotel by now.'

Stinky looked worried. 'They will look for us, won't they? The rescue people, I mean?'

'Of course!' Spearman took out a firestarter and held the steady flame to the pile of wood. Nothing happened for a moment or two, and then the smaller twigs caught and flames spread through the pile. 'That reminds me . . . you should gather a pile of green leaves. If you hear a jet or a rescue copter, throw them on the fire.'

'Won't that put it out?'

'No, it'll make a huge amount of white smoke. They'll spot it right away.'

'Unless it's night time.'

'Correct. If it's dark, throw dry branches on to make the flames bigger. Something with lots of old leaves on.'

'Green leaves in the daytime, dry leaves at night.'

'You've got it.' Spearman glanced at the sky. 'Can you fetch some more wood? I don't know how cold it's going to be overnight, so we'd better lay in a good supply.'

Cold! Hal hadn't thought of that. Aboard the Space Station you just turned a dial and the climate control did the rest. He knew about snow and ice, of course, but he hadn't actually thought about sleeping outdoors, in real weather.

'Don't look so worried,' said Spearman. 'We have food, water and warmth. By tomorrow those rescue teams will be combing the forest, and we'll be back to civilisation in no time.'

Hal nodded.

'Listen, I saw a roll of fishing line in the emergency kit. Once you've got the wood I'll show you how to make a bow and arrows. How about that?'

'Really?' Hal's eyes widened. 'Can I go hunting?'

'Maybe just the trees, for now.' Spearman looked into the flames, and Hal could almost read his

457

thoughts. If they weren't rescued soon, hunting and fishing might be the only way to survive!

— 15 —

Bow done

Hal and Stinky traipsed up and down the hill, fetching armfuls of wood, and by the time it got dark their legs were aching like crazy. Hal dumped the final load of branches onto the pile and sat down on a log. Mr Spearman had built the fire to a roaring blaze, and the warmth soon dealt with Hal's frozen nose and ears.

Spearman passed them a ration bar each, and Hal chomped his down in seconds. It hardly made a dent in his hunger, but a big drink of water helped. Then he noticed Spearman sorting through the pile of firewood. The pilot selected several straight branches, bending each one before setting them aside. When he had half a dozen he limped back to the log and sat down.

'How's your ankle?' asked Hal.

'Not too bad, thanks.' Spearman pulled up the leg

of his flightsuit, revealing a neat bandage. 'I can move around a bit, but I wouldn't want to walk far on it.'

'Are you making a bow?'

'Yes, I'll make a couple of them. Hopefully one of them will work.' Spearman took out a large pocket knife and cut notches at each end of the poles. Then he unwound several metres of fishing line. 'Do you know how to plait?'

Hal shook his head. As far as he knew, it was something you did with hair.

'This stuff isn't strong enough for a bowstring, but it'll be okay if we plait it.' Spearman measured off two metres of fishing line, then cut another dozen lengths the same. 'We'll double-plait it, six strands to a string. Here, take these.'

Hal was given six lengths of fishing line. They kept curling up, and before he knew it there was a big tangle in his lap.

'Tie the end off like this.' Spearman demonstrated, and Hal copied him. 'Okay, now separate them into pairs and start crossing them over.'

Hal tried, but the lines tangled up worse than ever. Instead of a bowstring, he ended up with a plate of spaghetti. Mmm. Spaghetti.

Spearman laughed. 'Was that a peal of thunder?'

'No, it was my stomach.'

'Try not to think about food.' Spearman took the hunting knife and cut a deep notch in the log, then trapped one end of his string in the V. 'You work on this one, and I'll try and sort yours out.'

Hal crouched by the log and started plaiting the bowstring, hand over hand. It didn't look very straight, but he figured the bow would soon take care of that.

Meanwhile Spearman dealt with Hal's first effort, picking at the jumbled ball of fishing wire until he'd separated the strands. By the time he'd finished Hal was at the end of his own bowstring, and he held the loose threads until Spearman could tie it off.

Stinky did really well with the bowstring, working quickly and accurately. Hal's was a bit rougher, with a couple of knots and one spot where he'd looped the line back on itself.

'Not bad,' said Spearman, as he inspected the result in the firelight. 'Good job.'

Hal felt a rush of pride.

Next, Spearman took one of the notched poles and hooked the bowstring over one end. He stood up and turned the pole over, sticking the tied end into the ground just outside his left foot. He stepped over the pole with his right foot, and the wood creaked as he bent it forward, pressing it against the back of his leg. It bent further and further until Hal thought it was going to snap, but Spearman slipped the loose end of the bowstring over the tip. When he was done the pole was bent into a curve, and the plaited string was stretched tight. Hal was impressed, and he resolved to smuggle some wooden poles aboard the Space Station when they eventually went home. Maybe they could hold an archery tournament in the recycling centre!

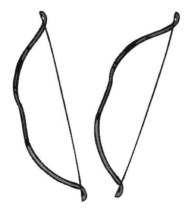

Spearman plucked the string, which made a deep twang. Then he strung a second bow using the spare string.

'What about arrows?' asked Hal, who'd just realised they had nothing to shoot.

'Try and find some straight sticks, about as thick as your little finger.'

Hal dug through the pile of firewood with gusto, tossing aside branches and snapping off anything that might make a decent arrow. When he was finished he had about two dozen sticks, and he carried them back to the fire.

Spearman took the bundle and held them over the flames, turning them whenever they started smouldering. Then he reversed them to harden the other end, holding the hot sticks with a rag. When he was happy, he took up the hunting knife and sharpened the sticks to a point. 'We need vanes to make them fly properly. I don't suppose you saw any feathers when you were gathering wood?'

Hal shook his head.

'Never mind. I'll use wrappers from the ration bars.'

Hal watched, fascinated, as Spearman cut triangles from the plastic wrappers. Then the pilot split the blunt end of the arrows, cutting a slot six or seven centimetres deep, before sliding the triangle inside. Finally, he tied around the split end with some fishing line, tying it off neatly.

'Want to try it?' he asked, offering Hal one of the bows.

Did he ever! Hal took the bow and tested the string, pulling it back to his ear. He let go and the bow went twannggg!

'Don't fire it without an arrow,' said Spearman. 'The shock will destroy the wood.'

'Sorry. I didn't know.'

Spearman passed him the arrow and showed him how to fit it to the bow. When he was ready, Hal pulled back on the string until his muscles creaked, aimed at a tree and . . . twanngggg! The arrow sped into the darkness.

Thunk!

'Good shot!' said Spearman.

Hal beamed. His first go with a bow and arrow, and he'd hit the target! He fetched the arrow, which was lying on the ground next to the thick tree trunk. Of course, animals were a lot smaller than trees, so they'd be much harder to hit. And truth be told, he didn't like the idea of killing anything. He decided he'd practice with the bow as much as possible, but he wouldn't shoot creatures unless he was desperate for food.

Kent Spearman seemed to read his thoughts. 'We'll follow that stream tomorrow and see if it turns into something bigger. If so, you can hunt fish with the bow and arrow.'

Hal brightened. Fish were different somehow, and they were getting short of food. He sat on the log and watched Spearman making arrows, and all of a sudden he yawned. It was getting late, and the warmth of the fire was sending him to sleep.

'You two kip inside the capsule,' said Spearman. 'I'll sit here and keep the fire going for a bit.'

The boys didn't argue. They crawled inside and settled on two of the couches with a blanket each. Firelight played on the walls, and the crackling flames lulled them to sleep in no time.

— 16 —

Hunting

Captain Spacejock checked his weapons one last time. They'd landed in darkness, hoping to take the pirates by surprise, and every member of his team was under strict orders: no noise! They were outnumbered, outgunned, and if they tipped their foes off too soon ... they'd lose the battle for sure.

Bzzzz-glglglgl!

Hal woke with a start, and for a second or two he thought he was in his bunk aboard Space Station Oberon. From the sound of it, someone was in his cabin, making holes in the wall with a very loud hammer drill.

Bzzzz-glglglgl!

It was very dark, but a small amount of light came through a door near his feet. Then it all came back: the damaged passenger ship, the escape pod, and the wild flight through space.

Bzzzz-glglglgl!

What *was* that noise? It sounded like wild boars, or hunting dogs, or maybe a whole gang of angry bunny rabbits. Did rabbits roar? Hal wasn't sure, but whatever it was, it sounded pretty angry.

Bzzzz . . . glglglgl.

Hal peered across the capsule and saw Kent Spearman lying on the bunk opposite. The pilot was fast asleep, and his snoring was loud enough to wake the dead.

Bzzzz . . . glglglgl.

Hal threw off his blanket and hopped down onto the floor. He was very hungry, but he had a brilliant idea: They'd find the river, catch some fish and get breakfast cooking before Mr Spearman woke up! Hal put his shoes on, then shook Stinky out of his sleep.

'Wassat? Whoozat? Where am I?' Stinky rubbed his eyes. 'What time is it?'

'Breakfast time. Come on.'

Bzzzz . . . glglglgl.

'Who's drilling holes in the wall with a hammer drill?'

Hal nodded towards Kent Spearman.

'Oh.' Stinky got up, and together they crawled out of the pod via the trench. The forest was very still and cold, and there was a light mist between

467

the trees. The campfire was almost out, but Hal managed to get it going again with a handful of leaves and sticks. The flames were barely visible in daylight, but there was plenty of smoke.

'You mentioned breakfast?' said Stinky, looking around hopefully.

'Sure. We just have to catch it.'

Stinky groaned. 'Hal, I was dreaming about eggs and bacon!'

'You can't eat dreams. Come on, grab a bow.'

They went to collect the weapons Spearman had made the night before, but they discovered the pilot had unstrung them. Instead of the fearsome bows Hal was expecting, they were just wooden poles with a knotted string tied to one end.

Stinky picked one up and swished it back and forth. 'Maybe we could tie a hook on the string and go fishing?'

'What are you going to use for bait? Ear wax?'

'No, big green bogies!'

They both laughed. Then their stomachs rumbled. 'You look for hooks and I'll get the bows set up. Maybe the fish will bite on chunks of food ration.'

While Stinky went to look in the emergency kit, Hal inspected the bows. Spearman had unhooked the strings and Hal wasn't sure how to put them back again. He tried bending one around a tree but it didn't work: he needed two hands to bend the bow and another to fit the string. Then he remembered how Mr Spearman had stepped over the bow and bent it across the back of his leg. Hal tried it, but the wooden pole tripped him over and he fell headlong into the dirt. He brushed himself down and tried again, straining the wood until he got the string near the end, but he wasn't strong enough to bend it all the way.

Stinky came back with a small tin. 'I found some hooks, and there's a packet of dried bait.'

'Good.'

'Mr Spearman was waking up, so I told him we were going fishing. He said we should try not to drown.'

'Okay, give me a hand getting this string back on.' Hal bent the pole around a tree, straining and puffing, and Stinky attached the plaited bowstring. Then they spotted a small problem: they'd strung the bow with the tree in the middle, and there was no way to get it off. Muttering under his breath, Hal bent the pole again while Stinky removed the string . . . again.

'Forget the bow,' said Stinky. 'We'll fish instead.'

'I'm not going without a bow,' said Hal stubbornly. He looked around for inspiration and saw two big logs nearby. He laid the pole across them and got

Stinky to sit on it. The bow bent all the way to the ground and Hal had no trouble hooking the string on. He raised the bow and twanged it a couple of times, pretending to shoot wild bears and space monsters.

'Mr Spearman said not to fire it without an arrow.'

'I wasn't firing it, I was checking the string.' Hal looked around and saw the arrows leaning against the escape pod. He took half, then slung the bow over his shoulder and led Stinky down the hill. His stomach was grumbling, and when he found the stream he stopped for a good long drink. Suitably refreshed, he decided to follow the running water downhill.

As they picked their way down the valley, jumping rocks and pushing through the undergrowth, Hal wished the rest of their class could be there to share the adventure. This was *real* camping: surviving in the wild, not sitting around in brightly-coloured tents in the corner of a park! He just wished they had something to eat.

— 17 —

Fish food

The stream got bigger the further it went downhill, then vanished into the undergrowth. Hal barged through the bushes and stopped. He'd almost fallen headlong into the river.

The river was five or ten metres wide, and Hal could see the bottom through the sparkling clear water. He saw a shadow, and when he looked closer he made out the outline of a fish. Was it really going to be that easy? Hal nocked an arrow, drew back and . . . Twanng! Splash!

The fish darted off, and Hal saw the arrow slowly floating away. That's when he remembered the important thing about fishing with a bow: you had to tie your arrow to the fishing line.

Oh well, he still had five arrows.

Stinky handed him the fishing reel, and Hal took the loose end and tied it around an arrow with

471

one of his special patented knots. By the time he finished, half the reel was knotted around the arrow, which now weighed twice as much as before.

Stinky laughed at the sight. 'If you don't hit anything with the pointy end you can always use it as a club.'

Hal ignored him and fitted the arrow to the bowstring. He drew the bow back and peered into the river, looking for fish. The big one had vanished, but there were several smaller ones swimming around in the shallows. He took aim, then released the arrow.

Twanng! SPLASH!

The fish scattered, and the arrow bobbed on the surface of the water. Hal retrieved it hand over hand, muttering under his breath. Why couldn't the fish stay still?

'Maybe we could throw stones at them,' said Stinky.

'Maybe I could throw you at them,' growled Hal. The arrow was soaking wet, and the big ball of twine on the end now weighed as much as a brick. He was beginning to think fishing with arrows was impossible, and he'd have given anything for a stale ration bar. Still, he wasn't one to give up, so he drew the arrow back and waited for the fish to settle.

'You need to aim below them,' said Stinky. 'Do you remember Teacher's lesson on refraction?'

Hal never remembered any of Teacher's lessons, especially maths. 'How are fractions going to help me catch fish?'

'Not fractions . . . refractions,' said Stinky. 'Light bends when you shine it through water.'

'Don't be a feeb. I'm not shining anything, am I?'

Stinky rolled his eyes. 'Listen, when light travels through water it slows down, and that makes things look bigger than they really are. It even makes them look like they're in a different place.'

'Don't be silly. It's just water, not some magical liquid.'

'Try it. Hold the end of the arrow in the water.'

Hal did so, and nearly fell in. The straight piece of wood looked like it had a sharp bend! He swished it around and tried moving it in and out of the water.

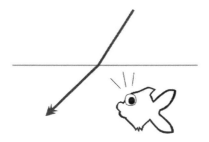

'You see? When you were shooting at the fish you were aiming over their heads. That's why you kept missing.'

'You could have mentioned this fraction stuff before I wasted an arrow,' grumbled Hal. 'That big fish would have made a great breakfast.'

'I'm sure there are plenty more.'

'Not here there aren't. They took one look at the arrow and cleared off.'

'I don't think they'd have recognised it.'

Hal pointed at the water. 'Do you see any fish?'

'No,' admitted Stinky.

'Right then. Now what?'

'We should think of it like a chess game.'

'You mean we should make swords, like knights, and chop the fish up?'

'No, nothing like that. Teacher says you have to think like your opponent, and then you'll know how to defeat them. Put yourself in your enemy's shoes.'

'Did Teacher mention fish don't have shoes?'

Stinky ignored him. He thought for a moment then opened his eyes wide, made his mouth into a big O, and starting opening and closing it. Next he walked around in circles, weaving his head from side to side and waving his hands like fins.

'It's okay, you can stop now,' said Hal.

'You mean you know how to catch the fish?' said Stinky hopefully.

'No need. They all died laughing.'

'This is serious, Hal! Unless we think like a fish . . .'

'You don't need to think like a fish!' said Hal. 'What would you do if someone fired arrows at you?'

'Hide behind a tree.'

'Exactly.' Hal pointed down-river, where a dead tree was lying in the shallows. The thick trunk was halfway out of the water, and the tip of the longest branch almost reached the opposite bank. 'There's bound to be fish hiding underneath.'

They made their way along the bank, fighting the thick undergrowth. They had to cross several streams, and their shoes were heavy with mud by the time they reached the fallen tree. Roots stuck into the air like splayed fingers, and there was a big hole where they'd been buried in the ground. Hal bent a root back so he could get past, then released it.

Thwack!

'Ow!' shouted Stinky. 'Do you mind?'

The root had flicked back and caught him across the chest, almost knocking him off his feet. Worse, the blow had knocked the metal tin out of his hand, and the contents were scattered all over the ground. They found the fishing line and bait easily enough, but could only find two hooks.

'How many were there?' asked Hal.

'Lots more than that,' said Stinky. He peered in the tin. 'Mr Spearman won't be happy.'

'He'll be fine if we take some fish back.'

— 18 —

Eddy's in the river

When they got to the tree, they discovered it was covered in slippery green moss. Stinky favoured fishing from the safety of the bank, but Hal wasn't having that. He stepped onto the log, holding the bow out like a balancing pole. He'd only taken two steps when he froze.

'What is it?' demanded Stinky. 'Is it a really big fish?'

Hal shook his head. He'd spotted something far more interesting: there was a little wooden boat tied up in the shelter of the log. It was half-filled with leaves and water, but imagine if they could empty it out! They could follow the fish wherever they went . . . maybe even cross the river!

Hal heard Stinky gasp. His friend had climbed onto the log, and was staring at the little rowing boat as though it were an alien battlecruiser. 'Hal, do you know what this means?'

'No more walking.'

'Well yes, but it also means people. Civilisation. Food!'

Hal looked doubtful. The boat had plants growing inside it, and it looked very old. For all he knew it might have a big hole in the bottom. 'We need something to empty it out. And we'll need a couple of poles to push it along with.'

'We need oars,' said Stinky.

'Those too.'

They both looked around hopefully, but there were no oars to be seen.

'Maybe they're inside the boat, under that mucky water,' said Stinky.

Neither of them made a move. The water inside the boat was green and murky, and for all they knew there could be water snakes or vicious crabs or rats or slimy wriggly creatures living under the surface. Crocodiles, even, if they were little ones.

'We could tip it over,' suggested Hal.

'Let's see whether the boat is sitting on the bottom. If there's a big hole in it, we can forget about using it.'

They stumbled down the steep bank to the river, slipping and sliding in the mud. Hal pulled his shoes off, rolled up his trousers and waded into the water. He winced as the mud squidged between his toes, and he was worried the water might get deeper and deeper. Fortunately it only came up to his knees before levelling off. He put one hand on the wooden boat and tried rocking it. It moved sluggishly, but was definitely afloat.

'Try pulling it closer to the shore,' said Stinky, who was hovering on the bank like a mother duck watching her babies.

Hal grabbed hold of the rope and pulled on it to find out what it was tied to. To his surprise he came up with a loose, ragged end. 'It's not tied to anything. Why didn't it float away?'

'It must be eddies,' said Stinky.

Hal frowned. 'How do you know who it belongs to?'

'It's the swirls in the water.' Stinky pointed at the river. 'It flows past the trunk and some of it comes around here and moves backwards. That's why the boat got stuck here.'

'Do you think Eddy will mind if we borrow it?'

'Who's Eddy?'

'You said this was Eddy's boat.'

'I didn't!'

'Yes you did. You said it was Eddy's, and he was keeping it here.'

Stinky laughed. 'I didn't say it was Eddy's boat, I said it was trapped by the eddies in the river.'

'So now it's his river too? Does this Eddy guy own everything?'

'Oh, for goodness sake!' Stinky pointed with both hands. 'Look, will you? Eddies in the river!'

Hal stared, expecting to see the mysterious Eddy swimming around in a pair of trunks. All he could see was the big fallen tree and a whole lot of water. 'Where is he, then?'

'Swirls, Hal. Whirlpools.' Stinky pointed again. 'Look, those ripples. They're called eddies.'

'Why didn't you say that instead of using someone's name?' demanded Hal bitterly. 'Here I was thinking Eddy was going to tell me off for messing with his boat.'

'Teacher explained all about eddies. Remember that lesson ... ' Stinky paused. 'All right, forget about eddie.'

'About time,' grumbled Hal. 'And if you see Tom or Dick in the river, keep them to yourself too.'

Stinky muttered under his breath, but Hal ignored him. He managed to drag the boat to the bank, where Stinky took the rope gingerly between finger and thumb. 'It's not going to bite you,' said Hal.

'No, but it's dirty.'

Hal saw red at this. He'd been wading around in the freezing cold river, getting muddy and wet while Stinky rabbited on about Invisible Eddy and his magical whirlpools. Now that he'd rescued the boat all by himself, Stinky was too fussy to grab a wet rope? 'If you don't hold it properly I'll dunk your head in the mud.'

Stinky held the rope properly, while Hal peered into the murky water. 'I can see something on the bottom. And,' he said, before Stinky could speak, 'it is not Eddy or any of his friends.'

'Is it a pair of oars?'

'No. It looks like a tin.' Hal rolled his sleeve up and reached into the water, pulling a face at the nasty rotting smell. His fingers closed on a small tin, and he pulled it out for a closer look. It was a tin can, still sealed, but the label had long since disappeared.

'What do you think is inside?'

'I don't know, but I bet it belongs to Eddy,' muttered Hal.

'It might be food. Is there an expiry date?'

Hal turned the can over and saw a grey touchpad on the bottom. Underneath the pad there was a tick and a cross. He touched the pad, and the tick turned green. 'Hey, it's still okay!'

Stinky eyed the can doubtfully. 'I bet it isn't. It's been sitting in that slime for years. Anyway, you don't know for sure that it's food.'

Hal looked into the water, hoping to spot the label floating around. Instead, he saw another can. This one was bigger, but when he fished it out he discovered it was empty. He was about to throw it away when Stinky stopped him.

'No, wait,' he said. 'We can use that for a bailer.'

Hal's eyes narrowed. 'Is Bailer another of your imaginary friends?'

'No, a bailer is used to scoop the water out of a boat.'

'Like this, you mean?' Hal dipped the can in the water and tipped the contents over the side. It didn't move much water, but as he continued, the level started to drop little by little. Within a few minutes the water was low enough to see a dozen tin cans and a metal box. Hal reached for the box, then drew back in alarm as a large frog leapt from the water and sat on top of it. Hal stared at the frog, fascinated. The frog stared right back.

'I don't think they bite,' said Stinky doubtfully.

Hal wasn't so sure. The frog had a pretty big mouth, and there was plenty of room for two rows of fearsome teeth. He'd seen a movie once where things like this leaped across rooms to attack their prey. And here he was, face to face with it.

All of a sudden the frog puffed out its cheeks, and . . . *Ribbit!*

Startled, Hal stepped back, losing his balance and sitting down in the squidgy mud.

Ribbit ribbit! went the frog.

'I think it's laughing at you,' said Stinky.

Hal leapt up, dripping mud. The frog didn't sound very dangerous, and he wondered whether he could put it in his pocket and smuggle it back to the Space Station. But no, it looked like it lived in water, and that was something they were very short of at home. 'Go on, shoo!' he said, flapping his hands at it.

The frog gave him a disgusted look and sprang into the river, landing with a plop and a splash.

Hal wasted no time. He took hold of the box, snapped the catches and opened the lid. Water poured out, and then inside he saw ... a chrome-plated blaster! It had a checkered black hand grip and a long slender barrel, and it was the most amazing thing Hal had ever seen.

'Is that real?' asked Stinky.

'I bet it is.' Hal reached into the box for the gun, then stopped. Guns were dangerous at the best of times, and this one had been underwater for years. Imagine if it went off when he touched it? Or imagine if the charge pack exploded? Carefully he closed the lid, and then he tucked the box under the big tree. 'We'll tell Mr Spearman about it. He'll know what to do.'

Stinky nodded.

'Come on, help me get the other tins out.'

The boys tipped the boat to remove the last of the water, then plucked the tins from the goopy green mess in the bottom. There were fourteen of them, all different shapes and sizes, and not one of them had a label. Hal and Stinky used the freshness tester on each, and they ended up with nine good tins and five which had gone bad.

'We should take them back to Mr Spearman,' said Stinky. 'He'll be getting worried, and he's probably twice as hungry as we are.'

Hal eyed the boat. He really wanted to try it out, but Stinky was right. They would take the food to the capsule, have breakfast and come back afterwards. He grabbed some leaves and covered the tin box with the gun inside, and then he and Stinky set off back to camp.

— 19 —

Hot food

When they arrived at the escape pod there were no signs of life. Stinky went inside to get Kent, but he re-appeared in the doorway immediately. 'He's not here.'

'Don't be daft. He must be.'

'Check for yourself.'

Hal crawled through the tunnel and stood up. After the bright daylight, it was dark inside the capsule, and he felt his way around carefully. There were blankets, and a pair of shoes, but there was definitely no Kent Spearman. After a few minutes his eyes adjusted, and he could see at a glance that the capsule was empty. 'He can't have gone far, not with a bad ankle.'

'Maybe it got better.'

'Not that quickly.' Hal had twisted his ankle once, and afterwards it was several days before he could put weight on it.

'Hal . . . you don't think he went looking for us?'

'Even Captain Spacejock wouldn't trek around the forest with an injury like that.'

'But if he did . . . do you think he left a message?'

'A secret message?' Hal looked hopeful. 'In code?'

They searched the pod, but apart from the blankets all they found were a couple of empty storage compartments. 'Let's check outside,' said Hal. 'He might have pinned a note to a tree with his hunting knife. Maybe he wrote something in the blood of his enemies.'

'There aren't any enemies.'

'Oh yeah? What if he's been captured?'

'If he was captured, he wouldn't have time to run around pinning notes to trees, would he?'

Hal thought for a moment. 'He might have scratched a message in the dirt.'

They spent five minutes scouring the area around the pod, but all they found were lots of footprints - mostly their own. Hal did find something which could have sort have been a message, if you looked at it sideways, until Stinky pointed out it was caused by a branch they'd dragged to the fire the night before.

'What next?' asked Stinky.

It was approaching lunchtime and they hadn't

even had breakfast yet. Back on the Space Station he'd dreamed about camping in the woods: sleeping in a snug tent, cooking eggs and bacon and swimming in the river. Instead he'd spent an uncomfortable night in the capsule, he'd had nothing to eat and the river had been freezing cold and teeming with dangerous frogs and skittish fish. At that moment, if someone offered to wave a magic wand and transport him back to Space Station Oberon he'd have been sorely tempted. If only he wasn't so hungry! 'I know. Let's try one of the cans.'

'It might be off.'

'We'll sniff it first. If it smells okay we'll try a tiny bit each, and then we'll wait an hour or two. If we feel all right, we'll eat the rest of the tin.'

'That's pretty good thinking.'

'No need to look so surprised.' Hal returned to the pod and selected the biggest tin. He pressed down in the middle of the lid and turned his thumb sideways, and the can opened with a hiss. Inside there were half a dozen cylinders, all vacuum sealed in foil.

'What are they?' asked Stinky. 'Biscuits? Cheese sticks? Cured sausages?'

'No,' said Hal, who'd just finished reading the label. 'They're battery packs for that pistol.'

Stinky started to back way. 'Do you . . . do you think the rest might be hand grenades?'

Hal went pale as he remembered the rough way they'd handled the tins. They'd had to carry five or six each, and they'd dropped them all several times on the way back. They could have set off a huge explosion! Then he relaxed. If dropping them hadn't blown them up, opening them would be safe enough. 'Hide behind a tree if you like. One of them might have food in, and I'm going to find it.'

Stinky hesitated, then came back. 'I'll do the next one.' He examined the tins, then picked a small square one. The lid was dented where Hal had dropped it on a rock, but it popped open with a hiss under Stinky's thumb. Inside were two slabs of brown . . . plasticine?

'Great. Now we can make zoo animals,' said Hal.

'It might be food.' Stinky sniffed the pale brown slabs, then coughed and wrinkled his nose in distaste. 'No,' he wheezed. 'Not food. Chemicals of some kind.'

489

Hal picked up a flat tin with rounded corners. Hiss! went the lid, and he peered inside hopefully. Success! There was a thick stew with a spoon in, and he had to put the can down quickly as it became too hot to hold. The heating element warmed the food up in seconds, and Hal's stomach growled at the delicious smell.

'Remember, it might be off,' said Stinky.

Hal breathed deeply, and his mouth watered. 'If that's off I'm a teacher's pet,' he declared.

'One spoonful each. That was the rule.'

'But then it'll get cold!'

'Just one spoonful, then we wait.'

'Who put you in charge?' grumbled Hal. He plucked the spoon out of the stew and scooped up as much as he could, then shovelled it into his mouth. The taste was heavenly, and it was all he could do not to gulp it down. Instead, he passed the spoon to Stinky and chewed on the mouthful for as long as possible, enjoying the rich meat and vegetable flavours to the very last drop.

Stinky took a mouthful and chewed in silence, his face a study of concentration. Gulp! The food was gone, and he sighed. 'Now we have to wait an hour.'

Hal looked at Stinky. Stinky looked at Hal. They both looked at the tin.

'It was a silly rule anyway,' said Hal, and he

reached for the spoon.

The can of stew lasted two minutes, and they each got half a dozen mouthfuls of delicious food. It was very tasty, but they were both still hungry and they longed for more. There were only a few tins left, though, and they couldn't afford to open another.

After a few minutes of silence, Hal filled the empty tin from the stream. They both drank deeply, draining every last drop. 'That's breakfast dealt with,' said Hal at last. 'Now let's find Kent Spearman.'

— 20 —

Meeting

They climbed to the top of the hill, hoping it would give them a better view of the surroundings. Unfortunately, all they could see was trees.

'Maybe we should wait for him near the pod,' said Stinky.

'What if his ankle got worse?' Hal gestured down the other side of the hill. 'He could be stuck out there somewhere.'

'We should never have left this morning. Not without telling him where we were going.'

'We didn't know where we were going,' said Hal shortly. He wasn't a big fan of 'we should have' and 'we ought to have'. What was done, was done.

'Maybe we could try whistling.'

Hal frowned. Out of the entire class, he was the only one who hadn't mastered the really loud whistle Teacher had tried to show them all. He

492

suspected Stinky had only suggested whistling so he could show his own off. Then his face cleared. 'Of course! He's gone hunting!'

'Do you think so?'

'I bet he has. He probably made another bow and arrows, and set off to get dinner.' Hal realised something. 'If he's hunting we'd better not make a sound. We'll scare the game away.'

'What are we going to do, then?'

Hal thought for a moment. 'Okay, we'll go down the other side of the hill then circle round. He can't be far away, and he might see us.'

'He might shoot us,' said Stinky in alarm.

'Do I look like a rabbit to you?'

Stinky looked him up and down. 'I guess not,' he said doubtfully.

'Right. Follow me, then.'

They made their way down the steep slope, pushing through the undergrowth and keeping an eye out for Kent Spearman. At the bottom of the hill they turned left, and after half an hour they heard something totally unexpected: voices!

'Do you hear them?' whispered Hal.

'Of course,' Stinky whispered back. 'And Hal . . . '

'Yes?'

'Why are we whispering?'

'We don't know who it is, do we?'

'Maybe Mr Spearman found help.'

'Yeah, and maybe it's those fugitives from the news flash.'

'The bank robbers?' Stinky gulped, then realised Hal was leaving. 'Hey, where are you going?'

'To get a better look.' Hal crawled under a bush, parted the branches and peered between the leaves. He imagined he was Captain Spacejock tracking a deadly enemy, and he was disappointed to see two ordinary-looking adults sitting on tree stumps near a blazing campfire. They were wearing dark clothing, and had broad webbed belts with knives and pouches. Hal realised they weren't fugitives or bank robbers . . . they were hunters! The man had red hair and a freckled face, while the woman was darker with short black hair. Then Hal sniffed. There was a pot hanging over the fire, and the contents smelled delicious. His spirits rose. Not only had they found help, they might get lunch too!

'It's going to be another cold night,' said the woman.

'I hate these woods,' said the man. 'They give me the creeps.'

'That's because you're scared of your own shadow.' She laughed. 'If someone leapt out of the bushes right now –'

'Excuse me,' said Hal loudly.

The adults jumped, springing to their feet. They stared into the bushes, directly towards the boys' hiding place. 'Who is it?' demanded one. 'Show yourself!'

Hal set the bow and arrows down and crawled out of the bush.

'It's just a kid,' said the woman.

'There are two of us,' said Hal, as Stinky appeared at his side. 'Our ship fell apart, and we crashed last night. We . . . we don't have any food.'

'You look all in, the pair of you,' said the man kindly. He had a good-humoured face with lots of freckles, and Hal warmed to him straight away. 'Here, come and sit down. There's plenty of hot grub to go around.'

The boys didn't need to be asked twice. They sat on the tree stump, took bowls of stew and wolfed them down.

The man tapped himself in the chest. 'I'm Ted and this is Amber. And you are?'

'I'm Hal, and this is Stink–, er, Stephen.'

'Nice to meet you both.' Ted hesitated. 'So, are you out here alone?'

Stinky shook his head. 'Mr Spearman is back at the escape pod. He hurt his ankle during the landing.'

'Sounds like you had a lucky escape.'

495

With the food now warming his stomach, Hal turned his mind to other matters. 'You're hunters, aren't you? Have you caught anything yet?'

Amber laughed. 'Hunters. Yes, that's us.'

Hal looked around curiously. 'Where are you staying? Do you have a tent?'

'More of a shelter. We came out here a week ago in a neat little flyer, but this dummy left the lights on.' Amber slapped Ted on the shoulder. 'The battery went flat, and now we can't open the ship. Isn't that a laugh?' Despite her words, she looked a long way from laughter. In fact, she looked seriously annoyed.

'You had to bring that up again, didn't you?' Now Ted sounded angry. 'I already told you –'

'Lucky for him,' interrupted Amber, speaking to Hal, 'we got the gear out of the ship first.'

'So it's just the two of you?' asked Hal.

'That's right. Me and my best buddy Ted.'

496

'Don't you have enough power to radio for help?' asked Hal. 'I think Mr Spearman needs a doctor.'

Ted shook his head. 'No radio. We can make a splint though, maybe get him comfortable.'

'I have an idea,' said Stinky.

Everyone turned to look at him.

'I–I was just thinking, we might be able to take batteries from the capsule and use them to power up your ship.'

'Aren't you the bright one?' said Amber, with a tight smile.

'They'll be heavy, but we could manage with a travois.'

Hal frowned. Was Travis another one of Stinky's imaginary friends?

'Mr Spearman is good with ships, and I know a thing or two about electronics,' added Stinky. 'Between us I'm sure we could rig something up.'

'This Spearman. Is he your teacher?'

'No, he's the pilot.'

The adults exchanged a glance. 'Pilot, eh? That's handy.'

Hal liked the sound of the plan. They could find Mr Spearman, get the batteries, fix the hunters' ship and call for help. 'Hey, maybe we could fly out of here,' he said suddenly.

'Sounds perfect to me,' said Ted. 'What do you think, Amber?'

'One hundred percent agreement,' said Amber. 'Let's go talk to Mr Spearman.'

— 21 —

Travis

When they reached the pod there was still no sign of Kent Spearman. Amber glanced inside, then frowned at Hal and Stinky. 'So where's this pilot of yours?'

'We think he went hunting,' said Hal.

Ted and Amber exchanged a glance. 'He has a gun?'

'No, we made bows and arrows out of sticks and fishing line.'

Amber nodded, and immediately started giving orders. 'Take the cushions off the seats, rip lengths of wire from the pod's console, and if you can loosen any wall panels grab those too. You never know what we might need.'

While Ted and the boys stripped everything of use from the capsule, Amber took the axe and chopped down a couple of small trees. She stripped the branches with half a dozen strokes, then lashed the narrow ends together to make a large 'A'. When it was ready she laid a blanket on top and called for the equipment, which she piled in the middle. 'Anything else?'

Ted held up a shovel. 'I found this in a compartment under the seat.'

'Good. That could be useful.'

Once everything was sitting on the blanket, Amber wrapped it up and tied it to the poles with lengths of wire. She tested the weight, and nodded. 'It's heavy, but we'll manage.'

Hal looked around the clearing. 'We should leave a note for Mr Spearman, telling him where we are.'

Ted and Amber exchanged a glance. 'I'll do it,' said Amber. 'You go ahead.'

Ted stood between the poles, holding one in each hand like a wheelbarrow in reverse. Hal and Stinky stood in front of him, holding one end each. On the count of three they all lifted together and staggered forwards. The travois bumped and scraped over the rough ground, and Hal couldn't help being impressed. The pole was rough on his hand, but the load was manageable. It would have been a lot worse if they'd had to carry everything.

It was a good hour before they arrived at the hunters' ship. It was a sleek grey flyer with swept-back wings, and Hal could see two seats inside, one behind the other. One wing had green branches over it, woven together to form an A-shaped shelter. Underneath the body of the flyer, on the ground, he could see a small pile of supplies: tinned food, a plastic drum of water and a couple of crates.

They set the travois down carefully, and Hal and Stinky flexed their hands and shoulders to ease the aches and pains. Ted had a quick drink before unpacking the salvaged equipment, dividing it up into piles. 'We'll build you a shelter under the other wing,' he said. 'Can you fetch some branches? Those trees with the big leaves are best.'

Hal and Stinky headed into the woods, where they spent twenty minutes pulling green leafy branches from the trees. Hal was careful to break the branches off cleanly, instead of pulling them down and tearing great strips of bark from the trunk. They'd taught him that in the hydroponics lab aboard the Space Station, explaining that the branches would eventually regrow that way.

They ended up with armfuls of bushy branches, which they dragged back to the clearing. Ted selected the three largest and propped the splintered ends against the flyer's wing. Then he showed the boys how to weave and twist smaller branches between them, filling the gaps to block out cold wind and - hopefully - any rain.

After several hours, and many more trips to fetch branches, the new shelter was finally ready. There were two leafy green walls, one on either side of the wing, and the entrance was finished off with a blanket from the escape pod. Inside was snug, like a living tent, and Hal couldn't wait to try it out at night.

He clambered outside again and found Ted inspecting a pile of equipment from the escape pod. 'You should get Stinky to look at those batteries. He might be able to wire them into your ship so you can call for help.'

Ted smiled. 'I'm sure you're both very clever, but I'm not risking things getting even worse.'

'Stinky wouldn't make things worse. He'd have that thing going in no time.'

'No, it'll be dark soon. We'll take another look in the morning.'

❧

It was late at night, and Hal was snug and warm inside his blankets. Stinky was nearby, fast asleep and snoring gently. They'd enjoyed a dinner of hot stew, and afterwards Ted told them funny stories about his childhood. Amber barely spoke a word all evening, just sitting and gazing into the fire.

After one particularly hair-raising tale involving a jetbike, a length of rope and an old wooden crate, Stinky had given a huge yawn. Not long after, Ted had sent the boys to their tent. He and Amber stayed up, tending the fire.

Hal gazed up at the underside of the flyer's metal wing, wondering what might have happened to Kent Spearman. He hadn't shown up yet, and Hal hoped the blanket and food they'd left at the capsule would keep the pilot going until the morning. Hal wondered where he'd got to, especially with his injured ankle. He felt they could have done more to search for the missing pilot, but night had closed in quickly and they might have ended up with two or three people missing instead of just one.

Moments later his eyes closed, and he drifted off to sleep.

❖

Hal woke with a start. He wasn't sure how long he'd been asleep, and as the fog in his brain cleared he realised he could hear raised voices. In the next shelter, on the other side of the flyer, Ted and Amber were arguing about something. Hal strained his ears, trying to pick out a word or two, but their voices were muffled.

He lay there in the blankets, snug and warm. Hal knew their argument was none of his business, but he suspected they might be arguing about him and Stinky, or about the search for Kent Spearman. They were probably saying things they didn't want Hal to hear, but that made him even keener to hear them.

Unfortunately it was dark, it was very cold, and the last thing he wanted to do was sneak around in the bushes listening to private conversations.

'They know too much, that's all I'm saying.'

Amber's voice was loud, and no sooner had she spoken than Hal heard Ted's reply.

'They're just kids, Amber. What can they do?'

'Plenty, if they talk to the wrong people.'

'They swallowed the hunters story, didn't they?'

'Yeah, they believed it. Their pilot is another matter.'

'I thought you took care of him?'

'Hopefully. I left a note telling him we were heading North.'

Hal frowned. No wonder they hadn't found

Kent Spearman. Amber had sent him the wrong way! But why? Ted and Amber weren't hunters, apparently, so who were they?

'Is the stuff still in the cockpit?' asked Ted.

'Under the seat.' Amber hesitated. 'They'll have to be dealt with, you know.'

'Relax, will you? I know a guy we can sell them to.'

'Eh?'

'The gold bars. I know a guy.'

Gold? Hal's eyes widened. These two *were* the bank robbers everyone was looking for. And he and Stinky had been hanging out with them all day!

'I'm not talking about the gold,' snapped Amber. 'I meant we'd have to take care of those kids!'

Hal was wide awake now, and despite the warm blankets he was chilled to the core. He remembered when Amber found the shovel in the escape pod, and how she'd said it would prove useful 'later'.

'You can't mean –' began Ted.

'No, of course not. We'll leave them out here when we go. We'll put some food aside, maybe get word to the authorities in a day or two.'

'After the fuss dies down, you mean.'

'Yeah. In the meantime we'll have to lie low.'

There was no reply, and Hal strained his ears for all they were worth. Why had they stopped

505

speaking? Were they whispering? Hal peeled back the blankets, and he was just about to crawl out of the shelter when he got the shock of his life.

Someone clamped a rough, muddy hand over his mouth!

— 22 —

Midnight foray

Hal struggled to get free, until he heard a frantic whisper in his ear. 'Keep still, Hal. It's me, Kent Spearman! I'm going to take my hand away, but don't make a noise. Understood?'

Hal nodded, and Kent removed his hand. 'Where have you been all day?' whispered Hal.

Kent explained quickly. He'd been hunting, as Hal had guessed, but he'd got lost on the way back. He found the pod in the end, and then he'd spotted the note.

'How did you find us here?' whispered Hal. 'I thought Amber sent you on a wild duck chase?'

'Wild goose chase,' said Kent, with a grin. 'I headed North, just like the note said, but after a couple of hours my ankle was much worse so I doubled back. It got dark, but I spotted your firelight through the trees. I crept closer to find out who it was, and then I saw you two come in here. That's when I heard the adults talking, and I realised I'd have to rescue you both. You do realise who they are, don't you?'

'Yes, they're the bank robbers from the news.'

'They might be dangerous. We have to get away from here, as far as possible, before they discover you're gone.'

'Where will we go? Back to the pod?'

Kent shook his head. 'That's the first place they'll look.'

'But your ankle. How will you get away?' Hal wondered whether he and Stinky could move Mr Spearman on the travois, but he doubted it. Anyway, Ted and Amber would catch them up in no time.

'We'll go as far as possible, and then we'll climb a tree. It's a big forest and there's a good chance we'll be able to avoid them.' Kent glanced up at the flyer. 'Unless they use this, of course.'

'They said it had a flat battery.'

'I wouldn't believe everything they told you.'

Hal thought for a moment. 'What if Stinky and I drew them away, and you started the flyer? We could meet you near the river.'

'That's not a bad idea, but I can't put you in that kind of danger. These people are desperate, and I don't like to think what might happen if they caught up with you.'

Hal shivered. Ted seemed okay but Amber was another matter. He didn't mind admitting it: she scared him. 'Hey, we left the bows and arrows under a bush. We could arm ourselves and –'

'No.' Kent shook his head. 'I'm not having either of you fighting pitched battles with these people. Is that clear?'

'I guess,' mumbled Hal. Then he remembered something. The boat! 'Mr Spearman, when Stinky and I went fishing we found something useful. There was a wooden boat next to a big tree.'

'That could be handy. Was it far?'

'No, just near the river. And . . . there was another thing.' Hal hesitated. 'There were tins of food in the bottom of the boat, as well as a metal box. We opened the box and found . . . a gun.'

Kent's eyebrows shot up. 'A what?'

'A blaster.' Hal indicated the size with his hands. 'It was about this big, and dark grey.'

'This isn't one of your games, is it?'

'No, it's true! I wanted to hunt fish with it but Stinky wouldn't let me.'

'At least one of you is sensible,' said Spearman drily. 'So what did you do with the gun?'

'I hid it under a fallen tree.'

509

Kent thought for a moment. 'Okay, here's what we'll do. You fetch the gun and make sure the boat is still there. Meanwhile, I'll wake Stinky and explain everything.'

Hal frowned. He thought Stinky would be coming to the boat too. He wasn't wild about tackling the woods on his own.

'One last thing,' said Kent. 'Is there any food around? I've barely eaten all day.'

'Wait here.' Hal crept under the flyer and felt around until his fingers brushed the cans of food. He grabbed two and clambered out again. When he got back to the shelter he found Stinky awake and rubbing sleep from his eyes. 'Here,' said Hal, passing Kent the tins. 'I don't know what's in them.'

'Right now I'd eat lumpy custard and raw beef . . . all mixed together.'

'Did you explain the plan to Stinky?'

'Sure did. Just one little change . . . we've decided he's going with you.'

Hal glanced at Stinky, who looked worried. He doubted Stinky had volunteered, which meant Kent had told him to go to the river with Hal . . . probably to keep an eye on him. 'It's all right, he doesn't have to come. I'll be quicker on my own.'

'I'd rather you both went,' said Kent firmly.

Hal realised this was one of those 'adult

suggestions' which were pretty much the same as direct orders. 'All right, fine.'

'Thank you. And Hal . . . '

'Yes, Mr Spearman?'

'Be careful out there.'

The boys crept out of the shelter and got to their feet. Hal had no idea how late it was, but the fire was out and the forest was silent and dark. Looking up, he could see tiny patches of night sky between the leaves and branches of the overhanging trees, and when he waved his hand in front of his face he discovered there was just enough light to see movement.

Hal turned this way and that, trying to get his bearings. He could just hear the rush and splash of moving water in the distance, and he set off in the general direction. On the way he stopped at the bush where he'd hidden with Stinky earlier that day. They dug around inside until they found the bows, grabbing as many arrows as they could find in the darkness. Mr Spearman had told him not to take the weapon, but the forest was dark and spooky. Actually, it was so dark Hal wouldn't be able to see what he was shooting at, not unless their enemies waved torches in the air and shouted 'hit me, hit me!'

With the bows slung over their shoulders and the arrows gripped in their hands, Hal and Stinky marched confidently towards the river. Five minutes later they were moving a lot more carefully: their faces and arms were scratched from low-hanging branches, and their toes hurt where they kept stubbing them on half-buried rocks.

Hal wasn't sure how far they'd come, but the river didn't seem to be getting any louder. In fact, he was starting to wonder whether they were even heading in the right direction. He would have gone back to the flyer to start again, but he wasn't sure which way that was either. Kent Spearman had used the campfire to home in on the camp, but the fire was out now.

Hal shrugged and pressed on. First they'd find the gun and the boat. Then they'd worry about getting back again.

— 23 —

Seeking

The river was a lot closer now, and there was more light filtering through the trees. Hal found a stout branch along the way, and he used it to swish a path through the leafy undergrowth. Not only did this protect his arms and face from scratches, but it also left a handy trail he could follow to get back to camp.

Swish! Crack!

'Could you make a bit more noise?' whispered Stinky. 'I think there are still a few people on this planet who don't know where we are.'

Annoyed, Hal swung the branch even harder.

Swish! CRACK!

Eventually he chopped his way through the final bushes, and they saw the river laid out in front of them. The water gleamed like polished silver in the starlight, but the far bank was like a solid black cloud. Then Hal realised something: there was no fallen tree!

Hal looked left and right, but the river was empty in both directions. Which way should he go? The escape pod had been up-river from the flyer earlier in the day, but if he'd passed it in the darkness it could be down-river now, off to his left. He was just about to head that way when Stinky spoke up.

'I think it's to our left.'

Hal frowned. Who was in charge of the expedition anyway? He was! 'Well I think it's off to the right.'

'All right, I'll go the other way.'

'I don't think we should split up,' said Hal. 'Mr Spearman said –'

'Oh, who cares what Mr Spearman said!' growled Stinky. 'He got us into this mess in the first place! If his ship hadn't broken down, if all the pods had been working, if he were a proper pilot . . . we'd be camping in proper tents with proper food instead of running around in the dark like this!'

Hal eyed his friend in surprise. He'd never known Stinky to get angry, and he wasn't sure he liked it. Stinky was calm and dependable, and if he was having a breakdown, the whole situation had to be worse than Hal thought. 'We could go left if you like.'

'I don't care which way we try first. I just want to

go home.'

'All right, follow me.' Hal was was just about to set off up-river when he remembered to mark his way. He took a fallen branch and jammed the end in the ground, creating a makeshift signpost. If he ran into that coming back again, he'd know exactly where he was.

Following the river bank sounded like an easy plan, but it was a lot tougher than they expected. Thick bushes and trees grew right down to the water's edge, which meant constant detours, and there were muddy inlets hidden under spongy moss and creepers. In the dark these looked just like any other patch of ground . . . until Hal stepped on them. Each time he did, he'd cry out in alarm as he sank right up to his knees in cold water. Stinky would help him out, and they'd make their way around the edge until they arrived at the next one . . . where Hal would promptly get another soaking.

After ten or twenty minutes they finally made it to the river bank. They were a long way up-stream, and there was no sign of the fallen tree. 'This is hopeless,' grumbled Hal. 'It's going to be light soon, and those crooks will wake up and discover we're missing.'

'It's not even midnight yet,' said Stinky.

Hal checked his impressive space watch, illuminating the big flashy screen with a flick of his wrist. He checked the time and discovered his friend was right . . . it seemed like they'd been walking for hours, but it had only been forty or fifty minutes. Hal covered his watch and stood on the river bank, deciding what to do next. They could make their way further up the river, hoping the boat would come into view. Or they could turn around and tramp all the way down-stream again. 'What do you think?' he asked Stinky.

'I think we should have turned left.'

Hal didn't bother replying. 'What if we built a raft and floated down the river? That way we wouldn't have to walk through the mud again.'

'It'll take all night to build a raft. Anyway, we don't have any logs and we certainly don't have any rope.'

Hal frowned into the darkness. The river bank was wider here, and it looked a lot easier to follow. 'Okay, we'll keep going until we hit a rough patch, and then we'll turn back.'

They walked in silence under the stars ... silent, that is, except for the squish-squish-squish of Hal's soggy shoes. Eventually they rounded the next bend, and he squinted into the darkness. Was that a shadow on the water up ahead? 'Hey, is that the tree?'

Stinky shaded his eyes. 'I think it's more bushes.'

Hal muttered under his breath. 'Come on, we'd better check.'

They hurried forward, and as they got closer Hal's expression grew more and more hopeful. It was definitely a fallen tree, but was it the right tree? Then ... joy! He spotted the wooden boat lying on the shore. 'That's it, Stinky. We found it!'

Hal didn't waste any time on the boat. He went straight to the fallen tree and felt underneath for the metal box. It was exactly where he'd left it, but he still held his breath as he popped the lid. If the gun wasn't there . . .

But it was, still wrapped in its protective cloth. 'Okay, give me a hand with the boat.'

Stinky looked puzzled. 'What for?'

'I'm not walking all the way back again. We'll sit in the boat and sail down the river.'

'We can't do that. We don't know how to use it!'

'Of course we do. You just get in and float along.'

'It's not that simple. We need oars to row it.'

Hal gestured at the river. 'What for? The water's already moving, isn't it?'

'How will we stop when we reach the right place?'

'We'll paddle back to shore with our hands.'

'No, I don't like it. We could get into real trouble.'

'Stinky, we survived an exploding spaceship, crash-landed in the middle of nowhere, and we're stuck in a huge forest with a wounded pilot and a pair of dangerous criminals. I'd say we're already in trouble.'

'And if the river carries us out to sea? You think we'll be better off then?'

'If that happens we'll shout for help.' Hal started to drag the boat towards the water. 'Come on, give me a hand.'

Stinky shook his head. 'It's too dangerous.'

'Fine, walk back on your own. I'll wait for you.' Hal expected Stinky to cave in, like he always did, but his friend stood firm.

'I'm not getting into that boat. You don't know what you're doing, and even if it works you'll only save a few minutes.'

'But . . . '

'No!' Stinky set off for the bushes without another word, leaving Hal alone with the boat.

'Stinky, wait!'

No reply.

'Stinky!' Hal thumped his fist on the boat. For a moment he considered pushing it onto the river anyway, heading out alone if he had to. Then he gave up and tramped into the bushes after his friend.

— 24 —

Wild animals

Hal caught up with Stinky straight away, and they made their way through the bushes together. They hadn't gone far when Hal froze. 'Did you hear that?' he whispered.

'What?'

Hal cupped his hand to his ear. 'There it was again.'

Stinky cupped *both* hands to his ears and turned his head this way and that. In the darkness he looked like a faulty radar dish, and Hal almost burst out laughing. 'I still can't hear anything,' hissed Stinky.

'Maybe it's circling round behind us.'

'Maybe *what* is?'

'I don't know. It sounded like a growl.'

Stinky turned his head even faster.

'It might have been a moan,' said Hal. 'Do bears moan in the woods, or is that wolves?'

'W-wolves?'

Hal smiled to himself. Teacher had shown them a documentary on wolves, and it had given Stinky nightmares for days. 'Oh well, it was probably nothing. Come on, time's wasting.'

Stinky didn't move. 'I think I heard it.'

'Really?' said Hal in surprise.

'I-I think maybe we should try the boat,' said Stinky.

'You said it was dangerous.'

'It's safer than a pack of wolves.'

Hal pretended to think about it. He didn't want to sound too eager in case Stinky smelled a rat . . . or a bear, or a wolf. 'All right,' he said at last. 'I agree with you. Let's take the boat instead.'

They turned tail and hurried out of the woods. When they reached the boat Hal went to push it out, but Stinky stopped him. 'Look around for a couple of branches. We can use them to fend off obstacles, and if the water isn't too deep we can pole the boat along by pushing against the riverbed.'

Hal searched the undergrowth but all he found was a short piece of stick.

'You'll want something just a bit longer than that,' said Stinky. 'It'll need to be twice your height.'

Hal roamed further afield, and he came across a fallen tree. The branches were dry and brittle, and he managed to snap two of the bigger ones off. Stinky nodded his approval, and Hal laid them in the bottom of the boat.

'Ready?' he said.

'On three,' said Stinky. 'One . . . Two . . . Three!'

They pushed the boat into the water, throwing themselves on board as it sailed away from the shore. They ended up in a heap in the bottom, and Hal made a face as his fingers encountered a layer of gooey, squishy mud. He cleaned his hands by dipping them in the water.

'I wonder if there are any sharks?' said Stinky innocently.

Hal yanked his hand out of the water.

'Then again,' said Stinky, 'your wolves and bears probably ate them all.'

The boat turned slowly as it floated down river. They were moving very slowly, and Hal decided to help it along. He grabbed one of the poles and stood up.

'Hal, sit down!' hissed Stinky, as the boat rocked like crazy. 'You'll have us over!'

Hal didn't need telling . . . he'd already sat down, and a lot harder than he meant to. He clung to the sides as the boat settled, then took the pole and tried sticking it in the water. He leant over the side, reaching down as far as he could, but the pole just moved around in the water. He opened his mouth to tell Stinky, then closed it again. Instead, he pretended to push the boat along, groaning and heaving as he struggled with the pole.

'That's working,' said Stinky. 'We're moving quicker now.'

They continued like this for several minutes, with Hal pretending to push them along. He kept his eyes on the bank, looking for the branch he'd poked into the ground. Unfortunately he could barely make out tree trunks, let alone a skinny stick. The water was bright enough, flickering and dancing with reflected starlight, but under the trees it was gloomy and dark.

'Do you want me to take a turn with that?' asked Stinky, nodding towards the pole.

'Er, no. I can manage.'

'You sound worn out.'

'It's nothing, believe me.' Hal redoubled his efforts, lifting the pole and pushing it into the water, and all the while pretending it was touching the ground.

'We're going the wrong way,' said Stinky. 'Take us closer to the shore.'

'I'm doing my best,' puffed Hal.

'Wait, I'll give you a hand.' Stinky took up the

second branch, and before Hal could stop him he stuck it in the water. He frowned, then stretched further and further until the water reached his elbow. 'Hal . . . '

'Your pole must be shorter than mine.'

'They were both the same.'

Hal gave up the deception, throwing his branch into the bottom of the boat. 'Oh, all right, I admit it. I was just pretending.'

'For how long?' demanded Stinky.

'Ever since we set off.'

Stinky opened and closed his mouth, unable to speak. Then, with big round eyes, he turned to look down-river. Hal knew exactly what his friend was thinking, because he'd already gone over it in his head. Even if they saw the marker in the darkness, they'd still float past. In fact, they could float for hours before the river washed them out to sea.

'You should have told me,' said Stinky. 'I'd have thought of something.'

'Like swimming to shore?'

'Don't be silly. Neither of us could do that.'

'What about –'

'Let me think!' snapped Stinky. He eyed the branches, then stared across at the bank, then rubbed his chin. Meanwhile, the boat continued to sail down-river. 'Okay, what we need is a longer pole.'

'Brilliant,' said Hal. 'I wish I'd thought of that.'

Stinky ignored the interruption. 'What we have is two short poles. My solution is ... tie them together.'

Hal smiled to himself. High-tech or low-tech, Stinky always had an answer! There was just one problem. 'What about rope?'

'Shoelaces.' Stinky looked down at Hal's feet. 'They're not elastic, are they?'

'No, these are new.'

Stinky looked again. 'Er ... is it just me, or is there a bit more water in the boat?'

'You're right. It's getting deeper.' Hal removed his shoelaces, then grabbed the big bailing tin and started emptying water over the side.

Five minutes later Stinky was ready. He'd used all four shoelaces to bind the poles together, tying the lashings off with a simple knot. Hal wanted to use one of his special knots, but the laces weren't long enough.

'Be careful with it,' said Stinky. 'It'll snap in half if you jam it into the ground.'

Hal dipped the end of the pole in the water, lowering it hand over hand. Three-quarters disappeared beneath the surface before he felt resistance. 'That's it. I can feel the river bed.'

'Try pushing us towards the shore.'

Hal did so, leaning on the pole. It bent alarmingly, but they did seem to be getting closer to the bank.

'Keep going,' said Stinky. 'It's working!'

Hal pushed again, and the boat moved. Again, and they were in the shallows. One final push and the boat grounded, heeling over as the river tried to carry it away. Hal was over the side in a flash, and he hauled the boat towards the bank. Stinky hopped out, and together they pulled it to safety.

Then Hal laughed. Five metres away, standing up from the muddy bank, was the branch he'd stuck into the ground.

— 25 —

Sail away

It was almost an hour before Hal and Stinky arrived back at camp. They were muddy and exhausted, and Hal's shoulder ached from carrying the metal tin. All the way back, he'd been wondering how they'd find the flyer in the darkness, but Kent Spearman had thought of that. He was flashing a torch into the trees every few seconds, lighting the way.

'Here, warm yourselves up,' he whispered, passing the boys a blanket each. Then he saw the tin. 'Is that the gun?'

Hal nodded and handed it over. He watched carefully as Kent took the bundle of fabric out, and he waited for the congratulations and thanks which were sure to follow. With the gun, they could arrest the bank robbers, tie them up and take their ship to the spaceport. Maybe even claim a big reward!

Instead, Kent took one look at the gun and shook his head. 'Sorry Hal. I'm afraid it's no good.'

'Is it broken?'

'No, it looks fine. Problem is, it's a flare pistol.'

Hal and Stinky exchanged a glance, but for once Stinky didn't have an answer.

'It's for emergencies,' explained Kent. 'When you're in trouble, you fire it into the sky. That way people know where you are.'

'I see,' said Stinky. 'And we're so far from anywhere, nobody would see the flare.'

'Exactly.'

Hal felt cheated. 'But if you point it at Ted and Amber . . .'

'They'll just laugh at us,' said Kent. 'It's dangerous enough, but it's not deadly.'

'But we walked all night to fetch it!' grumbled Hal.

'Oh, I'm sure it'll be useful. Just not the way we thought.'

'So what are we going to do?'

Kent thought for a moment. 'First, we have to get away from here. We'll take as much food and gear as we can carry, and follow the river down to the sea. It's going to be a long walk, and I'm afraid we'll have to live rough.'

'We don't need to walk,' said Hal. 'We can use the boat. It's got a leak, but there's a tin to bail it out.'

'Excellent. That'll make a big difference. Now, can you and Stinky grab some more food? I'll make up a few bundles with the blankets.'

Hal crawled under the ship to the supplies, and he passed items back to Stinky one by one. Ted and Amber were sleeping just a few metres away, and every time a tin scraped or clinked he held his breath, worried the noise might wake them up. Worse, he couldn't use a light to identify the tins, and for all he knew he was grabbing pickled cabbage, lumpy custard and washing powder.

After a few minutes collecting supplies, Hal felt Stinky tugging his ankle. He backed out and saw Kent Spearman separating tins into three piles: two small and one large. He tested the weight now and then, and when he was happy he bundled up the blankets and tied the tops together. 'At least we won't have to carry water,' he said. 'The river will supply all we need.'

Even so, the bundle of tins was heavy across Hal's shoulder, and he was glad they wouldn't be walking to the coast.

Spearman tucked the flare pistol into his belt. 'All set?'

Hal and Stinky nodded.

'Okay. To the boat!'

The sky was lighter by the time they reached the river, and Hal realised the sun would soon be up. He was tired and cold after the long night, and he was looking forward to a bit of warmth.

Kent was limping badly, even though his ankle was heavily strapped. He'd carried the heavy bundle of food all the way from the flyer, using a stout branch as a crutch, and he looked relieved to see the boat. After the disappointment with the gun, he'd probably been expecting a pair of wooden planks or a waterlogged raft. 'That'll do the job,' he said, nodding in approval. 'Put your stuff on the seats and we'll get her onto the water.'

They loaded the boat quickly, and Hal volunteered to push off. Before he did so, Stinky showed Kent the two branches, and he watched closely as the pilot lashed them together with good strong rope.

Then they were ready. They moved the boat to the shallows, Kent and Stinky climbed in, and as soon as they were settled Hal gave the wooden boat a shove and vaulted over the side.

They sailed into the middle of the river, where the current took hold of the boat. Kent used the branch like a tiller, straightening their course, and before long they were slipping past the silent trees. After a few minutes he passed the tiller to Hal, and picked up the bow. He unstrung it, then dug in the salvaged equipment for the tin of hooks.

'Are you going to fish?' asked Hal.

'We're all going to fish. We'll trail lines out the back, and maybe catch ourselves a nice breakfast.'

Hal's mouth watered. They'd had frozen fish cutlets on the Space Station once, with lots of tasty white flakes that had melted in his mouth. Imagine how much better fresh fish would be, especially when it was cooked over a fire!

Kent prepared several lines as well as the rod,

and he selected a tin of ham for the bait. They all dangled lines over the side, and nothing happened for several minutes. Then . . .

'It's pulling!' shouted Stinky. 'I've got one, I've got one!' He yanked on the line, and a big tangle of green weed landed in the boat.

Hal laughed at his friend's expression. 'Yum. Seaweed fritters. My favourite.'

'Try to keep the hook off the bottom,' said Kent.

Hal was still smiling to himself when his line went taut. At first he thought it was another weed, until the line shot sideways towards the bank. He pulled with all his might, and a mottled green fish landed in the bottom of the boat. It leapt and twisted, tangling the line, until Kent despatched it with a blow.

'Sorry, fish,' he muttered under his breath. 'Not your lucky day.'

Hal eyed the fish with mixed emotions. A minute ago it had been swimming around happily, and now it was breakfast. Still, they had to eat, and the fish hadn't suffered.

Ten minutes later there were half a dozen fish in the boat. Three were Hal's, Stinky caught two and Kent only caught one . . . the smallest of the lot. 'That'll do for now,' he said. 'We can't save the leftovers, so we'll just take what we can eat.'

'Are we going to cook them?'

'In a minute. Let me know if you see a dead tree.'

It was more like thirty minutes, but eventually Hal spotted a fallen tree in the woods. The branches were bare, white with age, and after a quick inspection Kent poled the boat towards the shore. They landed on a patch of sand, tied the boat up, and began snapping branches off the tree to make a fire.

Once it was alight Kent took the fish back to the river for cleaning, a process Hal wasn't too keen to watch. When the pilot came back the fish were skewered on branches. He gave the boys two each, and once the fire died down a little he showed them how to hold the skewers over the coals. The fish started to sizzle, and they turned them over and over until they were browned on both sides. When they were ready, Kent tried a mouthful. 'Its good. Just watch out for bones. Make sure you chew every mouthful.'

Hal tried his fish, and he gasped at the amazing flavour. Compared to this, the processed fish aboard the Space Station tasted like stale cardboard! Stinky was silent too, savouring every mouthful as though he'd never tasted anything better.

When they were finished Kent dug a hole, and

they buried the fish bones and scraped the remains of the fire in on top. Then he buried the ashes in dirt, stamping it down hard. 'That's how you leave a camping spot,' he said to the boys. 'As if nobody had ever been there.'

They returned to the boat, happy and full, and were just about to set off when Hal heard a rumble of thunder. 'Is that rain coming?'

'That's not thunder,' said Kent, staring up at the sky. 'It's a ship!'

— 26 —

Rapid escape

'You mean rescuers?' said Hal in excitement. 'Have they found us?'

'It seems like it,' said Kent thoughtfully. 'Unless . . .'

The thunder grew louder, and Hal saw a flash above the trees. He was about to wave both arms at it when Kent grabbed his wrist and hauled him under cover. 'Wh-what is it? What's the matter?'

'It's your friends, Ted and what's her name.'

'Amber?'

Kent nodded. 'I recognise the flyer.'

'It can't be,' said Stinky. 'They said the batteries were flat. They said –'

Hal snorted. 'They said they were hunters, Stinky. It was all lies.'

'They must be looking for us.' Kent gestured at

the boat. 'When they see that, they'll work out where we are soon enough.'

Roar! The flyer shot overhead, and Hal spotted a face in the sleek cockpit. It was Amber, and she seemed to be looking right at him. The flyer roared past and banked sharply, the ground shaking from the raw power of its engines.

'Why don't they land?' shouted Hal.

'Nowhere suitable,' said Kent. 'The bank isn't wide enough and they can't set down in the water.'

The flyer roared away, and everything was quiet again. 'Have they gone?'

'They'll land nearby and walk the rest. Come on, back to the boat.'

They hurried down to the water and pushed off. Once they were moving, Hal piped up again. 'I don't understand. What do they want us for?'

'They're hiding out in the woods, right? When we make it out of here we're going to report them, and the Peace Force will shut the whole area down. They'll never get away.'

'But they could fly away now. They have a whole planet to hide in.'

Kent shook his head. 'Every ship has a unique ID. If they fly anywhere else they'll be picked up by ground control.'

'So they're stuck in the woods?'

'Yep. Trapped.'

'But surely a proper search . . .'

'Hal, there are escape pods scattered all over Gyris, and this planet only has one rescue ship. The authorities will be looking for your classmates first, and until they're safe they can't turn their attention to Ted and Amber.'

'Maybe we could shoot the flyer down?'

'I admire your spirit, but our best bet is to evade them. We have the boat, so they'll never catch us on foot. All they can do is fly around until we fetch up somewhere with a landing spot.'

'Wh-what will they do to us?' asked Stinky.

'Nothing,' said Kent. 'They want to lie low until the fuss dies down, and they won't want us giving away their position.'

'We could promise not to tell.'

'I don't think they'd believe us, Hal.'

They floated down the river in silence, with Hal keeping one eye on the bank and another on the sky. Being hunted wasn't pleasant, and for all he knew Ted and Amber might be armed. Then he tilted his head. Was that more thunder? It was very faint, but getting louder all the time. 'They're coming back!' he shouted. 'Quick, to the bank!'

Kent stood up, making the boat wobble, and dug the pole into the river. He gave a huge push, sending the boat towards the bank, then dragged the pole from the water for an even bigger heave.

Snap!

The pole broke in two, leaving half sticking out of the water with their shoelaces still attached. Hal could only watch helplessly as the boat continued on its way. Meanwhile, the roaring got louder. He searched the sky for the flyer, but the noise seemed to be coming from further down the river, as if Ted had landed and was waiting for them round the next bend.

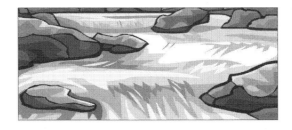

Hal glanced towards the bank. The boat was travelling faster now, and the trees were moving past at quite a speed. It was too far to jump or swim, and their only option was to stay with the boat. The roar got louder and louder, and then they rounded the corner. Hal stared. It wasn't the flyer waiting for them, it was a narrow canyon filled with boulders. And the nice, gentle river wasn't flowing between the banks, it was smashing over the rocks with violent waves and vicious white water.

'Rapids!' shouted Kent in alarm. 'Hold on for your lives!'

The next ten minutes were the most frightening of Hal's life. Worse than getting stranded in space without any air, worse than the time he'd set fire to the Space Station's canteen . . . it was even worse than the time his mum discovered he hadn't washed his face for two weeks.

The boat leapt forward like a startled deer, plunging into the rapids before anyone was ready. Water came over the sides in waves, and the boat cannoned into one rock after another, shaking from end to end and nearly tipping over more than once. The noise was unbelievable, with shouting and roaring and the crashing of timber, and it was all Hal could do to hang on. Half their equipment flew out, vanishing without trace into the churning water, and the rest was hurled around the boat. Hal caught a tin can with his shin, which made him gasp in pain, and he saw Stinky clutching his elbow. His friend looked stunned and frightened, and Hal tried to give him a reassuring grin. Unfortunately his face was frozen in a fearsome grimace, which only made things worse.

Then . . . silence. They cleared the rapids, with the boat turning slow, soggy circles as it floated down the middle of the river.

'Is everyone okay?' asked Kent.

Stinky nodded, while Hal managed a brief 'yep'.

Kent found the bailer and set to work, throwing waves of water over the side. Hal gathered the remaining tins and stretched the blankets out to dry. It was mid-morning, and he wondered whether they'd still be damp by nightfall. Then he remembered the fishing gear, and he looked around the boat in growing despair. They'd lost the lot! And the gun? What about that? He couldn't see it at first, then spotted the tin jammed under Kent's seat.

'We had a lucky escape,' said Kent. 'If you hear a noise like that again, let me know straight away.'

'How will we get to the bank? The pole broke.'

'We'll paddle with our hands. Try it now.'

The river widened, and Hal saw a big sandbank to the right. He leant over the side and paddled for all he was worth, and with the other two assisting they moved the boat slowly to the edge of the river. They were just staggering out of the boat when he heard a low growl. 'Not wild animals too!' he muttered.

541

But no, it wasn't wild animals. It was the flyer.

Caught

Hal glanced at Kent, waiting for the next step in the escape plan, but the pilot shook his head. 'Sorry lads. It's time to call it quits. We barely have any food, and there could be more rapids around the corner.'

Hal pressed his lips together. How could they give up without a fight? Then he glanced at Stinky, and he realised Mr Spearman was right. They'd done their best, but his friend was out on his feet.

The flyer settled on the sandbank, blowing clouds of sand with its jets. Hal shielded his eyes from the grit, scowling as he saw Ted and Amber climbing out of the cockpit. They didn't seem to be armed, but the two of them could take Mr Spearman easily enough, and Hal and Stinky were no match for a pair of adults.

'There you are!' said Ted. 'We were worried about

you.'

'Give it up,' said Kent. 'We know who you are.'

Ted and Amber exchanged a glance. 'Fair enough,' said Ted at last. 'You're the pilot, right?'

'Kent Spearman.'

'Good. We need you to fly us out of here.'

Whatever Hal was expecting, that wasn't it.

'I'm sorry?' said Kent.

Ted jerked his thumb at the flyer. 'You're going to fly that to the next planet, with us onboard.'

Kent looked from one to the other. 'Why do you need me? Fly the thing yourself.'

'Neither of us is qualified for space flight.'

'It's easy. Just point the flyer straight up and hit the boost.'

'Neither of us knows the first thing about navigation.' Ted glanced at the sky. 'We don't want to get lost in space, do we?'

'That's a two seater,' said Kent, nodding towards the flyer. 'With you two and me ... '

'It'll take three at a stretch.'

'What about the boys?' demanded Kent. 'You can't leave them out here on their own.'

'We'll leave them food and blankets, and when we're free and clear we'll notify the authorities.'

'That could be a day or two.'

'They'll survive,' said Amber shortly. 'It's either that or . . .'

'Okay, okay,' said Kent. 'I'll do it.'

Ted gestured towards the flyer. 'After you.'

'Wait. Let me talk to the boys first.'

'You've got five minutes.'

Kent turned to Hal. 'Sorry about this, but it's the only way. Now, do you remember how to make a fire?' Despite Hal's nod, Kent explained every step again, getting Hal to repeat them one by one. Once he'd got it, Kent explained how to build shelters and make their food last. Ted and Amber listened at first, but eventually started talking between themselves.

'I've got all that,' said Hal. 'But what about you? Will you be all right?'

'Don't worry, they'll let me go.'

'I don't trust them,' whispered Hal.

'Frankly, neither do I.' Kent glanced at Ted and Amber, who were arguing about something. Amber

545

was gesturing with her finger, making a point, and Ted had both hands up. 'She's the danger. I don't think she likes loose ends.'

Then, before Hal knew what was happening, Kent pushed the flare pistol into his hands. It was heavy and warm to the touch.

'Hide it quickly,' murmured Kent. 'Behind your back.'

Hal did as he was told.

'Now, look at the flyer. Do you see the intake just behind the wing?'

Hal nodded.

'I'm going to lift off and hover above the ground, and then I'll turn the ship away from you. When I do, run up to it, aim the flare pistol at the intake and pull the trigger. Get close, one shot and run for it.'

Now that was more like it! Hal's heart thudded in his chest. 'What if the ship explodes? You might get hurt!'

'It won't, but the distraction will be very handy.'

'Come on, your time's up!' shouted Ted.

'Remember the plan,' murmured Kent. 'And keep that thing out of sight, or the game will be up.'

— 28 —

Flare

Hal watched Kent Spearman working the flyer's controls. When the pilot was ready he closed the cockpit and fired up the engines, blasting the boys with clouds of dust and grit. Hal squinted through the murk, trying to spot the signal. There! The lights flashed three times, and the ship rose into the air. It stopped about two metres up, and slowly turned away. Hal ran into the dust cloud, clutching the gun and struggling to breathe. The noise was intense, the engines hammering his ears.

The blast increased, and the flyer started to move. Desperately, Hal raised the gun and pulled the trigger.

Blam!

The gun bucked, and a bright spark bounced off the flyer and vanished into the trees. Hal frowned and aimed again.

Blam! Blam!

Two more shots, both wide of the mark. The first buried itself in the river, while the second almost parted Stinky's hair. Hal took the gun in both hands and sighted carefully, watching the wavering, dancing air intake through one eye. He didn't know how many shots the gun had left, and this one had to count.

Blam!

The shot streaked towards the flyer, and for a split second Hal thought he'd done it. The bright spark was heading for the air intake, just as Kent wanted. Then, at the last second . . . disaster! The flyer turned suddenly, and instead of hitting the intake, the flare went straight into the engine.

For a second, nothing happened. Hal lowered the gun, and the flyer's engines roared as it began to gain height. Surely they wouldn't get away?

Then . . . *crump!* The nearest engine exploded, bits of metal blasting from the exhaust. The flyer wobbled in mid-air, a loose engine cover flapping like a sheet of cardboard, and Hal and Stinky dived for the ground as the ship sailed overhead, trailing black smoke.

Hal uncovered his eyes just as the flyer splashed down, right in the middle of the river. There was a hiss as the cold water met the searing hot engines, and steam billowed up in waves, completely hiding the ship from view.

'Wow,' breathed Stinky. 'You've really done it this time.'

'He *told* me to do it!' protested Hal.

All was quiet, except for the cracking, bubbling noises from the ruined flyer. When the steam cleared Hal saw the ship sinking, with Kent struggling to get the cockpit open from the inside. Water was already lapping around the edge, and any second now the flyer was going to disappear for good.

The boys raced for the boat, pushing it out on the water and paddling like crazy, hurling spray far and wide as they crossed the river. Hal saw Kent waving him away, but he ignored the gestures. As soon as the boat bumped against the flyer he leapt up with a tin can in both hands, smashing it on the canopy with all his might. The toughened plastic didn't yield, and he saw Kent pointing at something. Under the cockpit there was a red and yellow handle, and Hal twisted and pulled until it came free.

Whoosh! The canopy rose into the air, and Kent immediately ducked out of view. Hal peered over the edge and saw Ted and Amber crammed into the rear seat, still struggling to undo their seatbelt.

Kent gave them a hand with the catch, then hauled them out one by one, helping them into the boat.

The flyer continued to settle, and water started pouring over the edge of the cockpit. 'Get clear!' shouted Kent.

'What about you?'

'I'm going to activate the emergency beacon. Go!'

Hal and Stinky paddled for shore, ignoring the stunned adults lying in the bottom of the boat. Behind them, the flyer started to list, electronics sparking and flashing inside the cockpit. Hal saw Kent Spearman with a microphone to his mouth, and then, without warning, the flyer slipped beneath the surface. Apart from an oil slick, there was nothing to show where it had been.

Hal stopped paddling and held his breath. Mr Spearman would emerge any second now, for sure. He had to!

— 29 —

The Deep

Seconds passed, and the water remained flat and still. Hal glanced at Stinky, who was frozen with shock. In the bottom of the boat, Ted and Amber looked as though the sky had just fallen on their heads.

Hal felt totally helpless. He didn't know how to swim, and he didn't have anything to reach underwater and hook Mr Spearman out of the cockpit. And even worse - Hal was the one who'd shot the flyer down. Nobody was going to believe Mr Spearman told him to!

There was a roar in the distance, and Hal stared at the sky. Was that thunder or another flyer?

Splaaassh!

At that second Kent Spearman broke the surface, his long hair plastered to his skull. He took a huge shuddering breath, shook the water from his eyes, then looked around for the boat.

'Over here!' shouted Hal.

Kent swam towards the boat with powerful strokes, and when he reached it he hooked one arm over the edge and guided it to the shore by kicking his legs. They were halfway there when Hal heard the low rumble again, and he scanned the sky. There was a dark spot in the distance, and as he watched it glinted in the sunlight. It *was* another flyer - maybe even rescuers looking for them!

They reached the shore, and Hal jumped out of the boat. 'I thought you'd drowned,' he told Kent. 'You were gone for ages!'

'I was trying to send a signal before the water killed the radio.'

'Did you do it?'

Kent shook his head.

'So what about that?' demanded Hal, pointing at the flyer. It was a long way away, and it seemed to be flying back and forth over a patch of sky.

'We need smoke, and lots of it. Time to light a fire.'

They'd completely forgotten about Ted and Amber, but Stinky's warning shout soon reminded them. Hal spun round and saw Stinky struggling in Amber's grip. 'Hey, let him go!'

'Nobody's going to get hurt,' said Ted. 'It's just a little insurance.'

'Help! Murder! Kidnap!' shouted Stinky, struggling for all he was worth.

'All right, take it easy,' said Kent. 'Everyone calm down.'

'You,' shouted Amber. 'Get that boat under the trees. Now!'

Hal realised what they were doing. If they hid the boat and got everyone under cover, the rescuers wouldn't see them from the air. Then he remembered the flare pistol, which was still tucked into his waistband. He reached behind his back and grabbed it, then pointed it directly at Amber. 'Hands up. Let Stinky go!'

Amber started to obey, then laughed. 'That's just a flare pistol! What are you going to do, light me?'

'Not quite.' Hal raised his hand above his head and pulled the trigger. There was a *whump!* as the gun fired, and a *whoosh!* as the flare shot into the sky. It sailed higher and higher, a tiny spark against the bright blue, and then . . . *Fizzz!* It burst into a dazzling white light.

The distant flyer continued on the same course for a few seconds, and then they heard it: a deep roar as it banked sharply and accelerated towards them. Amber and Ted took one look and bolted for the woods.

'Stop!' shouted Hal. 'Hands up!' The adults disappeared into the trees, and Hal was about to race into the forest waving the flare pistol.

Instead, Kent grabbed his arm. 'Let them be. The Peace Force will track them down in no time.'

'They couldn't find them before.'

'No, but they had a whole planet to search. Now they just have to cordon off this part of the woods. Trust me, those two will never get away.'

Hal felt cheated. He wanted to see the crooks marched away in handcuffs.

— 30 —

Camping

It was several days later, and Hal was sitting on a red plastic chair in front of a bright blue tent. There was a picnic table in front of him, with plastic knives and forks, paper serviettes and a tablecloth decorated with trees and plants. Hal was toying with a plate of food, with vegetables and cheese and cubes of meat all cut into neat shapes, and he wasn't happy.

'This isn't real camping,' he muttered under his breath. 'This is a picnic in the playground!'

Stinky rolled his eyes. They'd joined their classmates at the campsite after the rescue, and Hal had done nothing but complain ever since. 'The beds are too soft, the water's too clean, the grass is all smooth and even . . . is there anything you like about this place?'

'No,' said Hal shortly.

'So you'd rather be lost in the woods with a pair of criminals?' Stinky waved his arms. 'You'd prefer that to swimming, and games, and campfires, and sing-alongs?'

Hal groaned.

'And eggs and bacon for breakfast, and steak for dinner, and –'

'The food out of those old cans tasted better than this.'

Stinky was about to protest, but then he nodded. 'I suppose eggs and bacon does get boring after a while.'

'And they ring bells for lunch, and dinner,' muttered Hal. 'And they won't let us fish, or hunt, or build a real shelter.'

Stinky nodded. The bows had been confiscated within minutes, and hadn't been seen since. Hal's attempts to make more had failed dismally, and he'd been banned from cutting any more branches, or 'borrowing' twine.

'I wish they'd never rescued us,' said Hal.

'Never mind. We're going home tomorrow.'

'Is that supposed to make me feel better? My new tutor is making up so many lesson plans I'll still be studying when I'm fifty.' There was a commotion near the gift shop, and Hal's voice tailed off as he watched a dark blue car pulling up. It had Peace

Force badges on the side, and a dozen lights and sirens on the roof. Two officers stepped out, one of them a short, overweight man, and the other a tall, slender woman. The short man went into the shop, and a few seconds later there was an announcement over the PA system.

Would all children please come to the barn for an important event. I repeat –

'Quick, let's sneak away,' said Hal.

Stinky displayed the orange band on his wrist. 'We're all tagged, remember?'

Hal remembered all right. The campsite was surrounded by a safety fence, and crossing it triggered an alarm. He'd set it off half a dozen times on his first day, until they threatened to feed him nothing but spinach for the week.

'Come on,' said Stinky. 'It might be something interesting.'

Hal snorted, but he followed his friend to the barn. It was a large building, with mock timber walls that were actually made from sheets of plastic. There were rows of seats for the audience, and Hal and Stinky sat at the back. The two Peace Force officers glanced at their watches, then took to the stage.

'Good afternoon,' said the female officer. 'Tell me, are Hal Junior and Steven Binn here?'

Everyone looked at Hal and Stinky.

'Would you come up the front please?'

Hal groaned. Now what? Was it the home-made porridge he'd cooked over the campfire, or the boat he'd tried to make out of picnic tables, or his repeated attempts to remove the hated orange band from his wrist? Whatever it was, it had to be bad. They didn't send two Peace Force officers for nothing.

Hal and Stinky made their way to the front, ignoring the whispers from the crowd. When they got there, the officers smiled, and the female one took up the microphone again. 'As you know, these two boys had quite an adventure, and thanks to their initiative and bravery two dangerous criminals are behind bars.'

Hal was shocked. They weren't there to punish him, they were saying thanks!

'As a reward, we'd like to present you with these Peace Force cadet medals.' The officer nodded to her partner, who gave each of the boys a polished wooden box. Hal peeked in his, and his eyes widened as he saw the official-looking badge. How cool was that!

'There's also a small gift for each of you, by way of thanks.'

The sweating officer returned with two brand-new rucksacks in Peace Force blue, setting them on the floor. Hal opened his, and his eyes lit up when he saw the compact tent, the super-light sleeping bag, the neat little cooking stove and the clever stack of pots, pans and plates. Then his face fell. They were going back to the Space Station the next day. What was he going to do with camping equipment?

The officer glanced at her watch, then continued. 'There was supposed to be another guest, but –' She stopped. A groundcar had just drawn up nearby, and there was a thud as the door closed. They heard pounding footsteps, and everyone turned to the door just as Kent Spearman hurried in. Instead of wearing his pilot outfit, he was decked out in jeans and a padded jacket, and he was wearing big black hiking boots.

'Sorry I'm late! I got a speeding ticket.'

'I'm sure we can sort that out for you,' said the officer drily. 'Now, would you like to say a few words?'

'Sure thing. Thanks to these two I've been offered a great new job. I just wanted to say thanks in public, and give them a gift of my own.' Kent reached into his pocket and took out a matching pair of utility knives, with blades, scissors, pliers and even a little magnifying glass. He gave one each to Hal and Stinky, and Hal resolved to try the sharpest blade on his orange bracelet the minute he was alone.

The officer wrapped up the ceremony, and after the applause died down, Hal drifted outside with the rest.

'So, how are you both?' asked Kent.

Hal shrugged.

'Enjoying the camping?'

Hal pulled a face.

'That good, huh? Here, take a look at this.' Kent led them to his car and opened the trunk. Inside was a big rucksack, stuffed with camping gear. There was also a bundle of fishing rods. 'I start my new job in a week, but before that I'm going to explore these woods properly. Fishing, camping, sleeping under the stars . . . it's going to be great.'

Hal sighed. 'It sounds fantastic.'

'So, I got to wondering. How'd you two like to come along? I never did show you how to hunt properly.'

A whole week of real camping! Hal's eyes shone. 'That would be amazing!'

'Fantastic!' added Stinky.

'Do we get bows and arrows?' asked Hal quickly.

'Of course!' said Kent. 'And fishing rods, too.'

Then Hal remembered something, and his spirits crashed. 'It's no good. We're going home tomorrow. We can't miss our flight or we'll get in trouble.'

Kent laughed. 'I'm a space pilot, remember? When the week's up I'll fly you home myself.'

'Yes, but . . . ' Hal sighed. 'My new tutor's got lessons ready for me, and mum won't let me miss school, and –'

'Don't worry, I've already cleared it with your folks. Your dad says the Space Station will survive without you for a few more days. In fact, your dad says they're enjoying the peace and quiet.'

— 31 —

Real camping

The next week was the most exciting - and exhausting - of Hal and Stinky's lives. They hiked over hills, climbed mountains, and explored deep valleys with thundering waterfalls. They camped wherever they liked, they hunted their own food and learned to clean & cook it for themselves. They used their bows, the fishing rods, their special utility knives, and all their brand new camping equipment. Kent Spearman showed them how to navigate by the stars so they didn't get lost, and he taught them how to set a proper fire, build a shelter, and survive in the rough. The boys grew tanned under the sun, and fitter than they'd ever been aboard the Space Station.

When the glorious week finally ended, and they boarded the shuttle for the flight home, Hal Junior promised himself that one day he'd live in the wild, sharing with nature and getting away from civilisation.

In between piloting his own spaceship and saving the Galaxy from evil, of course!

Acknowledgements

With thanks to my loyal readers, Tricia and Ian.

If you enjoyed this book, please leave a brief review at your online bookseller of choice. Thanks!

About the Author

Simon Haynes was born in England and grew up in Spain. His family moved to Australia when he was 16.

In addition to novels, Simon writes computer software. In fact, he writes computer software to help him write novels faster, which leaves him more time to improve his writing software. And write novels faster. (www.spacejock.com/yWriter.html)

Simon's goal is to write fifteen novels before someone takes his keyboard away.

Update 2018: goal achieved and I still have my keyboard!

New goal: write thirty novels.

Simon's website is spacejock.com.au

Manufactured by Amazon.com.au
Sydney, New South Wales, Australia

10105458R00330